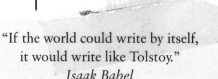

"If the world could write by itself,
it would write like Tolstoy."
Isaak Babel

"Tolstoy's greatness lies in not turning the story
into sentimental tragedy… His world is huge and
vast, filled with complex family lives and great social
events. His characters are well-rounded presences.
They have complete passions: a desire for love,
but also an inner moral depth."
Malcolm Bradbury

"What an artist and what a psychologist!"
Gustave Flaubert

"The pure narrative power of his work is unequalled."
Thomas Mann

"Tolstoy is the greatest Russian writer of prose fiction."
Vladimir Nabokov

"The greatest of all novelists."
Virginia Woolf

Childhood, Boyhood, Youth

Leo Tolstoy

Translated by Dora O'Brien

ALMA CLASSICS

ALMA CLASSICS
an imprint of

ALMA BOOKS LTD
3 Castle Yard
Richmond
Surrey TW10 6TF
United Kingdom
www.almaclassics.com

Childhood first published in 1852
Boyhood first published in 1854
Youth first published in 1857
Childhood, Boyhood, Youth First published by Alma Classics in 2010
This new edition first published by Alma Classics in 2016
English translation and Notes © Dora O'Brien, 2010
Extra Material © Alma Classics, 2010

Printed in Great Britain by CPI Group (UK) Ltd, Croydon CR0 4YY

ISBN: 978-1-84749-600-3

Contents

Leo Tolstoy (1828–1910)

Nikolai Ilyich Tolstoy,
Tolstoy's father

A young Leo Tolstoy
in 1848

Tolstoy's wife Sofya with her younger children: left to right, Mikhail
(Misha), Andrei (Andryusha), Alexandra (Sasha) and Ivan (Vanechka)

The house in which Leo Tolstoy was born

Yasnaya Polyana, where Tolstoy spent most of his life

Notes and sketches made by Leo Tolstoy
on the field of the Battle of Borodino

Childhood, Boyhood, Youth

Childhood

1

Karl Ivanych, the Tutor

O N 12TH AUGUST 18**, exactly three days after my tenth birthday, when I had received such wonderful presents, Karl Ivanych woke me up at seven o'clock in the morning by swatting a fly right above my head with a fly-swatter made of sugar paper on a stick. He did this so clumsily that he brushed against the small icon of my guardian angel hanging on the oak headboard of my bed and the dead fly fell straight on my head. I stuck my nose out from beneath the blanket, steadied the small icon, which was still rocking, with my hand, flicked the dead fly onto the floor and with grumpy if still-sleepy eyes glanced over at Karl Ivanych. He, however, wearing his colourful quilted dressing gown tied with a belt of the same material, his red knitted skullcap with a tassel and his soft goatskin boots, continued to move close to the walls, taking aim and swatting flies.

"I may only be little," I thought, "but why must he disturb me? Why doesn't he hit flies around Volodya's bed? There are plenty over there! No, Volodya is older than me; I am the youngest of the lot, which is why he torments me. That's all he thinks about in life," I whispered, "how to create trouble for me. He sees perfectly well that he woke me up and scared me, but he acts as if he hasn't noticed... repulsive man! And his dressing gown, and his cap and his tassel – how repulsive they are!"

While I was mentally expressing my annoyance with Karl Ivanych this way, he went over to his bed, glanced at his watch, which was hanging above it in a small beaded slipper, hung the fly-swatter on a nail and turned to us, clearly in a most happy frame of mind.

"*Auf, Kinder, auf... s'ist Zeit. Die Mutter ist schon im Saal,*"* he called out in his kind German voice. He then came over to me, sat by my feet and took his snuffbox out of his pocket. I pretended to be asleep. Karl Ivanych first took a pinch of snuff, wiped his nose and snapped his fingers and only then did he pay attention to me. Chuckling, he began to tickle my heels. "*Nu, nun, Faulenzer!*"* he said.

Much as I feared being tickled, I still did not leap out of bed or answer him, but just hid my head deeper under the pillow and kicked as hard as I could with my legs, trying my utmost not to laugh.

"How kind he is and how he loves us; how could I have thought so badly of him!"

I was annoyed with myself and with Karl Ivanych. I felt like laughing and crying all at once: my nerves were on edge.

"*Ach, lassen sie, Karl Ivanych!*"* I cried out with tears in my eyes, poking my head out from under the pillow.

Karl Ivanych looked surprised, let go of the soles of my feet and began asking me anxiously what all that was about? Had I perhaps had a bad dream? His kind German face and the concern he showed, trying to guess the reason for my tears, made them flow even more profusely: I felt ashamed and could not understand how a moment before I could have disliked Karl Ivanych and found his dressing gown, cap and tassel repulsive. Now, on the contrary, they all seemed particularly endearing and even the tassel seemed to be a clear proof of his goodness. I told him that I was crying because I had had a bad dream – Maman had died and they were carrying her away to be buried. I made all this up because I certainly did not remember what I had dreamt that night, but when Karl Ivanych, touched by my story, began to comfort and reassure me, I really felt as if I had had that horrible dream and now my tears were pouring down for a different reason.

When Karl Ivanych left me and I, sitting up in bed, began to pull my stockings up my little legs, my tears dried up somewhat, but sad thoughts about my made-up dream would not leave me. *Dyadka** Nikolai came in – a neat little man, always serious, precise and respectful and a great friend of Karl Ivanych. He brought in our clothes and footwear: boots for Volodya and for me still those detestable shoes with bows. I would have felt ashamed to cry in front of him, and besides, the morning sun was shining merrily through the window and Volodya, mimicking Mimi (our sister's governess), was laughing so loudly and happily as he stood at the washbasin that even the usually serious Nikolai, a towel over his shoulder and with soap in one hand and a water jug in the other, smiled and said:

"That'll do, Vladimir Petrovich. Please get washed."

I had completely cheered up.

"*Sind sie bald fertig?*"* Karl Ivanych's voice could be heard from the schoolroom.

His voice was stern and no longer had that expression of kindness that had moved me to tears. In the schoolroom Karl Ivanych was a completely different person: he was the teacher. I hastily dressed, washed and, with my hairbrush still in my hand to smooth down my wet hair, I responded to his call.

Karl Ivanych, his glasses on his nose and a book in his hand, sat in his usual place, between the door and the small window. To the left of the door were two small shelves: one was ours, the children's shelf, the other was Karl Ivanych's *very own*. On ours there were all sorts of books – school books and non-teaching books: some were upright, others lay flat. Only two large volumes, *Histoire des Voyages** in red bindings, were properly placed against the wall, and then came tall and thick, big and small books, covers without books and books without covers; you would often squeeze and shove them all in before break time when told to tidy up the "library", as Karl Ivanych loudly named this small shelf. The collection of books on *his own* shelf, if not as large as ours, was even more diverse. I remember three of them: a German pamphlet without binding on how to manure a cabbage patch, one volume on the *History of the Seven Years' War* in parchment, burnt at one corner, and a complete course on hydrostatics. Karl Ivanych spent a large part of his time reading, and even spoilt his eyesight doing so; yet he never read anything besides those books and *The Northern Bee.**

Among the items lying on Karl Ivanych's shelf, there was one that reminds me of him most of all. It was a small round piece of cardboard stuck on a wooden foot, and this circle could be moved by means of some pegs. A small picture was glued on the circle showing the caricatures of a lady and a hairdresser. Karl Ivanych was very good at pasting things and had devised this round cardboard himself to protect his weak eyes from the bright light.

I see the tall figure before me, as if it were now, in the quilted dressing gown and red cap beneath which thin strands of grey hair are showing. He is sitting by a small table on which stands the cardboard circle with the hairdresser on it, casting a shadow across his face; he holds his book in one hand and rests the other on the arm of the chair; by him lies his watch with a hunter painted on the dial, a checked handkerchief, a round black snuffbox, a green spectacle case and snuffers on a small tray. All this lies so neatly and properly in its rightful place that from this orderliness alone one could conclude that Karl Ivanych has a clear conscience and a soul at peace.

There were times, having had enough of running around the reception room downstairs, when I would steal upstairs to the school-room on tiptoe and look in – Karl Ivanych would be sitting alone in his armchair, reading one of his favourite books with a calm, solemn expression. Sometimes I came upon him in such moments when he was not reading: his glasses had slipped down his big aquiline nose, his blue eyes, half-closed, gazed ahead with a somewhat peculiar expression and his lips smiled sadly. It was quiet in the room; all you could hear was his even breathing and the ticking of the watch with the hunter on the dial.

Sometimes he would not notice me and I would stand in the doorway thinking: "Poor, poor old man! There are many of us. We play and have fun and he – he is so alone with no one to show him affection. He's not wrong when he says he's an orphan. And how awful his life story is! I remember how he told Nikolai all about it – it is awful to be in his position!" And I would begin to feel so sorry for him that I would go up to him, take his hand and say: "*Lieber* Karl Ivanych!"* He loved it when I spoke to him this way; he would always be affectionate in response and was visibly moved.

On the second wall of the schoolroom hung some maps, almost all torn but skilfully glued back together by Karl Ivanych. On one side of the third wall, in the middle of which was a door leading downstairs, hung two rulers: one, a scratched one, was ours; the other – a brand-new one – was *his own*, used by him more as "encouragement" than to draw lines. On the other side was a blackboard on which our major offences were marked with small circles and our lesser ones with small crosses. To the left of the board was the corner where we were made to kneel.

How well I remember that corner! I remember the stove damper, its air vent and the noise it made when it was turned. At times, you would stand and stand in the corner until your knees and back began to ache and you would think: "Karl Ivanych has forgotten about me: he must be comfortable sitting in his soft armchair reading his hydrostatics book – but what about me?" And to remind him of your existence, you would begin very softly to open and close the damper or pick at the wall plaster, but if a very large piece of plaster suddenly fell noisily onto the ground – then truly the fear alone would be worse than any punishment. You would glance round at Karl Ivanych, but he would sit with his book in his hand and appear not to have noticed a thing.

In the middle of the room stood a table covered with a tattered black oilcloth beneath which you could see the table edge, slashed in many places with penknives. Around the table were some unpainted stools, shiny from long use. Three small windows took up the last wall. This was the view from them: immediately beneath the windows was a road on which every pothole, every pebble and every rut had long been familiar and dear to me; beyond the road there was an avenue of cropped lime trees, and here and there you caught sight of a wattle fence. Across the avenue you could see a meadow, with a barn on one side of it and a wood opposite; far into the wood you could spot the watchman's hut. The window on the right overlooked part of the veranda where the grown-ups usually sat before dinner. Sometimes you would look out that way while Karl Ivanych was correcting a dictation sheet, and you would see Mother's dark head or someone's back and you would hear the muffled sounds of chatter and laughter; you would be so annoyed that you could not be there and would think to yourself: "When will I ever be big enough to stop studying and be able to sit with those I love instead of with these *Dialogues*?" Annoyance would turn to sadness and, God only knows why and how, you would be so lost in thought that you would not hear Karl Ivanych getting cross about your mistakes.

Karl Ivanych took off his dressing gown, put on a dark-blue tailcoat with ruched padded shoulders, adjusted his cravat before the mirror and led us downstairs to greet Mother.

2

Maman

MOTHER WAS SITTING in the drawing room pouring tea; she held the teapot with one hand and with the other the tap of the samovar, from which water was dripping over the top of the teapot onto the tray. Yet, even though she was watching closely, she did not notice this, nor did she notice that we had come in.

So many memories of the past spring up when you try to envision the features of a loved one, that you see them hazily through those memories as through tears. Those are tears of the imagination. When I try to remember my mother such as she was then, all I can see are her brown eyes, always with the same expression of kindness and love, the birthmark on her neck, just below the spot where tiny hairs curled, her white embroidered collar, her thin, tender hand, which had so often caressed me and which I had so often kissed, but her overall appearance eludes me.

To the left of the sofa stood an old English piano at which sat my olive-skinned little sister Lyubochka; with her little, pink fingers, which she had just washed in cold water, she played Clementi's* *Études* with obvious concentration. She was eleven; she wore a short cotton dress and white lace-trimmed pantalettes and she could manage octaves only in arpeggio. Beside and half-facing her sat Marya Ivanovna* in a bonnet with pink ribbons and a loose-fitting blue jacket, with an angry red face that took on an even sterner expression when Karl Ivanych came in. She looked forbiddingly at him and, without acknowledging his bow, continued to count, beating time with her foot: "*Un, deux, trois; un, deux, trois,*" louder and more assertively than before.

Karl Ivanych, not paying any attention to this at all, walked straight over to my mother and, as was his custom, greeted her in German. She collected herself and shook her head as if wanting to chase away sad thoughts, gave her hand to Karl Ivanych and kissed his wrinkled temple as he kissed her hand.

"*Ich danke, lieber Karl Ivanych,*"* and continuing to speak in German, she asked: "Have the children slept well?"

Karl Ivanych was deaf in one ear and now, with the piano noise, heard nothing at all. He bent closer to the sofa, resting one hand on the table and, standing on one foot, lifted his cap with a smile, which at the time I considered the height of refinement, and said:

"Will you excuse me, Natalya Nikolayevna?"

Karl Ivanych never took off his cap for fear of his bald head catching cold, but each time he came into the drawing room he would ask for permission to keep it on.

"Put it back on, Karl Ivanych... I asked you whether the children had slept well?" said Maman quite loudly, moving closer to him.

But again he did not hear anything, covered his bald head with his red cap and smiled even more engagingly.

"Do stop for a moment, Mimi," said Maman with a smile to Marya Ivanovna, "we can't hear a thing."

When Mother smiled, her face, beautiful as it was, became infinitely more so and everything around it seemed to brighten up. If I could catch but a glimpse of that smile in the painful moments of my life, I would not know the meaning of sorrow. It seems to me that what is called beauty in a face lies in its smile: if a smile adds to the charm of a face, then the face is beautiful; if it doesn't change it, it is ordinary; if it spoils it, it is ugly.

After saying good morning to me, Maman took my head in both her hands, tilted it back, then looked intently at me and said:

"Have you been crying today?"

I did not reply. She kissed my eyes and asked in German:

"What were you crying about?"

When she talked to us in that affectionate way, she always spoke in German, which she knew to perfection.

"I cried in my sleep, Maman," I said, remembering the made-up dream in all its detail and instinctively shuddering at the thought of it.

Karl Ivanych confirmed my words, but kept silent about the dream. After chatting about the weather, with Mimi joining in, Maman put six sugar lumps on a tray for a few favoured servants, got to her feet and went over to the embroidery frame that stood by the window.

"Well, go to Papa now, children, and tell him to come and see me without fail before going to the threshing floor."

The music, the counting and the forbidding looks resumed and we went off to see Papa. Passing through the room, still known, as in my grandfather's day, as "the servants' pantry", we entered the study.

3

Papa

H E WAS STANDING BY HIS DESK, pointing to some envelopes, papers and small piles of money, and became very animated as he heatedly explained something to the steward Yakov Mikhailov, who, standing in his usual place between the door and the barometer with his hands behind his back, rapidly moved his fingers in all directions.

The more animated Papa became, the faster the fingers moved and vice versa – when Papa stopped talking, the fingers also stopped moving – but when Yakov himself began to speak, his fingers became hugely agitated and jumped about desperately. From their movements I imagine that you could guess Yakov's secret thoughts; his face after all remained calm throughout, reflecting an awareness of his own merit as well as of his subordinate position – in other words: I'm right, but then again you'll do as you please!

When he saw us, Papa merely said:

"Just a minute, I'll be right with you."

And with a nod of his head he indicated that one of us should close the door.

"Oh, dear God! What's the matter with you today, Yakov?" he continued, addressing the steward and twitching his shoulder (a habit of his). "This envelope with 800 roubles enclosed…"

Yakov moved the abacus, put in 800 and directed his gaze at an indeterminate spot, waiting for what would come next.

"…is for expenses on the estate during my absence. Do you understand? You should be getting 1,000 roubles from the mill… am I right? You should be getting 8,000 in loans back from the Treasury; for the hay, of which we could sell 7,000 *poods*,* according to your calculations – let's say at forty-five copecks a *pood* – you'll get 3,000: consequently, how much money will you have in total? 12,000… Am I right or not?"

"That's right, sir," said Yakov.

But judging by his rapid finger movements, I noticed that he wanted to retort; Papa cut him short:

"So, from that money you'll send 10,000 to the Council for Petrovskoye. As for the money that is in the office," continued Papa (Yakov cancelled the previous 12,000 and put in 21,000), "bring it to me and you'll enter it under today's expenses." (Yakov shook the abacus and turned it over, probably to show that the 21,000 would also disappear.) "You'll deliver this envelope here with money in it to the person to whom it is addressed."

I was standing close to the table and glanced at the address. It was to "Karl Ivanych Mauer".

Papa, having probably noticed that I had read something I should not have, put his hand on my shoulder and nudged me gently away from the table. I did not understand whether this was meant as a caress or as a reprimand, so to be on the safe side I kissed his big veined hand, which lay on my shoulder, anyway.

"Very well, sir," said Yakov. "And what do you instruct me to do with the Khabarovka money?"

Khabarovka was Maman's estate.

"Leave it in the office and on no account must it be used for anything without my permission."

Yakov remained silent for a few seconds, then suddenly his fingers began to twirl with intensified speed, and the dutifully dull expression with which he listened to his master's orders changed to one of cunning alertness which was more natural to him; he drew the abacus towards him and began to speak:

"Allow me to report to you, Pyotr Alexandrych, that it may be as you please, but it is impossible to pay the Council on time. You were good enough to explain," he continued deliberately, "that we should get money from the loans, the mill and the hay…"(Having enumerated these items, he put them in on the abacus.) "So I fear that we may have made some errors with the calculations," he added, and briefly fell silent, glancing very seriously at Papa.

"Why?"

"Be so kind as to look, sir: as regards the mill, the miller has already been to see me twice to ask for a delay in payment and he swore to God that he had no money… He's actually here right now: would you perhaps like to speak to him yourself?"

"What does he have to say?" asked Papa, indicating with his head that he did not want to speak to the miller.

"Well, it's the same old story, isn't it? He says that there has been no grinding at all and that whatever little money there was, he's spent it all on the dam. Even if we were to dismiss him, sir, what would we gain by it? As regards the loans you were pleased to mention, I believe that I have already reported to you that our money is deposited there and that we are not about to get it back any time soon. The other day I sent a cartload of flour to Ivan Afanasych with a note on the subject: he again replied that he was happy to do his best for Pyotr Alexandrych, but that the matter was out of his hands and that it looked unlikely that you would get your payment within two months. As regards the hay you were pleased to mention, let's say it gets sold for 3,000…"

He put in 3,000 on the abacus and was silent for a moment, looking now at the abacus, now into Papa's eyes, as much as if to say, "You can see for yourself how little it is! And we'll lose out again if we sell it now, as you yourself may be good enough to know…"

It was clear that he still had a large store of arguments; this must have been why Papa interrupted him.

"I will not alter my arrangements," he said, "but if there is indeed to be a delay in receiving this money, then there is nothing to be done and you'll have to take as much as is needed from the Khabarovka estate."

"Yes, sir."

From the expression on Yakov's face and the movement of his fingers it was obvious that this last instruction afforded him much satisfaction.

Yakov was a serf, a diligent and devoted man; like all good stewards, he was extremely stingy on his master's account and had the strangest notions as to what was of benefit to his master. He was constantly concerned about increasing his master's property at the expense of his mistress's property, trying to prove that all her estate's income should be used towards Petrovskoye (the estate we lived in). In this instance he was triumphant because he had scored his point.

After greeting us, Papa said that we had idled away our time in the country long enough, that we were not little boys any more and that the time had come to study in earnest.

"I think you already know that I'm leaving for Moscow tonight and that I'm taking you with me," he said. "You'll live with your grandmother and Maman will stay here with the girls. And you know that the only consolation for her will be to hear that you are studying well and that everyone is pleased with your progress."

The last few days there had been some noticeable preparations going on and, although we had expected something unusual to happen, this news did affect us terribly. Volodya turned red and in a trembling voice passed on Mother's message.

"That's what my dream foretold!" I thought. "Please God may nothing worse happen."

I began to feel very, very sorry about Mother and at the same time I was happy at the thought of us really being big boys now.

"If we are indeed leaving today, then there won't be any lessons; that's splendid!" I thought. "However, I'm sorry for Karl Ivanych. They are probably letting him go; otherwise they wouldn't have prepared that envelope for him. It would be better to go on doing lessons for ever and not go away and part with Mother and hurt poor Karl Ivanych. He's so very unhappy as it is!"

These thoughts were flashing through my mind; I did not move an inch and stared at the black bows on my shoes.

After exchanging a few more words with Karl Ivanych about a drop in the barometer and instructing Yakov not to feed the dogs as the plan was to ride out and test the young hounds in farewell after dinner, Papa, against our expectations, sent us off to our lessons, consoling us however with the promise that he would take us hunting.

On my way upstairs I ran onto the veranda. In the sunshine by the doorway, with eyes half-closed, lay Father's favourite wolfhound, Milka.

"Milochka," I said, stroking and kissing her nose, "we're off today. Goodbye! We'll never see each other again."

Deeply moved, I burst into tears.

4

Lessons

KARL IVANYCH WAS EXTREMELY OUT OF SORTS. This was apparent from the way he knit his brows, flung his coat into the cupboard and furiously tied on his belt, and from the way he jabbed at the book of *Dialogues* with his nail to point out how much we had to learn off by heart. Volodya applied himself well, but I was so upset that I really could not do anything. For a long time I stared vacantly at the book of *Dialogues*, but was unable to read because of the tears that welled up in my eyes at the thought of the impending separation; when the time came for me to recite to Karl Ivanych, who listened to me with his eyes screwed up (this was a bad sign), just at the place where one person says: "*Wo kommen sie her?*"* and the other one replies: "*Ich komme vom Kaffee Haus,*"* I could no longer keep back my tears, and sobs prevented me from saying: "*Haben sie die Zeitung nicht gelesen?*"* When we turned to writing, my tears falling on the paper made such a smudged mess that it was as if I had been writing with water on wrapping paper.

Karl Ivanych became angry and made me get down on my knees. He repeated several times that I was being stubborn, that this was play-acting (a favourite expression of his), threatened me with the ruler and demanded that I apologize, although I could not utter a single word through my tears. He must finally have felt that he was being unfair, and went off to Nikolai's room, slamming the door behind him.

From the schoolroom we could hear the conversation next door.

"Have you heard, Nikolai, that the children are going to Moscow?" said Karl Ivanych, as he went in.

"Yes, indeed, I heard."

Nikolai must have attempted to get to his feet, because Karl Ivanych said: "Sit down, Nikolai!" And he shut the door behind him. I left the corner and went over to the door to eavesdrop.

"However many kind deeds you do for people, however much you become attached, you must not expect gratitude, isn't that so, Nikolai?" said Karl Ivanych with feeling.

Nikolai, who sat by the window mending boots, nodded in agreement.

"I have now lived twelve years in this house and I can say, before God, Nikolai," continued Karl Ivanych, lifting his eyes and his snuffbox towards the ceiling, "that I have loved them and looked after them better than if they had been my own children. Do you remember, Nikolai, when Volodyenka had a fever, do you remember how I sat by his bedside for nine days without once shutting my eyes. Yes! Then I was kind, dear Karl Ivanych, then I was needed, and now," he added, smiling ironically, "now *the children have grown up: they have to study in earnest.* As though they are really not learning anything here, Nikolai!"

"I can't think what more they could learn," said Nikolai, laying down his awl and pulling at the thick wax thread with both hands.

"So now I am no longer needed and I have to be sent away, and where are the promises? The gratitude? I love and respect Natalya Nikolayevna, Nikolai," he said, laying his hand on his chest. "But what is she? Her wish in this house counts for no more than this." And he threw a piece of leather on the floor with an expressive gesture. "I know who's behind this and why I'm no longer needed: because I don't flatter them or indulge them in everything like *some people.* I'm used to always stating the truth in front of everyone," he said proudly. "God be with them! They won't grow richer by my not being here, and I, please God, will find myself a crust of bread, don't you agree, Nikolai?"

Nikolai raised his head and looked at Karl Ivanych as if wanting to reassure himself that he would indeed be able to find a crust of bread – but said nothing.

Karl Ivanych continued talking in this vein for a long time: he spoke of some general, in whose home he had lived and where his services had been so much more appreciated (I felt very hurt to hear that), he spoke of Saxony, of his parents, of his friend Schönheit the tailor and so on and so forth.

I felt for his grief and it pained me that Father and Karl Ivanych, both of whom I loved almost equally, did not understand one other. I returned to the corner, sat on my heels and mulled over ways to restore peace between them.

After returning to the schoolroom, Karl Ivanych told me to get up and to prepare my exercise book for a dictation. When everything was ready, he majestically lowered himself into the armchair and with a voice that seemed to come from some cavernous depths he began to dictate the following: "*Von al-len Lei-den-schaf-ten die grau-samste ist… haben sie geschrieben?*"* Here he stopped, slowly sniffed some tobacco and continued with renewed vigour: "*Die grausamste ist die Un-dank-bar-heit… Ein grosses U.*"* After writing the last word, I looked up at him expecting the next phrase.

"*Punctum*,"* he said with a barely discernible smile and he signalled for us to hand over the exercise books. He read this dictum – a reflection of his own intimate thought – a few more times with various intonations and with an expression of great satisfaction; then he set us a history lesson and sat by the window. His face was no longer glum; it now reflected the satisfaction of a man who had taken fitting revenge for an injury inflicted upon him.

It was a quarter to one, but Karl Ivanych gave no sign that he was going to let us go: he kept on setting us new lessons. Boredom and hunger grew in equal measure. Highly impatient, I looked out for all the signs that indicated that dinner* was near. The maid was setting off with her dishcloth to wash the plates, there was a clattering of plates and dishes in the pantry, the table was being extended and the chairs placed around it, and Mimi, Lyubochka and Katyenka (Katyenka was Mimi's twelve-year-old daughter) were coming in from the garden, but no sign of Foka, the butler, who always came in and announced that dinner was ready. Only then would we be allowed to throw aside our books and run downstairs without regard to Karl Ivanych.

17

Footsteps could be heard on the stairs, but it was not Foka! I knew his step and always recognized the squeaking of his boots. The door opened and in its frame appeared a figure totally unknown to me.

5

The Holy Fool

A MAN OF ABOUT FIFTY, with a pale, pockmarked, oblong face, long grey hair and a scant, reddish beard, entered the room. He was so tall that he had to lower his head as well as bend his whole body to get through the door. He wore a tattered garment that could be a kaftan or a cassock; in his hand he held a huge staff. When he came into the room, he hit the floor with it as hard as he could and then, contorting his eyebrows and opening his mouth excessively wide, he burst into a frightful and unnatural cackle. He was blind in one eye, and that eye's white pupil continually darted about, giving his face, unappealing as it was, an even more repulsive expression.

"Aha! I have found you!" he shouted and, running up to Volodya with tiny steps, he grabbed his head and carefully began to examine his crown; then he moved away from him with a perfectly serious expression, walked over to the table and began blowing under the oilcloth and making the sign of the cross over it. "Oh, what a pity! Oh, oh, it's painful! The dear ones... will fly away," he said in a voice shaky with tears and, peering at Volodya with feeling, he began to wipe away with his sleeve the tears which were indeed falling.

His voice was gruff and wheezy, his movements hurried and jerky, his speech irrational and incoherent (he never used pronouns), but the emphasis of his words was so poignant and his yellow misshapen face at times assumed such a candid, sorrowful expression that when you listened to him you could not help but experience a mixture of pity, fear and sorrow.

This was Grisha, the holy fool* and pilgrim.

Where was he from? Who were his parents? What inspired him to choose a pilgrim's life? No one knew. I only know that from the age of fifteen he became known as a holy fool who went around barefoot in winter and summer, visited monasteries, gave small icons to those he took a liking to and spoke in riddles which some interpreted as prophecies, that no one had ever known him in any other guise, that he occasionally went to my grandmother's and that some people said that he was the unfortunate son of wealthy parents and a pure soul, and others said that he was simply a bone-idle peasant.

At last the longed-for and punctual Foka arrived and we went downstairs. Grisha, sobbing and still uttering various absurdities, followed us, banging his staff on the stairs. Papa and Maman were walking arm in arm up and down the drawing room talking softly to each other. Mimi sat primly in one of the armchairs adjoining the sofa at right angles. She admonished the girls, who sat next to her, with a stern but muted voice. As soon as Karl Ivanych came into the room, she looked up at him and immediately turned away and her face took on an expression which could have been interpreted as, "I'm not aware of you being here, Karl Ivanych". It was clear from the girls' eyes that they very much wanted to communicate some all-important news to us as soon as possible, but it would have been breaking Mimi's rules for them to jump up from their seats and join us. We had to go up to her first and say, "*Bonjour* Mimi!" and click our heels, and only then would we be allowed to speak.

What an insufferable creature that Mimi was! It was impossible to talk about anything in her presence: she considered everything unseemly. What is more, she constantly nagged us with: "*Parlez donc français,*"* just when, as luck would have it, we wanted to chat in Russian. Or at dinner when you had just begun to enjoy some dish or other and wanted to be left in peace, she would say without fail: "*Mangez donc avec du pain,*"* or, "*Comment est-ce que vous tenez votre fourchette?*"* "What business is it of hers?" you would think to yourself. "Let her look after the girls, we have Karl Ivanych to see to us." And I totally shared his hatred for *some people*.

"Ask Mama to let us go out on the hunt," whispered Katyenka, pulling me by my jacket as the grown-ups walked ahead into the dining room.

"All right, we'll try."

Grisha ate in the dining room but at a separate small table. He did not raise his eyes from his plate, gave an occasional sigh, pulled some frightful faces and said, as if talking to himself: "What a pity! It flew off, the dove will fly up to heaven... Oh, there's a stone on the grave!" and so on.

19

Maman had been upset since morning; Grisha's presence, his words and actions noticeably aggravated her mood.

"Oh yes, I'd almost forgotten to ask you something else," she said, handing Father a plate of soup.

"What's that?"

"Do please order those dreadful dogs of yours to be locked up, because they nearly bit poor Grisha as he walked across the yard. They could attack the children too."

When he heard that they were talking about him, Grisha turned towards the table, began to show them the torn flaps of his clothes and, still chewing, began to repeat over and over again:

"He wanted me to be torn to pieces… God wouldn't let it happen. It's a sin to set the dogs on me! A grave sin! Don't beat, *bolshak*,* why beat? God is merciful… times have changed."

"What's he talking about?" asked Papa, sternly looking him over. "I don't understand a thing."

"But I do," replied Maman. "He told me that some huntsman let the dogs loose on him on purpose and that's why he says: 'He wanted me to be torn to pieces, but God wouldn't let it happen,' and he's asking you not to punish the huntsman for this."

"Oh, I see!" said Papa. "But why does he imagine I want to punish that huntsman? You know that on the whole I am not too fond of these gentlemen," he went on in French, "and I particularly don't like this one and he should be—"

"Oh, don't say that, my dear," interrupted Maman, as if afraid of something. "What do you know about it?"

"I have had plenty of opportunity to learn something about this sort of person, with so many of them coming to you – they're all the same. It's always the same story…"

It was plain that Mother had a completely different view on the matter and did not want to argue.

"Please pass me a pasty," she said. "Aren't they good today?"

"No, it makes me angry," went on Papa, taking a pasty and holding it beyond Maman's reach. "No, it makes me angry when I see intelligent and educated people being taken in."

And he struck the table with his fork.

"I asked you to pass me a pasty," repeated Maman, holding out her hand.

20

"And it is an excellent thing," went on Papa, moving his hand further away, "that they take these people into custody. All they do is upset some people who already suffer from weak nerves," he added with a smile, noticing that Maman did not take to this conversation at all, and he handed her the pasty.

"I'll say just one thing on the subject: it is hard to believe that a man who, in spite of being aged sixty, goes around barefoot winter and summer and wears chains weighing two *poods* under his clothes without ever removing them, and has more than once refused any offer of a quiet life – it is hard to believe that such a man does all this out of laziness. As for the prophecies," she added with a sigh after a brief pause, "*je suis payée pour y croire.** I believe I told you how Kiryusha foretold my late father's death to the day and the hour."

"What have you done to me!" said Father, smiling, cupping his mouth with his hand on the side where Mimi sat. (When he did that I used to listen very attentively, expecting something funny.) "Why did you remind me of his feet? I've just looked at them and now I won't be able to eat anything."

Dinner was nearing its end. Lyubochka and Katyenka kept on winking at us and fidgeted on their chairs, generally expressing huge restlessness. The winks signified: "Why don't you ask them to let us go out on the hunt?" I nudged Volodya with my elbow. Volodya nudged me and finally made up his mind: he explained, first with a timid voice, then quite firmly and loudly, that, as we were leaving that day, we would like the girls to come hunting with us in the wagonette. After some deliberation among the grown-ups, the matter was settled in our favour and – what was even nicer – Maman said that she would come too.

6

Preparations for the Hunt

O VER DESSERT Yakov was summoned and given instructions regarding the wagonette, the dogs and the saddle horses – everything in great detail, mentioning each horse by name. Volodya's horse was lame; Papa ordered a hunter to be saddled for him. This expression "hunter" sounded somehow odd to Maman's ears; it seemed to her

21

that a hunter must be some kind of rabid beast, which would undoubtedly bolt and kill Volodya. Despite Papa's assurances and Volodya saying with remarkable spirit that it was fine and that he loved it when a horse bolted, poor Maman reiterated that she would be in agony throughout the outing.

Dinner came to an end; the grown-ups went into the study to drink coffee and we ran into the garden to shuffle our feet along the paths covered in yellow fallen leaves and to chat. We talked first about Volodya riding a hunter, and what a shame it was that Lyubochka did not run as fast as Katyenka, and about how interesting it would be to see Grisha's chains and so on; yet the fact that we were about to part was not mentioned at all. Our conversation was interrupted by the clatter of the wagonette driving up, with a serf boy sitting on each of its springs. Behind the wagonette came the huntsmen with the dogs; behind the huntsmen – the coachman Ignat on the horse intended for Volodya, leading my old *klepper** on the rein. At first we rushed to the fence where you could see all these interesting things, then, shrieking, we tramped upstairs to get dressed, trying to look as much as possible like huntsmen. One of the best ways to do this was by tucking our trousers inside our boots. We got down to this without delay, rushing to finish quickly and run down to the porch where we could enjoy both seeing the dogs and the horses and chatting with the huntsmen.

It was a hot day. Oddly shaped small white clouds had been appearing on the horizon since morning; then a light breeze began to drive them closer and closer, so that at times they covered the sun. However much the clouds gathered and darkened, they were apparently not destined to gather into a storm and disrupt our enjoyment this one last time. Towards evening they began to disperse again: some turned pale, lengthened out and fled to the horizon; others just above our heads turned into transparent white scales; only one large black storm cloud hovered in the east. Karl Ivanych always knew which cloud would go where; he declared that this cloud would float towards Maslovka, that it would not rain and the weather would be wonderful.

Foka, despite his advancing years, ran very niftily and quickly down the stairs, called out, "Drive up!" and, placing his legs far apart, stood firmly in the middle of the entrance, between the threshold and the spot to which the coachman was to drive up the wagonette: he had the look of a man who did not need to be reminded of his responsibilities.

The ladies came out and after some debate as to who would sit where and who would hold on to whom (though I felt that that there was no need at all to hold on), they sat down, opened their parasols and set off. As the wagonette started moving, Maman, pointing at the "hunter", asked the coachman with a trembling voice:

"Is that Vladimir Petrovich's horse?"

When the coachman said that it was, she gestured with her hand and turned away. I was in a state of great impatience: I climbed on my horse, looked straight between his ears and did several manoeuvres around the yard.

"Watch you do not crush the dogs," one of the huntsmen said to me.

"Don't worry: this isn't my first time," I replied haughtily.

Volodya mounted his "hunter" not without a shudder in spite of his strong character and, patting her, asked several times:

"Is she docile?"

He looked very good on a horse, like a grown-up. His thighs were pressed so firmly and neatly around the saddle that I felt envious – especially because I, as far as I could make out from my shadow, did not look like that at all.

Papa's steps could now be heard on the stairs; the whipper-in drove on the unleashed hounds; the huntsmen with the *borzois** called them up and began to mount their horses. The groom led a horse to the porch. Papa's pack of dogs, which had been lying in various picturesque poses nearby, rushed up to him. Milka, with a small bead collar, its metal clip rattling, ran up happily from behind him. She always greeted the kennel dogs when she came out: she played with some, sniffed a few and growled, or looked for fleas on others.

Papa mounted his horse and we set off.

7

The Hunt

THE MASTER OF THE HOUNDS, nicknamed Turka, rode ahead on a blue-grey hook-nosed horse, wearing a shaggy hat, with a huge horn over his shoulders and a knife in his belt. Judging by the man's joyless and fierce appearance, you might have thought that he was on his way to mortal combat rather than on a hunting expedition. Close on his horse's heels, in a rippling mass of mixed colours, ran the hounds, closely packed. It was sad to see what fate befell any unfortunate hound that took it upon herself to lag behind. She would have to drag along her leash-mate with all her might, and when she succeeded, one of the whippers-in coming in from behind would be sure to crack at her with his whip, saying: "Back in the pack!" When we emerged from the gate, Papa ordered us to ride along the road with the huntsmen and he turned into a field of rye.

The grain harvest was in full swing. The vast, glistening yellow field was hemmed in only on one side by a tall dark-bluish forest, which in those days seemed to me a very distant, secret place beyond which the world either ended or uninhabited lands began. The whole field was covered with sheaves and people. Among the tall thick rye stalks you could, here and there, catch a glimpse, where a strip had been reaped, of a reaper's bent back, of the sweep of the ears as she shifted them between her fingers, of a woman in the shade stooping over a cradle, and of scattered sheaves among the stubble dotted with cornflowers. On the other side peasants, standing on carts wearing only their shirts, loaded the stacks, raising clouds of dust over the dry scorching field. The village elder, in boots, his *armyak** slung over his shoulder and with a notched stick in his hand, caught sight of Papa in the distance and took off his woollen hat, wiped his ginger hair and beard with a towel and shouted at the women. The chestnut horse which Father rode was trotting lightly and playfully, occasionally dropping her head down to her chest, or pulling at the reins and with her thick tail swishing off flies and gadflies that were greedily clinging on to her. Two *borzois*, their sickle-shaped tails curved up tautly and lifting their legs high, jumped gracefully over high stubble behind the horse's legs. Milka ran ahead, turning up her head in expectation of titbits. The chatter of people, the clatter of horses and carts, the merry whistle of quails, the buzzing of insects hovering in the air in motionless swarms, the smell of wormwood, straw and horses' sweat, thousands of different colours and shadows cast by the burning sun across the bright yellow stubble, the dark blue of the distant forest and the pale lilac clouds, white gossamer threads suspended in the air or lying across the stubble – all of these I saw, heard and felt.

When we reached the Kalinovo woods, we found the wagonette already there and, beyond our expectations, another cart, with one horse, and the butler sitting in the middle of it. Underneath the straw we could see a samovar, a tub of ice cream and some enticing small bundles and boxes. There was no mistaking it: this was to be a picnic tea, with ice cream and fruit. At the sight of the cart we cried out with joy because we considered having a picnic tea in the woods on the grass, in a place where no one had ever had tea before, a great treat.

Turka rode up to the spot where all the hounds were gathered,* stopped, listened carefully to Papa's detailed instructions on how to line up and where to come out (incidentally, he never took any notice of those instructions and did as he pleased), unleashed the dogs, took his time strapping the leashes to his saddle, mounted his horse and, whistling softly, disappeared behind the young birches. The unleashed hounds showed their appreciation first of all by wagging their tails and shaking themselves; then, sniffing around and still wagging their tails, they darted off in various directions.

"Do you have a neckerchief?" asked Papa.

I pulled one out of my pocket and showed it to him.

"Well, take that grey dog with you with the neckerchief…"

"Zhiran?" I asked with the air of a connoisseur.

"Yes, and run along the road. When you get to the clearing, stop and watch: don't come back without a hare!"

I wound my neckerchief round Zhiran's shaggy neck and rushed off to the appointed place. Papa laughed and called after me:

"Hurry up or you'll be too late."

Zhiran kept stopping, pricking up his ears and listening to the hallooing of the huntsmen. I did not have the strength to drag him onwards, and began to shout: "Halloo! Halloo!" Zhiran then strained so hard that I could hardly hold him back, and I fell over more than once before I reached the clearing. I chose a shady level spot by the roots of a tall oak tree, lay on the grass, sat Zhiran next to me and waited. My imagination, as usual in such circumstances, ran away with me. I was imagining that I had already coursed my third hare by the time the first hound responded in the woods. Turka's voice rang out stronger and more animated through the trees; a hound bayed and her voice could be heard more and more frequently; she was soon joined by another deeper voice, then a third, then a fourth… Their voices now stopped, now drowned each other out. The sounds

25

became increasingly loud and continuous and finally merged into one resounding tumultuous din. *The hounds were in full cry, in hot pursuit of their prey.*

When I heard this, I froze to the spot. With my eyes fixed on the edge of the wood, I smiled inanely; I was sweating profusely and, although the drops running down my chin tickled me, I did not wipe them off. I felt that there could not be a more crucial moment than this one. This state of tension was too unnatural to last for long. The hounds were spilling out at the very edge of the wood one moment, while the next they were gradually moving away from me; there was no hare. I began to look in all directions. It was the same with Zhiran: at first he strained and yelped, then he lay down next to me, put his nose on my knees and calmed down.

By the exposed roots of the oak under which I sat, along the grey earth, in between dry oak leaves, acorns, dry moss-covered twigs, yellowy-green moss and a few thin blades of grass forcing their way upwards, swarmed countless ants. One behind the other they hurried along their beaten track: some with a load, others without. I picked up a stick and blocked their passage. It was fascinating to watch how some, scorning danger, crept under it, others climbed over it, and some, particularly those with a load, became totally lost and did not know what to do: they stopped, looked for a way round, turned back or else reached my arm via the stick and were apparently prepared to climb under the sleeve of my jacket. I was distracted from these interesting observations by a butterfly with little yellow wings that fluttered particularly enticingly in front of me. No sooner had I turned my attention towards her, than she flew away from me and hovered over a wilting white clover bloom and then settled on it. I do not know whether the sun was warming her or whether she was drawing the sap from this little plant – it was plain to see that she was feeling very happy. She occasionally fluttered her wings and pressed against the flower, and finally just froze. I leant my head on my hands and watched her contentedly.

Suddenly Zhiran began to howl and tugged so hard that I almost fell over. I glanced back. At the edge of the woods skipped a hare, one ear flattened and the other slightly raised. The blood rushed to my head and in that instant I forgot everything: in a frenzied voice I shouted something out, let the dog go and rushed ahead. No sooner had I done so, than I already began to regret it: the hare cowered, took a leap and was no longer to be seen.

But how mortified I felt when, following the hounds driven in full cry to the edge of the woods, Turka appeared from behind the bushes. He saw my mistake (which was my failure to hold on) and, looking at me scornfully, just said:

"Oh, master!" But you had to know how he said this! I would have found it easier had he hung me on his saddle like a hare.

I stood rooted to the spot for a long time in great despair; I did not call my dog and only kept on repeating as I slapped my thighs:

"Dear God, what have I done!"

I heard the hounds being driven further on, the hallooing on the other side of the thicket, the hare being caught and Turka summoning the dogs with his huge horn – and still I did not move an inch…

8

Games

THE HUNT WAS OVER. A rug had been spread out in the shade of some young birch trees and the whole company sat on it in a circle. Gavrilo the butler, having flattened the green lush grass near him, wiped some plates and took plums and peaches wrapped in leaves out of a small box. The sun shone through the green branches of the young birches and cast quivering circles of light on the pattern of the rug, on my legs and even on Gavrilo's perspiring bald head. A light breeze darted through the leaves of the trees, through my hair and my clammy face, refreshing me beyond measure.

After we had finished the ice cream and fruit, there was nothing left to do on the rug and we got up and went off to play despite the scorching slanting rays of the sun.

"Well, what shall we do?" said Lyubochka, squinting in the sunlight and skipping along the grass. "Let's play *Robinson*."

"No… it's boring," said Volodya, who had lazily collapsed on the grass and was chewing on some leaves, "always *Robinson*! If you really want to, then let's rather build a small bower."

Volodya was clearly giving himself airs: he was no doubt proud of having ridden a hunter, and pretended to be very tired. It could also be that he already had too much sense and too little imagination to fully enjoy playing *Robinson*. The game consisted of performing scenes from *Robinson suisse*,* which we had recently read.

"Please, why won't you go along with us?" insisted the girls. "You can be Charles or Ernest or the father, whatever you want," said Katyenka, attempting to pull him up from the ground by his jacket sleeve.

"I really don't want to – it's boring!" said Volodya, stretching himself and smiling smugly.

"We'd be better off at home if no one wants to play," stated Lyubochka through her tears.

She was a terrible cry-baby.

"Well let's do it then; only don't cry, please; I can't stand it!"

The fact that Volodya was indulging us gave us very little pleasure; on the contrary, his idle, bored look ruined all the game's appeal. When we sat down on the ground, imagining ourselves on a fishing expedition, and began to row with all our might, Volodya sat with arms folded in a pose that was anything but a fisherman's. I pointed this out to him, but he replied that we could wave our arms about as much as we liked: we would not win or lose or get anywhere far. I was forced to agree with him. When I set off into the woods, imagining myself going hunting with a stick on my shoulder, Volodya lay on his back, put his hands behind his head and told me to pretend he was going too. Such behaviour and words dampened our enjoyment in the game and were extremely disagreeable, the more so because I secretly had to agree that Volodya was acting reasonably.

I knew that you could not kill a bird, let alone shoot with my stick. It was a game. If you were to reason that way, then you would not ride on chairs, and I believe Volodya himself remembered how on long winter evenings we covered an armchair with shawls and turned it into a carriage; one was the coachman, another the footman, the girls sat in the middle and three chairs were the three horses – and off we went on our way. And what adventures we encountered along that way! And how joyfully and swiftly those winter evenings went by!... If you go by what is real, then there would be no games. And without games, what would be left?

9

Something Akin to First Love

PRETENDING to pick some American fruit from a tree, Lyubochka tore off a leaf with a huge worm on it, threw it on the ground in horror, lifted her arms up in the air and sprang back as if fearful that something might spurt out of it. The game stopped; we all dropped to the ground with our heads close together to look at this rarity.

I looked over Katyenka's shoulder as she tried to lift the worm onto a small leaf that she placed in its path.

I had noticed that many girls had the habit of wriggling their shoulders, attempting with this movement to adjust their low-necked dress that had slipped down back into place. I also remember that Mimi always got cross when they did this, saying: "*C'est un geste de femme de chambre.*"* Bending down over the worm, Katyenka made just this movement and at the same time the breeze lifted the scarf off her little white neck. Her shoulder was two fingers' length away from my lips. I no longer watched the worm; I just stared and stared at Katyenka's shoulder and kissed it as hard as I could. She did not turn round, but I noticed that her neck and ears had turned red. Volodya, without raising his head, said scornfully:

"What's this display of affection?"

But I had tears in my eyes.

I did not take my eyes away from Katyenka. I had long grown used to her fresh fair little face and had always loved it; but now I began to look at it more closely and loved it even more. When we went over to the grown-ups, Papa declared to our great joy that at Mother's request our trip was postponed to the following morning.

We rode home along with the wagonette. Volodya and I, wanting to outdo each other in horsemanship and bravado, pranced alongside it. Judging by my shadow, which was now longer than before, I assumed that I cut the figure of a rather fine horseman, but this feeling of self-satisfaction was soon crushed by the following incident. Wanting once and for all to dazzle all those who sat in the wagonette, I fell back a little; then, aided by the whip and my heels, I drove my horse forwards and assumed a casually charming attitude, wanting to fly past them like a whirlwind on the side where Katyenka sat. But I did not know what would be better: to gallop past in silence or with a loud cry. But that insufferable horse, despite all my efforts, halted so suddenly when she came level with the carriage horses, that I vaulted over the saddle onto her neck and very nearly flew off.

10

What Kind of a Man Was My Father?

H E WAS A MAN of the previous century and, in common with that century's youth, had an indefinable personality, a blend of chivalry, enterprise, self-confidence, courtesy and licentiousness. He looked with scorn upon people of this century, and this stemmed as much from innate pride as from a secret resentment that in our century he could not have the same influence or success he had enjoyed in his. The two overriding passions in his life were cards and women; he won several millions with cards in his lifetime and he had liaisons with countless women from all walks of life.

A tall and well-proportioned figure, a strange way of walking with tiny steps, a habit of twitching his shoulder, small perpetually smiling eyes, a large aquiline nose, irregular, somewhat awkwardly yet pleasingly shaped lips, a speech defect – a slight lisp – and not a hair on his head: such was my father's appearance from when I first remember him, an appearance with which he not only could hold a reputation for being a man *à bonnes fortunes*,* but which made him liked by everyone without exception, people from all backgrounds and stations, and particularly those he wanted to please.

He could prevail in his dealings with everyone. Never having belonged in *very high society*, he always moved in those circles in a manner that won their respect. He knew the exact degree of pride and self-assurance needed to boost him in the opinion of society without offending others. He was original, though not always, and in some cases used this originality as a substitute for good breeding and wealth. Nothing on earth surprised him: whatever resplendent situation he found himself in, he had the air of being born to it. He was such an expert at hiding from others and pushing away from himself the dark side of life, familiar to all and full of petty irritations and afflictions, that it was impossible not to envy him. He was a connoisseur of all things that afforded comfort and enjoyment and knew how to make the most of them. His fixation was his brilliant connections made partly through my mother's family, partly through companions from his youth, with whom he was secretly angry because they had risen high in the ranks while he would remain a retired Lieutenant of the Guards for good. Like all ex-military men he did not know how to dress fashionably; on the other hand he dressed with originality and elegance. He always wore very loose-fitting light clothes, top-quality linen and wide turned-down cuffs and collars... But then, everything suited his tall frame and strong physique, bald head and calm self-assured movements. He was sensitive and even easily moved to tears. Often, when he read aloud, on reaching an emotional passage, his voice would begin to tremble, tears would appear and he would irritably put the book down. He loved music and sang, to his own piano accompaniment, romances composed by his friend A.* or Gypsy songs and arias from operas, but he disliked classical music and, disregarding the general consensus, he openly said that Beethoven's sonatas made him sleepy and bored and that the best music he knew was 'Don't Wake Me Up, Young Girl' as sung by Semyonova and 'Not Alone' as sung by the Gypsy girl Tanyusha.* His nature was such that he needed an audience to perform a good deed. And he only considered good what the public accepted as such. God only knows whether he had any moral convictions. His life was so full of all manner of distractions that he would have had no time to form them and he was so fortunate in life that he saw no need to have them.

In old age he had formed a steady view on things and on set rules, but only based on practical matters: those actions and that lifestyle that provided him with happiness and satisfaction he considered good and he believed that everyone should act likewise. He spoke very convincingly and that ability, it seems to me, reinforced the flexibility of his rules: he was able to describe the same act as an endearing prank or as the meanest of tricks.

11

What Went on in the Study and in the Drawing Room

I T WAS ALREADY GETTING DARK when we reached home. Maman sat down at the piano and we children brought some paper, pencils and paints and settled at the round table to paint. I had only blue paint, but I still resolved to paint the hunt. I painted a very vivid picture of a blue boy riding a blue horse and some blue dogs, but I felt unsure whether you could paint a blue hare and I ran to the study to ask for Papa's advice on the subject. Papa was reading something and to my question: "Are there such things as blue hares?" he replied without raising his head: "Yes, there are, my dear, there are." I returned to the round table, painted a blue hare and then felt the need to turn it into a shrub. I did not like the shrub either, so made it into a tree and the tree became a haystack, the haystack a cloud and I had finally stained the whole sheet of paper so badly with blue paint that I was annoyed and tore it up, and went off to doze in the Voltairean armchair.

Maman played the second concerto by Field,* who had been her teacher. I dozed, and light-hearted, bright and flimsy memories sprang up in my imagination. She began to play Beethoven's *Sonata Pathétique* and my memories became sad, heavy and gloomy. Maman often played those two pieces, which is why I remember the feelings they stirred up in me very well. Those feelings were like memories, but memories of what? It felt as though you were remembering something that never was.

Opposite me was the door to the study and I saw Yakov going in there with some other bearded men wearing kaftans. The door soon shut behind them. "Well, business has started!" I thought. It seemed to me that nothing in the world could be more important than what went on in the study; this thought was also borne out by the fact that everyone usually approached the study whispering and on tiptoe; you could hear Papa's loud voice from inside and catch the smell of his cigar, which, I do not know why, always attracted me strongly. Half asleep, I was suddenly startled by the very familiar squeaking of boots in the servants' room. Karl Ivanych, with a grim determined face and holding some notes in his hand, tiptoed up to the door and gave a light knock. They let him in and the door banged shut again.

"I do hope nothing terrible has happened," I thought. "Karl Ivanych is angry and capable of anything…"

I dozed off again.

Nothing terrible did happen; an hour later the same squeaking boots woke me up again. Karl Ivanych, using his handkerchief to wipe away tears, which I detected on his cheeks, came through the door muttering to himself under his breath and went upstairs. Papa came out after him and entered the drawing room.

"Do you know what I've just decided?" he said cheerfully, resting his hand on Maman's shoulder.

"What's that, my dear?"

"I'll take Karl Ivanych along with the children. There's room in the *britzka*.* They have become used to him and he to them; in fact he is very attached to them, and seven hundred roubles a year won't make any difference, *et puis au fond c'est un très bon diable*."*

I could not grasp at all why Papa was berating Karl Ivanych.

"I'm very glad," said Maman, "both for the children's sake and for his: he's a wonderful old man."

"If you could have seen how touched he was when I told him to look upon those five hundred roubles as a gift... But the funniest of all is the bill that he brought me. It's worth having a look at," he added with a grin, handing her the note written by Karl Ivanych. "It's a gem!"

This is what was in the note:*

For children, two fishing rod – 70 copeck.
   Colour papers, gold edging, glues for boxes for present – 6 r. 55 c.
   Book and bow, present for children – 8r. 16 c.
   Pant for Nikolai – 4 rouble
   *Gold watch promised by Pyotr Alexandrovich from Moscow in 18** at 140 rouble.*
   Such is expected to receive Karl Mauer beside wages – 159 rouble 79 copeck.

When reading this note, where Karl Ivanych demanded to be paid money spent by him on presents and even wanting to be paid for a present he had been promised, anyone would have thought that Karl Ivanych was nothing but an insensitive, mercenary egotist; yet everyone would have been mistaken.

When he went into the study with his notes in his hand and a well-prepared speech in his head, he had planned to spell out eloquently before Papa all the injustices suffered by him in our house, but when he began to speak with that same affecting voice and sensitive intonation which he usually used to dictate to us, he was the one who ended up most affected by his own eloquence; so that when he reached the point where he said "as sad as it will be to part from the children", he was quite overcome, his voice started shaking and he was forced to pull his checked handkerchief out of his pocket.

"Yes, Pyotr Alexandrych," he spoke through his tears (this had not been part of his prepared speech at all), "I have become so accustomed to the children that I don't know what I will do without them. I'd rather stay in your service without wages," he added, wiping away his tears with one hand and handing over the bill with the other.

I can confirm that Karl Ivanych was speaking sincerely at that moment, because I know his kind heart, but how he reconciled the bill with his words remains a mystery to me.

"If it is sad for you, then it is even sadder for me to part from you," said Papa, patting his shoulder. "I've now changed my mind."

Not long before supper, Grisha came into the room. He had not stopped sighing and weeping since he had arrived at the house, which, according to those who believed in his prophetic skills, was a sign that some misfortune was to befall us. He began to say goodbye, and announced that he was off somewhere else the next morning. I winked at Volodya and left the room.

"What?"

"If you want to have a look at Grisha's chains, then let's go straight away to the men's quarters upstairs – Grisha sleeps in the second room – and we can easily sit in the storage room and see everything."

"Excellent! Wait here; I'll call the girls."

The girls ran out and we went upstairs. After deciding, not without arguing, who should step into the dark storage room first, we settled down and began to wait.

12

Grisha

WE WERE ALL SCARED IN THE DARK; we pressed up close to each other and no one said a word. Grisha came in almost straight away, stepping softly. He held his staff in one hand and in the other a tallow candle in a brass candlestick. We held our breath.

"Lord Jesus Christ! Holy Mother of God! Father, Son and Holy Ghost…" Drawing in a deep breath, he repeated this over and over with different intonations and abbreviations peculiar to those who often repeat those words.

After putting his staff in a corner while saying a prayer, he inspected his bed and began to undress. Unfastening his old black girdle, he slowly removed his tattered nankeen coat, folded it carefully and hung it over the back of the chair. His face no longer expressed its usual haste and obtuseness; on the contrary, he was calm, pensive and even dignified. His movements were slow and considered.

Left only in his underclothes, he quietly lowered himself onto the bed, made the sign of the cross all over it and adjusted the chains under his shirt; this was plainly with some effort, because he winced. He sat for a while and carefully examined his underclothes, torn in various places; then he got up, praying while he raised the candle to the level of the icon case, in which stood a few icons, made the sign of the cross before them and turned the candle upside down. It went out with a splutter.

An almost full moon was casting its light on the windows which looked towards the forest. The long white figure of the holy fool was lit up on one side by the pale silvery rays of the moon, on the other it fell as a dark shadow that, merging with the shadow of the window frames, dropped to the floor, ran up the walls and reached the ceiling. In the courtyard the watchman struck the iron gong.

Grisha stood silently in front of the icons, his huge arms folded across his chest, his head bowed and continually sighing heavily; then he lowered himself with difficulty onto his knees and began to pray.

At first he quietly intoned the usual prayers, with the emphasis on just a few words, then he repeated them, louder this time and with more animation. He began to speak in his own words, trying to express himself in Church Slavonic with obvious effort. His words were incoherent, yet poignant. He prayed for all his benefactors (as he called those who took him in), including my mother; he prayed for us, for himself; he asked God to forgive him his grievous sins and he kept on repeating: "God, forgive my enemies!" He lifted himself up with a groan and, again and again repeating the same words, he prostrated himself, and rose to his feet again, despite the weight of his chains, which let out a dull jarring sound as they knocked against the floor.

Volodya pinched my leg very painfully, but I did not even look up: I just rubbed the spot with my hand and with a feeling of childish wonder, compassion and reverence I continued to follow all Grisha's words and movements.

Instead of the fun and laughter I had counted on when we went into the storage room, I shivered and had a sinking feeling.

For a long time Grisha continued in this state of religious fervour and he improvised prayers. Now he repeated a few times in sequence: "Lord have mercy," but each time with renewed strength and expression; now he said: "Forgive me, Lord, teach me, Lord, what to do, teach me what to do, Lord!" with such a voice as though expecting an immediate answer to his words; now we could only hear plaintive sobbing... He sat up on his knees, folded his hands across his chest and fell silent.

I poked my head very quietly round the door and held my breath. Grisha did not move; his chest heaved with sighs. One tear, lit up by the moonlight, had lodged itself in the dull pupil of his blind eye.

"May your will be done!" he suddenly cried out with an inimitable expression, fell with his forehead to the ground and began to sob like a child.

Much water has flowed under the bridge since then, many memories of the past have lost all meaning for me and have turned into hazy dreams; even Grisha the pilgrim completed his last journey long ago, but the impression he made on me and the feeling he awoke in me will never die in my memory.

Oh Grisha, you great Christian! Your faith was so strong that you felt the nearness of God; your love was so immense that words just poured of their own volition from your lips – you did not let reason verify them. And what height of praise you offered His greatness, when, at a loss for words, you fell to the ground in tears!

The deep emotion with which I listened to Grisha could not go on for long; firstly because my curiosity was satisfied and secondly because I had pins and needles in my legs from sitting in one position, and I wanted to join the general whispering and goings on I could hear behind me in the dark storage room. Someone took hold of my hand and whispered: "Whose hand is this?" It was completely dark in the room, but by the touch alone and the voice whispering just above my ear, I immediately recognized Katyenka.

Quite without thinking, I grabbed her arm, with its short sleeve, by the elbow and pressed my lips to it. Katyenka was surprised at this and drew back her arm: in doing so she touched the broken chair standing in the storage room. Grisha raised his head, quietly looked round and, reciting some prayers, began to make the sign of the cross in all the corners. We ran out of the room whispering noisily.

13

Natalya Savishna

IN THE MIDDLE OF THE LAST CENTURY, Natashka, a little girl in a faded dress, barefoot, but cheerful, chubby and red-cheeked, used to run about the farmyards of the village of Khabarovka. At her father's request and in recognition of his services – her father was the clarinet player Sava – my grandfather took her into service to be one of my grandmother's female servants. The housemaid Natashka distinguished herself in her duties by her gentle temperament and her diligence. When my mother was born and there was need of a nanny, they entrusted Natashka with this task. In this new role she won praise and rewards for her hard work, loyalty and devotion to her young mistress. But the powdered head, stockings and buckles of the young, lively servant Foka, who came into frequent contact with Natalya through work, captivated her simple but loving heart. She even decided to go to my grandfather herself to ask permission to marry Foka. My grandfather took this wish as a sign of ingratitude, and in anger he sent poor Natalya off to a cattle farm in his village in the steppes as punishment. After six months, however, seeing that no one could replace her, Natalya was brought back to her previous employment. Back from banishment to her old routine, she appeared before my grandfather, fell at his feet and begged him to restore his favour and kindness and to forget her previous foolishness, which she swore would never be repeated. And indeed, she kept her word.

From then on Natashka became Natalya Savishna and she wore a bonnet; she now transferred all that love, stored up inside her, to her mistress.

When a governess replaced her to look after my mother, she was given the keys to the storeroom and was put in charge of the linen and the provisions. She fulfilled those new responsibilities with similar diligence and love. She lived her life entirely for her master's property, saw waste, damage and theft all around her and tried to counteract this by all means possible.

When Maman married, wishing to thank Natalya Savishna in some way for twenty years of work and devotion, she sent for her and, expressing all her gratitude and love with words of great praise,

37

she handed her an official document with which she granted her her freedom;* she added that whether or not she continued to serve in our house, she would always receive her yearly pension of three hundred roubles. Natalya Savishna listened to all this in silence, then, taking the document in her hand, glanced at it crossly, muttered something through her teeth and ran out of the room, slamming the door. Not understanding the reason for such strange behaviour, Maman waited before going into Natalya Savishna's room. She was sitting on a chest, with tear-stained eyes, wringing her handkerchief through her fingers and staring at the pieces of the torn certificate lying on the floor before her.

"What's the matter with you, dearest Natalya Savishna?" asked Maman, taking her hand.

"Nothing, my dear mistress," she replied. "I must be hateful to you in some way for you to turn me out of the house... Anyway, I'm going."

She snatched her hand away and, hardly containing her tears, tried to leave the room. Maman held her back, put her arms round her and they both burst into tears.

From then on, as long as I remember being alive, I remember Natalya Savishna, her love and tenderness, but only now am I able to appreciate them – at that time it never even entered my head what a rare and marvellous creature that old woman was. Not only did she never talk about herself, she never seemed to think about herself: her whole life was love and self-sacrifice. I was so used to her selfless and tender love for us that I did not imagine it could be otherwise. I never felt grateful towards her nor did I ever ask myself: is she happy? is she contented?

Sometimes, on the pretext of needing something, I would leave my lessons and go to her room. I would sit down and begin to daydream out loud, without in any way feeling inhibited by her presence. She was always busy with something: either knitting a stocking or rummaging in the chests that filled her room, or making a list of the linen and listening to the nonsense I would spout: about how, when I was a general, I'd marry an amazing beauty, I'd buy myself a chestnut horse, I'd build a glass house and I'd send for Karl Ivanych's relatives from Saxony, and so on. In response she would repeat several times: "Yes, my dear little man, yes." Usually, when I stood up and prepared to go, she would open the blue chest, where, inside the lid, as I remember, were stuck a coloured picture of a hussar, a picture from a pomade jar

38

and a drawing by Volodya. She would take a stick of incense from that chest, light it and, waving it to and fro, she would say: "This, my dear, is incense from Ochakov. When your late grandfather – God rest his soul – fought the Turks, he brought this back from there.* This is the last piece," she would add with a sigh.

In the chests that filled her room there was absolutely everything. Whatever we needed, we would usually say: "You'll have to ask Natalya Savishna," and indeed, after some rummaging, she would find the required item and say: "Well, it's a good thing I put it by." In those chests there were thousands of such items which no one, except herself, bothered or even knew about.

Once I became very angry with her. This is how it happened. At dinner, as I poured myself some *kvas*,* I knocked over the carafe and soaked the tablecloth.

"Call Natalya Savishna, so that she may be really pleased with her darling boy," said Maman.

Natalya Savishna came in and, taking in the mess I had made, shook her head; then Maman whispered something in her ear and with a threatening gesture she left the room.

After dinner I went skipping to the reception room in the best of moods, when suddenly Natalya Savishna sprang out from behind the door with the tablecloth in her hand, caught hold of me and, despite desperate resistance on my part, began to rub my face with the wet cloth, repeating over and over again: "Don't stain the tablecloth, don't stain the tablecloth!" I felt so offended that I began to howl with rage.

"How can this be?" I said to myself, pacing up and down the hall, choked up with tears. "Natalya Savishna, or simply Natalya, uses a familiar tone with me and hits me about the face with a wet cloth as if I were a servant boy. That's just awful!"

When Natalya Savishna saw me snivelling, she immediately ran off as I continued to pace up and down, working out in my mind how to repay that insolent Natalya for the insult she had inflicted on me.

A few minutes later Natalya Savishna returned, approached me timidly and began to plead with me:

"That's enough, dearest, don't cry... Forgive me, I'm a fool... I'm to blame... So please forgive me, my little dove... This is for you."

She produced from under her handkerchief a red paper cornet with two toffees and one dried fig in it and she offered it to me with a trembling hand. I could not look that kind old woman in the face. I turned away, took the gift and my tears flowed even more profusely, but this time not from anger but from love and shame.

14

Parting

A T MIDDAY on the day after the events I have just described, the barouche and the *britzka* stood in front of the porch. Nikolai was dressed for the road; in other words, his trousers were tucked into his boots and his old frock coat was tightly belted. He stood in the *britzka* stacking coats and cushions under the seat; when he thought it was too high, he bounced up and down to press them down.

"Be so kind, Nikolai Dmitrych, is it not possible to put the master's box in there too?" said Papa's valet, puffing and panting, leaning out of the barouche. "It's only a small one…"

"You should have said so before, Mikhei Ivanych," replied Nikolai, rushing his words as he crossly flung a small bundle with all his might into the bottom of the *britzka*. "Oh God, my head is spinning already and now there's you with your small boxes…" he added, lifting his cap and wiping away large drops of sweat from his sunburnt brow.

Menservants in coats, kaftans or shirts and without hats, women in everyday clothes and striped scarves with infants in their arms, and barefoot children, stood near the porch watching the carriages and chatting among themselves. One of the coachmen, a bent old man in a winter hat and an *armyak*, was holding the carriage shaft, running his hand over it and intently checking its movement; another one, a fine-looking young lad, wearing a white shirt with red calico gussets and a black cone-shaped felt hat, which he pushed first towards one ear then towards the other as he scratched his blond curls, put his *armyak* on the coach box, tossed the reins over it and, cracking his braided whip, stared either at his boots or at the coachmen who were greasing the *britzka*. One of them was making a supreme effort to hold it up; another, bending over the wheel, was carefully greasing the axle and ball bearing, and in order not to waste any of the grease left on the brush, he even greased around the rim below. The weary post horses, differently coloured, stood by the railing, swishing off the flies with their tails. Some of them, their shaggy swollen legs splayed forwards, narrowed their eyes and dozed; others rubbed against one other in boredom or nibbled at the leaves and stalks of the tough dark-green fern that grew near the porch. There were several *borzois* – some lay panting heavily in the sun, others moved about in the shade under the carriages, licking the grease near the axles. A kind of dusty haze filled the air all around and the horizon was lilac-grey, yet there was not a single cloud in the sky. A strong westerly wind raised columns of dust from the roads and fields, bent the tops of the tall limes and birches in the garden and swept the fallen yellow leaves far away. I sat by the window and waited impatiently for all the preparations to come to an end.

When everyone had gathered in the drawing room near the round table to spend a few minutes together for the last time, it simply did not occur to me what a sad moment we were facing.* The most trivial thoughts went through my head. I asked myself questions such as: which coachman was going to drive the *britzka* and which one the barouche? Who would go with Papa and who with Karl Ivanych? And why is it so important to wrap me up in a shawl and a quilted *chuika*?*

"Am I some kind of sissy? I probably won't freeze to death. I wish all this were over quickly: if we could just get into the carriage and go."

"Who do you want me to give the list of the children's linen to?" said Natalya Savishna, who had come in with tear-stained eyes, turning to Maman with the list in her hand.

"Give it to Nikolai, and come back afterwards to say goodbye to the children."

The old woman wanted to say something, but suddenly stopped, covered her face with her handkerchief, made a gesture with her hand and left the room.

I felt a slight tug in my heart when I saw that gesture, but my impatience to be off was stronger than that feeling and I continued to listen with complete indifference to Papa's conversation with Maman. They were talking about things that obviously did not interest either of them: what should be bought for the house? What should they say to Princess Sophie or Madame Julie? And would the road be good?

Foka came in and with exactly the same voice with which he usually announced "Dinner is ready", stopped at the doorway and said: "The horses are ready." I noticed Maman flinch and turn pale at this news as if she had not expected it.

Foka was told to shut all the doors in the room. I found this highly amusing, as if we were all hiding from someone.

When everyone was seated, Foka also sat down on the edge of a chair, but no sooner had he done so than the door creaked and everyone looked round. Natalya Savishna hurriedly entered the room and, without looking up, sought refuge by the door on the same chair as Foka. I can see them now: Foka's bald head and his fixed wrinkled face and the kind bent figure in a bonnet with some grey hair showing under it. They squeeze together on the one chair and they both feel awkward.

I remained unconcerned and impatient. The ten seconds during which we sat with the doors closed felt like a whole hour to me. Finally everyone stood up, made the sign of the cross and began to say their goodbyes. Papa put his arms round Maman and kissed her several times.

"Enough, my dear," said Papa, "after all we are not parting for ever."

"It's sad all the same!" said Maman in a voice shaky with tears.

When I heard that voice and saw her trembling lips and her eyes full of tears, I forgot everything and began to feel so sad, hurt and terrified that I would have preferred running off to saying goodbye to her. I understood in that instant that when she embraced Father she was already saying goodbye to us.

She began to kiss and make the sign of the cross over Volodya so many times that I pushed forwards, imagining she was now going to turn to me, but she continued to bless him and press him to her bosom. Finally I hugged her and, clinging to her, I cried and cried, thinking of nothing beyond my grief.

When we made our way to the carriages, the tiresome servants approached us in the hallway to say goodbye. Their "please may I kiss your hand", their noisy kisses on our shoulders, the smell of their greasy heads, awoke in me a feeling of irritation very like that of short-tempered people. Inspired by that feeling, I kissed Natalya Savishna extremely coldly on her bonnet as she said goodbye to me in floods of tears.

It is strange that I can see all the servants' faces as if it were now and could draw them all in the most minute detail; yet Maman's face and demeanour resolutely slip my mind: perhaps because all that time I could not pluck up the courage to look at her once. It seemed to me that had I done so, her grief and mine would have reached impossible limits.

I threw myself into the barouche before anyone else and settled down on the back seat. I couldn't see anything behind the raised hood, but some instinct told me that Maman was still there.

"Shall I look at her or not? Well, for the last time!" I said to myself and leant out of the barouche towards the porch. At that moment Maman walked over to the opposite side of the barouche with the same thought in mind and called out my name. When I heard her voice behind me, I turned towards her so quickly that we bumped our heads together; she smiled sadly and kissed me very, very tenderly for the last time.

When we had gone a few *sazhen*,* I decided to take a look at her. The wind had lifted the small blue scarf that was tied round her head; she had bowed her head and covered her face with her hands, and she was slowly climbing up the steps to the porch. Foka was holding on to her.

Papa sat next to me and did not say anything; I was choked up with tears and my throat felt so tight that I was afraid I would suffocate. Driving onto the main road, we saw someone waving a white handkerchief from the balcony. I began to wave back with mine and doing this calmed me down a little. I continued to cry and the thought that my tears were proof of my sensitiveness gave me pleasure and comfort.

When we had travelled a verst* or so, I settled down more quietly and began to stare persistently at the nearest object before my eyes – the hindquarters of the horse running on my side. I watched how this piebald horse swung her tail, how she put one leg before the other, how the coachman's braided whip caught up with her and how both her legs began to leap forwards together. I watched her harness bounce up and down as well as the rings on it and I watched until the harness was covered with foam around the tail. I began to look around: at the fields stirring with ripened rye, at the dark fallow land where in places you could spot a plough, a peasant, a mare with her foal, the verst posts; I even glanced at the coach box to find out which coachman was driving us, and the tears had not yet dried on my face before my thoughts had wandered far away from Mother, from whom I had parted perhaps for ever. But each memory led me back to thoughts of her. I remembered the mushroom I had found the day before in the birch avenue; I remembered how Lyubochka and Katyenka had quarrelled about who should pick it, and I remembered how they cried when they said goodbye to us.

I felt sad about them! And about Natalya Savishna, and the birch avenue and Foka. I even felt sad about nasty Mimi. I felt sad about everything! And poor Maman? And again tears welled up in my eyes, but not for long.

15

Childhood

O H HAPPY, happy time of childhood, never to return! How can you help but love and cherish its memories. Those memories refresh and lift up my soul and are the source of my greatest pleasures.

Sometimes, after running about to my heart's content, I sit at the tea table in my tall chair. It is already late, I have long since finished my cup of milk with sugar, my eyes have begun to close, but I do not stir from my place, I just sit and listen. And how could I not listen? Maman is talking to someone and the sound of her voice is so sweet and warm. That sound alone speaks so fully to my heart! I stare at her face with eyes blurred by drowsiness and she suddenly becomes tiny, tiny – her face is no bigger than a button, but I can still see it quite clearly. I see her glance at me and see her smile. I like to see her so tiny. I squint even more and she becomes no bigger than those little boys reflected in the pupil of one's eye, but I move and the spell is broken. I screw up my eyes, twist round, I do all I can to bring it back, but in vain.

I get down and settle comfortably in the armchair, tucking my legs beneath me.

"You'll fall asleep again, Nikolyenka," says Maman. "You'd better go upstairs."

"I don't want to go to sleep, Mama," you reply, and faint sweet visions fill your imagination, the healthy sleep of childhood bears down on your eyelids and a moment later you doze off and sleep until you are woken up. While half-asleep, you may feel someone's tender hand touching you; by the touch alone you recognize her and still in your sleep you instinctively catch hold of her hand and press it firmly, firmly against your lips.

Everyone has already retired; only one candle burns in the drawing room; Maman has said that she would wake me up herself; she sits down on the armchair where I sleep and runs her wonderfully tender hand through my hair, and I can hear the sound of her dear familiar voice in my ear:

"Get up, my darling: it's time to go to bed."

No one is there to constrain her with an indifferent glance: she is not afraid to pour all her tenderness and love on me. I do not move, but kiss her hand even harder.

"Get up now, my angel."

She puts her other hand under my neck and her fingers move quickly and tickle me. It is quiet and almost dark in the room; my nerves are all on edge from being tickled and woken up. Mama sits right beside me; she touches me; I catch her scent and her voice. All this makes me spring up, throw my arms around her neck, press my head against her breast and, catching my breath, say:

"Oh, dear Mama, how I love you!"

She smiles her sad enchanting smile, takes my head in both her hands, kisses me on the forehead and lifts me onto her lap.

"So you love me very much, do you?" She pauses for a moment, then says: "Love me always, mind, don't ever forget. If your Mama is no longer there, you won't forget her, will you? You won't forget, will you, Nikolyenka?"

She kisses me even more tenderly.

"Don't! Don't say such things, my darling, my dearest Mama!" I cry out, kissing her knees, with tears streaming from my eyes – tears of love and rapture.

After this, when I might be upstairs and standing before the icons in my quilted dressing gown, what a delightful feeling I experience as I recite: "Oh Lord, save Papa and Maman." When repeating those prayers, which my baby lips had babbled for the first time in imitation of my beloved mother, my love for her and my love for God in some strange way merge into the same feeling. After prayers I might wrap myself up in my blanket; my soul feels light, bright and comforted. Dreams are chasing one another – but what are they about? They are

45

elusive but filled with pure love and hopes of radiant happiness. I might remember Karl Ivanych and his bitter lot – the only man whom I knew to be unhappy – and I feel so sorry for him and love him so much that tears begin to flow and I think: "May God grant him happiness; give me the chance to help him, to lighten his burden. I am prepared to sacrifice everything for him." Then I might bury my favourite china toy – a little hare or a dog – in the corner of my downy pillow and think with pleasure how warm and comfortable it must be lying there. I say an additional prayer to ask God to grant everyone happiness, for everyone to be contented and for the weather to be good for next day's walk. I turn over, my thoughts and dreams become entangled, mingle and I sink into a peaceful sleep, my face still wet with tears.

Will that freshness, that light-heartedness, that need for love and that strength of faith which you possess in childhood ever come back? What time of life can be better than that in which the two finest virtues – innocent high spirits and a boundless need for love – are the only impulses in life?

Where are those passionate prayers now? Where is that best gift of all – those pure tears of emotion? The angel of comfort would fly down to wipe away those tears with a smile and blow sweet dreams into the innocent imagination of the child.

Has life left such heavy marks in my heart that those tears and raptures have left me for ever? Are memories all that remain?

16

Verses

NEARLY A MONTH AFTER OUR MOVE TO MOSCOW, I sat upstairs in Grandmother's house, writing at a large table; opposite me sat our drawing master, adding the final touches to a black-pencil drawing of the head of a Turk in a turban. Volodya, craning his neck, stood behind the teacher, looking over his shoulder. This head was Volodya's first black-pencil drawing and it was to be presented to Grandmother on that very day, her name day.*

"Wouldn't you add some more shading here?" Volodya asked the master, standing on tiptoe and pointing to the Turk's neck.

"No, that's not necessary," the master said, putting his pencils and his drawing pen away in their case. "It looks fine now, so don't do anything more to it. Now you, Nikolyenka," he added, standing up and still glancing at the Turk from the corner of his eye, "will you finally reveal your secret to us? What are you going to give your grandmother? Of course it would have been best to offer her a drawing of a head also. Goodbye, gentlemen," he said as he picked up his hat and lesson slip,* and left.

At that moment I too thought that a head would have been better than what I was working on. When we were told that Grandmother's name day was coming up soon and that we were to prepare gifts for her for that day, it occurred to me to write some verses for the occasion, and at once I made up two rhyming verses, hoping to make the rest up as quickly as I had those two. I do not remember at all how such an idea – a strange one for a child – entered my head, but I do remember that I liked the thought very much and that to all questions on the subject I replied that I would definitely present Grandmother with a gift, but I would not tell anyone what it would be.

Contrary to my expectations, it turned out that despite my best efforts I could not write anything beyond the two verses I had thought up in the heat of the moment. I began to read poems I found in our books, but neither Dmitriev nor Derzhavin* were of any help to me – quite the reverse: they convinced me even further of my incompetence. Knowing that Karl Ivanych loved to copy out poetry, I began to rummage secretly through his papers and among some German verses I found one Russian poem, which he must have written himself.

To Mrs L   Petrovskoye   1828   3rd June

Remember near
Remember far
Remember me
Now and for ever
Remember to my grave
How true and loving I am

Karl Mauer

47

That poem, written in a beautiful round handwriting on thin writing paper, pleased me for the touching sentiment which permeated it. I immediately learnt it off by heart and decided to use it as a model. It all worked out quite well. A poem of congratulations in twelve verses was ready on the name day and, sitting at the schoolroom table, I copied it out on vellum paper.

Two sheets of paper had already been spoilt... not because there was anything I felt needed changing in the verses – they seemed outstanding to me – but from the third line onwards the end of each line began to curve upwards more and more, so that you could see from a distance that the writing was all askew and would not do at all.

The third sheet came out equally crooked, but I decided not to copy it out again. In my poem I congratulated Grandmother, wishing her many years of good health, and ended with:

> *We'll try to comfort you as no other*
> *And we love you as our own dear mother*

It seemed not bad at all, but that last verse somehow strangely offended my ear.

"And we love you as our own dear mo-ther," I kept on repeating to myself under my breath. "What other rhyming word could I use instead of *mother*? Brother, bother? Oh well, it will do! It's still better than Karl Ivanych's poem!"

And I wrote down the last verse. Then in my bedroom I read the whole poem out loud with expression and gestures. Some of the verses had no metre at all, but I did not dwell on that; the last line struck me still more forcefully and unpleasantly. I sat down on my bed deep in thought...

"Why did I write *as our own dear mother*? She's not here, so there's no need to mention her; of course I love Grandmother, I respect her, but she's not... Why did I write that, why did I lie? Even if these are only verses, I shouldn't have done that."

At that moment the tailor came in bringing our new jackets.

"Well, so be it!" I said highly impatiently and I crossly shoved the verses under my pillow and ran up to try on our Moscow outfits.

They turned out to be superb: the brown tailored jackets with brass buttons were close-fitting – not like those made in the country, with room to grow – and the black trousers were also tight-fitting; it was wonderful how they outlined our muscles and how well they sat on our boots.

"At last I own trousers with foot straps, real ones!" I reflected, inspecting my legs from every angle, beside myself with joy. Although I felt very constricted and uncomfortable in my new outfit, I hid this from everyone and on the contrary said that it was very comfortable and that, if anything, it was a little loose-fitting. After that I stood before the mirror for a long time brushing my lavishly pomaded head, but much as I tried I could not flatten the tufts of hair on the top of my head: no sooner did I stop pressing them down with my brush to test their compliance than they rose up again and twisted in all directions, giving my face the funniest look.

Karl Ivanych was dressing in the other room and they brought him his dark-blue tailcoat and also some white accessories through the schoolroom. The voice of one of Grandmother's maids could be heard at the door leading downstairs; I went to find out what she wanted. She was holding a stiffly starched shirt front and told me that she was bringing this to Karl Ivanych and that she had not slept all night in order to have it laundered in time. I undertook to deliver the shirt front and asked the maid if Grandmother was up yet.

"Well, of course, sir! She's already had her coffee and the priest has arrived. What a dashing young gentleman you look!" she added smiling, examining my new outfit.

That remark made me blush. I twirled on one leg, snapped my fingers and skipped, wanting to make her realize that she had so far not fully appreciated what a truly dashing young gentleman I was.

When I brought Karl Ivanych the shirt front, he no longer needed it; he had put on another one and was bending down in front of a small table mirror, holding the splendid bow of his cravat with both hands to check whether his clean-shaven chin could move about freely in it. He smoothed down our outfits on all sides and asked Nikolai to do the same for him, and then he led us to Grandmother. I am amused at the thought of how strongly we all three smelt of pomade as we set off down the stairs.

Karl Ivanych held in his hands a little box he had made himself; Volodya had his drawing and I my poem; we each had a greeting ready to accompany the presentation of our gift. Just as Karl Ivanych opened the drawing-room door, the priest was putting on his vestments and the first words of the service rang out.

Grandmother was already in the drawing room: she stood near the wall, bowing her head and leaning on the back of a chair, and prayed devoutly. Next to her stood Papa. He turned to us and smiled when he noticed us hurriedly hide our presents behind our backs and stop at the door, trying to remain inconspicuous. The whole element of surprise we had counted on was lost.

When they began to move towards the cross, I was suddenly seized by an insurmountable paralyzing shyness and felt that I would never have the courage to offer my gift. I hid behind Karl Ivanych, who congratulated Grandmother in the most flowery terms, passed the box from his right hand to his left, handed it over to her and stepped aside to give way to Volodya. Grandmother appeared delighted with the box, which had gilt edgings, and expressed her thanks with the warmest of smiles. It was obvious, however, that she did not know where to put the box and it was probably for that reason that she suggested to Papa to take a look at how skilfully it had been made.

Having satisfied his own curiosity, Papa passed it on to the priest, who appeared to like this trinket very much indeed; he shook his head and looked intrigued first at the box, then at the craftsman who could make such a beautiful object. Volodya presented his Turk and he too won the most flattering praises from all sides. Now it was my turn: Grandmother turned to me with an approving smile.

Those who suffer from shyness know that the feeling grows in direct relation to time and that one's determination decreases in equal measure; in other words: the longer the situation lasts, the more it becomes insurmountable and the less determination there is left.

The last remnants of courage and determination left me as Karl Ivanych and Volodya presented their gifts and my shyness reached its culminating point: I felt the blood rushing relentlessly from my heart to my head, one shade of red replacing the other on my face and thick beads of sweat breaking out on my forehead and my nose. My ears were burning. I felt shivers and cold sweat coursing through my whole body; I shifted from one foot to the other, but did not move from the spot.

"Well, show me, Nikolyenka, what you have – a box or a drawing?" said Papa. There was nothing for it: with a trembling hand I handed over the fateful crumpled roll of paper, but my voice completely refused to cooperate and I stopped silent in front of Grandmother. I could not bear the thought that instead of the expected drawing, they would read, in front of everybody, my worthless verses and the words: *as our own dear mother*, which would clearly prove that I never loved her and that I had forgotten her. How can I describe my suffering when Grandmother began to read my poem aloud, and when, unable to decipher it, she stopped in the middle of the poem to look at Papa with what to me seemed a mocking smile; when she delivered the words not as I wanted her to, and when, because of her feeble eyesight, she did not read it to the end, but passed the paper to Papa, asking him to read it again from the beginning? It seemed to me that she was doing this because she was bored with reading such bad poetry, written in such a skewed hand, and in order for Papa himself to read that last verse, which so clearly proved my lack of feeling. I expected him to flick me across the nose with those verses and say: "You bad boy, you must not forget your mother… that's what you get for this!" But nothing of the kind happened; on the contrary, when the poem had been read to the end, Grandmother said: "*Charmant*,"* and kissed me on the forehead.

The box, the drawing and the poem were laid out beside two linen handkerchiefs and a snuffbox with a portrait of Maman on it, on a sliding table attached to the Voltairean armchair, on which Grandmother always sat.

"Princess Varvara Ilinishna," announced one of the two huge footmen who rode on the back of Grandmother's carriage.

Grandmother, deep in thought, looked at the portrait set on the tortoiseshell snuffbox and gave no reply.

"Shall I show her in, Your Highness?" repeated the footman.

17

Princess Kornakova

"SHOW HER IN," said Grandmother, sinking deeper into her armchair. The Princess was a woman of about forty-five, small, frail, wizened and sallow with tiny unappealing grey-green eyes whose expression clearly contradicted the unnaturally appealing set of her small mouth. Light reddish hair was showing beneath her velvet hat adorned with an ostrich feather; against the sickly colour of her face her eyebrows and eyelashes looked even lighter and redder. For all that, her ease of movement, her tiny hands and a certain dryness of all her features gave her an aristocratic and energetic air.

The Princess talked a great deal, and in her manner of talking belonged to that category of people who always speak as if they are being contradicted, even if no one has uttered a word: at times she would raise her voice and then lower it gradually, and then suddenly she would begin to talk with renewed vivacity, looking round at those people present who were not taking part in the conversation, as though trying to bolster herself with that look.

Although the Princess kissed Grandmother's hand and continually addressed her as *ma bonne tante*,* I noticed that Grandmother was not pleased with her: she raised her eyebrows somewhat peculiarly while she listened to the Princess explain why Prince Mikhailo had not been able to come and congratulate Grandmother in person, despite wanting to so very badly, and, answering in Russian to the Princess's French, she said, drawing out her words:

"I'm very grateful to you, my dear, for your thoughtfulness; as for Prince Mikhailo not coming, why mention it at all… he always has lots to do, and anyway, what pleasure would it give him to sit with an old woman?"

And without giving the Princess time to retort, she continued:

"And how are your children, my dear?"

"Thank God, *ma tante*, they are growing, doing their lessons and misbehaving… especially Étienne; he's the eldest and is becoming so wild that he is nothing but trouble. He is a bright boy, however – *un garçon qui promet*.* Just imagine, *mon cousin*," she went on, turning exclusively to Papa, because Grandmother, not having any interest in the Princess's children and wanting to boast about her own grandchildren, had carefully reached under the little box for my poem and begun to unroll the paper, "just imagine, *mon cousin*, what he did the other day…"

And the Princess, leaning over to Papa, began to tell him something with great animation. When she finished her story, which I did not hear, she at once burst out laughing and, looking enquiringly up at Papa, she said:

"What a boy, don't you think, *mon cousin*? He deserved a beating, but it was such an amusing, clever trick that I forgave him, *mon cousin*."

And the Princess, fixing her eyes on Grandmother, went on smiling without saying a word.

"Do you *beat* your children, my dear?" asked Grandmother, raising her eyebrows meaningfully and particularly stressing the word *beat*.

"Oh, *ma bonne tante*," the Princess replied with a sweet voice after a quick glance at Papa, "I know your opinion on that score, but allow me to differ on this one: however much I have thought, read or sought advice on the subject, experience has nevertheless led me to the conviction that children should be governed by fear. To make something of your children, you need fear… is that not so, *mon cousin*? And what do children, *je vous demande un peu,** fear more than the birch?"

At this she looked questioningly at us and, I have to admit, I felt rather uncomfortable at that moment.

"Whatever you say, a boy of twelve and even fourteen is still a child; a girl, of course, is another matter."

"How lucky I am," I thought to myself, "that I am not her son."

"That's all very well, my dear," said Grandmother, rolling up the paper with my verses again and placing it under the little box as though she did not consider the Princess worthy of hearing such a work, "that's fine, only please tell me, how can you expect your children to have any sensitive feelings after that?"

And considering this argument incontestable, Grandmother added in order to stop the conversation short:

"However, each to his own on that subject."

The Princess did not reply, but only smiled indulgently, implying that she forgave those strange prejudices in someone she had so much respect for.

"Oh, do introduce me to your young people," she said, looking at us and smiling amiably.

We stood up and, fixing our eyes on the Princess's face, did not know what we should do to show that we had been introduced.

"Do kiss the Princess's hand," said Papa.

"I beg you to love your old aunt," she said, kissing Volodya on the hair. "Even though I am a distant relative, I set much more store on friendly ties than on the degree of kinship," she added, addressing herself primarily to Grandmother. But Grandmother was still displeased with her and replied:

"Oh, my dear, does such kinship count for anything these days?"

"This one will be my young man of the world," said Papa, pointing at Volodya. "And this one will be a poet," he added, while I, kissing the

Princess's small dry hand, imagined with extraordinary clarity a birch in that hand, and under the birch a little bench and so on.

"Which one?" asked the Princess, detaining me by the hand.

"This one, the small one, with the unruly tufts!" replied Papa, smiling gaily.

"What have my tufts ever done to him... has he nothing else to talk about?" I thought and moved away to the corner.

I had the strangest notions of beauty – I even regarded Karl Ivanych as the most handsome man in the world, but I also knew very well that I was not good-looking, and I was not at all mistaken about that; therefore any comments about my looks offended me deeply.

I remember well how once at dinner – I was six then – there was a discussion about my looks and Maman tried to find something good to say about my face; she said that I had intelligent eyes and a pleasant smile, and finally, giving way to Papa's arguments and to the obvious, she was forced to admit that I was ugly, and then, when I thanked her for dinner, she patted me on the cheek and said:

"You should know, Nikolyenka, that no one will love you for your face; that's why you must try and be a good and clever boy."

Those words not only convinced me that I was not handsome but also that I would definitely be a good, clever boy.

In spite of this, I often suffered moments of despair. I imagined that there was no happiness on earth for a person like me, with such a broad nose, thick lips and small grey eyes. I asked God to perform a miracle – to turn me into a good-looking man, and I would have given anything I had then and everything I would have in the future in return for a handsome face.

18

Prince Ivan Ivanych

WHEN THE PRINCESS HAD HEARD THE VERSES and showered their author with praise, Grandmother relented, began to speak to her in French, stopped addressing her formally and calling her *my dear*, and invited her to come back that evening with all her children, to which the Princess agreed and, after staying a little while longer, she left.

So many visitors came that day to congratulate Grandmother that the whole morning at any given time there were several carriages drawn up by the entrance in the courtyard.

"*Bonjour, chère cousine*,"* said one of the visitors, as he came into the room and kissed Grandmother's hand.

He was a man of about seventy, tall, dressed in military uniform with large epaulettes, a big white cross showing beneath its collar, and a calm, frank expression on his face. I was struck by the ease and simplicity of his movements. Although he had only a thin semicircle of hair left on the back of his head and the position of his upper lip clearly indicated a lack of teeth, his face was still remarkably handsome.

At the end of the last century, Prince Ivan Ivanych, while still very young, had made himself a brilliant career, thanks to his noble character, good looks, remarkable courage, distinguished and powerful connections and, especially, his good fortune. He continued to serve and his ambitions were soon satisfied to a point when he could no longer wish for anything more. From a very early age he had behaved as though he was preparing to fill that brilliant position in the world where Fate subsequently placed him. Therefore, despite encountering, as everyone else does, setbacks, disappointments and ordeals in his brilliant if somewhat self-important life, he never once lost his usual calm disposition or his lofty mindset, his fundamental religious and moral principles, and he acquired universal respect not so much for his brilliant position as for his consistency and firmness. He had no great intellect but, thanks to his position, which allowed him to look down on all the petty ups and downs of life, he remained high-minded. He was kind and sensitive, but came across as cold and somewhat arrogant, the reason being that, placed in a position in which he could be of assistance to many people, he tried to protect himself by his coldness from the constant demands and flatteries from those only wanting to take advantage of his influence. This coldness, however, was tempered by the indulgent courtesy of a man of *very high society*. He was well educated and well read, but his education had stopped with what he had acquired in his youth, at the end of the last century. He had read everything of note that had been written in France in the eighteenth century on philosophy and rhetoric; he had a thorough knowledge of all the best French literary works, so that he could and often loved to quote passages from

Racine, Corneille, Boileau, Molière, Montaigne and Fénelon. He had a brilliant knowledge of mythology and, to his advantage, had learnt ancient texts of epic poetry in French translation; he had sufficient knowledge of history, gleaned from Ségur,* but beyond arithmetic he had no understanding at all of mathematics, nor of physics, nor of contemporary literature. In conversation he could remain silent or contribute a few general remarks about Goethe, Schiller and Byron, but had never read them. Despite his classical French education, of which in our day so few examples still exist, his conversation was simple and that simplicity concealed his ignorance of certain things as well as displaying good taste and a tolerant nature. He was strongly against any kind of originality, saying that it was a ruse used by people of bad taste. He needed society, wherever he lived. Whether in Moscow or abroad, he kept open house and received the whole town on set days. Such was his standing in town that an invitation from him meant a passport to any drawing room, and many beautiful young women eagerly offered him their rosy cheeks, which he kissed with apparent paternal feeling, and some seemingly very important and respectable people were overjoyed beyond words when allowed to join his entourage.

Now the Prince had very few people left such as Grandmother who had moved in the same circles as he had, who had had the same upbringing and view of things and were of the same age; that is why he particularly treasured his old ties of friendship with her and always showed her a great deal of respect.

I could not gaze enough at the Prince: the respect he was being shown by everyone, the large epaulettes, the particular joy Grandmother expressed when she saw him and the fact that he was the only one who was apparently not afraid of her, was completely relaxed with her and even dared to call her *ma cousine*, inspired me with a respect towards him equal to, if not greater than the respect I felt for Grandmother. When he was shown my poem, he called me to him and said:

"Who knows, *ma cousine*, he might yet be another Derzhavin."

With that he pinched my cheek so painfully that if I did not cry out it was only because I guessed that it was to be taken as a token of affection.

The visitors had left; Papa and Volodya went out. Only the Prince, Grandmother and I were left in the drawing room.

"Why did our dear Natalya Nikolayevna not come?" asked Prince Ivan Ivanych suddenly, after a moment's silence.

"Ah, *mon cher*," replied Grandmother, lowering her voice and laying her hand on his uniform sleeve, "she would have come had she been free to do as she wanted. She wrote to me that, although Pierre did suggest she come, she refused because they've apparently had no income at all this year, and she adds: 'I have no reason to move the whole household to Moscow this year. Lyubochka is still too young, and as for the boys who are to live with you, I feel even more at ease about them than if they lived with me.' That's all very well," continued Grandmother in a tone clearly indicating that she did not think it was very well at all, "it was high time the boys were sent here to study and become accustomed to society; what kind of an education could they get in the country? The eldest is almost thirteen and the other one eleven... Have you noticed, *mon cousin*, how uncouth they are here... they don't even know how to enter a room."

"I still don't understand, however," replied the Prince. "Why these constant complaints about the sad state of their affairs? *He* has a very good fortune, and I know Natasha's Khabarovka – where you and I once acted on the stage – like the back of my hand; it is a wonderful estate which should always produce an excellent income!"

"I'll tell you as a true friend," interrupted Grandmother with a sad expression, "it seems to me that all those excuses are there only to give *him* the chance to live here alone, to wander from club to dinner party and God knows where else, and she doesn't suspect a thing. You know what an angelic kind soul she is – she believes *him* implicitly. He assured her that the children should be brought to Moscow and that she should stay behind in the country alone with that stupid governess – and she believed him; if he told her that the children ought to be flogged, like Princess Varvara Ilinishna flogs hers, she would agree to it as well, it seems," said Grandmother, turning round in her armchair with a look of total contempt. "Yes, my friend," went on Grandmother after a brief pause, having taken one of her two handkerchiefs in her hand to wipe away a tear that had just appeared, "I often think that *he* can neither treasure nor understand her and that, despite all her goodness and love for him and her efforts to conceal her grief – I know this very well – she cannot be happy with him, and mark my words, if he doesn't..."

Grandmother hid her face in her handkerchief.

"Eh, *ma bonne amie*,"* rebuked the Prince, "I see you have not grown more sensible – you're always distressed and weeping over some imagined grief. Shouldn't you be ashamed of yourself? I have known *him* a long time and know him to be an attentive, kind and excellent husband, and most important – a most noble man, *un parfait honnête homme*."*

Having unintentionally overheard a conversation not meant for my ears, I tiptoed out of the room, greatly agitated.

19

The Ivins

"VOLODYA! Volodya! The Ivins!" I shouted, watching through the window as three little boys in dark-blue overcoats with beaver collars crossed over to our house from the pavement opposite, following their young dandyish tutor.

The Ivins were related to us and were almost the same age; we had met them and become friends soon after our arrival in Moscow.

The second Ivin – Seryozha – was a dark-complexioned curly-haired boy with a solid little snub nose, very fresh red lips that rarely fully covered the upper row of slightly protruding white teeth, beautiful dark-blue eyes and an unusually lively expression on his face. He never smiled, but either looked totally serious or laughed wholeheartedly: a clear, distinctive and very bewitching laugh. I was struck at first sight by his unusual beauty. I felt irresistibly attracted to him. Just to see him was enough to make me happy and at one time all my energies were focused on this longing. When I happened to spend three or four days without seeing him, I felt bereft and sad to the point of tears. All my dreams, whether asleep or awake, were about him: when I lay down to sleep, I wanted him to appear in my dreams; when I closed my eyes, I saw him before me and cherished this vision as the utmost delight. This feeling was so dear to me that I could not bring myself to tell anyone in the world about it. He evidently preferred to play and chat with Volodya rather than me, perhaps because he was tired of feeling my restless eyes constantly fixed on him, or simply because he did not really like me. I was nevertheless contented, wished for nothing, demanded nothing and was prepared to sacrifice everything for him. Besides being passionately drawn to him, his presence aroused in me another, no less powerful feeling – a fear of causing him pain, offending him in some way, displeasing him: I felt as much fear of him as love for him, perhaps because of his haughty expression or because, despising my own looks, I valued too much in others the advantages of beauty – or most likely, because this is an essential symptom of love. The first time Seryozha spoke to me, I lost my head so completely from such unexpected happiness that I turned pale, then red and could not utter a word in reply. When lost in thought he had the bad habit of fixing his eyes on one spot and blinking incessantly, twitching his nose and eyebrows at the same time. Everyone found this habit very unbecoming, but I found it so endearing that I unwittingly began to do the same thing, and a few days after our first meeting, my grandmother asked me whether my eyes were hurting since I was blinking like an owl. We never, either of us, mentioned a word about love, but he sensed his power over me and exercised it unconsciously but tyrannically in our childish relationship. And I, much as I longed to express to him everything I had in my heart, was too afraid of him to bring myself to be open; I tried to appear indifferent and submitted to him without a murmur. Sometimes his influence seemed burdensome and intolerable, but it was not within my power to extricate myself from it.

I feel sad when I recall that beautiful pure feeling of unselfish boundless love, which died away without ever being expressed or reciprocated.

It is strange how I wanted to be like a grown-up when I was a child and why as soon as I was no longer a child I so often wanted to be like one again. How many times did that longing not to be like a small boy check the feeling that was ready to pour out and forced me to dissemble in my relations with Seryozha. Not only did I not dare to kiss him, as I sometimes longed to do, or take him by the hand and say how happy I was to see him, but I did not even dare to call him Seryozha, and always used the formal Sergei, as was customary in our house. Every expression of feeling denoted childishness and anyone indulging in such things was still *a little boy*. Without having lived through those bitter ordeals that drive grown-ups to behave carefully and coldly in their dealings with others, we deprived ourselves of the pure joys of a tender childish affection only for the strange reason of wanting to imitate the *grown-ups*.

I met the Ivins when they were still in the entrance hall, greeted them and rushed straight over to Grandmother: I announced the arrival of the Ivins to her in a way that presumed that this news would fill her with joy. Then, without taking my eyes off Seryozha, I followed him into the drawing room and watched his every movement. When Grandmother said that he had grown a great deal and fixed her penetrating eyes on him, I experienced that feeling of fear and hope that an artist must experience when he awaits the verdict on his work from a respected critic.

The Ivins' young tutor, Herr Frost, with Grandmother's permission, went to the front garden with us, sat down on a green bench, crossed his legs prettily, placed his cane with a bronze knob between them, and lit a cigar with the air of a man pleased with his actions.

Herr Frost was a German, but a German of a completely different kind than our dear Karl Ivanych: firstly, he spoke correct Russian, and French with a bad accent, and generally enjoyed the reputation of being a learned man, especially among the ladies; secondly, he had a red moustache, a large ruby-coloured pin stuck in a black satin cravat, its ends tucked under his braces, and shimmery light-blue trousers with foot straps; thirdly, he was young, had a handsome self-satisfied appearance and unusually prominent muscular legs. It was obvious that he was particularly proud of the latter: he considered them irresistible to the female sex and, probably with that in mind, tried to position his legs conspicuously and, whether he was sitting down or on his feet, he always wiggled his calves. He was the type of young Russo-German who aspires to be dashing and a ladies' man.

It was great fun in the garden. Our game of robbers went extremely well, but one incident almost upset everything. Seryozha was the robber: as he pursued some travellers at full speed, he stumbled and struck his knee against a tree so hard that I thought that it would be smashed to smithereens. Although I was the gendarme and my duty was to catch him, I went up to him and asked with some concern whether he was in pain. Seryozha was furious with me: he clenched his fists, stamped his foot and yelled at me in a voice that clearly indicated that he had hurt himself badly:

"What's the matter? We won't be able to play after this! Well, why don't you catch me? Why don't you catch me?" he repeated several times, glancing sideways at Volodya and the older Ivin, who, in the guise of travellers, ran skipping along the path, and suddenly he shrieked and, laughing loudly, rushed ahead to catch them.

I cannot convey how impressed and enthralled I was by this heroic act: in spite of terrible pain, not only did he not burst into tears, but he did not even show that he was in pain, nor did he for a moment forget the game.

Soon after this, when we were joined by Ilyenka Grap and made our way upstairs before dinner, Seryozha had another opportunity to impress and captivate me even more with his amazing courage and strength of character.

Ilyenka Grap was the son of a poor foreigner, who had lived at one time at my grandfather's and was indebted to him in some way and now considered it his vital duty to send his son frequently over to us. If he supposed that his son would gain some kind of honour or pleasure by being acquainted with us, then he was sadly mistaken in that respect, for not only did we not make friends with Ilyenka, but we only paid attention to him when we wanted to poke fun at him. Ilyenka Grap was a boy of about thirteen, thin, tall, pale, with a small bird-like face and a kindly meek expression. He was very poorly dressed, but his hair was so abundantly pomaded that we were sure that on a sunny day the pomade would melt on his head and trickle down his jacket. When I remember him now, I find that he was a very obliging, quiet and kind boy; at that time he appeared to me such a contemptible creature that there was no point feeling sorry for him or even giving him a second thought.

When the game of robbers had ended, we went upstairs and began to play around boisterously, showing off a variety of gymnastic tricks to one another. Ilyenka looked on with a timid smile of amazement and, when we invited him to try and do the same, he refused, saying that he was not strong enough. Seryozha was delightful; he took off his jacket – his face and eyes were on fire – and he laughed incessantly as he made up new tricks: leaping across three chairs placed side by side, executing cartwheels across the whole room, or standing on his head on Tatishchev's dictionaries,* which he had placed in the middle of the room to form a pedestal, and he performed such hilarious tricks with his legs that it was impossible not to laugh. After that last trick he thought for a while, blinked and suddenly went up to Ilyenka with a perfectly serious face: "You try and do that; it really isn't hard." Grap blushed, aware that everyone's attention was focused on him, and declared with a barely audible voice that he could not possibly do it.

"What's this, why doesn't he want to show us anything? What kind of a girl is he... he's got to stand on his head!"

And Seryozha took him by the hand.

"He's got to stand on his head!" we all shouted, clustering around Ilyenka, who at that moment was visibly frightened and had turned pale; we grabbed his arm and dragged him towards the dictionaries.

"Let me be, I'll do it myself! You'll tear my jacket!" cried the unhappy victim. But those cries of distress excited us even more; we were dying of laughter; his little green jacket was splitting at every seam.

Volodya and the eldest Ivin pushed Ilyenka's head down and placed it on the dictionaries; Seryozha and I grabbed the poor boy by his skinny legs, which he was waving in all directions, rolled his trousers up to his knees and, roaring with laughter, pulled his legs up in the air; the youngest Ivin held on to his body to keep the balance.

Suddenly, after that noisy laughter, we all fell silent and it became so quiet in the room that all we could hear was the unfortunate Grap's laboured breathing. At that moment I was not totally convinced that all this was so funny and enjoyable.

"That's a good lad," said Seryozha, slapping him with his hand.

Ilyenka remained silent and, trying to extricate himself, flailed around with his legs. In one of those desperate movements he struck Seryozha in the eye with his heel so badly that Seryozha immediately let go of his legs, covered his eye, which was by now shedding involuntary tears, and pushed Ilyenka as hard as he could. Ilyenka, no longer being held up by us, came crashing down to the floor like a lifeless object and could only stammer through his tears:

"Why do you bully me so?"

We were all struck by the weeping figure of the unfortunate Ilyenka, with his tear-stained face, his tousled hair and rolled-up trousers showing the unpolished tops of his boots, and we stood silent, trying to force a smile.

Seryozha was the first to come to his senses.

"Look at this old woman, this cry-baby," he said, lightly prodding him with his foot, "you can't have a joke with him... Well that's enough, get up."

"I told you, you are a nasty boy," said Ilyenka spitefully and, turning away, burst into loud sobs.

"Oh! You kicked me with your heels and now you are calling me names!" cried out Seryozha; he grabbed hold of the dictionary and swung it over the head of the unfortunate boy, who did not even think of defending himself and just covered his head with his hands.

"Take that, and that! Let's leave him be, as he can't take a joke. Let's go downstairs," said Seryozha, laughing unnaturally.

I looked at the poor boy with sympathy; he was lying on the floor, hiding his face among the dictionaries, and was crying so hard that it seemed that he would die of the convulsions that shook his whole body if this went on just a little longer.

"Oh Sergei," I said to him, "why did you do that?"

"So what! I didn't burst into tears when I smashed my leg almost to the bone."

"Yes, that's true," I thought. "Ilyenka is nothing but a cry-baby and look at Seryozha – he's a fine fellow, what a fine fellow he is!"

I did not consider that the poor boy was probably crying not so much from physical pain as at the thought that five boys he had perhaps liked had all, for no reason at all, agreed to hate and persecute him.

I really cannot explain to myself the cruelty of my own behaviour. How did it not occur to me to go up to Ilyenka and defend and comfort him? Where had my feelings of compassion disappeared to, those feelings that at times had caused me to sob uncontrollably at the sight of a jackdaw pushed from its nest, or a puppy taken away to be thrown over the fence, or chickens carried off by the kitchen boy for soup.

Was that fine feeling stifled within me by my love for Seryozha and by my desire to appear in front of him just as fine a fellow as he was himself? In which case that love and desire to appear a fine fellow were not to be envied. They produced the only dark blots on the pages of my childhood recollections.

20

We Have Visitors

JUDGING by the distinct flurry of activity in the pantry, and by the bright lights imparting a kind of new, festive air to objects long familiar to me in the drawing room and the ballroom, and in particular judging by the fact that Prince Ivan Ivanych had sent over his musicians not without good reason, a large group of guests were expected that evening.

At the sound of each carriage driving past I ran over to the window and with the palms of my hands against my temples I pressed against the window pane and looked out onto the street with impatient curiosity. Out of the darkness which at first hid everything outside the window, things gradually became discernible: directly opposite was the familiar small shop with the lantern; diagonally across stood the large house with two windows lit up downstairs; halfway along the street was some poor cab driver with two passengers or else an empty carriage slowly driving home. Just then a carriage drove up to the porch and, absolutely sure that it was the Ivins who had promised to come early, I ran over to meet them in the entrance hall. Instead of the Ivins, two persons of the female sex appeared from behind the liveried hand that opened the door: one was big, in a dark-blue coat with a sable collar, the other was small, all bundled up in a green shawl, beneath which all you could see were tiny feet in small fur boots. Without paying the slightest attention to my presence in the hall, although I considered it my duty to bow to those two persons as they appeared, the small one went over silently to the big one and stopped in front of her. The big one unwound the scarf which entirely covered the small one's head, undid the buttons of her coat and, when the liveried footman had been handed those things for safe-keeping and had pulled off her fur boots, there emerged from that bundled-up creature an amazing twelve-year-old girl in a short low-necked muslin dress, white pantalettes and tiny black shoes. She had a black velvet ribbon around her white neck; her little head was covered in dark-brown curls, which suited her pretty little face as well in front as they did her bare little shoulders in the back, so that I would not have believed anyone, not even Karl Ivanych, that her hair curled like that because it had been rolled up since morning in bits of *The Moscow News* and then been pressed with hot tongs. It seemed as though she had been born with that curly head.

A striking feature of her face was the unusual size of her prominent half-closed eyes, which formed a strange, yet pleasing contrast to her tiny mouth. Her lips were pressed together and her eyes looked so serious that from the general expression on her face you did not expect her to smile; when she did, it was all the more enchanting.

In an attempt to remain unnoticed, I sneaked through to the ball-room and found it necessary to pace up and down pretending to be lost in deep thought and totally unaware of guests arriving. When the guests had reached the middle of the room, I acted as if I had suddenly come to my senses, bowed, feet scraping together, and announced that Grandmother was in the drawing room. Madame Valakhina, whose face I liked very much, especially because I found it looked a lot like her daughter Sonyechka's face, kindly nodded her head.

Grandmother seemed to be very happy to see Sonyechka: she asked her to come closer, adjusted one of her curls, which had slipped down over her forehead, and looking at her intently said: "*Quelle charmante enfant!*"* Sonyechka smiled, blushed and seemed so sweet that I in turn blushed as I looked at her.

"I hope that you won't be bored here, my dear," said Grandmother, tilting her little face up by the chin. "Please do have fun and dance as much as possible. Here we already have one lady and two dancing partners," she added, addressing Madame Valakhina and touching me with her hand.

This act of bringing us together pleased me so much that I was compelled to blush again.

Aware of my growing shyness and having heard the sound of a carriage drawing up, I thought it best to leave. I found Princess Kornakova in the entrance hall with her son and an incredible number of daughters. The daughters were all alike: they looked like the Princess and were ugly, therefore not one of them held your attention. As they removed their coats and fur wraps, they suddenly all started talking with high-pitched little voices, fussed about and laughed for some reason – probably at there being so many of them. Étienne was a boy of about fifteen, tall, fleshy, with a gaunt look, hollow eyes with dark-blue circles under them and with huge hands and feet out of keeping with his age; he was clumsy, had an unpleasant, croaky voice, but he did appear very pleased with himself and was precisely the sort of boy who, in my opinion, would get whipped.

We stood for quite some time facing one another and sizing each other up in silence; then moving closer, we looked ready to embrace, but after staring at each other some more, we unaccountably changed our minds. After all his sisters' dresses had noisily swished past us, I wanted somehow to start a conversation, and I asked whether they had not been too squashed in the carriage.

"I don't know," he answered casually. "You see, I never ride in the carriage because the moment I sit down I begin to feel sick and Mama knows this. Whenever we go somewhere in the evening, I always sit on the box – it's a lot more fun and you can see everything; Filipp lets me drive and sometimes I even use the whip. And so now and then, you know, the passers-by get..." he added with a telling gesture. "It's great!"

"Your Highness," said the footman, coming into the entrance hall, "Filipp is asking where you may have put the whip?"

"How do you mean, where did I put it? I gave it back to him."

"He says that you did not give it back."

"Well, then I hung it up on the lantern."

"Filipp says that it is not on the lantern and it would be better if you admitted that you took it and lost it or else Filipp will have to pay up from his own money for your tricks," the footman continued, getting more and more worked up.

The footman, who looked a respectable and grave man, appeared to be ardently on Filipp's side and wanted at all costs to clear the matter up. With instinctive tactfulness I moved aside as though I had not noticed anything, but the other footmen present behaved very differently; they came closer and gave the old footman approving looks.

"Well, if I've lost it then I've lost it," said Étienne, avoiding further explanations. "So what does that whip cost? I'll pay for it. It's hilarious!" he added, coming towards me and dragging me to the drawing room.

"No, excuse me, master; what are you going to pay for it with? I know how you'll pay: for eight months running you have been paying Marya Vasilyevna twenty copecks, and you owe me too for the second year now. As for Petrushka—"

"Shut up!" screamed the young Prince, turning pale with fury. "I'll tell."

"I'll tell, I'll tell!" repeated the footman. "It's not right, Your Highness!" he added most expressively as we entered the ballroom, and he went off with the coats to the cloakroom.

"That's quite right!" Someone's approving voice could be heard behind us in the entrance hall.

Grandmother had a particular gift, that of using the plural and singular pronouns "you", with a certain tone and in certain circumstances, to express her opinion about people. Although she used the formal or the familiar "you"* against the prevailing trend, these nuances took on an entirely different meaning coming from her lips. When the young Prince approached her, she said a few words to him using the formal *vy*, and she glanced at him with such disdain that if I had been him I would have completely lost my head, but Étienne was obviously not of the same mould: he took no notice at all of Grandmother's reception, nor of her person, and exchanged bows with everyone present if not deftly, certainly with perfect ease. Sonyechka was the focus of all my attention: I remember that when Volodya, Étienne and I were chatting together in a part of the ballroom from where we could see Sonyechka and she could equally see and overhear us, I enjoyed talking; when I happened to say something that seemed to me funny or clever, I spoke louder and looked round towards the drawing-room door; when we moved to another place from where we could neither be seen nor heard from the drawing room, I kept silent and found no pleasure at all in the conversation.

The drawing room and the ballroom had gradually filled up with people; among them, as is always the case at children's parties, there were some older children who did not want to miss the chance of having fun and dancing with the pretext of doing so to please their hostess.

When the Ivins arrived, instead of feeling the usual pleasure at meeting Seryozha, I felt strangely annoyed with him because he would see Sonyechka and would be seen by her.

21

Before the Mazurka

"OH! It looks as if there's going to be dancing," said Seryozha, leaving the drawing room and taking a new pair of kid gloves out of his pocket. "I must put my gloves on."

"What's to be done? We have no gloves," I thought. "I'll have to go upstairs and look for some."

But although I searched through all the drawers, I only found our green travelling mittens in one and one kid glove in another, which could be of no use to me at all: firstly because it was particularly old and dirty, secondly because it was too big for me and mainly because its middle finger was missing, probably cut off a long time ago by Karl

Ivanych because of a sore hand. I did however put on what was left of the glove, and stared intently at that middle finger, which was always ink-stained.

"If only Natalya Savishna were here now: we would most likely find some gloves among her things. I can't go down looking like this, because if I'm asked why I am not dancing, what can I say? And staying here is also impossible, because my absence will surely be noticed. What shall I do?" I said, throwing up my arms.

"What are you doing here?" asked Volodya, who came running in. "Go and ask a lady to dance... it's all about to start."

"Volodya," I said to him, showing him my hand with two fingers stuck inside the dirty glove and with a voice bordering on despair. "Volodya, you haven't thought about this!"

"About what?" he said impatiently. "Ah! Gloves?" he added completely indifferently when he noticed my hand. "No, I haven't; we must ask Grandmama... we'll see what she says." And without giving it another thought, he ran downstairs.

His cool response to a situation that had seemed to me so important calmed me down and I hurried to the drawing room, having completely forgotten about the hideous glove, which I was still wearing on my left hand.

Cautiously approaching Grandmother's armchair and lightly touching her gown, I whispered to her:

"Grandmama! What shall we do? We have no gloves!"

"What, my dear?"

"We have no gloves," I repeated, moving closer and closer and leaning both hands on the arm of her chair.

"Oh, what's this?" she said, suddenly grabbing my left hand. "*Voyez, ma chère,*" she went on, addressing Madame Valakhina, "*voyez comme ce jeune homme s'est fait élégant pour danser avec votre fille.*"*

Grandmother held tightly onto my hand and looked earnestly and questioningly at all those present until everyone's curiosity had been satisfied and there was general laughter.

I would have been mortified if Seryozha had seen me at that moment, as, wincing with shame, I tried in vain to pull my hand away, but in front of Sonyechka, who laughed so much that tears came to her eyes and all her curls bounced up and down round her flushed little face, I did not feel embarrassed at all. I understood that her laughter was too loud and natural to be mocking; quite the opposite, the fact that we laughed together and looked at each other somehow drew us closer. The episode with the glove, although it might have had a bad ending, gave me the advantage that it put me at ease within the drawing-room circle, which always felt a most frightening place to me; as it was, I did not feel shy at all in the ballroom.

With shy people suffering is caused by being ignorant of the opinion people have of them; as soon as this opinion is expressed, whatever it may be, the suffering ceases.

How sweet Sonyechka Valakhina was when she danced the French quadrille opposite me with the clumsy young Prince! How sweetly she smiled as she gave me her hand for the *chaîne*!* How sweetly her brown curls leapt on her head to the rhythm of the music and how innocently she performed her *jeté-assemblé* with her tiny feet! In the fifth figure, when my partner ran across to the other side away from me, and when I, waiting for the beat, got ready to do the solo, Sonyechka earnestly pressed her lips and looked away. But she need not have been afraid for me; I boldly performed *chassé en avant*, *chassé en arrière*, *glissade* and, as I moved towards her, I playfully showed her my glove with its two fingers sticking out. She roared with laughter and darted about with her little feet more sweetly than ever on the parquet floor. I also remember how she bent her little head as we formed a circle and held hands and how, without pulling away her hand, she scratched her little nose with her glove. I can see it all as if it were now, and I can still hear the quadrille from *The Danube Maiden*,* to the strains of which all this took place.

The second quadrille began, which I danced with Sonyechka. When I sat next to her before our turn, I felt particularly awkward because I really did not know what to say to her. When my silence went on for too long, I began to be afraid that she might take me for a fool and decided to disabuse her at all costs. "*Vous êtes une habitante de Moscou?*"* I asked her and after she nodded I continued: "*Et moi, je n'ai encore jamais fréquenté la capitale,*"* counting particularly on the effect of the word *fréquenter*. Although I had begun brilliantly and had displayed my excellent knowledge of the French language, I felt that I was not in a position to continue the conversation in this vein. Our turn to dance was still a little while away and silence resumed: I looked at her anxiously, wanting to find out what impression I had made and expecting her to be of some help. "Where did you find such a hilarious glove?" she suddenly asked, and I was very pleased and relieved by that question. I explained that the glove belonged to Karl Ivanych, expanded even with some irony on the person of Karl Ivanych, telling her how funny he was when he took off his red cap and how he once fell off a horse in his green overcoat – straight into a puddle, and so on. The quadrille proceeded without further ado. That was all very well, but why had I made fun of Karl Ivanych? Would I have lost Sonyechka's good opinion of me had I described him with the love and respect that I felt for him?

When the quadrille ended, Sonyechka said *merci* with such a sweet expression as though I really did deserve her gratitude. I was ecstatic, beside myself with joy and did not even recognize myself: where had the courage, the self-confidence and even the audacity come from? "Nothing can daunt me now!" I thought, light-heartedly wandering through the ballroom. "I'm ready for anything!"

Seryozha asked me to be his vis-à-vis.* "That's fine," I said, "though I don't have a partner. I'll find one." Resolutely scanning the room, I noticed that all the ladies were taken, with the exception of one young lady, who stood near the drawing-room door. A tall young man was going up to her with the purpose, I concluded, of asking her; he was two steps away from her and I was at the opposite end of the room. In the twinkling of an eye, sliding gracefully across the parquet, I flew the whole distance that divided her from me and, clicking my heels, I invited her in a firm voice for the next quadrille. The young lady smiled patronizingly and gave me her hand and the young man remained without a partner.

I was so conscious of my power that I did not even pay attention to the young man's annoyance, but I heard afterwards that he asked who that dishevelled boy was who had raced past him and stolen the lady away under his very nose.

22

The Mazurka

THE YOUNG MAN from whom I had stolen the lady danced in the first pair of the mazurka. He leapt up from his place holding his partner by the hand and instead of performing the *pas de Basques*,* which Mimi had taught us, he just ran forwards; reaching the corner, he came to a halt, moved his feet apart, clicked his heels, turned round and with a skip ran on.

As I did not have a partner for the mazurka, I sat behind Grandmother's tall armchair and looked on.

"What is he doing?" I wondered. "It's not at all the way Mimi taught us: she assured us that everyone dances the mazurka on their toes, performing circular sliding moves with the feet, and it turns out that it's not danced like that at all. The Ivins and Étienne are all dancing, but they are not performing the *pas de Basques*. And even our Volodya has acquired the new fashion. It's rather nice! And that darling little Sonyechka! There she goes…" I was having a really good time.

The mazurka was drawing to an end. A few elderly gentlemen and ladies went up to say goodbye to Grandmother. The footmen, avoiding the dancers, carefully carried the table settings to the back rooms. Grandmother was clearly tired, seemed to be speaking reluctantly and very slowly; the musicians idly began to play the same tune for the thirtieth time. The young lady I had danced with caught sight of me as she was performing a dance figure and, smiling treacherously – probably wanting to please Grandmother – led Sonyechka towards me as well as one of the innumerable princesses. "*Rose ou ortie?*"* she said to me.

"Ah, there you are!" said Grandmother, turning round in her armchair. "Go on, my dear boy, go."

Although at that instant I would have much preferred to hide my head under Grandmother's chair than to step out from behind it, how could I refuse? I stood up, said *rose* and looked up timidly at Sonyechka. I scarcely had time to collect myself before someone's hand in a white glove came to be in mine and the Princess stepped forwards with a very pleasant smile and without an inkling that I really did not know what to do with my feet.

I knew that the *pas de Basques* was inappropriate and unseemly and might even disgrace me, but the familiar strains of the mazurka affected my ears and communicated a certain movement to my acoustic nerves, which in turn passed it on to my feet, and the latter instinctively, and to all the spectators' surprise, began to perform those fatal circular sliding steps on the tips of the toes. Whilst we were moving in a straight line things went more or less well, but at the turn I noticed that if I did not take some precautions I would definitely end up too far in front. To avoid such a calamity I stopped short, planning to perform the same clever turn so beautifully executed by the young man in the first pair. But at the very moment that I moved my feet apart and prepared to skip, the Princess, hastily running round me, looked at my feet with an expression of dazed curiosity and amazement. That look finished me off. I lost my nerve so completely that instead of dancing I stamped my feet on the spot in the strangest way with no connection to the rhythm of the music or anything else and finally I came to a complete halt. Everyone stared at me: some in surprise, some with curiosity, some mockingly, some with sympathy; only Grandmother looked at me with complete indifference.

"*Il ne fallait pas danser si vous ne saviez pas!*"* said Papa's angry voice just above my ear and, gently pushing me aside, he took my partner's hand, did a twirl in the old-fashioned way, to the loud approval of the onlookers, and led her back to her seat. The mazurka ended there and then.

"Oh Lord, why do you punish me so terribly!"

* * *

Everyone despises me and will despise me for ever... the path to friendship, love and honour – to everything, is now closed to me... I'm done for! Why did Volodya make signs to me, which everyone could see and which could not help me? Why did that disagreeable Princess look at my feet like that? Why did Sonyechka... she's so very sweet, but why did she smile just then? Why did Papa blush and grab me by the hand? Was he perhaps ashamed of me too? Oh, this is awful! Had Mama been there, she would not have blushed for her Nikolyenka... and my imagination carried me far away following that sweet vision. I remembered the meadow in front of the house, the tall lime trees in the garden, the clear pond above which swallows hovered, the blue sky in which lingered white transparent clouds, fragrant stacks of fresh hay and many other peaceful rosy memories swirled about in my confused imagination.

23

After the Mazurka

A T SUPPER the young man who had danced in the first pair sat down at our children's table and paid particular attention to me, which would have considerably flattered my pride had I been able to feel anything at all after my recent mishap. But the young man seemed determined to cheer me up at any cost: he was playful with me, called me a fine fellow and, when no grown-up was watching, filled my glass with wine from various bottles and made me drink it up. Towards the end of supper, when the butler had poured me only a quarter of a glass of champagne from a bottle wrapped in a napkin and the young man had insisted that he should fill the glass right up and forced me to drink it up in one go, I felt a pleasant warm feeling run through my whole body and particular goodwill towards my cheerful protector, and for some reason burst out laughing.

Suddenly the strains of the *Grossvater** resounded from the ballroom and everyone began to leave the table. My friendship with the young man came to a sudden end: he went to join the grown-ups, and I, not daring to follow him, walked over to Valakhina, curious to make out what she and her daughter were saying.

"Just another half-hour," implored Sonyechka.

"It's really impossible, my angel."

"Just for me, please," she said coaxingly.

"And will you be happy if I am ill tomorrow?" said Madame Valakhina, and she made the mistake of smiling.

"Ah, I'm allowed! We are staying?" burst out Sonyechka, jumping for joy.

"What can I do with you! Go, dance... you even have a partner," said Valakhina, pointing to me.

Sonyechka gave me her hand and we ran into the ballroom.

The wine, Sonyechka's presence and her high spirits made me completely forget the unhappy incident of the mazurka. I performed the funniest tricks with my legs: one moment I trotted along like a horse, lifting my legs up proudly, the next I stamped my feet on the spot like a ram getting angry at a dog, and all the time laughing loudly and taking no notice at all of how I might look to those watching. Sonyechka did not stop laughing either: she laughed as we twirled round holding hands, she laughed loudly watching some elderly gentleman step over a handkerchief, lifting his legs slowly and giving the impression that this was a very difficult thing for him to do, and she very nearly died of laughter when I jumped almost up to the ceiling to prove my agility.

As we went through Grandmother's room, I glanced at myself in the mirror: my face was covered in sweat, my hair tousled, my tufts stuck up more than ever, but the general expression on my face was so happy, good-natured and full of well-being that I liked the way I looked.

"If I could only be like this always," I thought, "I could yet be attractive."

But when I glanced again at my partner's pretty little face, where, besides that expression of happiness, well-being and light-heartedness which I had liked on mine, there was such elegant and tender beauty, I grew annoyed with myself and understood how stupid it was of *me* to hope to attract the attention of such an amazing being.

I could not hope to be loved in return, nor did I think of it: my soul was filled with happiness without it. I did not understand that in exchange for the love filling my soul with delight I could ask for an even greater happiness and wish for more than for this feeling never to end. I was happy as I was. Blood pounding, my heart was beating like a dove and I felt like crying.

When we walked through the corridor past the dark storeroom under the stairs, I glanced at it and thought: "What bliss it would be if I could spend a lifetime with her in that dark storeroom! And no one would know that we lived there."

"Today has been a lot of fun, hasn't it?" I said in a soft trembling voice, and I quickened my pace, afraid not so much of what I had said as of what I intended to say.

"Yes… lots of fun!" she replied, turning her little head towards me with such a frankly good-natured expression that I was no longer afraid.

"Particularly after supper… but if you only knew how sorry I am" (I wanted to say sad, but did not dare) "that you are leaving soon and that we'll no longer see each other."

"Why won't we see each other?" she said, staring intently at the tips of her shoes and running her finger along the latticed screens past which we were walking, "Mama and I go out on the Tverskoy boulevard every Tuesday and Friday. Don't you ever go out?"

"We'll definitely ask to go out on Tuesday, and if they won't let me, I'll run off by myself – without a hat. I know the way."

"You know," said Sonyechka suddenly, "I always use the familiar *ty* with some of the boys who come and visit us: let us do the same. Do you want to?" she added, tossing her little head and looking me straight in the eye.

By that stage we had entered the ballroom and another more lively section of the *Grossvater* was starting up.

"Yes, you and I should do that," I said, when the music and the noise could drown the fact that I had still used the formal *vy*.

"Let's! *Ty*, not *vy*," she corrected and laughed.

The dance ended and I had not once managed to use the familiar *ty*, although I constantly thought of phrases which would have included it several times. I did not feel bold enough. "Do you want to?" "Let's use *ty*," resounded in my ears and made me feel somewhat intoxicated. I saw nothing and no one except for Sonyechka. I saw how her curls were gathered up and tucked behind her ears, uncovering part of her forehead and her temples, which I had not yet seen; I saw her being bundled up in the green shawl so tightly that only the tip of her tiny nose remained visible; I noticed that, had Sonyechka not made a little opening near her mouth with her little pink fingers, she would have suffocated, and I saw how, following her mother downstairs, she quickly turned towards us, nodded her little head and disappeared through the door.

Volodya, the Ivins, the young Prince and I were all in love with Sonyechka and, standing on the stairs, we followed her with our eyes. To whom in particular she addressed that nod I do not know, but at that moment I was firmly convinced that it was to me.

As we said goodbye to the Ivins, I chatted quite unconcernedly, even somewhat coldly, with Seryozha and I shook his hand. If he understood that on that day he had lost my love and his power over me, then he probably regretted it, although he tried to appear completely indifferent.

For the first time in my life I had been unfaithful in love and for the first time I tasted the sweetness of that sensation. I was delighted to exchange the worn-out feeling of familiar devotion for the newer feeling of a love filled with mystery and uncertainty. Moreover, to fall out of love and in love at the same time means loving twice as deeply as before.

24

In Bed

"How could I have loved Seryozha so passionately and for so long?" I thought to myself, lying in bed. "No! He never understood my love, he was not able to appreciate or deserve it… and Sonyechka? How lovely she is! *'Do you want to?'*"

I jumped up in bed on my hands and knees, vividly picturing her little face; I covered my head with the quilt, tucked it under me on all sides and, when there was nothing left uncovered, I lay down and, feeling pleasantly warm, lost myself in sweet fantasies and recollections. I kept my gaze fixed on the quilt lining and I saw her just as clearly as I had an hour before; I mentally chatted with her, and that conversation, although making absolutely no sense, caused me indescribable joy, because we used familiar terms throughout.

Those fantasies were so lucid that the sweetness of my emotions prevented me from sleeping and I wanted to share the fullness of my happiness with someone.

"Darling!" I said almost out loud, abruptly turning over to my other side. "Volodya! Are you asleep?"

"No," he replied with a sleepy voice. "Why?"

"I'm in love, Volodya! I'm really in love with Sonyechka."

"Well, what of it?" he replied, stretching himself.

"Oh, Volodya! You can't imagine what is happening to me… I was lying down just now, wrapped up in my quilt, and I saw her clearly, so clearly, and I chatted with her and it's simply amazing. And do you know what else? When I lie down and think of her, God only knows why, I become sad and badly want to cry."

Volodya stirred.

"I only wish for one thing," I continued, "it's to be with her always, see her always and nothing more. And are you in love too? Do tell me the truth, Volodya."

It was strange, but I wanted everyone to be in love with Sonyechka and everyone to speak about it.

"What's it to you?" said Volodya, turning to face me. "Maybe."

"You don't want to sleep, you were just pretending!" I shouted, noticing by his shining eyes that he was not thinking of sleep at all, and I threw off my quilt. "Let's rather talk about her. Isn't she lovely? So lovely that if she were to say to me: 'Nikolyenka! Jump out of the window or throw yourself into the fire,' well, I swear," I said, "I'd jump straight away and with delight! Oh, how lovely she is!" I added, vividly imagining her before me, turning impulsively over to my other side and sticking my head under the pillow to delight fully in that image. "I want to cry so badly, Volodya."

"What a fool!" he said, smiling, and after a brief pause: "I'm not at all like you: I think that if it were possible I would first want to sit next to her and chat."

"Ah! So you are in love too?" I interrupted him.

"Then," went on Volodya, smiling tenderly, "then I would shower her little fingers, her eyes, her lips, her little nose, her tiny feet, with kisses – I would kiss her all over…"

"What nonsense!" I cried out from under the pillow.

"You don't understand anything," said Volodya contemptuously.

"Yes, I do understand and it's you who doesn't understand and are talking nonsense," I said through my tears.

"There's really nothing to cry about. You're just like a girl!"

25

The Letter

O N 16TH APRIL, nearly six months since the day I have just described, my father came upstairs during lessons and announced that we were going to the country with him that night. My heart ached at the news and my thoughts immediately turned to Mother.

The reason for this unexpected trip was the following letter:

Petrovskoye, 12th April

I have only just now, at ten o'clock at night, received your kind letter of 3rd April and, as is my habit, I am replying straight away. Fyodor did bring it over from town yesterday, but as it was late, he gave it to Mimi this morning. Mimi, on the pretext that I was unwell and upset, didn't give it to me all day. I did indeed have a mild fever and, to tell you the truth, I have not been very well for four days now and have not got out of bed.

Please don't be alarmed, my darling: I feel quite well and if Ivan Vasilych agrees, I think I'll get up tomorrow.

On Friday last week I went for a drive with the children, but near the exit to the main road, next to that small bridge which has always inspired me with horror, the horses became stuck in the mud. It was a beautiful day and I took it into my head to reach the road on foot while they dug out the carriage. When we reached the chapel, I was very tired and sat down to rest and, as it took about half an hour to get hold of enough people to help pull out the carriage, I began to feel cold, especially my feet, because I was wearing thin-soled boots and they were soaked through. After dinner I felt shivery and feverish, but I stayed up as usual and after tea I sat down with Lyubochka to play a duet on the piano with her. (You wouldn't recognize her: she has made such progress!) But imagine my surprise when I noticed that I couldn't keep time. I tried to count several times, but everything was getting very confused in my head and I felt a strange buzzing in my ears. I counted: one, two, three, then all of a sudden: eight, fifteen, but the main thing was that I saw that it was all wrong, but I couldn't put it right at all. Finally Mimi came to my assistance and almost forced me to lie down in bed. There, my dear, a detailed account of how I fell ill and how I am to blame for it myself. The next day I had quite a high fever and our dear old Ivan Vasilych came and has stayed with us until now and is resolved to get me back on my feet. What a wonderful old man Ivan Vasilych is! When I had a fever and was delirious, he sat near my bed without closing his eyes all night, and now, as he knows that I am writing to you, he is in the sitting room with the girls, and from the bedroom I can hear him telling them German fairy tales and them dying of laughter as they listen to him.

La belle Flamande,* as you call her, has been staying with me for over a week now, because her mother has gone to visit somewhere, and the way she takes care of me shows genuine affection. She entrusts me with all her intimate secrets. Were she in good hands, with her pretty face, kind heart and youth, she could emerge as a wonderful young woman in all respects, but, judging by her stories, she will sink completely in the environment she lives in. It occurred to me that if I did not have so many children myself, I would be doing her a good turn by taking her under my wing.

Lyubochka wanted to write to you herself, but has already torn up three sheets of paper and says: "I know what a tease Papa is; if I made just one mistake, he would show it to everyone." Katyenka is as sweet and Mimi as kind and boring as ever.

Now let's speak of serious things: you write that your affairs are not doing so well this winter and that you'll need to use the income from Khabarovka. I am indeed surprised that you are asking for my consent for this. Is not everything that is mine also yours?

You are so kind, my darling, that from fear of upsetting me you are hiding the real state of your affairs. But I am guessing: you have probably gambled away a great deal, and I am not at all distressed by that, I swear; so if you can put matters right, please don't think about it too much and don't torment yourself for nothing. I have become accustomed not only not to count on your winnings for the children but, forgive me, not even to count on all your property. I rejoice as little at your winnings as I feel upset at your losses; I am only distressed at your unhappy passion for gambling, which denies me part of your tender affection and forces me to speak such bitter truths as now, and God knows how painful this is to me! I never stop praying to him about one thing: to spare us... not from poverty (what is poverty?) but from that terrible situation when the children's interests, which I'll have to protect, will clash with ours. Up to now God has answered my prayers: you have not crossed the limit beyond which we would have to sacrifice our fortune, which does in fact not belong to us but to our children or... And to think of it is terrible, yet that awful fate is always threatening us. Yes, this is a heavy cross that God has sent us both!

You write again about the children and return to our long-standing quarrel: you ask me to agree to send them to an educational institution. You know my prejudice against such an education...

I don't know, my dear, if you will agree with me, but in any case I beg you, out of love for me, to promise me that as long as I live and after my death, if it's God's will to part us, that you will not let it happen.

You write that you need to go to St Petersburg to deal with our affairs. May Christ be with you, my darling, go and come back as *soon as possible. We all miss you so very much! It's a wonder how beautiful spring is: the balcony door has already been taken down, the path to the greenhouse was completely dry four days ago, the peach trees are covered in blossom, there is only a little snow left here and there, the swallows have flown in and today Lyubochka brought me the first spring flowers. The doctor says that I will be quite recovered in about three days' time and I'll be able to breathe in the fresh air and warm up in the April sunshine. Goodbye, my darling, don't worry, please, about my illness, or about your losses; sort out your affairs as soon as possible and come to us with the children for the whole summer. I am making wonderful plans on how we'll spend it, and it only needs you to make them come true.*

The next part of the letter was written in French, in a tight uneven handwriting, on another scrap of paper. I will translate it word for word:

Don't believe what I have written to you about my illness; no one suspects how serious it is. I only know that I will not get up from this bed again. Don't waste a single moment, come here immediately and bring the children. I may be able to embrace you one more time and bless them: that is my one last wish. I know what a terrible blow I am inflicting on you, but all the same, you would have received it from me or from others sooner or later; let us try to endure this misfortune with fortitude and hope in God's mercy. Let us submit to His will.

Don't think that what I write are the ravings of a sick imagination; quite the opposite: my thoughts are extremely clear right now and I am completely calm. Do not find consolation in the vain hope that these are lies, faint forebodings of a timid soul. No, I feel and know – know because it pleased God to reveal this to me – that I have very little time left to live.

Will my love for you and the children end with my life? I have understood that this is impossible. I feel too deeply right now to believe that that feeling without which I cannot comprehend existence could somehow some day be obliterated. My soul cannot exist without my love for you: and I know that it will exist for ever, if only because such a feeling as my love could never have arisen if it had to end at some point.

I won't be with you all, but I am firmly convinced that my love will never leave you, and this thought is so comforting to my heart that I await my impending death calmly and fearlessly.

I am at peace and God knows that I have always considered and do still consider death as the passage to a better life, but why then are my eyes heavy with tears? Why deprive children of their beloved mother? Why inflict upon you such a heavy, unexpected blow? Why must I die, when your love has made my life infinitely happy?

May His holy will be done.

I cannot write any longer for my tears. Perhaps I won't see you again. I thank you, my precious friend, for all the happiness you have surrounded me with in this life; over there I will ask God to reward you. Goodbye, my darling; remember, I won't be there, but my love will never leave you. Goodbye, Volodya, goodbye, my angel, goodbye my Benjamin – my Nikolyenka.

Is it possible that they will forget me some day?

In that letter was inserted a note in French by Mimi with the following content:

The sad forebodings she tells you about have been fully corroborated by the doctor. Last night she ordered this letter to be posted immediately. Thinking that she was delirious when saying this, I waited until this morning and decided to unseal it. No sooner had I done so than Natalya Nikolayevna asked me what I had done with the letter and told me to burn it if it had not been sent. She keeps on talking about it and believes that it will kill you. Do not delay your journey if you want to see this angel before she leaves us. Excuse this scribble. I have not slept for three nights. You know how much I love her.

Natalya Savishna, who spent the whole night of the 11th of April in my mother's bedroom, told me that, after writing the first part of the letter, Maman put it on the little table beside her and fell asleep.

"I must admit," said Natalya Savishna, "that I myself dozed off in the armchair and my knitting fell from my hands. Only I heard in my sleep – some time after midnight – that she seemed to be talking; I opened my eyes and saw her, my little dove, sitting up in bed, her arms crossed so, and tears streaming down. 'So is it all over?' she said and covered her face with her hands. I leapt up and asked: 'What's the matter with you?'

"'Oh, Natalya Savishna, if only you knew who I just saw.'

"For all my asking she said nothing more, only ordered the little table to be brought over to her, wrote something else down, asked for me to seal it in her presence and to send it off at once. After that things went from bad to worse."

26

What Awaited Us in the Country

O N 18TH APRIL we stepped down from our carriage at the front porch of the Petrovskoye house. Papa was in a pensive mood as we left Moscow, and when Volodya asked him whether Maman was ill, he looked at him sorrowfully and nodded silently. He grew visibly calmer during the course of the journey, but as we drew nearer to the house, his face looked increasingly sad and, when he stepped down from the carriage and asked Foka, who had come running and out of breath: "Where is Natalya Nilolayevna?" his voice was unsteady and there were tears in his eyes. Kind old Foka, glancing furtively at us, lowered his eyes and, opening the door to the entrance hall, turned away and replied:

"This is the sixth day that she has not come out of her room."

Milka, who, as I later learnt, had not stopped howling pitifully since the day Maman was taken ill, threw herself happily at Father: she jumped on him, yelped, licked his hands, but he pushed her aside and went into the drawing room, then into the sitting room from where the door led straight to the bedroom. The closer he came to that room, the more his whole body betrayed his anxiety: he entered the sitting room on tiptoe, hardly breathing, and made the sign of the cross before bringing himself to grasp the handle of the closed door. At that moment Mimi, unkempt and tear-stained, ran in from the corridor: "Oh! Pyotr Alexandrych!" she whispered with an expression of genuine despair and, when she noticed that Papa was turning the door handle, she added almost inaudibly: "You can't get in through here. The entrance is through the maids' room."

Oh, how gravely all this affected my childish imagination, already attuned to grief by a terrible foreboding.

We went to the maids' room; on the way, in the corridor, we ran into Akim the fool, who always amused us with the faces he pulled; yet not only did I not find him funny right then, but nothing struck me so painfully as the sight of his vacant, indifferent face. In the maids' room two girls who sat doing needlework half rose up to bow to us with such sad expressions that I felt terrified. Going through Mimi's room next, Papa opened the bedroom door and we went in. To the right of the door were two windows, curtained off with shawls; Natalya Savishna sat by one window, her glasses on her nose, knitting a stocking. She did not kiss us as she usually did, but only half rose, looked at us through her glasses, and tears poured down her face. I did not at all like the way everyone started to cry the moment they first caught sight of us, when they had been quite composed before.

To the left of the door were some screens and behind the screens a bed, a small table, a cabinet crammed with medicines and a big armchair in which the doctor dozed; beside the bed stood a very fair-haired young girl of remarkable beauty in a white housecoat with its sleeves slightly rolled up; she was placing ice on Maman's head, but I could not see Maman herself at the time.

That young girl was *la belle Flamande* Mother had written about, and who was later to play such an important role in the life of our whole family. As soon as we came in, she withdrew one hand from Maman's head and adjusted the folds on the front of her housecoat, then whispered: "She's unconscious."

I was struck with grief at that moment, but I unwittingly noticed the slightest details. It was almost dark in the room; it was hot and there was a combined smell of mint, eau de Cologne, camomile and Hoffmann's Drops.* That smell struck me so forcibly that when I smell it now, and even when I just remember it, my mind instantly takes me back to that gloomy, stuffy room and recreates every minute detail of that awful moment.

Maman's eyes were open, but she saw nothing... Oh, I will never forget that terrible look! So much suffering reflected in it!

We were led away.

When I later asked Natalya Savishna about Mother's last moments, this is what she told me:

83

"After they led you away, she tossed about for a long time, my little dove, as though something was weighing her down; then her head slipped from the pillow and she dozed off so peacefully and quietly, like an angel from heaven. I had just gone out to see why they hadn't brought in a drink: when I came in again, she, my dearest one, had already scattered everything around her and kept on beckoning to your Papa to come to her. He bent over her, but it was obvious that she didn't have enough strength left to say what she wanted; she only parted her lips and again began to lament: 'Oh my God! Oh Lord! The children! The children!' I wanted to go after you, but Ivan Vasilych stopped me and said: 'It will alarm her unduly, it's better not.' After that she would just raise her arm and drop it again. And what she meant by it God only knows. I think that she blessed you from afar; yes, the Lord evidently didn't mean her to see her little children before the end. Then she raised herself, my little dove, made a movement with her hand like this, and suddenly said in a voice that I can't bear to recall: 'Mother of God, don't abandon them!...' Then the pain reached her heart and her eyes told of her terrible struggle, the poor dear. She fell back on the pillow, grabbed hold of the sheet with her teeth, and her tears, my dear little one, were streaming down."

"Well, what then?" I asked.

Natalya Savishna could no longer speak: she turned away and wept bitterly.

Maman died in terrible agony.*

27

Grief

LATE THE FOLLOWING EVENING, I wanted to take a look at her one more time. Overcoming an involuntary feeling of fear, I softly opened the door and tiptoed into the room.

The coffin lay on a table in the middle of the room and around it were low burning candles in tall silver candlesticks; in the distant corner sat the chanter quietly intoning the psalter.

I paused by the door to look round, but my eyes were so full of tears and my nerves in such turmoil that I could not make anything out.

Everything somehow became a strange blur: the light, the brocade, the velvet, the tall candlesticks, the pink lace-trimmed pillow, the band on her forehead,* the bonnet with ribbons and something else, transparent, the colour of wax. I climbed onto a chair to look at her face, but in its place I was again confronted with a pale, yellowy, transparent thing. I could not believe it to be her face. I began to look at it more intently and little by little began to recognize the dear familiar features. I winced with horror when I felt certain it was she, but why were the closed eyes so sunken? Why that deathly pallor and on one cheek a darkish spot beneath the transparent skin? Why was the expression on the face so stern and cold? Why were her lips so pale and so beautifully and nobly set in an expression of such unearthly peace that cold shivers ran up my spine and my hair when I looked at them?

I looked and felt that some incomprehensible, irresistible force drew my eyes to that lifeless face. I did not take my eyes off her, yet my imagination drew me pictures blooming with life and happiness. I forgot that the dead body which lay before me and which I was gazing at senselessly as though it were an object, with nothing in common with my memories, was *she*. I would imagine her one way, alive, joyful, smiling, then another: all of a sudden I would be struck by some feature on the pale face that my eyes had fixed on; I remembered the terrible reality, shuddered, but continued to look. And again dreams replaced reality, and again awareness of reality destroyed the dreams. In the end my imagination grew weary and ceased to deceive me; all perception of reality also disappeared and I lost all consciousness of myself. I do not know how long I remained in that state, nor do I know what it was; I only know that for some time I lost consciousness of my own existence and experienced some lofty, inexpressibly bittersweet pleasure.

Perhaps her beautiful soul, having flown off to a better world, looked back with sadness at the world she had left us in; she saw my grief, took pity on it and with a heavenly smile of compassion she came down to earth on the wings of love to comfort and bless me.

The door creaked and a chanter came in to relieve the first one. The noise roused me and the first thought that came to mind was that I was not crying and, as I was standing on the chair in a pose that had nothing poignant about it, the chanter might take me for an insensitive boy who had climbed on the chair out of curiosity or for a prank:* I made the sign of the cross, bowed down and burst into tears.

As I recall those impressions now, I find that that moment of losing myself was the only one that denoted genuine grief. Before and after the burial I wept constantly and felt sad, but I am ashamed to recall that grief, because it always included some feeling of pride – a desire to show that I was more upset than anyone else – concerns about the effect I was having on others or even aimless curiosity which made me observe Mimi's bonnet and the faces of those present. I despised myself for not experiencing unadulterated grief and I tried to conceal all other feelings; that is why my grief was insincere and unnatural. Furthermore, I felt some pleasure in knowing that I was unhappy; I tried to stimulate an awareness of my unhappiness and this egotistical feeling more than any other stifled any genuine sorrow I had.

After sleeping deeply and peacefully that night, as always happens after great distress, I woke up with my tears dried up and my nerves calmed. At ten o'clock we were summoned to the funeral service, which was held before the burial procession. The room was filled with weeping servants and peasants, who had come to bid farewell to their mistress. During the service I wept as was fitting, made the sign of the cross, bowed down to the ground, but I did not pray with my soul and remained quite detached. I was concerned that the new jacket I was wearing felt very tight under the arms, I thought about not getting my trousers dirty at the knees and I surreptitiously carried out my own observations of all those present. Father stood at the head of the coffin, as white as a sheet, and he had obvious trouble holding back his tears. His tall figure in its black tailcoat, his pale expressive face and, as always, his graceful and confident movements were very striking when he made the sign of the cross, bowed down touching the ground with his hand, took the candle from the priest's hand or approached the coffin. I do not know why, but I did not like the way he could appear so striking at such a time. Mimi stood leaning against the wall and hardly seemed able to stay on her feet; her dress was crumpled and specked with fluff, and her bonnet knocked sideways; her puffy eyes were red, her head shook; she did not stop sobbing heart-rendingly and kept her face covered with her handkerchief and her hands. It seemed to me that she hid her face from the others so that she could have a moment's rest from her fake sobbing. I remembered how on the previous day she had told Father how Maman's death was such a terrible blow for her, from which she could never hope to recover, that it had now deprived her of everything, that that angel (as she called Maman) had not forgotten her before her death and had expressed her wish that she and her Katyenka would be taken care of for the rest of their lives. She shed bitter tears when saying this, and perhaps her grief was genuine, but it was not pure and did not exclude other feelings. Lyubochka, in her small black dress with white trimming,* her face wet with tears, held her head down, glancing from time to time at the coffin, and then her face only expressed childish terror. Katyenka stood next to her mother and despite her sad little face she was as rosy as ever. Volodya's open nature was open even in grief: he either stood lost in thought, fixing his gaze on some object, or his mouth would suddenly begin to quiver and he would hastily make the sign of the cross and bow down. I found all the other people present at the burial insufferable. The comforting phrases they said to Father – that she was better off over there, that she was not of this world – irritated me somehow.

What right did they have to speak of her and weep over her? Some of them, when mentioning us, called us *orphans*. As if we would not actually have known, without them telling us, that children who do not have a mother are called by that name? They were probably pleased that they were the first ones to call us that, just as people are usually in a hurry to call a young girl who has just been married Madame for the first time.

In the far corner of the room, almost hidden behind the open pantry door, knelt a bent grey-haired old woman. Clasping her hands and raising her eyes to heaven, she did not weep but prayed. Her soul reached out to God, she asked Him to reunite her with the one she loved most in the world and firmly hoped this would be soon.

"There's someone who truly loved her!" I thought, and I felt ashamed of myself.

The funeral service ended; the face of the deceased was uncovered and one by one all those present, except for us, began to approach the coffin and kiss her.

One of the last to come up to bid farewell to the deceased was a peasant woman holding a pretty little five-year-old girl in her arms, who, God knows why, she had brought with her. Right then I had inadvertently dropped my wet handkerchief and wanted to pick it up, but no sooner had I bent down than I was startled by a terrible piercing shriek, so full of terror that I will never forget it if I live to be a hundred. When I do remember it, a cold shiver runs through my entire body. I raised my head: on the stool next to the coffin stood that same peasant woman, having trouble holding on to the little girl, who, waving her little arms about and throwing back her frightened little face, her wide-open eyes fixed on the deceased's face, went on shrieking with a terrifying frenzied voice. I gave a scream in a voice that I think was even more frightful than the one that had startled me, and ran out of the room.

Only at that moment did I understand where that strong oppressive smell mixed with the smell of incense that filled the room came from, and the thought that that face, which a few days before had been full of beauty and tenderness, that face I loved above all on earth, could inspire horror, revealed to me, as though for the first time, the bitter truth and filled my soul with despair.

28

Last Sad Memories

Maman was no longer there, but our life resumed its normal course: we went to sleep and got up at the usual time and in the usual rooms; morning tea and evening tea, dinner, supper – everything happened at its normal time; the tables and chairs stood in the usual places; nothing changed at home or in our way of life; only she was not there…

It seemed to me that everything should change after such a misfortune; our ordinary way of life appeared to me an insult to her memory and reminded us too keenly of her absence.

The day before the burial, after dinner, I felt sleepy and I went to Natalya Savishna's room, planning to settle under a warm quilt on her soft feather bed. When I went in, Natalya Savishna was lying on her bed, probably asleep. When she heard the sound of my footsteps, she raised herself, threw off the woollen shawl that protected her head from flies and, adjusting her bonnet, sat on the edge of the bed.

Since I quite often used to come to sleep in her room after dinner, she guessed why I was there and asked me as she got up from the bed:

"Well? So you've come for a rest, my little dove, have you? Do lie down."

"What are you thinking, Natalya Savishna?" I said, holding her arm. "I haven't come for that at all… I just came… and you are tired yourself: you'd better lie down."

"No, my dear little man, I have slept all I want," she said (I knew that she had not slept for three days). "And I'm not in the mood for sleep now," she added with a deep sigh.

I wanted to talk with Natalya Savishna about our misfortune; I knew of her sincerity and her love, and it would be of comfort to me to shed a few tears with her.

"Natalya Savishna," I said, after a brief pause and sitting down on the bed. "Did you expect this to happen?"

The old woman looked at me bemused and intrigued, probably not understanding why I had asked her this.

"Who could have expected it?" I repeated.

"Oh, my dear little one," she said, looking at me with the most tender compassion, "not only did I not expect it, but I can't even think of it now. I, an old woman, should long ago have laid my old bones to rest, and now see where living on has led me to: I have buried my old master, your grandfather, Prince Nikolai Mikhailovich, God rest his soul, two of my brothers, my sister Annushka, and they were all younger than I, my dearest, and now, for my sins, I have to outlive her. His holy will be done! He took her because she was worthy and He needs good people over there."

That simple thought struck me as comforting and I moved closer to Natalya Savishna. She folded her arms across her breast and looked up; her sunken eyes, moist with tears, expressed a deep but calm sorrow. She firmly hoped that God had not separated her for long from the one on whom she had focused all the power of her love for so many years.

"Yes, dearest one, it seems a long time ago that I nursed and swaddled her and that she called me *Nasha*.* Sometimes she would run up to me, put her little arms around me, start kissing me and chant:

"'My Nashik, my little beauty, you're my little turkey hen.'

"And I would sometimes say in jest:

"'It's not true, dear little one, you don't love me; as soon as you grow up you'll get married and you'll forget your Nasha.' Then she would hesitate. 'No,' she'd say, 'I'd rather not marry than not take Nasha with

89

me; I'll never abandon our Nasha.' And now she has abandoned me and hasn't waited. And she did love me, the dearly departed one! And, to be truthful, was there anyone she didn't love? Yes, my dearest one, you must never forget your Mama; she was not an ordinary mortal but an angel from heaven. When her soul reaches the kingdom of heaven, she will love you and rejoice over you from up there."

"Why are you saying: when she will be in the kingdom of heaven, Natalya Savishna?" I asked. "I thought she was over there already."

"No, my dear little man," said Natalya Savishna, lowering her voice and settling down closer to me on the bed, "her soul is here now."

And she pointed upwards. She was almost whispering and spoke with such feeling and conviction that I instinctively lifted up my eyes towards the cornices, looking for something.

"Before the soul of a righteous person goes to paradise, it has to undergo forty trials, dearest, for forty days and it can stay in its own home..."

She went on talking in that vein for a long while and she spoke with such simplicity and confidence, as if she was telling me the most ordinary things that she had witnessed herself and which no one would think to doubt at all. I listened to her with bated breath and, although I did not understand all that well what she was talking about, I absolutely believed her.

"Yes, dearest one, she is here now looking at us and perhaps listening to what we're saying," concluded Natalya Savishna.

And lowering her head, she fell silent. She needed a handkerchief to wipe her streaming tears; she got to her feet, looked me straight in the face and said in a voice shaking with emotion:

"The Lord has drawn me through this many steps closer to Him. What have I got left here now? Who do I have to live for? Who to love?"

"But don't you love us?" I said reproachfully, hardly able to hold back my tears.

"God knows how much I love you, my little darlings, but I have never loved nor can I ever love anyone as I loved her."

She could no longer speak, turned away from me and sobbed loudly.

I did not think of sleep now; we silently sat opposite each other and wept.

Foka came into the room; noticing how we were and most likely not wanting to trouble us, he stopped silently and timidly at the door.

"Why are you here, Fokasha?" enquired Natalya Savishna, wiping her face with her handkerchief.

"One and a half pounds* of raisins, four pounds of sugar and three pounds of rice for the *kutya*."*

"Right away, my dear, right away," said Natalya Savishna; she hurriedly took a pinch of snuff and walked briskly over to the chest. The last traces of sorrow following our chat disappeared as soon as she set about her duties, which she considered extremely important.

"What are the four pounds for?" she asked grumpily, getting hold of the sugar and weighing it on the scales. "Three and a half should be enough."

And she took a few lumps off the scales.

"And I'll ask again: what's this supposed to mean when I handed over eight pounds of rice last night. Do what you will, Foka Demidych, I will not give you any more rice. That Vanka is happy right now with all this commotion in the house: he thinks that no one will notice. But I won't do anyone any favours at my master's expense. Did you ever hear of such a thing – eight pounds?"

"What can I do? He says everything has been used up."

"Well, here then, take it! Let him have it!"

I was startled by the transition from the poignant emotion she had expressed when talking to me to this grumpiness and these petty calculations. When I thought about it afterwards, I understood that whatever went on in her soul, she had enough presence of mind left to go about her business, and force of habit drew her to normal tasks. Grief had such a profound effect on her that she found it unnecessary to hide the fact that she could attend to things outside of it; she would not even have understood how anyone could think otherwise.

Vanity is a feeling quite incompatible with genuine grief, but at the same time a feeling so firmly rooted in man's nature that it can rarely be driven out by even the deepest grief. Vanity as part of grief manifests itself by the wish to appear either distressed or unhappy or strong, and those base desires, which we do not admit to, but which hardly ever leave us, even in moments of the most intense grief, rob it of power, dignity and sincerity. Natalya Savishna, however, was so deeply affected by her unhappiness that there was no desire left in her and she lived by habit alone.

Having given Foka the requested provisions and reminded him of the pie that had to be baked for the clergy, she dismissed him, picked up her knitting and sat down next to me again.

The conversation resumed around the same subject and once more we wept and wiped our tears.

Those chats with Natalya Savishna were repeated each day; her gentle tears and calm devout discourses gave me comfort and relief.

But we were soon parted: three days after the burial we arrived in Moscow with the whole household and I was destined never to see her again.

Grandmother only received the terrible news on our arrival and her grief was exceptional. We were not allowed in to see her, because she remained unconscious for a whole week; the doctors feared for her life, especially as not only would she not take any medication, but neither would she speak with anyone, she did not sleep and took no food at all. Sometimes, sitting alone in her armchair in her room, she would all of a sudden burst into laughter or into tearless sobs; she was seized by convulsions, and she shouted incoherent or dreadful words in a frenzied voice. It was the first intense grief that had ever affected her and that grief threw her into despair. She had to blame someone for her unhappiness and she would say awful things, threaten someone with unusual force, leap up from her chair, pace up and down the room with big hasty steps and then fall unconscious.

Once I went into her room; she sat as usual in her armchair and appeared to be calm, but her look startled me. Her eyes were wide open, but her gaze was uncertain and vacant: she looked straight at me, but probably did not see me. Her lips slowly formed a smile and she began to speak in a moving tender voice: "Come here, my friend, come, my angel." I thought she was speaking to me and came closer, but it was not me she was looking at. "Oh, if you only knew, my darling, in what torment I have been and how happy I am that you have come..." I understood that she imagined she saw Maman and so I held back. "But they told me that you were gone," she went on frowning, "what nonsense! Could you possibly die before me?" and she laughed loudly, a terrifying hysterical laugh.

Only people who are capable of loving deeply can experience intense grief, but such a need to love serves as an antidote to grief and heals them. This is why man's spiritual nature is more tenacious than his physical one. Grief never kills anyone.

After a week Grandmother was able to cry and she felt better. Her first thought, when she came to, was for us and her love for us grew. We never left her armchair; she wept softly, talked about Maman and caressed us tenderly.

It would not have entered anyone's head, when watching Grandmother's grief, that she might be exaggerating; the expressions of her grief were intense and moving, but for some reason unknown to me I felt more sympathy for Natalya Savishna, and I have been convinced ever since that no one loved or mourned Maman so sincerely and purely as did that simple loving creature.

With my mother's death ended that happy period of childhood and a new phase began – the boyhood phase, but as the memories of Natalya Savishna, whom I never saw again and who had such a strong and good influence on my life and the development of my sensibility, belong to that first period, I will say a few more words about her and her death.

After our departure, as I was later told by those people who remained in the country, she became very bored with having nothing to do. Although all the chests were still in her care and she continuously rummaged in them, rearranged, spread and repacked things, she missed the noise and the hustle and bustle of the country house when inhabited by its masters, as she had been used to since childhood. Sorrow, the change in her way of life and the absence of activity soon gave rise to an illness of old age she was prone to. Exactly one year after Mother's death, she developed dropsy and took to her bed.

I think that it was very hard for Natalya Savishna to live and even harder to die alone in that big empty house at Petrovskoye, without family or friends. Everyone in the house loved and respected Natalya Savishna, but she made no close friends and was proud of the fact. She believed that in her position as housekeeper, holding her masters' trust and having in her care so many chests full of all sorts of goods, being friends with anyone would inevitably lead her to partiality and criminal indulgence: that was why, or perhaps just because she had nothing in common with the other servants, she withdrew from everyone and said that as far as she was concerned she had no family or friends in the house, and that she would not do anyone any favours at her master's expense.

She sought and found solace in entrusting her feelings to God with fervent prayers. But sometimes, in those moments of weakness we are all susceptible to, when the best comfort for someone is the sympathy and the tears of another living being, she would take her little pug dog (who licked her hands and fixed her yellow eyes on her) into her bed; she talked to her and cried softly, stroking her. When the pug began to howl pitifully, she tried to calm her down, saying: "That's enough, I don't need to be told that I shall die soon."

A month before her death she took some white calico, white muslin and pink ribbons from her chest; with the help of her maid she made herself a white dress and a bonnet and arranged everything needed for her funeral to the last detail. She also went through her masters' chests and passed everything on to the steward's wife with the greatest precision, in line with the inventory; then she took out two silk dresses, an ancient shawl, given to her some time ago by my grandmother, and grandfather's gold embroidered military uniform that had also been entrusted to her. The embroidery and the braids on the uniform were, thanks to her care, in pristine condition and the fabric untouched by moths.

Before the end she expressed the wish that one of those dresses – the pink one – should be given to Volodya to be made into a dressing gown or a quilted jacket; the other one – in soft thick checked material – was for me for the same use, and the shawl was for Lyubochka. She bequeathed the uniform to whichever one of us would first be an officer. The remainder of her belongings and her money, except for forty roubles set aside for her burial and memorial services, she left to her brother. The latter, who had long before been given his freedom, lived in some distant province leading a very dissolute life, which is why she had had no dealings with him in her lifetime.

When her brother came to claim his inheritance and it turned out that all that was left of the deceased's property were twenty-five roubles in notes, he would not believe it and said that it was impossible that an old woman who had lived for sixty years in a wealthy household and had been in charge of everything, who had lived frugally all her life and had watched every penny, should have left nothing. But it was indeed so.

Natalya Savishna suffered for two months from her illness and bore her sufferings with real Christian endurance: she did not grumble or complain, but constantly turned to God, as was her habit. An hour before her death she made her confession, received communion and extreme unction with quiet joy.

She begged forgiveness of all the house servants for any offence she might have caused and she asked her confessor, Father Vasily, to convey to us all that she did not know how to thank us for our kindness and asked us to forgive her if she had upset anyone through foolishness, "but I have never once stolen and can say that I've never so much as made a penny from taking even a thread from my master." That was the one quality she valued in herself.

After putting on the prepared gown and bonnet and propping herself on the pillow, she did not stop talking to her priest until the very end. She remembered not having left anything for the poor, took out ten roubles and asked him to distribute them at the church entrance; then she made the sign of the cross, lay back and breathed for the last time with a joyful smile, invoking God.

She left life without regret, was not afraid of death and accepted it as a blessing. This is often said, but how seldom is it true. Natalya Savishna was not afraid of death, because she died with an unshakeable faith and fulfilling the laws of the Gospel. Her whole life had been pure, unselfish love and selflessness.

So what if her beliefs could have been loftier, her life directed to a higher goal; was that soul perhaps less deserving of love and wonder because of that?

She achieved the best and greatest thing in life – she died without regret or fear.

She was buried according to her wishes, not far from the chapel that stands over my mother's grave. The mound overgrown with nettles and burdock beneath which she lies is enclosed by black railings and I never forget to go from the chapel to those railings and bow down to the ground.

At times I stop in silence between the chapel and the black railings. Painful recollections suddenly stir in my soul. A thought occurs to me: has Providence linked me to those two beings just to make me grieve for them for ever?

Boyhood

1

A Long Journey

ONCE AGAIN two carriages are brought round to the front porch of the Petrovskoye house: one, a coach, in which Mimi, Katyenka, Lyubochka and the housemaid take their seats, with the steward Yakov himself on the box; the other, a *britzka*, in which Volodya and I ride, together with Vasily the footman, who has recently been brought in from the estate to become a house servant.*

Papa, who is to follow us to Moscow a few days later, stands hatless on the porch and makes the sign of the cross over the coach window and over the *britzka*.

"Well, may the Lord be with you! On your way!" Yakov and the coachmen (we are using our own horses and carriages)* raise their caps and make the sign of the cross. "Gee up, gee up! May God be with us!" The coach and the *britzka* begin to bob up and down along the uneven road and the birches on the wide avenue fly past us one by one. I am not sad at all: mentally I am looking ahead to what awaits me, not back at what I leave behind. As I put distance between myself and everything linked to the painful memories that until now have filled my mind, those memories lose their impact and are soon replaced by a joyful awareness of a life full of vigour, newness and hope.

I have seldom spent a few days – I won't say merrily: I still felt quite guilty succumbing to high spirits – but so pleasantly and enjoyably as the four days of our journey. I no longer had to face Mother's closed door, which I could not walk past without a shudder, nor the closed piano, which we did not go near and looked at with some kind of dread, nor the mourning clothes (we wore simple travelling clothes), nor all those things which keenly reminded me of my irrevocable loss and made me wary of any manifestation of life for fear of somehow offending *her* memory. Here on the other hand charming new places and objects constantly held my attention and entertained me, and nature in spring filled my soul with pleasant feelings of contentment with the present and bright hopes for the future.

Very, very early in the morning the heartless and – as is always the case with people with new responsibilities – ultra-zealous Vasily tugs off my blanket and assures us that everything is ready and it is time to go. However much you huddle, pretend, get cross, in order to prolong morning's sweet sleep by at least a quarter of an hour, you can tell by Vasily's determined face that he is unbending and prepared to tug off your blanket another twenty times; so you leap up and run over to the yard to wash.

In the passageway the samovar is already bubbling, fanned by Mitka the postillion, who has turned as red as a lobster. The yard is damp and misted over with the sort of steamy haze that rises from a fuming dung heap. The sun with its cheerful bright glow lights up the eastern sky and makes the dew glisten on the thatched roofs of the spacious open structures around the courtyard. Beneath them we can see our horses tied up by the feeding troughs and we can hear their rhythmic champing. A shaggy house dog, which until dawn was curled up on a dry dung heap, lazily stretches itself and trots lightly over to the other side of the yard wagging its tail. The bustling landlady opens the creaking gates and drives the pensive cows outside, where the tramping, bleating and mooing of flocks and herds can already be heard, and where she exchanges a word or two with her sleepy neighbour. Filipp, his shirt sleeves rolled up, winds a bucket up from the deep well, splashing the clear water as he pours it into an oak trough; in a puddle formed beside it some ducks, just awakened, are already paddling about and I look with pleasure at Filipp's expressive face with its broad beard and at the distinct outline of the thick veins and muscles that appear on his strong bare arms whenever he exerts himself.

There are sounds of movement behind the partition where Mimi and the girls have slept and across which we chatted the night before. Masha keeps rushing past us with various objects, which she tries to conceal from our inquisitive eyes behind her dress and finally the door opens and they call us in to tea.

Vasily, in a fit of excess zeal, repeatedly runs into the room, carrying away one thing after another, winks at us and does his utmost to persuade Mimi to leave sooner. The horses are harnessed and convey their impatience by now and then jangling their bells. Cases, trunks, small boxes and tiny boxes are piled up again and we take our places. But each time we look for a seat in the *britzka* we find mountains of luggage and we really cannot understand how everything was packed in the day before and how we will find room to sit down this time. In particular a walnut tea caddy with a triangular lid, which has been placed in the *britzka* beneath me, provokes strong indignation on my part. But Vasily says that it will not trouble me for long and I have no option but to believe him.

The sun has only just risen above a solid white cloud blanketing the east, and all the surroundings are lit up by its quietly joyful glow. Everything is so beautiful around me and my soul feels so light and peaceful... The road winds forwards like a wide dark-grey ribbon through fields of dried stubble with patches of green, shiny with dew; here and there along the road we come across a forlorn crack willow or a young birch with tiny sticky leaves casting a long motionless shadow over the dried-up clay tracks and green grass shoots on the road... The monotonous sound of the wheels and little bells does not muffle the song of the skylarks hovering close to the road. The smell of moth-eaten cloth, dust and some kind of acid odour peculiar to our *britzka* is covered up by the fragrance of early morning and a delightful restlessness stirs in my soul, a desire to do something – a sign of genuine enjoyment.

I had not found time to say my prayers at the coaching inn, but as I have noticed many times before that some misfortune occurs on those days when I for some reason forget to perform this ritual, I try to put this right: I take off my cap and, turning round to a corner of the *britzka*, I recite my prayers and make the sign of the cross under my jacket so that no one can see. But thousands of different things draw my attention and I absent-mindedly repeat the same words several times.

Some slow-moving figures can be spotted on the footpath that winds along the road: these are female pilgrims. Their heads are muffled in dirty scarves, they carry birch-bark knapsacks on their backs and their feet are wrapped in dirty torn *onuchas** inside heavy bast shoes. Swinging their sticks at an even pace and scarcely glancing at us, they move forwards in single file with a slow heavy step and I am full of questions: where are they going and why? Will their journey be long? And will the long shadows which they cast on the road soon meld with the shadow of the crack willow they must walk past? There is a four-horse carriage with post horses speeding towards us. Two seconds and the faces looking at us curiously and amiably from a distance of just over an *arshin** have already flashed past; it seems strange somehow that those faces have nothing in common with me and that I will most probably never set eyes on them again.

Two shaggy sweating horses, in collars with trace secured to their breast band, come galloping along one side of the road; behind them rides the driver, a young lad, his felt hat tipped over one ear as he drones some endless tune, his long legs in big boots dangling on either side of his horse, who has a shaft bow above her withers,* from which you can now and then hear the faint jingle of her little bell. The lad's face and posture express such idle, careless contentment that to me it seems the height of happiness to be a driver, to ride back and forth singing melancholy songs. There in the distance beyond the ravine a green-roofed country church is discernible against the light-blue sky; over there is a village and the red roof and green garden of a manor house. Who lives in that house? Are there children, a father, a mother, a tutor in it? Why could we not drive to that house and meet the owners? Here is a long line of large carts, each harnessed to three well-fed, thick-legged horses, and we are forced to drive to the side of the road to get round them. "What are you carrying?" Vasily asks the first driver, who, letting his huge feet hang over the edge of the cart and brandishing his whip, follows us with a vacant stare and only gives some kind of answer when we can no longer hear him. "What is your load?" Vasily turns to the next cart, its driver lying in the front section under new bast matting. A light-brown head with a red face and a reddish beard emerges for a moment from under the matting, casts his eye, expressing a mixture of scorn and indifference, over our *britzka* and vanishes again – and it occurs to me that these coachmen probably do not know who we are, where we come from or where we are going.

Engrossed for about an hour and a half in various observations, I do not pay attention to the crooked numbers displayed on the verst posts. But the sun begins to burn more hotly on my head and back, the road becomes dustier, the triangular lid of the tea caddy begins to bother me a lot more and I change position several times: I am beginning to feel hot, uncomfortable and bored. All my attention is now directed towards the verst posts and at the figures on them; I make various mathematical calculations regarding the time it will take us to reach the next stage. "Twelve versts make up one third of thirty-six and to Lipets it is forty-one, so we have driven one third and how much?" And so on.

"Vasily," I say when I notice that he is beginning to nod off on the box, "let me get on the box, my friend." Vasily agrees. We exchange places: he immediately begins to snore and sprawls out so much that there is no space left for anyone else in the *britzka*, and from my heightened position the most lovely picture now unfolds: our four horses, Neruchinskaya, Dyachok, Levaya the shaft horse and Aptyekar, each of which I had come to know down to the smallest detail and colouring.

"Why is Dyachok in the right trace today and not in the left-hand one, Filipp?" I ask him somewhat timidly.

"Dyachok?"

"And Neruchinskaya isn't pulling at all," I say.

"Dyachok mustn't be harnessed on the left," says Filipp, ignoring my last comment. "He's not the kind of horse you harness on the left. On the left you need a horse, well, in a word, that is a real horse, and he's not one of those."

And with these words Filipp leans over to the right and, tugging at the reins with all his might, he begins to whip poor Dyachok across the tail and legs in a peculiar manner from below, despite the fact that Dyachok is trying his hardest and is the one pulling the entire carriage. Filipp only ends this exercise when he feels the need to take a break and to push his cap for some unknown reason to one side, although it has sat very well until now squarely on his head. I make use of this happy moment to ask Filipp to let me drive. He passes me first one rein, then the second; finally all six reins and the whip are transferred into my hands and I am perfectly happy. I try to imitate Filipp in every way and ask him if I am doing well, but it usually ends with him being dissatisfied with me: he says that that one is pulling too much, the other one is not pulling at all, thrusts his elbow past my chest and takes the reins away from me. It is getting hotter all the time, small fleecy clouds begin to swell like soap bubbles higher and higher, and merge into dark-grey shadows. A hand holding a bottle and a small bundle is thrust out of the coach window; Vasily leaps off the coach box with amazing agility while we are still moving and brings us curd tarts and some *kvas*.

On steep slopes we all get out of the carriage and sometimes race to a bridge while Vasily and Yakov put the brakes on and hold on to each side of the carriage with their hands, as though by doing so they will keep it from toppling over. Then, with Mimi's permission, Volodya or I get into the carriage and Lyubochka or Katyenka sit in the *britzka*. These changeovers give the girls great pleasure, because they rightly find it much more fun in the *britzka*. Sometimes, in the heat of the day as we drive through a grove, we lag behind the coach, tear off some green branches and build a small bower in the *britzka*. The bower moving at full speed catches up with the coach and, when this happens, Lyubochka gives a loud piercing squeal, an opportunity she never misses, which affords her a great deal of pleasure.

But here is the village where we are to have dinner and a rest. Here are the village smells, of smoke, tar, *barankas** and the sounds of conversation, footsteps and wheels reach us. The little bells no longer ring like they did in the open field, and on both sides we catch a glimpse of peasant cottages with thatched roofs, carved wooden porches and little red-and-green shuttered windows, where here and there an inquisitive old woman thrusts out her face. Here are the peasant boys and girls wearing only long shirts; their eyes opened wide and their arms spread out, they stand motionless on one spot or, quickly tripping along in the dust on their bare feet, despite Filipp's threatening gestures, they run after the carriages and try to clamber up onto the luggage tied up behind. Reddish-haired innkeepers come running from both sides towards the carriages and one after another try to entice the new arrivals with winning words and gestures. Whoa! The gates creak, the harness crossbars scrape against the gate posts and we drive into the courtyard. Four hours of freedom and rest.

2

The Thunderstorm

THE SUN WAS DIPPING towards the west and its hot slanting rays burned my neck and my cheeks unbearably; it was impossible to touch the red-hot sides of the *britzka*; thick dust rose along the road and filled the air. There was not the slightest breeze to shift it. Keeping at an even distance ahead of us, the tall dusty body of the coach and its crossbars gently rocked in steady rhythm and you occasionally caught sight of a whip being swung by the coachman, of his hat and of Yakov's cap. I did not know what to do with myself: neither Volodya's face, black with dust as he dozed beside me, nor the movements of Filipp's back, nor the *britzka's* long shadow pursuing us at a slant, offered me any diversion. My whole attention was focused on the verst posts, which I noticed from afar, and on the clouds previously scattered along the horizon, which now, having adopted ominous black shadows, gathered to form one big sombre storm cloud. From time to time there was the distant rumble of thunder. It was this latest circumstance which more than anything else heightened my impatience to reach the coaching inn as soon as possible. Thunderstorms inspired in me an inexpressible feeling of anguish and fear.

The nearest village was still some nine versts away, but the large dark-purple cloud was moving swiftly towards us without there being any wind at all, appearing from God knows where. The sun, as yet not hidden by clouds, brightly lit up the sombre cloud mass and the grey streaks which streamed from it all the way to the horizon.

Occasional lightning flashes in the distance and a weak rumble can be heard, gradually strengthening, drawing nearer and turning into broken peals of thunder that engulf the heavens. Vasily lifts himself up slightly and raises the hood of the *britzka*. The coachmen put on their *armyaks* and at each clap of thunder they remove their hats and make the sign of the cross; the horses prick up their ears and puff out their nostrils as though getting used to the fresh air which carries the smell of the approaching storm cloud, and the *britzka* rolls faster along the dusty road. I am becoming terrified and feel the blood rushing through my veins. And now the foremost clouds begin to cover the sun; it has emerged one last time, lit up the terribly gloomy part of the horizon and has stolen away. Everything around us suddenly changes and assumes a sombre character. The aspen grove has begun to tremble; the leaves take on a dull whiteness and stand out clearly against the lilac backdrop of the storm cloud; they rustle and twirl. The tops of the tall birches begin to sway and wisps of dry grass fly across the road. Swifts and white-breasted swallows flutter around the *britzka* and even fly right by the horses' chests as though intent on stopping us; jackdaws with jagged wings fly at an angle somehow driven by the wind. The edges of the leather carriage apron, which has been done up to cover us, begin to lift, letting in gusts of moist air; they flap about and lash against the sides of the *britzka*. Lightning seems to flash right inside the *britzka*, blinding us, and for an instant it lights up the grey fabric, its braiding and Volodya's figure flattened against the corner. Within that same second an awe-inspiring rumble resounds right above our heads, which, as though rising higher and higher and spreading wider and wider in a huge spiral, gradually intensifies and turns into a deafening crash, making us instinctively tremble and hold our breath. The wrath of God! What poetry in that popular notion!

The wheels turn faster and faster. Judging by Vasily's back and that of Filipp's, who swings the reins about impatiently, I notice that they too are afraid. The *britzka* rolls along fast downhill and clatters across a plank bridge; I am afraid to move and am expecting us all to die at any moment.

Whoa! A crossbar has come off and, despite continuous deafening thunderclaps, we are forced to stop on the bridge.

Leaning my head against the side of the *britzka*, I hold my breath and with a sinking heart hopelessly follow the movements of Filipp's thick black fingers as he slowly secures the loop and aligns the traces, nudging the side horse with the palm of his hand and the handle of his whip.

Alarming feelings of anguish and fear grow within me as the thunderstorm intensifies, but when the awe-inspiring moment of total silence arrives, which usually precedes a thunder burst, my feelings reach such levels that if this continues for another quarter-hour I am convinced that I will die from anxiety. At that moment some kind of human being suddenly emerges from under the bridge, wearing only a dirty ragged shirt, with a blank puffy face, a clean-shaven wobbly head, puny crooked legs and some kind of shiny red stump instead of an arm, which he thrusts straight into the *britzka*.

"Some-thing for the crip-ple for Christ's sa-ke," whimpers a sickly voice and with each word the beggar makes the sign of the cross and bows from the waist down.

I cannot express the feelings of cold terror which clamp my soul at that moment. Shivers run through my hair, and my eyes, filled with irrational fear, are glued to the beggar...

Vasily, who is in charge of giving out alms en route, gives Filipp instructions on how to reinforce the crossbar, and only when everything is quite ready and Filipp gathers the reins and climbs back on the box does he take something out of his side pocket. But as soon as we move forwards, a blinding lightning bolt for a split second fills the entire hollow with fiery light, forces the horses to stop and is accompanied without a moment's grace by such a deafening thunderclap that it seems as if the entire vault of heaven is collapsing above us. The wind intensifies yet again: the horses' manes and tails, Vasily's overcoat and the edges of the apron all head in the same direction and desperately flutter in the gusts of the frenzied wind. A large raindrop falls heavily on the *britzka's* leather hood... then another one, a third, a fourth and suddenly it is as if someone is beating a drum above us and the surrounding countryside is filled with the steady sound of falling rain. I notice from the way Vasily moves his elbow that he is untying a small purse; the beggar, continuing to make the sign of the cross and to bow down, runs right alongside the wheels and it looks as though they will crush him. "Gi-ve for Christ's sa-ke." Finally a copper coin flies past us and the pitiful creature, soaked to the skin, his shirt stretched over his skinny body, swaying with the wind, stops bewildered in the middle of the road and disappears from my sight.

The slanting rain, driven by strong wind, pours down in bucket loads; it flows in streams down the back of Vasily's heavy woollen coat into a puddle of murky water forming on the apron. At first the dust, churned up into tiny pellets, is turned into watery mud by the wheels; the jolts become fewer and murky rivulets flow along the clay ruts. The lightning flashes grow more distant and paler and the peals of thunder are less startling with the steady patter of the rain.

And now the rain becomes finer. The storm cloud begins to break up into billowy clouds and is brighter in the place where the sun must be; you can just glimpse a patch of clear blue sky through its greyish-white edges. A moment later a timid sunbeam shines on the road puddles, on the streaks of fine vertical rain falling as through a sieve, and on the shiny newly washed green of the grass on the road. A black storm cloud obscures the far edge of the horizon just as forbiddingly, but I am no longer afraid of it. An inexpressibly comforting feeling of hope in life swiftly replaces my overwhelming feeling of terror. My heart smiles, as does nature, now refreshed and joyful. Vasily folds back the collar of his overcoat, takes off his cap and shakes it; Volodya folds back the apron; I lean out of the *britzka* and greedily drink in the fresh, fragrant air. The shiny, newly washed coach body, with its crossbars and its luggage, rocks gently ahead of us. The horses' backs, the breast bands, the reins, the wheels are all wet and sparkling in the sun as if covered in lacquer. On one side of the road is an immense winter field sliced across in places by shallow gullies; it sparkles with wet earth and greenery and unrolls like a shadowy carpet all the way to the horizon. On the other side an aspen grove, interspersed with walnut and bird cherry seedlings, does not stir, as though overflowing with joy, and slowly sheds bright drops of rain from its newly washed branches on last year's dry leaves. On all sides crested larks circle with a happy cry and swiftly swoop down; you can hear the busy movements of little birds in the wet bushes, and the call of the cuckoo clearly reaches us from the middle of the grove. This wonderful smell of the forest after a spring storm, the smell of birch, of violet, of decaying leaf, morel, bird cherry, is so enchanting that I cannot stay in the *britzka*. I leap down from the step, run over to the bushes and, showered by raindrops, I tear wet branches off the blossoming bird cherry, slap them across my face and am intoxicated by their wonderful smell. I pay no attention to the huge clods of mud sticking to my boots nor to my stockings that are soaked through; I tramp through the mud and run up to the coach window.

"Lyubochka! Katyenka!" I cry out, handing them some branches of bird cherry. "Look how wonderful!"

The girls squeal and exclaim; Mimi shouts at me to go away or I will certainly get crushed.

"But do smell it, do!" I cry.

3

A New View on Things

KATYENKA SAT BESIDE ME in the *britzka* and, bending down her pretty little head, she pensively followed the dusty road running away beneath the wheels. I looked at her silently and marvelled at the un-childlike, sad expression I saw for the first time on her rosy little face.

"We'll soon be arriving in Moscow," I said. "What do you think it's like?"

"I don't know," she replied reluctantly.

"Still, what do you think: is it bigger than Serpukhov or not?"

"What?"

"Nothing."

But that instinctive feeling which allows one person to guess the other one's thoughts and which serves as a guiding thread in a conversation made Katyenka aware that I was hurt by her indifference. She raised her head and turned to me:

"Did your Papa tell you that we are going to live with your grandmother?"

"He did; Grandmother really wants us to live with her."

"And are all of us to live there?"

"Of course; we'll live upstairs in one half of the house, you in the other half; Papa will be in the wing, and we'll all have dinner together downstairs at Grandmother's."

"Maman says that your grandmother is so grand and bad-tempered."

"Not at all! It only seems so at first. She is grand but not bad-tempered at all; on the contrary, she is very kind and cheerful. If you could have seen what a ball there was on her name day."

"All the same, I'm afraid of her, and anyway, God knows whether we…"

Katyenka suddenly fell silent and again became thoughtful.

"What?" I asked uneasily.

"Nothing. I was just saying."

"No, you did say something: 'God knows…'"

"And you were saying what the ball at your grandmother's was like."

"Well, it's a shame you weren't there; there were swarms of guests, about a thousand people, music, generals, and I danced… Katyenka!" I said, suddenly stopping in the middle of my description. "Aren't you listening?"

"Yes, I am listening; you were saying that you danced."

"Why are you so dull?"

"One can't be cheerful all the time."

"No, you've changed a lot since we arrived back from Moscow. Tell me the truth," I added, turning to her with a determined look, "why have you become rather strange?"

"Me strange?" Katyenka replied with spirit, proving that my remark had caught her interest. "I'm not strange at all."

"No, you're no longer the same as before," I went on. "Before it was obvious that you were one of us in everything, that you considered us your family and that you loved us as much as we love you, and now you have become so serious, you keep away from us—"

"Not at all—"

"No, let me finish," I interrupted, as I already began to feel the slight tickling in my nose that preceded the tears which welled up in my eyes whenever I expressed a long suppressed heartfelt thought, "you keep away from us, you only talk to Mimi, as though you didn't want to know us."

"Well, it's impossible to always remain the same; you have to change some time," replied Katyenka, who had a way of explaining away everything as some kind of fatalistic inevitability when she did not know what to say.

I remember how once, after quarrelling with Lyubochka, who had called her a "stupid girl", she had replied: "Not everyone can be clever, there have to be stupid people too." But I was not satisfied with the reply that "you have to change some time" and I continued to question her:

"Why does it have to be so?"

"Well, we won't always be living together," replied Katyenka, blushing slightly and staring fixedly at Filipp's back. "Mama could live with your late Mama, who was her friend: but God knows whether she'll get on with the Countess, who they say is so bad-tempered. Besides, we'll have to part some time: you are rich, you have Petrovskoye and we are poor – Mama has nothing."

"You are rich, we are poor": those words and the ideas connected to them seemed extremely strange. Only beggars and peasants could be poor, according to my understanding at that time, and I could not in any way reconcile that idea of poverty in my mind with graceful, pretty Katyenka. I thought that, if Mimi and Katyenka had always lived with us and shared everything equally, then they would always continue to do so. It was impossible for it to be otherwise. Now thousands of obscure new ideas regarding their lone situation came crowding into my head, and I felt so ashamed that we were rich and they were poor that I turned red and could not look Katyenka in the face.

"What does it mean that we are rich and they are poor?" I reflected. "And how does the need for a separation follow from that? Why not share equally what we have?" But I understood that it was no good talking to Katyenka about this; some practical instinct, as opposed to my logical reflections, told me that she was right and that it would be inappropriate to explain my thinking to her.

"Will you really be leaving us?" I said. "How will we live apart?"

"What can be done about it? It'll hurt me too. But if it happens, I know what I'll do—"

"You are going to become an actress... what nonsense!" I joined in, knowing that to be an actress had always been a favourite dream of hers.

"No, that's what I said when I was little..."

"So what will you do?"

"I'll go to a monastery and live there and I'll go about in a black robe and a velvet cap."

Katyenka burst into tears.

Has it ever happened to you, Reader, that at a certain time in your life you suddenly notice that your view on things has completely changed, as though everything you have seen until then has suddenly turned around to reveal a different, as yet unfamiliar side? It was that kind of moral turnaround that I experienced for the first time on our journey and I consider it was then that my boyhood began.

It occurred to me for the first time with great clarity that we, that is to say our family, were not the only ones to live in this world and that not all interests revolved around us, but that another life existed, that of people who had nothing in common with us, did not care about us and did not even conceive of our existence. I had undoubtedly known all this before, but I had not known, nor realized nor felt it the way I knew it now.

An idea becomes a conviction by following a particular path, often a completely unexpected and uniquely different path from the one other minds follow to arrive at the same conviction. The conversation with Katyenka, which had touched me deeply and had forced me to think of her future situation, was such a path for me. When I looked at the villages and towns we travelled through, where at least one such family as ours lived in every house, at the women and children who looked at the carriages with momentary curiosity and for ever disappeared from our sight, at the shopkeepers, the peasants who not only did not bow down to us, as I was used to seeing in Petrovskoye, but did not even favour us with a glance, for the first time the thought came to my mind: what can they have to do if they are not taking care of us? And that question gave rise to others: how and by what means do they live, how do they bring up their children, teach them, send them out to play, punish them? And so on.

4

In Moscow

WITH OUR ARRIVAL IN MOSCOW the change in the way I viewed things and people and my attitude towards them became even more pronounced.

When I first met Grandmother again and saw her thin wrinkled face and her lifeless eyes, the slavish respect and fear I used to feel for her gave way to compassion, and when she pressed her face against Lyubochka's head and sobbed as though the body of her beloved daughter were before her own eyes, compassion even gave way to love. I felt uncomfortable witnessing her grief when she saw us again; I was conscious that we ourselves were nothing to her and that we were only dear to her as reminders of *her*; I felt that with every kiss with which she covered my cheeks, she expressed but one thought: "She's not here, she has died, I shall never see her again!"

Papa, who in Moscow hardly ever bothered about us and with a perpetually preoccupied face only joined us for dinner in a dark frock coat or tailcoat – together with his large shirts with collars undone, his dressing gown, his village elders, his stewards, his trips to the threshing floor and his hunting – lost a great deal in my eyes. Karl Ivanych, whom Grandmother called *dyadka** and who had suddenly, God knows why, taken it into his head to replace his respectable, familiar bald patch with a red wig with a parting almost in the middle of his head, appeared to me so odd and ridiculous that I was surprised how I had failed to notice this before.

Some kind of invisible barrier rose up between the girls and us. We already had our own secrets. It was as though in front of us they showed off their skirts, which they now wore longer, as we did our trousers with foot straps. Mimi herself appeared at dinner on the first Sunday in such a magnificent dress and with such ribbons on her head that it was instantly clear that we were no longer in the country and that everything would now be different.

5

My Older Brother

I WAS ONLY A YEAR and a few months younger than Volodya; we grew up together and had always studied and played together. No distinction was made between the older and the younger. But just around the time I speak of, I began to understand that Volodya was not really close to me, in age, inclination or ability. It even seemed to me that Volodya was himself conscious of his advantage and was proud of it. That conviction, even if a false one, was inspired by my pride, which suffered whenever we clashed. He was ahead of me in everything: in games, studies, quarrels, in the way he held himself, and all this alienated me from him and made me suffer moral pangs I could not understand. Had I frankly admitted, the first time some Dutch pleated shirts were made for Volodya, that I found it very annoying not to have some as well, I am sure that I would have felt much better for it and I would not have thought that every time he adjusted his collar he was doing it purely to offend me.

What tormented me most of all was that at times Volodya seemed to know this about me, but tried to hide it.

Who has not noticed those secretive wordless connections manifested in an imperceptible smile, gesture or glance between people who constantly live together: brothers, friends, husband and wife, master and servant, particularly when people are not entirely honest with each other. How many unspoken wishes, thoughts and fears – of being understood – are expressed in one casual glance when our eyes meet timidly and hesitatingly!

But perhaps I was deceived in this respect by my excessive susceptibility and my tendency to analyse; perhaps Volodya did not at all feel the way that I did. He was passionate, frank, and fickle in his enthusiasms.

Carried away by the most diverse things, he surrendered to them heart and soul.

He would suddenly become passionate about pictures: he took up painting himself, spent on it all his own money, which he would wheedle out of his drawing master, Papa and Grandmother. Then there was his passion for ornaments with which to adorn his small table; he collected them from all over the house. Then his passion for novels which he got hold of on the quiet and read whole days and whole nights... I was instinctively drawn to his passions, yet was too proud to follow in his footsteps and too young and dependent to choose something new. But there was nothing I envied more than Volodya's happy, upright character, which was particularly sharply displayed when we quarrelled. I felt that he behaved well, but I could not be like him.

Once, at the height of his passion for ornaments, I approached his table and accidentally broke a small, empty, colourful scent bottle.

"Who asked you to touch my things?" asked Volodya as he came into the room, noticing that I had upset the symmetry of the various ornaments on his small table. "And where is the little scent bottle? You must have—"

"I accidentally dropped it: it broke; so what?"

"Do me a favour, don't ever *dare* touch my things," he said, picking up pieces of broken bottle and looking at them, quite upset.

"Please don't *order* me about," I replied. "So I broke it: what else is there to say?"

And I smiled, though I did not feel like smiling at all.

"It may mean nothing to you, but it does to me," Volodya went on, with a twitch of his shoulder, a habit he had inherited from Papa. "You broke it and on top of that you laugh; you are such an intolerable *little boy*!"

"I may be a little boy, but you're big and stupid."

"I have no intention of arguing with you," said Volodya, pushing me away, "go away."

"Don't push me!"

"Go away!"

"I told you not to push me!"

Volodya took me by the arm and wanted to pull me away from the table, but I was already put out to the extreme. I grabbed the table by its leg and overturned it. "Take that!" And all the china and crystal

114

ornaments flew to the ground with a crash. "Loathsome little boy!" cried Volodya, trying to save the falling objects.

"Now it's all over between us," I thought as I left the room. "We've fallen out for good."

We did not speak to each other until evening. I felt guilty, was afraid to look at him and could not get on with anything all day. Volodya on the other hand did his lessons well and chatted and laughed with the girls after dinner as usual.

As soon as the teacher ended the lesson, I left the room: I felt awful, uncomfortable and too conscience-stricken to stay in the same room as my brother. After the evening history lesson, I took my exercise books and made for the door. As I passed Volodya, I wanted to go up to him and make up, but I sulked and tried to look cross instead. Volodya raised his head right then and boldly looked at me with a barely perceptible, good-natured, mocking smile. Our eyes met and I understood that he understood me and also that I understood that he understood me, but some indefinable feeling compelled me to turn away.

"Nikolyenka!" he said in a voice that sounded natural and in no way pathetic. "Stop being cross. Forgive me if I have offended you."

And he held out his hand.

It was as though something rose higher and higher inside me and suddenly began to crush my chest, making me catch my breath, but this lasted only one second; tears came to my eyes and I felt better.

"Forgive... me, Vo... lodya!" I said, shaking his hand.

Volodya looked at me, however, as though he could not understand at all why there were tears in my eyes...

6

Masha

NONE OF THOSE CHANGES in the way I viewed things, however, shook me as much as when I stopped seeing one of our housemaids as a female servant and began to see her as a *woman* on whom my peace and happiness might to some extent depend.

I remember Masha being in our house as far back as my earliest memories, and I never paid her the slightest attention until the event which completely transformed my view of her and which I am about to mention. Masha was about twenty-five years old when I was fourteen. She was very pretty, but I am afraid to describe her, afraid that my imagination may reproduce the bewitching and deceptive image it formed at the time of my passion. To avoid any errors, I will only say that she had unusually white skin and a splendid figure and that she was a woman; also that I was fourteen.

In one of those moments when, textbook in hand, you wander around the room trying to step only on the chinks in the floorboards, or to hum some absurd tune, or rub ink along the edge of the table, or mindlessly repeat some set phrase, in short in one of those moments when your mind refuses to do any work and your imagination takes over in search of new impressions, I left the schoolroom and aimlessly wandered down to the landing.

Someone wearing shoes was coming up along the other flight of stairs. Of course I wanted to know who it was, but the footsteps suddenly ceased and I heard Masha's voice: "What are you up to? And what if Marya Ivanovna turns up, that wouldn't do, would it?"

"She won't come," Volodya's voice whispered and after this there was a sound of movement as though Volodya was trying to detain her.

"Keep your hands off! Shameless boy!" And Masha ran past me, her scarf pulled to one side, beneath which her full white breast was revealed.

I cannot express the extent of my amazement at this discovery; however the feeling of amazement soon gave way to a certain sympathy for what Volodya had done. It was not the deed so much that surprised me as wondering how he had come to discover that it was a pleasant thing to do. And I instinctively wanted to imitate him.

I sometimes spent whole hours on the landing without any thoughts, listening intently for the slightest movement coming from upstairs, but I could never steel myself to imitate Volodya, despite wanting to more than anything in the world. Sometimes I hid behind the door and with a painful feeling of envy and jealousy listened to the noise reaching me from the maids' room. Then the thought would come to me: "What would it be like if I, just like Volodya, went upstairs and wanted to kiss Masha? What would I, with my thick nose and unruly tufts of hair, say when she asked me what I wanted?" Sometimes I heard Masha say to Volodya: "What a nuisance you are! Why are you pestering me so, go away, you naughty boy... why doesn't Nikolai Petrovich ever come here to fool around..." Little did she know that I, Nikolai Petrovich, was at that very moment sitting under the stairs prepared to give up everything to be in that naughty Volodya's place.

I was bashful by nature, but my bashfulness was further increased by my conviction that I was ugly. I am indeed sure that nothing has such a forceful influence on a person's development as his appearance, and not so much his appearance as his conviction of its appeal or lack of it.

I was too proud to settle for my situation, and took comfort, as did the fox, in persuading myself that the grapes were still unripe. In other words I tried to scorn all those pleasures that come from good looks, such as those Volodya enjoyed in my eyes and for which I envied him from the bottom of my heart, and I harnessed all the powers of my mind and imagination to find pleasure in proud solitude.

7

Small Shot

"MY GOD, GUNPOWDER!" exclaimed Mimi, her voice breathless with emotion. "What are you doing? You are determined to burn the house down, destroy us all..."

With an indescribable expression of grim determination Mimi ordered everyone to make way and with big firm strides she approached the scattered shot and, scorning any danger that might result from an unexpected explosion, began to stamp it out with her feet. When she thought the danger was over, she called Mikhei and ordered him to throw all that gunpowder somewhere as far away as possible or, even better, into the water, and with a proud toss of her bonnet she walked away towards the drawing room. "They're well looked after, I must say!" she muttered.

When Papa came over from his wing of the house and we went over to Grandmother's with him, Mimi was already sitting in the room by the window and with a kind of mysteriously official expression looked forbiddingly past the door. She had in her hand something wrapped up in several bits of paper. I guessed that it was the small shot and that Grandmother already knew everything.

In Grandmother's room, besides Mimi, were Gasha the housemaid, who, judging by her angry flushed face, was very upset, and Doctor Blumenthal, a small, pockmarked man, who was trying in vain to calm Gasha down by making secret placatory signs to her with his eyes and head.

Grandmother herself sat slightly sideways and was laying out the *Traveller*'s game of Patience, which was always a sign of her being in a very unfavourable frame of mind.

"How are you feeling today, Maman? Did you sleep well?" said Papa, respectfully kissing her hand.

"Very well, my dear; I think you know that I'm always in great health," replied Grandmother in a tone which seemed to indicate that Papa's question was most inappropriate and offensive. "Well, are you going to hand me a clean handkerchief or not?" she continued, turning to Gasha.

"I have given you one," replied Gasha, pointing to a snow-white batiste handkerchief lying on the arm of the chair.

"Take that dirty old rag away and give me a clean one, my dear."

Gasha walked over to the chest of drawers, pulled out a drawer and slammed it so forcefully that the window panes in the room rattled. Grandmother looked menacingly at all of us and continued to follow the maid's movements intently. When Gasha gave her what seemed to me the same handkerchief as before, Grandmother said:

"When will you be grinding some snuff for me, my dear?"

"I'll grind it when I have time."

"What's that you're saying?"

"I'll grind it today."

"If you don't want to be in my service, my dear, you should have said so: I would have let you go long ago."

"Then let me go, I won't be crying," muttered the maid under her breath.

At that moment the doctor tried to wink at her, but she looked back at him so angrily and resolutely that he looked down at once and busied himself with his watch key.

"You see, my dear," said Grandmother, turning to Papa when Gasha had left the room still muttering, "how I'm spoken to in my own home?"

"Allow me, Maman, I'll grind some snuff for you myself," said Papa, evidently put into a very difficult position by this unexpected appeal.

"No, I thank you: she is so rude because she knows that no one can grind my snuff the way I like it as well as she can. Do you know, my dear," went on Grandmother after a moment's pause, "that your children nearly burned the house down today?"

Papa looked at Grandmother with respectful curiosity.

"Yes, that's what they play with. Show them," she said, turning to Mimi.

Papa took the shot in his hand and could not help smiling.

"This is small shot, Maman," he said, "it isn't dangerous at all."

"I am very grateful to you, my dear, for teaching me, only I'm really too old—"

"Nerves, nerves!" whispered the doctor.

And Papa turned to us at once:

"Where did you get this from? And how dare you play around with such things?"

"There's no point asking them, you must ask their *dyadka*," said Grandmother, pronouncing the word *dyadka* with particular disdain. "Is that the way to look after them?"

"Voldemar* said that it was Karl Ivanych himself who gave him that *powder*," put in Mimi.

"Now you see how good he is," went on Grandmother. "And where is he now, that *dyadka*, what's his name? Send him here."

"I gave him leave to go and visit friends," said Papa.

"That's not an argument; he should always be here. The children are not mine but yours and I don't have the right to give you my advice as you are wiser than I," Grandmother went on, "but it seems to me that it's time to hire a tutor for them, and not that *dyadka*, that German peasant. Yes, a stupid peasant who can teach them nothing besides bad manners and Tyrolean songs. Is it really necessary for the children to be able to sing Tyrolean songs, I ask you? However *now* there is no one to think about all this and you can do what you want."

The word "now" meant "now that they have no mother" and it conjured up sad memories in Grandmother's heart; she lowered her gaze to the snuffbox with the portrait on it and became lost in thought.

"I have long thought about that too," Papa hastened to say. "I wanted to ask your advice, Maman: could we not ask Saint-Jérôme, who already comes here, to give them lessons?"

119

"You'll do very well indeed, my friend," said Grandmother, her voice sounding less displeased than before. "At least Saint-Jérôme is a *gouverneur** who knows how to bring up *des enfants de bonne maison,** and not simply a *dyadka* who is only good for taking them out on walks."

"I'll speak to him tomorrow," said Papa.

And indeed two days after that conversation, Karl Ivanych gave up his post to the young French dandy.

8

Karl Ivanych's Story

L ATE ONE EVENING, on the eve of the day Karl Ivanych was due to leave us for good, he was standing next to his bed in his quilted dressing gown and his red cap, bending over his case and carefully packing his belongings in it.

Karl Ivanych's treatment of us had somehow been particularly cold lately; he seemed to be avoiding having anything to do with us. Just then, when I came into the room, he glared briefly at me and went back to what he was doing. I lay down for a while on my bed, but Karl Ivanych, who had previously forbidden me to do so, said nothing, and the thought that he would no longer tell us off or stop us from doing certain things, that he now had nothing more to do with us, reminded me sharply of the impending separation. I grew sad at the thought that he no longer loved us and wanted to express this to him.

"Please let me help you, Karl Ivanych," I said, going over to him.

Karl Ivanych glanced at me and turned away again, but in the fleeting look he cast at me I read that it was not indifference that explained his coldness, but heartfelt concentrated sadness.

"God sees all and knows all and may His holy will be done," he said, straightening up to his full height and sighing deeply. "Yes, Nikolyenka," he went on, noticing the genuine sympathy with which I looked at him. "It is my fate to be unhappy from my earliest childhood to my grave. I have always been repaid with evil for the good I have done to people and my reward is not here but up there," he said, pointing to heaven. "If only you knew my story and all I've suffered in this life...

I have been a shoemaker, a soldier, a deserter; I have been a factory worker, a teacher and now I'm a nobody! And I, like the Son of God, have nowhere to lay my head," he concluded and, closing his eyes, sank into his armchair.

Aware that Karl Ivanych was in that sensitive frame of mind in which he expressed his intimate thoughts for his own benefit and without taking any notice of his listeners, I sat down on the bed in silence, without taking my eyes away from his kind face.

"You are not a child, you can understand. I'll tell you my story and everything I have endured in this life. Some time you children will remember your old friend who loved you very much."

Karl Ivanych leant his arm on the table beside him, took a pinch of snuff and, rolling his eyes up to heaven, began his narrative with that particular measured guttural voice he used when dictating to us:

"I vas un'appy even ven in my moter's vomb," he said. "*Das Unglück verfolgte mich schon im Schosse meiner Mutter!*" he repeated in German with even more feeling.

As Karl Ivanych subsequently told his story to me a few more times, using many similar expressions in the same sequence with the same unchanging intonation, I hope to convey it almost word for word, excluding of course his linguistic mistakes (and the reader can be the judge of those with that first sentence). Whether it really was his story or a work of fantasy conceived during his lonely life in our house in which he himself began to believe due to frequent repetition, or whether he embellished the real events of his life with imaginary facts, I have not determined to this day. On the one hand, he told his story with too much live emotion and methodical consistency (the main signs of plausibility) for it not to be believable; on the other hand, there were too many poetic embellishments in his story and those very embellishments raised doubts.

"In my veins flows the noble blood of the Counts von Sommerblat! *In meinen Adern fliesst das edle Blut des Grafen von Sommerblat!* I was born six weeks after the wedding. My mother's husband (I called him Papa) was Count Sommerblat's tenant. He could not forget my mother's shame and didn't love me. I had a little brother Johann and two sisters: but I was a stranger in my own family. *Ich war ein Fremder in meiner eigenen Familie!* When Johann did something stupid, Papa would say, 'I'll never have a moment's peace with that child Karl.' They

121

told me off and punished me. When my sisters quarrelled with each other, Papa would say, 'Karl will never be an obedient boy!' Only my dear Mama loved me and showed me affection. She would often say to me, 'Karl, come here, into my room,' and she would stealthily kiss me. 'Poor, poor Karl!' she would say. 'No one loves you, but I wouldn't exchange you for anyone. Your Mama asks you for only one thing,' she said to me, 'do your lessons well and always be an honest man and God won't abandon you! *Trachte nur ein ehrlicher Deutscher zu werden,*' sagte sie, '*und der liebe Gott wird dich nicht verlassen!*' And I tried. When I was fourteen and allowed to go to communion, my Mama said to my Papa, 'Karl is a big boy now, Gustav; what will we do with him?' And Papa said, 'I don't know.' Then Mama said, 'Let's hand him over to Herr Schulz in town, let him be a shoemaker!' And Papa said, 'Fine,' *und mein Vater sagte, 'Gut.'* I lived six years and seven months in town with the master shoemaker and he loved me. He said, 'Karl is a good worker, and soon he'll be my *Geselle!*'* But man proposes and God disposes... In 1796 they introduced conscription and everyone who could serve between the ages of eighteen and twenty-one had to assemble in town.

"Papa and brother Johann came to town and we went to draw *Lose,** as to who was to be a *Soldat** and who wasn't. Johann drew a bad lot – he was to be a *Soldat*; I drew a good one, so I was not to be a *Soldat.* And Papa said, 'I have only one son and I have to part from him! *Ich hatte einen einzigen Sohn und von diesem muss ich mich trennen!*'

"I took him by the hand and said, 'Why did you say that, Papa? Come with me and I'll tell you something.' And Papa came along. Papa came along and we sat at a small table in a tavern. 'Give us two *Bierkrug,**' I said and they brought them over to us. We drank a mug each and so did brother Johann.

"'Papa!' I said, 'don't say such a thing: "I had only one son and I have to part from him." My heart wants to *leap out* when I hear *that*. Brother Johann will not serve – I will be a *Soldat*!... No one needs Karl here and Karl will be a *Soldat*.'

"'You are an honest man, Karl Ivanych!' said Papa to me and he kissed me. '*Du bist ein braver Bursche!*' sagte mir Vater und küsste mich.

"And I was a *Soldat*!"

9

The Story Continues

"THOSE WERE TERRIBLE TIMES, Nikolyenka," continued Karl Ivanych. "There was Napoleon then. He wanted to conquer Germany and we defended our fatherland to the last drop of blood! *Und wir verteidigten unser Vaterland bis auf den letzten Tropfen Blut!*

"I was at Ulm, I was at Austerlitz! I was at Wagram! *Ich war bei Wagram!*"

"Did you really fight?" I asked, looking at him in amazement. "Did you really kill people?"

Karl Ivanych promptly reassured me on that count.

"Once a French grenadier dropped behind his men and fell on the road. I ran to him with my rifle and wanted to run it through him *aber der Franzose warf sein Gewehr und rief Pardon** and I let him go!

"At Wagram Napoleon drove us onto an island and encircled us so that there was no escape. We were without provisions for three days and stood up to our knees in water. That scoundrel Napoleon would neither take us nor let us go! *Und der Bösewicht Napoleon wollte uns nicht gefangen nehmen und auch nicht freilassen!*

"On the fourth day, thank God, they took us prisoner and led us off to the fort. I wore dark-blue trousers, a uniform of good quality cloth, had fifteen *thalers** on me and a silver watch – a gift from Papa. A French *Soldat* took everything. Fortunately I had three gold coins sewn into my jersey by Mama and no one found them!

"I didn't want to stay long in the fort and decided to run away. Once, on an important festival, I said to the sergeant in charge of us: 'Herr Sergeant, today is a big festival and I want to celebrate it. Please bring two bottles of Madeira and we'll drink them up together.' And the sergeant said, 'Fine.' When the sergeant brought the Madeira and we had drunk a glassful each, I took his hand and said, 'Herr Sergeant, perhaps you have a father and a mother?' He said, 'I have, Herr Mauer…' 'My father and mother haven't seen me for eight years,' I said, 'and don't know if I'm still alive or whether my bones have been lying somewhere in the damp earth. Oh Herr Sergeant! I have two gold coins that I've kept inside my jersey; take them and let me go. Be my benefactor and my Mama will pray for you to the almighty God all her life.'

"The sergeant emptied his glass of Madeira and said: 'Herr Mauer, I love and pity you very much, but you are a prisoner and I'm a *Soldat*!' I shook his hand and said, 'Herr Sergeant!' *Ich drückte ihm die Hand und sagte: 'Herr Sergeant!'*

"And the sergeant said, 'You are a poor man and I won't take your money, but I'll help you. When I go to sleep, buy the soldiers a *vedro** of vodka and they'll sleep. I won't be watching you.'

"He was a good man. I bought a *vedro* of vodka and, when the soldiers were drunk, I put on my boots and an old overcoat and crept out of the door. I went onto the rampart and wanted to jump, but there was water below and I didn't want to spoil my last piece of clothing, so I went to the gates.

"The sentry went *auf und ab** with his rifle and looked at me. *'Qui vive?' sagte er auf einmal** and I kept silent. *'Qui vive?' sagte er zum zweiten Mal** and I kept silent. *'Qui vive?' sagte er zum dritten Mal** and I ran. I jumped in the water, climbed up on the other side and ran off. *Ich sprang ins Wasser, kletterte auf die andere Seite und machte mich aus dem Staube.*

"All night I ran along the road, but when day broke I was afraid I might be recognized and I hid in the tall rye. There I kneeled down, folded my hands, thanked God in heaven for having saved me and with a restful feeling fell asleep. *Ich dankte dem allmächtigen Gott für seine Barmherzigkeit und mit beruhigtem Gefühl schlief ich ein.*

"I woke up in the evening and continued on my way. Suddenly a large German wagon drawn by two black horses caught up with me. In the wagon sat a well-dressed man smoking a pipe and he looked at me. I slowed down to let the wagon overtake me, but when I walked slowly, the wagon went slowly and the man looked at me; I walked faster and the wagon moved faster and the man looked at me. I sat down on the road; the man stopped his horses and looked at me. 'Young man,' he said, 'where are you off to so late?' I said, 'I'm going to Frankfurt.' 'Get into my wagon, there is room and I'll take you... Why don't you have anything with you and why are you unshaven and why are your clothes covered in mud?' he asked me when I'd got in with him. 'I'm a poor man,' I said, 'I want to get a job in a factory, and my clothes are covered in mud because I fell down on the road.' 'You are lying, young man,' he said, 'the road is dry right now.'

"And I kept silent.

"'Tell me the whole truth,' said the kind man, 'who are you and where have you come from? I like your face and if you are an honest man, I'll help you.'

"And I told him everything. He said: 'That's good, young man, come with me to my rope factory. I'll give you work, clothes and money and you'll live in my house.'

"And I said: 'Fine.'

"We arrived at the rope factory and the kind man said to his wife: 'Here is a young man who fought for his country and escaped from captivity; he has no home, no clothes and no bread. He'll live with us. Give him clean linen and feed him.'

"I lived for a year and a half at the rope factory and my master loved me so much that he wouldn't let me go. And I was happy there. I was a handsome man then: I was young and tall, had blue eyes, a Roman nose... and Madame L. (I can't mention her name), my master's wife, was a pretty young lady. And she fell in love with me.

"When she saw me she said: 'Herr Mauer, what does your Mama call you?' And I said: 'Karlchen.'

"And she said: 'Karlchen, sit beside me.'

"I sat beside her and she said: 'Karlchen, kiss me.'

"I kissed her and she said: 'Karlchen! I love you so much that I can't bear it any longer,' and she began to tremble all over."

At that point Karl Ivanych took a lengthy pause and, rolling up his kind blue eyes and lightly shaking his head, he began to smile as people do when under the influence of pleasant memories.

"Yes," he began again, settling more comfortably in his armchair and wrapping his dressing gown around him, "I went through a lot, good and bad, in my life, but may this be my witness," he said, pointing to a small icon of the Saviour embroidered on canvas hanging above his bed, "no one can say that Karl Ivanych was a dishonourable man! I didn't want to repay what kindness Mr L. had done for me with black ingratitude... and I decided to run away. In the evening after everyone had gone to sleep, I wrote my master a letter and put it on the table in his room. I took my clothes, three *thalers* and crept outside. No one saw me and I set off along the road."

10

Continuation

" I HAD NOT SEEN MY MAMA for nine years and didn't know whether she was alive or whether her bones lay in the damp earth. I returned to my fatherland. When I arrived in town, I asked where Gustav Mauer, Count Sommerblat's tenant, lived, and I was told: 'Count Sommerblat died and Gustav Mauer now lives on the main street and has a liqueur shop.' I put on my new waistcoat and a smart frock coat, a gift from the factory owner, brushed my hair neatly and went to my Papa's liqueur shop. My sister Mariechen was sitting in the shop and asked me what I wanted? I said: 'May I have a glass of liqueur?' and she said: '*Vater!* A young man is asking for a glass of liqueur.' And Papa said: 'Give the young man a glass of liqueur.' I sat at a small table, drank my glass of liqueur, smoked my pipe and looked at Papa, Mariechen and Johann, who had also come into the shop. In conversation Papa said to me: 'You probably know, young man, where our *Armee** presently finds itself.' I said: 'I have myself just come from the *Armee* and it is now near Vienna.'

"'Our son,' said Papa, 'was a *Soldat* and it has now been nine years since he wrote to us and we don't know whether he is alive or dead. My wife weeps for him all the time…' I smoked my pipe and said: 'What was your son's name and where did he serve? Perhaps I know him…' 'His name is Karl Mauer and he served with the Austrian *Jäger*,'* said my Papa. 'He is tall and handsome like you,' said my sister Mariechen. I said: 'I know your Karl.' 'Amalia!' *sagte auf einmal mein Vater.** 'Come here, there is a young man who knows our Karl.' And my dear Mama came through the back door. I immediately recognized her. 'You know our Karl?' she said, looked at me and, turning pale, she began to tremble! 'Yes, I have seen him,' I said and didn't dare look up at her; my heart wanted to *leap*. 'My Karl is alive!' said Mama. 'Thank God! Where is he, my darling Karl? I would die in peace if I could look at him, my beloved son, one more time, but God does not want this.' And she wept… I could hold out no longer… 'Mama!' I said. 'I'm your Karl!' And she fell into my arms…"

Karl Ivanych closed his eyes and his lips began to quiver.

"'*Mutter,*' *sagte ich,* '*ich bin ihr Sohn, ich bin ihr Karl!*' *Und sie stürtzte mir in die Arme,*"* he repeated, calming down a little and wiping away the big tears rolling down his cheeks.

"But it didn't suit God to let me end my days in my homeland. Misfortune was my fate! *Das Unglück verfolgte mich überall...* I lived in my homeland only three months. One Sunday I was in a coffee house, bought a mug of beer, smoked my pipe and was chatting with my acquaintances about politics, Emperor Franz, Napoleon, the war and each one gave his opinion. Near us sat a stranger in a grey *Überrock.** He drank coffee, smoked a pipe and said nothing to us. *Er rauchte sein Pfeifchen und schwieg still.* When the *Nachtwächter** called out ten o'clock, I took my hat, paid and went home. In the middle of the night, someone knocked at the door. I woke up and said: 'Who's there?' '*Macht auf!*'* I said, 'Tell me who's there and I'll open up.' *Ich sagte: 'Sagt wer ihr seid, und ich werde aufmachen.'* '*Macht auf im Namen des Gesetzes!*'* he said behind the door. And I opened. Two soldiers carrying rifles stood behind the door and the stranger in *Überrock*, who had sat near us in the coffee house, came into the room. He was a spy! *Es war ein Spion!...* 'Come with me!' said the spy. 'Very well,' I said... I put on my boots and trousers, put on my suspenders and paced up and down the room. I was seething. I said: 'He's a scoundrel!' When I reached the wall where my sword was hanging, I suddenly grabbed it and said: 'You're a spy; defend yourself! '*Du bist ein Spion, verteidige dich!*' *Ich gab ein Hieb** on the right, *ein Hieb* on the left and one on the head. The spy fell! I grabbed my case and some money and leapt through the window. *Ich nahm meinen Mantelsack und Beutel und sprang zum Fenster hinaus. Ich kam nach Ems,** where I met General Sazin. He became very fond of me, obtained a passport for me from the envoy and took me with him to Russia to teach his children. When General Sazin died, your Mama summoned me to her. She said: 'Karl Ivanych! I am handing my children over to you; love them and I'll never abandon you; I'll look after you in your old age.' Now she is no longer there, everything is forgotten. After twenty years of service, I must now, in my old age, go to the streets and look for a stale piece of bread... God sees all and knows all and his will be done and I'm only sorry to leave you, children!" concluded Karl Ivanych, pulling me to him and kissing me on the head.

11

A Bad Mark

A T THE END OF THE YEAR'S MOURNING, Grandmother recovered a little from the grief that had struck her and began to receive visitors from time to time, particularly children – girls and boys of our own age.

On Lyubochka's birthday, the 13th of December, Princess Kornakova and her daughters, Valakhina and her daughter Sonyechka, Ilyenka Grap and the two younger Ivin brothers arrived before dinner.

The sounds of chatter, laughter and running about had already reached us from downstairs, where all those people had gathered, but we could not join in before the end of morning lessons. On a timetable hanging in the schoolroom it said: *Lundi, de deux à trois, Maître d'Histoire et de Géographie,** and so we had to wait for this *Maître d'Histoire*, then hear him out and see him off before being free. It was already twenty past two and the history master had not yet been heard or seen in the street along which he was to arrive and which I watched with the fervent wish never to see him again.

"Lebyedev doesn't seem to be coming today," said Volodya, tearing himself for just a moment away from Smaragdov's textbook,* from which he was learning the lesson.

"Please God, please God... I know absolutely nothing... however, I think he's here," I added in a gloomy voice.

Volodya got up and walked over to the window.

"No, that's not him, it's some *gentleman*," he said. "Let's wait a little longer until half-past two," he added, stretching himself and scratching the top of his head as he usually did when taking a short break from work. "If he's not here by half-past two, we can tell Saint-Jérôme to put away the exercise books."

"And he so wants to co-o-o-me," I said, stretching myself too and brandishing Kaidanov's book,* which I held in both hands, over my head.

Having nothing better to do, I opened the textbook where the lesson had been set and began to read it. It was a long and difficult lesson, I knew none of it and saw that I would not manage to even remember any part of it, particularly as I was in that excitable mood when thoughts refuse to focus on any subject, whatever it might be.

After the previous lesson of history, which always seemed to me the most boring and difficult of subjects, Lebyedev had complained about me to Saint-Jérôme and had put down a "two", which was considered a very bad mark, in the mark book.* Saint-Jérôme had told me then that if I were to get less than a "three" for the next lesson I would be severely punished. Now I was faced with that next lesson and I must admit that I was really scared.

I was so engrossed in reading the unprepared lesson that I was suddenly startled by the sound of galoshes being removed in the entrance hall. I hardly had time to look round before the pockmarked, to me repulsive, face and the all-too-familiar awkward figure of the master, in a dark-blue tailcoat done up with scholarly brass buttons, appeared in the doorway.

The master slowly put his hat down by the window, the exercise books on the table, spread his tails apart with both hands (as though this were essential) and sat down, puffing, in his seat.

"Well, gentlemen," he said, rubbing his sweaty hands together, "let's first go over what we covered last lesson and then I'll attempt to introduce you to the next events of the Middle Ages."

This meant: recite your lessons.

While Volodya answered him with the ease and assurance that comes with knowing a lesson well, I wandered out aimlessly to the stairs and, as I was not allowed to go downstairs, it was quite natural that, before I knew it, I should find myself on the landing. But just as I wanted to settle down at my usual observation post, behind the door, Mimi, as always the cause of my misfortunes, all of a sudden ran into me. "You're here?" she said threateningly, looking first at me then at the maids' room and then back at me.

I felt entirely to blame both for the fact that I was not in the school-room and because I was in a place that was out of bounds; so I kept silent and hung my head, displaying the most touching expression of remorse.

"No, this is beyond anything!" said Mimi. "What were you doing here?" I remained silent. "No, it won't be left like this," she repeated, drumming her knuckles against the banisters, "I'll tell the Countess everything."

It was already five to three when I returned to the schoolroom. The master, as though unaware whether I was there or not, was explaining the next lesson to Volodya. When he began to pile up the exercise books at the end of this and Volodya had gone into the next room to fetch the lesson slip,* the comforting thought came to me that it was over and they would forget about me.

But the master suddenly turned to me with a malevolent half-smile.

"I hope you've prepared your lesson," he said, rubbing his hands.

"I did," I replied.

"Then take the trouble to tell me something about St Louis's Crusade,"* he said, rocking on his chair and thoughtfully gazing down at his feet. "First you'll give me the reasons that prompted the French King to take up the cross," he said, raising his eyebrows and pointing his finger at the inkwell. "Then you'll explain to me the general characteristics of that crusade," he added, moving his whole hand as though trying to catch something, "and finally, the overall influence of that crusade on the European states," he said, striking the left side of the table with the exercise books. "And particularly on the kingdom of France," he concluded, striking the right side of the table and tilting his head to the right.

I swallowed several times, cleared my throat, tilted my head to one side and kept silent. Then, picking up a quill pen from the table, I began to pluck at it and continued to be silent.

"Do pass me that pen, please," said the master, putting out his hand. "It will come in handy. Well, sir?"

"Louis... Char... St Louis was... was... was... a good and clever tsar."

"A what, sir?"

"A tsar. He thought of going to Jerusalem and passed on the reins of government to his mother."

"What was her name?"

"B... b... lanka."

"How's that, sir? Bulanka?"*

I laughed somewhat wryly and uncomfortably.

"Well, sir, don't you know anything else?" he said with a sneer.

I had nothing to lose so I cleared my throat and began to utter any nonsense that came into my head. The master remained silent, sweeping dust from the table with the quill pen he had taken from me, stared past my ear and repeatedly said, "Good, sir, very good, sir." I felt that I knew nothing and that I was not expressing myself at all as I should, and I was terribly upset that the master did not stop or correct me.

"Why had he taken it into his head to go to Jerusalem?" he said, repeating my words.

"Because... out of... since..."

I became decidedly flustered, did not say another word and felt that if that villain of a master were to stare at me questioningly in silence for a whole year, I would still not be able to utter another sound. The master looked at me for about three minutes, then an expression of deep sadness suddenly appeared on his face and with a voice filled with emotion he said to Volodya, who by that time had come into the room:

"Let me have the mark book: I need to put down the marks."

Volodya gave him the book and mindfully put down the lesson slip beside it.

The master opened the book and in beautiful handwriting, carefully dipping the pen, he put down a "five" for Volodya in the columns headed Progress and Conduct. Then, holding the pen still above the column where my marks were recorded, he looked at me, shook the ink and hesitated.

Suddenly his hand made an almost imperceptible flourish, and in the first column appeared a beautifully formed "one" followed by a full stop; another flourish – and in the Conduct column another "one" followed by a full stop.

Having carefully put away the mark book, the master got up and walked to the door as though not noticing my look of despair, entreaty and reproach.

"Mikhail Larionych!" I said.

"No," he replied, quite aware of what I wanted to say to him, "that's not the way to learn. I don't want to take money for nothing."

The master put on his galoshes, his thick woollen coat, and tied his scarf round his neck with great care. How could anyone possibly concentrate on anything after what had just happened to me? To him it was just the stroke of a pen, to me a huge disaster.

"Is the lesson over?" enquired Saint-Jérôme, entering the room.

"Yes."

"Is the master pleased with you?"

"Yes," said Volodya.

"What marks did you get?"

"Five."

"And Nicolas?"

I was silent.

"Four, I think," said Volodya.

He understood that I had to be saved at least for that day. Let them deal out a punishment, only not on that day, when we had visitors.

"*Voyons, messieurs!*" (Saint-Jérôme had the habit of adding *voyons* before everything he said.) "*Faites vos toilettes et descendons.*"*

12

The Little Key

WE HAD BARELY MANAGED to greet all the guests after coming downstairs before we were called to the table. Papa was very cheerful (he was on a winning streak at the time). He gave Lyubochka an expensive silver tea set and remembered over dinner that he had left a *bonbonnière** behind in his room in the wing, which he also intended as a gift for her.

"Why send a servant? Perhaps you'd better go, Koko," he told me. "The keys are in the shell on the large writing table, do you know where I mean?... So take them and open the second drawer on the right with the largest key. There you'll find a small sweet box and some sweets wrapped in paper, and bring them here."

"And shall I bring you your cigars?" I asked, knowing that he always sent for them after dinner.

"Yes, do, and mind you don't touch anything in there!" he called after me.

I found the keys at the place he had indicated and was all ready to open the box, when I was stopped in my tracks by a desire to find out what a tiny key hanging on the same bunch would unlock.

On the writing table, among thousands of different kinds of objects, next to the rail was an embroidered portfolio with a small padlock hanging from it, and I wanted to see whether the little key would fit it. The attempt was crowned with complete success, the portfolio opened and in it I found a whole pile of papers. Curiosity prompted me so

132

persuasively to find out what those papers were that I did not have time to listen to the voice of conscience and began to inspect the contents of the portfolio.

* * *

A childish feeling of unconditional respect for all those older than me, and in particular for Papa, was so strong in me that my mind instinctively refused to draw any conclusions from what I saw. I felt that Papa should live in a completely unique, beautiful sphere, inaccessible and incomprehensible to me, and that any attempt to penetrate the secrets of his life would be tantamount to sacrilege on my part.

Therefore the discoveries that I almost accidentally made in Papa's portfolio did not leave me with any clear understanding beyond a dark recognition that I had acted badly. I felt ashamed and uncomfortable.

That feeling made me want to lock the portfolio as quickly as possible. But on that memorable day I was to suffer all possible misfortunes: after inserting the little key in the keyhole, I turned it the wrong way. Thinking it was locked, I pulled out the key when – oh horror! – the top of the key was all that was left in my hand. I tried in vain to join it to the other half left in the lock and by some magic to disengage it. I finally had to come to terms with the horrible thought that I had committed a new crime, which would be uncovered on that same day when Papa would return to his study.

Mimi's complaint, the "bad mark" and the little key! Nothing worse could happen to me now. Grandmother, because of the complaint, Saint-Jérôme, because of the bad mark, Papa, because of the key… and all that was to come down on me no later than that very evening.

"What will become of me? Oh-h what have I done?" I said out loud, pacing up and down on the study's soft carpet. "Oh well!" I said to myself as I picked up the sweets and the cigars. "What will be will be…" And I ran into the main house.

That fatalistic saying, overheard from Nikolai as a child, has had a salutary and temporarily calming effect on me in all the difficult moments in my life. As I went into the hall, I was in a slightly excitable and unnatural but exceedingly cheerful frame of mind.

13

The Traitress

A FTER DINNER the *petits jeux** began and I took a very active part in them. While playing Cat and Mouse, I ran rather clumsily into the Kornakovs' governess, who was playing with us, and inadvertently stepped on her dress and tore it. Having noticed that the girls, particularly Sonyechka, were deriving great pleasure from seeing their governess go off greatly upset to the maids' room to mend her dress, I decided to afford them the same pleasure again. With such an obliging end in view, I started to gallop around the governess as soon as she came back into the room and continued those manoeuvres until I found the right moment to catch her skirt with my heel again and tear it. Sonyechka and the Princesses could hardly restrain their laughter, which flattered my pride no end, but Saint-Jérôme, no doubt having noticed my tricks, came over to me and, knitting his brows (a thing I could not stand), said that my high spirits led to no good and that if I did not behave with more reserve he would make me repent, despite it being a day of celebration.

But I was in that excitable state of someone who has gambled beyond his means, is afraid to do his sums and who continues to put down those desperate cards not with any hope of recovering his losses but only so as not to give himself time to come to his senses. I smiled cheekily and walked away from him.

After Cat and Mouse someone organized a game, which we apparently called *Lange Nase*.* The game consisted in essence of placing two rows of chairs facing one another and the ladies and their partners were split into two groups and they had to choose one another in turn.

The youngest Princess chose the younger Ivin every time, Katyenka chose either Volodya or Ilyenka, but Sonyechka chose Seryozha every time and to my extreme surprise showed no embarrassment at all when Seryozha walked straight over and sat down opposite her. She laughed that sweet clear laugh of hers and nodded to him to indicate that he had guessed right. No one chose me. My pride was deeply wounded and I realized that I was superfluous, "the one left out", and that each time they had to say, "Who's left? Ah yes, Nikolyenka; you take him then." So when it was my turn, I walked straight over to my sister or to one of the ugly princesses and I was unfortunately never wrong. Sonyechka

134

appeared to be so busy with Seryozha Ivin that I did not even exist for her. I do not know on what grounds I mentally called her a "traitress", as she had never promised to choose me and not Seryozha, but I was firmly convinced that she had behaved abominably towards me.

After the game I noticed that "the traitress", whom I despised while not being able to take my eyes off her, went away to a corner with Seryozha and Katyenka, where they were secretly discussing something. Sneaking up to them behind the piano to discover their secret, I saw the following: Katyenka was holding a linen handkerchief up by two ends to form a screen hiding Seryozha's and Sonyechka's heads. "No, you lost and now you'll pay the price!" said Seryozha. Sonyechka stood before him with her arms hanging down as though guilty, and said, blushing: "No, I didn't lose, isn't that so, *mademoiselle Catherine*?" "I like the truth," replied Katyenka, "you lost your bet, *ma chère*."

No sooner had Katyenka uttered those words than Seryozha stooped down and kissed Sonyechka. Just like that, on her rosy lips. And Sonyechka laughed as though it was nothing, as though it was great fun. Horrible! *Oh perfidious traitress!*

14

Black-out

I SUDDENLY DESPISED THE WHOLE FEMALE SEX in general and Sonyechka in particular. I began to convince myself that there was no fun in those games, that they were only fit for *little girls*, and I desperately wanted to create a stir and do something bold which would amaze everyone. The opportunity did not take long to present itself.

Saint-Jérôme, having had a word with Mimi, left the room. His footsteps could at first be heard on the stairs, then above us in the direction of the schoolroom. It occurred to me that Mimi had told him where she had seen me in lesson time and that he had gone to check the mark book. I did not suppose at that time that Saint-Jérôme might have other aims in life besides the desire to punish me. I read somewhere that children between the ages of twelve and fourteen, who are in that transitional phase of boyhood, are particularly prone to arson and even murder. As I remember my own boyhood and particularly the mood I was in on that unfortunate day, I can only too clearly understand the possibility of committing the most terrible crime without planning or wanting to cause harm, but just like *that*, out of curiosity and an instinctive craving for action. There are moments when the future appears to you in such a sombre light that you are afraid to contemplate it; you stop your mind from functioning altogether and try to convince yourself that there will be no future and that there has been no past. It is in such moments – moments when the mind no longer looks ahead to consider what one's intentions are, and physical instincts are the only springboard to action – that I can understand how an inexperienced child particularly prone to such moods could, without the slightest hesitation or fear and with a smile of curiosity, build a fire and fan its flames under his own house, where his brothers, father and mother, all of whom he loves tenderly, are asleep. In the grip of just such a temporary mind lapse – almost distraction – a peasant lad of about seventeen, inspecting the newly sharpened blade of an axe lying next to a bench on which his old father lies asleep face down, suddenly swings the axe and with idle curiosity watches the blood from the severed neck trickling down under the bench. It is under the influence of that same absent-mindedness and instinctive curiosity that a person discovers some kind of pleasure pausing at the very edge of a ravine, thinking: "What if I were to hurl myself down?" Or placing a loaded pistol to his forehead and thinking: "What if I were to pull the trigger?" Or watching some very important person for whom all of society feels slavish respect and thinking: "What if I were to go up to him, grab him by the nose and say: 'Now then, my dear, let's go!'"

I was in the grip of just such inner turmoil and lack of reflection when Saint-Jérôme came down and told me that I had no right to be there that day, because I had behaved badly and not done my lessons well, and that I should immediately go upstairs: so I stuck my tongue out at him and said that I would not leave the room.

Astonishment and fury left Saint-Jérôme speechless for a moment.

"*C'est bien*,"* he said, catching up with me. "I have already several times promised you a punishment your Grandmother wanted you to be spared from, but I see now that nothing but the birch will make you obey, and today you have fully deserved it."

He spoke so loudly that everyone heard him. The blood rushed to my heart with unusual force and I felt its strong beat and the colour leaving my face, and my lips beginning to tremble quite beyond my control. I must have appeared terrifying in that instant, because Saint-Jérôme, avoiding my eyes, quickly walked up to me and grabbed me by the arm, but the moment I felt the touch of his hand, I was so overcome that, beside myself with fury, I tore my arm away and I hit him with all the child's strength I had in me.

"What's come over you?" said Volodya, approaching me, having witnessed my conduct with horror and amazement.

"Leave me be!" I screamed at him through my tears. "None of you love me and you don't understand how miserable I am! You're all loathsome, repulsive," I added, addressing everyone present in some sort of frenzy.

But at this point Saint-Jérôme walked up to me again with a pale, determined face and, before I had time to defend myself, he gripped both my arms forcefully in a vice and dragged me somewhere. My head was spinning with emotion; all I remember is that I fought desperately with my head and knees while I still had some strength left in me; I remember that my nose hit someone's thighs several times, that someone's coat ended up in my mouth, that all around me I could hear the presence of feet, sense the smell of dust and *violette*,* the scent used by Saint-Jérôme.

Five minutes later the door of the storeroom shut behind me.

"Vasily!" said he in a loathsome jubilant voice. "Bring the birch…"

15

Daydreams

COULD I EVER HAVE THOUGHT THEN that I would survive all of the disasters which struck me and that there would come a time when I would look back on them calmly?…

When I went over everything I had done, I could not imagine what would become of me, but I had a vague premonition that I had come to the end of the road.

Complete silence reigned downstairs and around me at first, or at least so it seemed to me in my overwrought state, but gradually I began to distinguish various sounds. Vasily came up and threw something looking like a broom against the window ledge; then he lay down yawning on a chest. Downstairs you could hear Saint-Jérôme's loud voice (no doubt talking about me), then children's voices, then laughter and running about and a few minutes later everything in the house went back to normal, as though no one knew or was thinking about my sitting in the dark storeroom.

I did not cry, but something lay heavy, like a stone, on my heart. Thoughts and imaginings flashed through my distracted mind with accelerated speed, but the memory of the disaster that had hit me continually interrupted their whimsical chain and I entered once more a hopeless maze of despair, fear and uncertainty about my impending fate.

One moment it occurred to me that there had to be some unknown reason for the general dislike and even hatred towards me. (At that time I was firmly convinced that everyone, from Grandmother down to Filipp the coachman, hated me and took pleasure in my sufferings.) "I am probably not my father and mother's son nor Volodya's brother but an unfortunate orphan, a foundling taken in out of charity," I told myself, and that absurd notion not only offered me some sad comfort but even seemed utterly plausible to me. It was gratifying to think that I was unhappy not because I was to blame, but because it had been my destiny from the day I was born and that my fate was similar to that of the unfortunate Karl Ivanych.

"But why keep this secret any longer now that I myself have exposed it?" I tell myself. "I'll go to Papa tomorrow and say to him: 'Papa! You are concealing the secret of my birth for no good reason; I know everything.' And he'll say, 'What can be done, my friend, you would have found out sooner or later; you are not my son, but I adopted you and if you are worthy of my love I'll never desert you,' and I'll say to him: 'Papa, although I don't have the right to call you by that name, I'll now pronounce it for the last time; I have loved you and will always love you and I'll never forget you as you are my benefactor, but I can no longer stay in your house. No one loves me here and Saint-Jérôme has sworn to destroy me. Either he or I must leave your house otherwise I won't be responsible for my actions; I hate that man so much that I'm prepared to do anything. I'll kill him.' I'll say just that: 'I'll kill him.' Papa will begin to entreat me, but I'll wave my arm and say to him: 'No, my friend, my benefactor, we cannot live together, so let me go,' and I'll embrace him and say to him, for some reason in French: '*Ô mon père,*

Ô mon bienfaiteur, donne-moi pour la dernière fois ta bénédiction et que la volonté de Dieu soit faite!* And as I sit on a trunk in the dark storeroom I sob at the thought. But I suddenly remember the shameful punishment that lies in store for me, reality appears in its true light and my dreams are instantly shattered.

Next I picture myself already free outside our house. I join the hussars and go to war. The enemy attacks me on all sides; I brandish my sabre and kill one, then I strike again and kill another and then a third. Finally, worn out by my injuries and exhaustion, I fall to the ground and cry out, "Victory!" The General rides up and asks: "Where is he, our saviour?" They point me out to him and he flings his arms around my neck and calls out with tears of joy: "Victory!" I recover and with my arm wrapped in a black sling I walk along Tverskoy Boulevard. I am a general! And now the Emperor sees me and asks who that wounded young man is? They tell him that he is the famous hero Nikolai. The Emperor comes up to me and says: "I thank you. I will do anything you ask me." I bow to him deferentially and, leaning on my sabre, I say, "I am happy, Your Majesty, that I could spill blood for my fatherland and would have wished to die for it, but since you are so gracious as to allow me to appeal to you, I'll ask for one thing – allow me to destroy my enemy, the foreigner Saint-Jérôme. I want to destroy my enemy Saint-Jérôme." I stop menacingly in front of Saint-Jérôme and say to him, "You caused my misfortune, *à genoux!*"* But it suddenly occurs to me that any minute now the real Saint-Jérôme could come in with the birch, and I see myself once more not as a general, the saviour of his fatherland, but as a very sad, pitiful creature.

And then the thought of God would enter my head and I would ask Him with impudence why He was punishing me: "I believe I have not forgotten to say my prayers morning and evening, so why must I suffer?" I can absolutely say that it was then that I took the first step towards the religious doubts that troubled me during my boyhood. This was not because misery provoked me to grumble and disbelieve, but because the thought of the injustice of Providence entered my head at a time of complete mental confusion and twenty-four hours of seclusion and it speedily grew and spread its roots, like a bad seed fallen on porous soil after rainfall. Or else I imagined that I would certainly die and sharply pictured to myself Saint-Jérôme's amazement when he found a lifeless body in the storeroom instead of me. Recalling

Natalya Savishna's tales about the soul of the deceased not leaving the house for forty days after death, I mentally roamed through every room of Grandmother's house, invisible to all, and overheard Lyubochka's heartfelt tears, Grandmother's regret and Papa's conversation with Saint-Jérôme. "He was a good boy," Papa would say with tears in his eyes. "Yes," Saint-Jérôme would say, "but also a great troublemaker." "You should respect the dead," Papa would say, "you were the cause of his death, you frightened him, he couldn't stand the humiliation you had in store for him… Get out of here, you villain!"

And Saint-Jérôme will fall on his knees, weep and ask for forgiveness. After forty days my soul flies up to heaven. There I see something amazingly beautiful, white, transparent and long, and I sense that it is my mother. This white thing surrounds me, caresses me, but I feel troubled, as though I do not recognize her. "If that's really you," I say, "then show yourself in a better guise so that I can hug you." And her voice answers, "Over here we are all like this, I cannot embrace you any better. Don't you like it this way?" "Yes, I'm very happy, but you can't tickle me and I can't kiss your hands…" "That is not necessary, it's nice here anyway," she says, and I feel that it is indeed very nice there, and she and I fly up together, higher and higher. At this point I seem to wake up and find myself again on the trunk in the dark storeroom, my cheeks wet with tears and senselessly repeating the words: "and we fly higher and higher". For a long time I use all my powers to clarify my situation, but right now I mentally face only one terribly gloomy, unfathomable prospect. I try to return again to those comforting happy dreams that interrupted my consciousness of reality, but as soon as I settle down to my former dreams, I realize to my surprise that it is not possible to go on and, what is even more surprising, that they no longer give me any pleasure at all.

16

All's Well that Ends Well

I SPENT THE NIGHT IN THE STOREROOM and no one came to see me. It was not until the following day, on the Sunday, that I was taken to a small room adjoining the schoolroom and locked in again. I began to hope that my punishment would be limited to confinement, and my thoughts, swayed by sweet, invigorating sleep, by bright sunlight playing against the frost patterns on the windows, and by the usual daily noise on the streets, began to settle. But being secluded was still very hard: I wanted to move about, tell someone about everything that had built up inside me, and there was not a living soul within reach. The situation was made even more unpleasant because I could not help – as loathsome as this was for me – hearing Saint-Jérôme walking around in his room and quite calmly whistling some cheerful tune. I was utterly convinced that he did not really feel like whistling at all, but that he did so purely to torment me.

At two o'clock Saint-Jérôme and Volodya went downstairs and Nikolai brought me my dinner; when I chatted to him about what I had done and what I was to expect, he said:

"Oh, master! Don't be sad; all's well that ends well."*

Although this saying, which subsequently offered me moral support more than once, brought me a degree of comfort, the fact that I had not been sent bread and water but a whole dinner, down to the *rozanchiki,** made me rethink the whole situation. Had they not sent me the *rozanchiki*, it would have meant that I was to be punished by being confined, but now it turned out that I had not yet been punished, that I had only been removed like a criminal from the others and that my punishment still lay ahead. While engrossed in solving this question, the key turned in the lock of my dungeon and Saint-Jérôme entered the room with a stern, official expression on his face.

"Come with me to see your grandmother," he said without looking at me.

I wanted to brush the sleeves of my jacket, which had become grubby with chalk, before leaving the room, but Saint-Jérôme told me that there was no point in doing this, as though I was already in such a wretched moral state that there was no point worrying about my appearance.

As Saint-Jérôme led me by the arm across the room, Katyenka, Lyubochka and Volodya all looked at me with exactly the same expression with which we usually watched the convicts being led past our windows on Mondays. When I approached Grandmother's armchair with the intention of kissing her hand, she turned away from me and hid her hand under her mantilla.

"Yes, my dear," she said after quite a lengthy silence, during which she examined me from head to toe with such a look that I did not know

141

where to put myself, "I can say that you value my love very highly and are a true comfort to me. Monsieur Saint-Jérôme, who at my request," she added, drawing out every word, "took on your education, no longer wishes to remain in my house. And why? Because of you, my dear. I had hoped you would be grateful," she went on, after a brief pause and in a tone demonstrating that she had prepared her speech beforehand, "for his efforts and his care and that you would be able to value his services, but you, a mere boy still wet behind the ears, decided to raise your hand against him. Excellent! Wonderful! I too am beginning to think that you are incapable of understanding decent treatment, that for you other, baser methods are called for... Beg for his forgiveness right now," she added in a stern commanding tone, pointing at Saint-Jérôme. "Do you hear me?"

I looked in the direction of Grandmother's hand and, catching sight of Saint-Jérôme's coat, I turned away and did not move, feeling my heart sink again.

"What's this? Do you perhaps not hear what I am saying?"

My whole body was trembling, but I did not move an inch.

"Koko!" said Grandmother, probably noticing my anguish. "Koko," she said in a voice that was rather more tender than commanding, "is this really you?"

"Grandmother! I won't beg him to forgive me for anything..." I said, suddenly stopping short, as I felt that I would be unable to hold back the floods of tears if I said another word.

"I order you, I beg you. What is the matter with you?"

"I... I... don't... want... I can't," I stuttered, and the suppressed sobs that had built up in my chest suddenly broke down the barriers that had been holding them back and burst into a desperate flood.

"*C'est ainsi que vous obéissez à votre seconde mère; c'est ainsi que vous reconnaissez ses bontés,*" said Saint-Jérôme in a tragic voice, "*à genoux!*"*

"My God, if she'd seen this!" said Grandmother, turning away from me and wiping away some tears that had just appeared. "If she had seen... It's all for the best. No, she could not have endured this grief, she could not have endured it."

And Grandmother cried harder and harder. I cried too, but had no intention of begging for forgiveness.

"*Tranquillisez-vous au nom du ciel, madame la comtesse,*"* said Saint-Jérôme.

But Grandmother no longer heard him; she covered her face with her hands and her sobs soon turned to hiccups and hysterics. Mimi and Gasha ran into the room with scared faces, there was a whiff of smelling salts, and all over the house there was much running about and whispering.

"See what you've done," said Saint-Jérôme, leading me upstairs.

"My God, what have I done? What a terrible criminal I am!"

As soon as Saint-Jérôme had gone downstairs after telling me to go to my room, I ran along the main staircase leading towards the street, oblivious of what I was doing.

I do not remember whether I wanted to run away from home for good or drown myself; I only know that, covering my face with my hands so as not to see anybody, I ran further and further down the stairs.

"Where are you off to?" a familiar voice suddenly asked me. "It's you I need right now, my boy."

I wanted to run past him, but Papa grabbed me by the hand and said sternly:

"Come with me, my dear! How dare you touch my portfolio in my study," he said, leading me behind him into the small sitting room. "Well? Why aren't you saying anything? Well?" he added, holding me by the ear.

"I'm sorry," I said, "I myself don't know what came over me."

"So you don't know what came over you, you don't know, you don't know, you don't know, you don't know," he repeated, pulling my ear with every word. "Will you poke your nose where it's not wanted in future? Will you? Will you?"

Although my ear hurt very badly, I did not cry, but experienced a pleasant feeling inside. As soon as Papa let go of my ear, I grabbed his hand and, now in tears, began to cover it with kisses.

"Beat me more," I uttered through the tears, "harder, make it more painful, I am a good-for-nothing, nasty, wretched person!"

"What's the matter with you?" he said, gently pushing me away.

"No, there's no way I am going back," I said, clinging to his coat. "They all hate me, I know it, but for God's sake listen to me, protect me or drive me out of the house. I cannot live with him, *he* tries to humiliate me in every way, orders me to kneel before him, he wants to flog me. I can't, I'm not a little boy, I won't stand it, I'll die, I'll kill myself. *He* told Grandmother that I was a good-for-nothing; now she's ill, she'll die because of me, I… with him… for God's sake… flog me… why do they… torment me."

The tears were choking me; I sat down on the sofa and, lacking the strength to utter another word, I fell with my head on his lap, sobbing so hard that I thought I must die there and then.

"What are you going on about, my little boy?" said Papa sympathetically, bending over me.

"*He* is my tyrant… tormentor… I'll die… no one loves me!" I could hardly speak and I was struck by convulsions.

Papa picked me up in his arms and carried me to the bedroom. I fell asleep.

It was already very late when I woke up. One candle burned near my bed and in the room sat our house doctor, Mimi and Lyubochka. By their faces it was clear that they feared for my health. I felt so well and light-hearted after my twelve-hour sleep that I would have leapt straight out of bed had I not been unwilling to upset their belief that I was very ill.

17

Hatred

YES, IT WAS REAL HATRED; not the sort of hatred only described in novels, which I do not believe in, hatred that appears to derive pleasure from causing someone harm, but rather the hatred that inspires you with insuperable revulsion for an individual who deserves your respect, yet whose hair, neck, walk, voice, whose every limb and every movement fill you with disgust, and meanwhile some incomprehensible force draws you to him and compels you to focus restlessly on everything he does. Such was the hatred I felt for Saint-Jérôme.

Saint-Jérôme had already lived with us for a year and a half. When I now consider this man in cold blood, I find that he was a fine Frenchman, but a Frenchman to the utmost degree. He was not stupid and was quite well educated. He fulfilled his responsibilities towards us conscientiously, but he suffered from thoughtless selfishness, vanity, impertinence and blind self-confidence, all characteristics he had in common with his fellow countrymen and that are in sharp contrast with the Russian character. I deeply resented this. It goes without saying that Grandmother explained her view on corporal punishment to him and that he did not dare beat us, but he nevertheless frequently threatened us, and me in particular, with the birch and he would pronounce the word *fouetter** (or as he said it: *fouatter*) in a disgusting way and with an intonation that seemed to indicate that flogging me would give him the utmost satisfaction.

I was not in the least afraid of the pain of such a punishment, nor had I ever experienced it, but the very thought of Saint-Jérôme striking me brought about in me a painful state of suppressed anger and despair.

There were times when Karl Ivanych himself, in a moment of vexation, would use a ruler or his braces to deal with us, but I do not recall that with the slightest vexation. Even at the time I speak of (when I was fourteen), had Karl Ivanych beaten me, I would have calmly endured his blows. I loved Karl Ivanych, remembered him from my earliest childhood and considered him a member of our family, but Saint-Jérôme was a proud, conceited man for whom I felt nothing but that instinctive respect all grown-ups inspired in me. Karl Ivanych was a comical old man, a *dyadka*, whom I dearly loved, but whom I nevertheless placed below me in my childish understanding of how society worked.

Saint-Jérôme, on the other hand, was an educated, handsome young dandy, who tried to be on an equal footing with everyone. Karl Ivanych always remained impassive when he scolded and punished us; it was clear that he regarded this a necessary if unpleasant duty. Saint-Jérôme on the contrary loved to assume the mantle of a master; when he punished us, it was obvious that he did this more for his own personal satisfaction than for our benefit. He was carried away by his own self-importance. His bombastic French phrases, with their pronounced stress on the last syllable and their *accents circonflexes*,* were unspeakably loathsome to me. When Karl Ivanych was cross, he would say: "It's play-acting, misbehaving boy or Shpanish fly." Saint-Jérôme called us *mauvais sujet, vilain garnement** and other such names that offended my pride.

Karl Ivanych would make us kneel facing the corner and the punishment consisted of the physical pain caused from being in such a position; Saint-Jérôme would draw himself up and make a grand gesture with his hand and cry out in a dramatic voice: "*À genoux, mauvais sujet!*"* ordering us to kneel facing him and to beg his pardon. The punishment lay in the humiliation.

I was not punished and no one even mentioned what had happened to me, but I could not forget all that I had suffered those two days: the despair, the shame, the fear and the hatred. Although from then on Saint-Jérôme appeared to have given up on me and hardly bothered about working with me, I could not bring myself to look at him with indifference. Each time our eyes accidentally met, it seemed to me that my glance betrayed too much overt hostility and I would hurriedly put on a careless air, but then it seemed to me that he was aware of my pretence and I would blush and turn away.

In short, it was unspeakably hard for me to have anything to do with him.

18

The Maids' Room

I BEGAN TO FEEL MORE AND MORE LONELY and my chief pleasures consisted of solitary reflections and observations. I will discuss the subject of my reflections in the next chapter; the stage for my observations was chiefly the maids' room, where what was to me a highly absorbing and moving romance was going on. The heroine of this romance was of course Masha. She was in love with Vasily, who had known her before she came into service at the house and who had promised at that time to marry her. Fate, which had separated them five years before, reunited them again in Grandmother's house, but laid an obstacle in the path of their mutual love in the person of Nikolai (Masha's uncle), who would not hear of a marriage between his niece and Vasily, whom he called "slow-witted" and "unruly".

It was this obstacle that made Vasily, who had previously been quite cold and offhand in his manner, suddenly fall in love with Masha, in love in a way only a house servant of tailor stock, with a pink shirt and pomaded hair, could be.

Although he manifested his love in very odd and irrational ways (for example, when he met Masha, he always tried to hurt her, and pinched or slapped or squeezed her so tightly that she could hardly breathe), his love was sincere. This was proven by the fact that after Nikolai had decisively refused him his niece's hand, Vasily took to drink from grief

146

and began to wander around taverns, to brawl – in short to behave so badly that he was subjected more than once to the shameful punishment of being kept in a police cell. But these actions and their consequences were, it seems, merits in Masha's eyes and only increased her love for him. When Vasily was confined to the cells, Masha would weep entire days without drying her eyes once and complain about her bitter lot to Gasha (who took a lively part in the unfortunate lovers' affairs) and, disregarding her uncle's swearing and blows, she would stealthily run over to the police station to visit and comfort her friend.

Reader, do not look down on the company I introduce you to. If the chords of love and sympathy have not weakened your heart, then there are sounds in the maids' room to which they will respond. Whether it suits you or not to follow me, I will move to the landing above the stairs, from where I can see everything that is going on in the maids' room. There is the stove bench,* on which stands an iron, a cardboard doll with a broken nose, a tub and a wash bowl; there is the window sill, where a piece of black wax, a skein of silk, a half-eaten green cucumber and a box of sweets lie in disarray; there is the big red table with a brick wrapped in calico lying on top of some unfinished sewing and behind which *she* sits wearing a pink gingham dress, my favourite, and a blue scarf which particularly attracts my attention. She is sewing, now and then stopping to scratch her head with her needle or to adjust the candle and I look at her and think to myself: "Why was she not born a lady with those bright blue eyes, that thick light-brown plait and full bosom? How well it would suit her to sit in the drawing room, in a bonnet with pink ribbons and a silk crimson housecoat, not like the one Mimi wears but the one I saw on Tverskoy Boulevard. She would do embroidery on a frame and I would look at her in the mirror and do anything she wanted: I would pass her her coat, food, I would pass her…"

And what a drunken face and a loathsome figure that Vasily has in his tight coat, worn over a dirty untucked pink shirt! In every movement of his body, in every twist of his back I think I see the unmistakable signs of the revolting punishment he has been subjected to…

"What is it, Vasya? Again," said Masha, sticking the needle in the pin cushion and not lifting her head to greet Vasily, who had come in.

"And so what? As if anything good will come from *him*," Vasily replied, "if only something could be decided. I'll be done for this way, for no good reason and all because of *him*."

"Will you have some tea?" asked Nadyezha, another maid.

"My humble thanks. And why does he hate me, that thief, that uncle of yours, what for? It's because I have a proper coat, and I'm such a strapping fellow, and because of the way I walk. That's it. Oh well!" Vasily concluded with a wave of his hand.

"We have to resign ourselves," said Masha, biting off a thread, "and you are so—"

"It's become intolerable, that's what!"

At that moment the sound of a door banging in Grandmother's room reached us as well as Gasha's grumbling voice as she approached along the stairs.

"Just try to please her when she herself doesn't know what she wants... Cursed life, this is hard labour! If there were just one thing... Forgive me, Lord, my sin," she muttered, throwing up her arms.

"My respects, Agafya Mikhailovna,"* said Vasily, rising to greet her.

"So you're here! I have no time for your respects," she replied menacingly, looking at him. "And why do you come here? As if the maids' room is a suitable place for a man to come to..."

"I wanted to enquire about your health," said Vasily timidly.

"I'll soon kick the bucket, that's how my health is," shouted Agafya Mikhailovna at the top of her voice, still more angrily.

Vasily burst into laughter.

"There's nothing to laugh at, and when I tell you to make yourself scarce, then quick march! Look at the rascal, and he wants to get married, the scoundrel! Well, quick march, off you go!"

And Agafya Mikhailovna walked off to her room stamping her feet, and banging the door so hard that the window panes began to rattle.

For a long time from behind the partition you could still hear her flinging her things around and taking it out on her favourite cat, while continuing to berate everything and everyone and to curse her existence. Finally the door opened slightly and through it flew the cat thrown out by its tail, miaowing pitifully.

"It's best I come and have tea another time," Vasily whispered. "Goodbye till next time."

"Don't worry," said Nadyezhda with a wink, "I'll just go and check the samovar."

"I'm going to put an end to all this," went on Vasily, moving closer to Masha as soon as Nadyezha had left the room. "Either I go straight to the Countess and say to her: 'It's like this... and this.' Or I'll leave everything behind and run to the ends of the earth, I will."

"And how will that leave me?"

"You alone I do feel sorry for, else I'd have sought my freedom long, long ago, really and truly."

"Why don't you bring me your shirts to be washed, Vasya," said Masha after a short pause. "And look how black this one is," she added, pulling him over by his shirt collar.

At that moment Grandmother's little bell rang downstairs and Gasha came out of her room.

"Well, what are you trying to get from her now, you scoundrel?" she said, pushing Vasily, who had quickly risen to his feet on seeing her, towards the door. "You have brought the girl to this and you still persist; you must enjoy watching her tears, you crazy man. Get off! And may you not be seen again. And what good do you find in him?" she went on, turning to Masha. "Is it nothing to you that your uncle beat you today because of him? No, you'll have it your own way: I'll marry no one but Vasily Gruskov. You foolish girl!"

"I'll marry no one then, I love no one else and you can kill me for it," said Masha, suddenly bursting into tears.

I watched Masha for a long time as she lay on a chest, wiping her tears with her scarf, and I tried in every way to alter my opinion of Vasily, wanting to find that angle from where he appeared so attractive to her. But despite my genuine sympathy for her sorrow, I could not even begin to understand how a creature as charming as Masha seemed to me could love Vasily.

"When I am grown-up," I reasoned with myself, after going back upstairs to my room, "Petrovskoye will be mine and Vasily and Masha will be my serfs. I'll be sitting in my study smoking a pipe and Masha will be going through to the kitchen with her iron. I'll say, 'Tell Masha to come here.' She'll come and there won't be anyone in the room... Suddenly Vasily will come in and, when he sees Masha, he'll say, 'That's the end of me!' And Masha will also weep, and I'll say, 'Vasily! I know you love her and she loves you, so here are a thousand roubles, marry her, and may God grant you happiness,' and I'll go off to the sitting room." Among the countless thoughts and dreams which go through the mind and imagination without leaving a single trace, there are some that do leave a deep sensitive groove. And often, without remembering what it was you actually thought about, you remember that something pleasant has passed through your head, you sense a trace of the thought and try to resurrect it. Just such a deep mark was left in my soul at the thought of sacrificing my own feelings for the sake of Masha's happiness, which she could only achieve by marrying Vasily.

19

Boyhood

YOU WOULD FIND IT HARD TO BELIEVE what the favourite and constant subjects of my reflections were during my boyhood, as they were so incompatible with my age and situation. But in my opinion incompatibility between a person's situation and his moral activity is the surest sign of truth.

For a year during which I led a solitary inner life, focused entirely on myself, I was already faced with all those abstract questions regarding the purpose of man, the hereafter, the immortal soul, and my feeble childish mind attempted to clarify those questions with all the fervour of inexperience; even though a person may never obtain the solutions, it is the very asking that will push his mind to its highest level.

It seems to me that the human mind develops in the same way for each individual as for entire generations and that ideas that serve as a basis for various philosophical theories are an integral part of the mind; I think, however, that every person is more or less conscious of those ideas even before becoming aware of the existence of philosophical theories.

These ideas came to my mind with such clarity and impact that I even tried to apply them to life, imagining that I was the *first* to discover such great and useful truths.

It once occurred to me that happiness does not depend on external causes, but on our attitude towards them, and that a person who is used to enduring suffering cannot be unhappy. So, to train myself for hardship I would hold Tatishchev's dictionaries on my outstretched arms for five minutes, despite terrible pain, or I would go into the storeroom and whip my bare back with a rope, causing such pain that unbidden tears came to my eyes.

Another time, after suddenly remembering that death was waiting for me at any hour, any minute, and, failing to understand how people had not grasped this before, I decided man could only be happy by making the most of the present and not thinking about the future. So, influenced by this idea, I abandoned my lessons for three days and lay on my bed doing only the things that I liked: reading a novel and eating gingerbread with honey, which I had bought with the last of my money.

Once, standing before the blackboard and drawing various figures on it with a chalk, I was suddenly struck by a thought: "Why is symmetry pleasing to the eye? What is symmetry? It is an innate feeling," I answered myself. "What is that feeling based on? Is there symmetry everywhere in life? On the contrary, here is life," and I drew an oval figure on the board. "After life the soul passes into eternity: here is eternity," and I drew a line from one side of the oval to the very edge of the board. "Why is there not a similar line on the other side? And indeed, how can there be eternity on one side only; surely we existed before this life, although we have lost the memory of it."

This argument, which seemed to me to be a particularly new and logical one – although I have difficulty grasping its thread now – pleased me enormously, so I picked up a sheet of paper and took it into my head to put it down in writing. But such a rush of ideas suddenly came crowding into my head, that I was forced to stand up and pace up and down the room. When I walked over to the window, my attention was drawn by a water-carrying horse being harnessed by the coachman and all my thoughts focused on solving the following problem: "Which person or animal will that horse's soul go into when it dies?" At that moment Volodya came walking across the room and smiled when he saw me so absorbed, and that smile was enough to make me understand that all my previous thoughts were the most awful nonsense.

I have recounted this incident, which I somehow remember, only to give the reader an idea of the nature of my philosophizing.

But no other philosophical school of thought swept me away as much as scepticism, which at one time drove me close to insanity. I imagined that, besides myself, no one and nothing existed in the whole world, that objects were not objects but forms that only appeared when I turned my attention to them and that as soon as I stopped thinking about them, those forms would also disappear. In short, I agreed with Schelling* that objects did not exist except in my relation to them. There were moments when, under the influence of that fixed notion, I reached such levels of erratic behaviour that at times I would quickly glance back in the opposite direction, hoping to catch the void (*néant*) unawares, there where I no longer was.

What a pathetic, insignificant coil of inner activity is the human mind!

My feeble mind could not penetrate the impenetrable, and during that exhausting exercise it lost, one by one, those convictions, which for the sake of my own life's happiness, I should never even have touched upon.

From all that painful soul-searching I took away only a resourceful mind that weakened my will-power and a habit of constant moral analysis that destroyed all spontaneity and clarity of judgement.

Abstract thoughts take shape through man's ability to detect consciously the state of his own soul at a given moment and transfer it to his memory. My propensity towards abstract thinking developed my consciousness so unnaturally that when I started thinking about something very simple, I often fell into the vicious circle of analysing my thoughts. I stopped thinking of the question in my mind and thought instead about what I had been thinking about. Asking myself: "What am I thinking about?" I replied: "I'm thinking about what I was thinking about. And now what am I thinking about? I'm thinking that I'm thinking about what I'd been thinking about," and so on. I was at my wits' end...

However, the philosophical discoveries that I made flattered my self-esteem no end. I often imagined myself to be a great man discovering new truths for the common good and I looked at other mortals, proudly conscious of my own merit. Yet strangely, when I came into contact with those mortals, I turned shy in front of each one of them; the higher I placed myself in my own judgement, the less able I was to display the consciousness of my own merit to others, nor could I get into the habit of not being ashamed of the simplest word I said or gesture I made.

20

Volodya

Yes, the further I progress in describing this period of my life, the more painful and difficult it becomes for me. Rarely, very rarely among the memories of that time do I find those moments of genuine warm feeling that had so brightly and constantly lit up the first years of my life. I instinctively want to skim across the wilderness of my boyhood and reach that happy time when once again a truly tender, noble feeling of friendship shed a bright light over the end of boyhood and marked the beginning of a new phase, full of charm and poetry, that of my youth.

I will not follow my memories hour by hour, but will cast a quick glance at the main ones from this point in my narrative until the time of my growing friendship with an unusual young man, who had a decisive and beneficial influence on my character and further development.

Volodya is to go to university some day soon. Masters now come to tutor him individually and I listen with envy and unwilling respect to the way in which, as he briskly taps the chalk against the blackboard, he explains functions, sines, coordinates and so on, which seem to me to be expressions of unattainable wisdom. And so, one Sunday after dinner, all the masters and two professors gather in Grandmother's room and, in the presence of Papa and a few guests, they run a rehearsal of the university entrance exam and, to Grandmother's great joy, Volodya displays extraordinary knowledge. They also ask me questions on some subjects, but I prove to be very bad at them and the professors obviously try to cover up my ignorance in front of Grandmother, which confuses me even more. But little attention is paid to me: I am only fifteen, therefore I have another year until the exam. Volodya only comes downstairs for dinner and spends entire days and even evenings upstairs studying, not because he has to, but because he wants to. He is extremely proud and wants to pass his exam with excellence, not just a pass mark.

And so the day of the first exam has come. Volodya puts on a dark-blue tailcoat with brass buttons, a gold watch and patent leather boots; Papa's phaeton is brought to the front porch, Nikolai folds back the apron and Volodya and Saint-Jérôme set off for the university. The girls, and especially Katyenka, look through the window with joyful excited faces at Volodya's stylish figure as he gets into the phaeton; Papa says:

"Please God, please God." Grandmother has also dragged herself to the window and tearfully makes the sign of the cross towards Volodya until the phaeton disappears round the corner of the street, and she mutters something.

Volodya returns. Everyone asks him impatiently: "Well? Was it all right? What did you get?" but his happy face already tells you it went well. Volodya was given a "five". The next day they send him off with similar anxiety and good wishes for success and they welcome him back with the same impatience and joy. This goes on for nine days. On the tenth day the last and hardest exam of all lies ahead – Divinity – and we all stand at the window and wait for him with even greater impatience. It is already two o'clock and there is no Volodya.

"My God! Everyone! They're here! They're here!" screams Lyubochka, pressed against the window pane.

And indeed next to Saint-Jérôme in the phaeton sits Volodya, no longer dressed in his dark-blue tailcoat and grey cap, but wearing the student uniform with a blue embroidered collar, a three-cornered hat and a gilt sword at his side.

"Oh, if only you were alive!" cries out Grandmother, having caught sight of Volodya in his uniform, and she faints.

Volodya runs into the entrance hall with a beaming face, kisses and hugs me, Lyubochka, Mimi and Katyenka, who turns bright red at this. Volodya is beside himself with joy. And how handsome he looks in his uniform! How well the blue collar goes with his barely apparent black moustache! How slim and long his waist is and how noble his step! On that memorable day, everyone has dinner in Grandmother's room and every face glows with joy; with dessert, the butler, with a suitably dignified yet genial expression on his face, brings in a bottle of champagne wrapped in a napkin. Grandmother drinks champagne for the first time since Maman's death; she even drinks a whole glassful, congratulating Volodya, and again weeps for joy as she looks at him. Volodya now drives off in his own carriage, has his *own* acquaintances over to his *own* room, smokes, attends balls and I even see him once in his room drink two bottles of champagne with his friends, toasting with each glassful some mysterious individuals and arguing as to who will have *le fond de la bouteille*.* He regularly dines at home, however, and after dinner settles down as before in the sitting room and is forever chatting about mysterious matters with Katyenka, but from what I can gather without participating in their conversation, they only talk about characters in novels they have read, about jealousy and about love; I cannot begin to understand what interest they can find in such conversations and why they smile so subtly and argue so heatedly.

In general I notice that between Katyenka and Volodya there exists, besides an understandable friendship between childhood friends, some strange connection, removing them from us and mysteriously binding them together.

21

Katyenka and Lyubochka

KATYENKA IS SIXTEEN; she is grown up. The angular figure, the bashful and awkward movements that characterize girls at that age of transition, have given way to the soft freshness and grace of a newly blossomed flower, but she herself has not changed. She has the same light-blue eyes and smiling expression, the same straight little nose with its firm nostrils, almost in one line with her brow, and the little mouth with its bright smile, the same tiny dimples in her delicate rosy cheeks, the same small white hands... and for some reason, the label of "neat little girl" still suits her extremely well: only the thick light-brown braid is new, which she wears like grown-ups do, as is her young bosom, which clearly pleases as well as embarrasses her.

Although Lyubochka has grown up and was brought up with her, she is in all respects a completely different kind of girl.

Lyubochka is short and, as a result of rickets, she still has goose-like legs and her figure is very ugly. Her eyes are the only attractive feature in her whole appearance, and those eyes are indeed beautiful – large, black, with such an indefinably pleasing expression of confidence and naivety, that they cannot help but hold your attention. Lyubochka is uncomplicated and natural in everything, whereas Katyenka seems to want to be like someone else. Lyubochka always looks straight at things and at times she rests her huge black eyes on someone and does not look away for so long that she is told off for being impolite; Katyenka, on the other hand, lowers her eyelashes, screws up her eyes and assures us that she is short-sighted when I know full well that she can see perfectly. Lyubochka does not like to put on airs in front of others, and if someone starts to kiss her in front of visitors, she pouts and says that she cannot stand "displays of affection"; Katyenka, on the other hand, is particularly affectionate towards Mimi in front of visitors and loves to walk up and down the room arm in arm with another girl. Lyubochka is a terrible giggler and sometimes runs around the room waving her arms in fits of laughter; Katyenka, on the other hand, covers her mouth with her handkerchief or her hands when she begins to laugh. Lyubochka always sits up straight and walks with her arms by her sides; Katyenka holds her head a little to one side and walks with her arms folded. Lyubochka is always terribly glad when she has the chance to talk to a grown-up man and says that she will definitely marry a hussar; Katyenka, however, says she finds all men vile and that she will never marry; when a man talks to her, she appears very different, as though afraid of something. Lyubochka is always indignant with Mimi because her corsets are laced so tight that she "can't breathe", and she loves to eat; Katyenka, on the other hand, inserts her finger under the bodice of her dress to show us how loose it is on her and she eats very little. Lyubochka loves drawing people's heads and Katyenka only draws flowers and butterflies. Lyubochka plays Field's concerts and some of Beethoven's sonatas with great precision, whereas Katyenka plays variations and waltzes, slows down the tempo, thumps the keys, continually uses the pedal and, before starting to play a piece, she plays three chords with much feeling in arpeggio...

But Katyenka, I felt then, was more like a grown-up to me and that was why I liked her a lot more.

22

Papa

PAPA HAS BEEN PARTICULARLY CHEERFUL since Volodya entered university and he comes to dine at Grandmother's more often than usual. However, the reason for his cheerfulness, as I later heard from Nikolai, is the fact that he has won a great deal of money lately. Some evenings he even drops in before going to the club. He sits down at the piano, gathers us all around him and, tapping his feet clad in soft boots (he cannot stand heels and never wears them), sings Gypsy songs. And then you should see Lyubochka's look of comical rapture: she is his favourite and in turn adores him. He sometimes comes to the schoolroom and listens with a stern face as I recite my lessons, but some of the words he uses to correct me make me realize that he does not know much of what I am being taught. Sometimes he winks slyly and makes signs at us when Grandmother begins to grumble and get cross with everyone without reason. "Well, we've really caught it this time, children," he says later. On the whole, he is coming down, little by little, in my eyes from that unattainable height on which my childish imagination had placed him. I kiss his large white hand with the same sincere feeling of love and respect, but I now allow myself to dwell on him in my mind and examine his actions, and certain thoughts about him spontaneously occur to me and scare me. I will never forget the incident which inspired many such thoughts in me and which caused me much moral suffering.

He came into the drawing room late one evening, in a black tailcoat and a white waistcoat, to take Volodya, who meanwhile was getting dressed in his own room, to a ball. Grandmother was waiting in her bedroom for Volodya to come and show himself to her (she used to summon him before each ball, to bless him, look him over and give him instructions). Mimi and Katyenka were walking up and down in the reception room, which was lit by only one lamp, and Lyubochka sat at the piano practising Field's second concerto, Maman's favourite piece.

I have never encountered such a family likeness as there is between my sister and my mother. This likeness did not lie in the face, nor the build, but in something elusive: in the hands, in the manner of walking, especially in the voice and certain expressions she used. When Lyubochka was cross and said "It won't be allowed for ages", she pronounced this phrase "for ages", which Maman was in the habit of using too, in just the same way, and it was as though I could hear Maman's somehow drawn out "*for a-a-ges*". But the most extraordinary thing of all was the way she played the piano, and every movement connected with this: the way she arranged her dress, turned the sheets from the top with her left hand, hit the keys with her fist when annoyed if a difficult passage escaped her, the way she said: "Oh, my God!" and that same elusive tenderness and clarity in the way she played, in that beautiful manner of Field's, so aptly named *jeu perlé*,* the charm of which all the clever tricks of modern pianists cannot make you forget.

Papa came into the room with short quick steps and went up to Lyubochka, who stopped playing when she saw him.

"No, do play, Lyuba, do play," he said, making her sit down again, "you know how much I love listening to you…"

Lyubochka went on playing and Papa sat facing her for a long time, leaning on his elbow; then he got up with a quick twitch of his shoulder and began to pace up and down the room. Every time he approached the piano, he stopped and stared at Lyubochka long and hard. I noticed from his movements and his walk that he was agitated. Having crossed the room several times, he stopped behind Lyubochka's chair and kissed her on her dark head and then, turning round quickly, he began walking again. When she had finished playing that piece, Lyubochka went up to him and asked: "Was it good?" and without saying a word he took her head with both his hands and began kissing her forehead and her eyes with such tenderness as I had never seen in him before.

"Oh, my God, you're crying!" said Lyubochka, suddenly letting go of his watch chain, and gazing in surprise at him with her big eyes. "Forgive me, dearest Papa, I completely forgot that that was *Mama's piece*."

"No, my darling, play it more often," he said with a voice trembling with emotion, "if you only knew how good it feels to be weeping with you…"

He kissed her again and, attempting to master his emotions and twitching his shoulder, he went out through the door that led via the corridor to Volodya's room.

"Voldemar! Will you be ready soon?" he called out, stopping in the middle of the corridor. At that same moment the maid Masha came walking past him and, when she saw the master, she cast down her eyes and tried to go round him. He stopped her:

"You are getting prettier and prettier," he said, bending over her.

Masha blushed and lowered her head even more.

"Please allow me," she whispered.

"Voldemar, well, is it to be soon?" repeated Papa, twitching and coughing when Masha had gone past and he caught sight of me…

I love my father, but a person's mind lives independently of his heart and often entertains unintelligible and harsh thoughts that offend that love. And although I do my best to keep them at bay, such thoughts come to me…

23

Grandmother

G RANDMOTHER IS BECOMING WEAKER by the day. Her little bell, Gasha's grumbling voice and the slamming of doors can be heard from her room more frequently, and by now she no longer receives us in her study in the Voltairean armchair but in her bedroom in her high bed with its lace-trimmed pillows. When I greet her, I notice a shiny, pale, yellowy swelling on her hand and that oppressive smell in the room that I was aware of five years ago in mother's room. The doctor visits her three times a day and there have already been several consultations. Yet her character and her proud formal ways with the whole household and with Papa in particular have not changed at all; she draws out her words, raises her eyebrows and says "My dear" just as before.

But it has been a few days now that they have not allowed us in to see her, and one morning during lessons, Saint-Jérôme suggests that I go out for a ride with Lyubochka and Katyenka. Although I notice, as I settle down in the sleigh, that the street in front of Grandmother's windows is covered with straw and that some people in dark-blue *chuikas** are standing near our gates, I cannot understand at all why we are being sent out for a drive at such an inopportune time. On this day, during the whole outing, Lyubochka and I are for some reason very high-spirited, and the slightest incident, word or gesture makes us laugh.

A pedlar, grabbing his tray, trots across the road and we laugh. A poor ragged sleigh driver, swinging the ends of his reins, overtakes our sleigh at a gallop, and we laugh out loud. Filipp's whip gets caught in the sleigh's runner; he turns round and says: "Oh my!" and we die of laughter. Mimi, looking displeased, says that only "fools" laugh without reason, and Lyubochka, all flushed with suppressed mirth, steals a look at me. Our eyes meet and we dissolve into such Homeric laughter that we have tears in our eyes and we cannot hold back the bursts of laughter that are choking us. We have just calmed down a little and I look at Lyubochka and utter a code word that has been in fashion with us lately and always provokes giggles and we are off again.

As we approach home, I have just opened my mouth to pull a really funny face at Lyubochka, when my eyes are struck by the black coffin lid leaning against our front door and my mouth freezes into that grimace.

"*Votre grand-mère est morte!*"* says Saint-Jérôme, looking pale as he comes out to meet us.

The whole time Grandmother's body remains in the house, I experience a painful fear of death; the corpse reminds me vividly and unpleasantly that I too must die some time, a feeling that for some reason we usually confuse with sadness.

I do not feel sad about Grandmother, and hardly anyone really feels sad about her. Although the house is filled with visitors in mourning, no one feels sorry for her death, except for one person, whose frenzied grief startles me beyond words. And that person is Gasha, the maid. She goes up to the attic, locks herself in, cries without stopping, curses herself, tears her hair, refuses to listen to any advice and says that death remains her only consolation after the loss of her beloved mistress.

I repeat once again that improbability in matters of feeling is the most reliable mark of sincerity.

Grandmother is no longer there, but memories of her live on in the house as well as various rumours about her. The rumours have mainly to do with the will which she made before her death, the contents of which no one knows except for her executor, Prince Ivan Ivanych. I notice some agitation among Grandmother's servants and often hear talk about who they will go to* and I confess that I cannot help rejoicing at the thought that we will receive an inheritance.

After six weeks, Nikolai, always the broadcaster of news in our house, tells me that Grandmother has left her whole estate to Lyubochka and has entrusted her guardianship until her marriage not to Papa but to Prince Ivan Ivanych.

24

Me

ONLY A FEW MONTHS ARE LEFT before I go to university. I'm studying well. Not only do I await my tutors without dread, but I even get some pleasure from my lessons.

I enjoy repeating a well-learnt lesson with clarity and precision. I am preparing to enter the Faculty of Mathematics and, to tell the truth, the only reason I have made that choice was purely that I just love the words "sines", "tangents", "differentials", "integrals" and so on.

I am considerably shorter than Volodya, broad-shouldered and chunky, still as ugly and it still torments me. I try to appear original. One thing comforts me: the fact that Papa once said about me that I had a "clever little mug", and I fully believe this.

Saint-Jérôme is pleased with me and praises me; not only do I not hate him, but when he says that "with my ability and my intellect" it is shameful not to do this or that, I even think I like him.

I have long since ceased watching the maids' room. I feel ashamed of hiding behind the door and besides I must confess that being convinced of Masha's love for Vasily has cooled me down somewhat. It is I who ask Papa to allow Vasily to marry, on the latter's request, and this cures me for good of that unfortunate passion.

When the young couple approach Papa to thank him, bearing sweets on a tray, and Masha, in a blue-ribboned bonnet, also thanks us all for something or other and kisses each one of us on the shoulder, I am aware only of the scent of pink pomade from her hair, but not of the slightest emotion.

On the whole I gradually begin to recover from my adolescent shortcomings, with the exception, however, of the main one, which is destined to cause me a great deal more harm in life – my tendency to philosophize.

25

Volodya's Friends

ALTHOUGH THE ROLE I PLAYED in the company of Volodya's friends offended my self-respect, I liked to sit in his room when he had visitors and silently watch everything that went on there. The two most frequent visitors were Dubkov, an aide-de-camp, and Prince Nekhlyudov, a student. Dubkov was a small, wiry, brown-haired man, no longer in his first youth, rather short-legged, but not unattractive and always cheerful. He was one of those people with limited intellect who are particularly pleasant because of those limitations; they are unable to see things from different perspectives and are always carried away by something. The opinions of such people can be one-sided and mistaken, but they are always sincere and beguiling. Even their narrow-minded selfishness seems forgivable and endearing somehow. Besides, for Volodya and me, Dubkov's charm was twofold: his military appearance and, more importantly, his age, which for some reason young people often confuse with their understanding of respectability (*comme il faut*), which was highly valued in our time. And Dubkov was indeed what they call *un homme comme il faut*.* One thing that I found unpleasant was that in front of him Volodya at times seemed ashamed of my most innocent actions and most of all of my youth.

Nekhlyudov was not good-looking: his small grey eyes, short jutting forehead, disproportionately long arms and legs could not be called handsome. What was attractive was that he was unusually tall, had a fine complexion and beautiful teeth. But his narrow shining eyes and his ever changing smile, now stern, now childishly uncertain, gave his face such an original and vigorous look that it was impossible not to notice him.

He seemed very bashful, because the slightest thing made him turn bright red, but his timidity was unlike mine. The more he blushed, the more his face expressed determination, as though he was angry with himself for his weakness.

Although he appeared very friendly with Dubkov and Volodya, it was clear that he was connected to them only by chance. They were poles apart: Volodya and Dubkov seemed to be afraid of anything that came close to serious discussions or feelings; Nekhlyudov, on the other hand, was the greatest enthusiast and would often throw himself into discussions on philosophical matters or feelings, despite being laughed at. Volodya and Dubkov loved to talk about the objects of their affection (and they could suddenly be in love with several ladies or both with the same ones). Nekhlyudov, on the other hand, always became seriously angry when they hinted at his love for a certain "redhead".

Volodya and Dubkov often ventured to poke fun, lovingly, at members of their family, but you could drive Nekhlyudov crazy by alluding unfavourably to his aunt, for whom he felt a kind of rapturous adoration. Volodya and Dubkov would go off somewhere after supper without Nekhlyudov and call him a "pretty girl".

I was struck from the beginning by Prince Nekhlyudov's conversation as well as by his appearance. Although I found that we had a lot in common in our outlook – or maybe just because of that – the feeling he inspired me with when I saw him for the first time was far from amicable.

I disliked his swift glance, his firm voice, his proud look, but most of all the complete lack of interest he showed in me. During the course of a conversation, I often badly wanted to contradict him; to punish him for his pride I wanted to get the better of him, prove to him that I was intelligent, even though he chose not to pay me any attention.

My shyness held me back.

26

Discussions

VOLODYA, lying with his feet up on the sofa and leaning on his elbow, was reading some French novel, when I came into his room, as usual, after evening lessons. He raised his head for a second to glance at me and returned to his reading – the simplest and most natural of movements, yet one that made me blush. It seemed to me that with his glance he questioned why I had come in, and with the swift lowering of his head he wished to conceal the meaning of that look. That tendency to assign a meaning to the very simplest gesture was characteristic of me at that age. I went up to the table and picked up a book too, but before beginning to read, it occurred to me that it was rather ridiculous not to exchange a single word after not seeing each other all day.

"Well, will you be home tonight?"

"I don't know, why?"

"No reason," I said and, aware that the conversation was going nowhere, I took up my book and began to read.

It was odd that, when alone with each other, Volodya and I spent hours on end in silence, but we needed only the presence of a third person, even if that person remained silent, to start off the most interesting and varied conversations between us. We felt that we knew each other too well. Knowing each other too well can stand in the way of intimacy just as much as knowing each other too little.

"Is Volodya at home?" Dubkov's voice could be heard in the entrance hall.

"I'm home," said Volodya, removing his feet from the sofa and putting his book down on the table.

Dubkov and Nekhlyudov came into the room in their overcoats and hats.

"Well, shall we go to the theatre, Volodya?"

"No, I don't have the time," replied Volodya, blushing.

"Well, whatever next! Let's go, please."

"But I don't have a ticket."

"There are plenty of tickets at the entrance."

"Wait, I'll be right back," replied Volodya evasively and with a twitch of his shoulder left the room.

I knew that Volodya really wanted to go to the theatre with Dubkov, that he had refused only because he had no money and that he had gone out to borrow five roubles from the butler until his next allowance.

"Good day, 'diplomat'!" said Dubkov, offering me his hand.

Volodya's friends called me "diplomat" because once, after dinner at Grandmother's, when discussing our futures, she had said in their presence that Volodya would join the military and that she hoped to see me become a diplomat in a black tailcoat, and with my hair *à la coq,** which she considered a necessary condition of being a diplomat.

"Where has that Volodya gone off to?" Nekhlyudov asked me.

"I don't know," I replied, blushing at the thought that they would probably guess why Volodya had gone out.

"I expect he has no money! Is that right? Oh 'diplomat'!" he added, interpreting my smile as affirmative. "I don't have any money either; do you have any, Dubkov?"

"Let's see," said Dubkov, getting hold of his purse and groping about in it with his squat fingers very carefully for a few coins. "Here is a five-copeck piece and here a twenty-copeck piece, but otherwise... pff... nothing!" he said, gesturing comically with his hand.

At that moment Volodya came into the room.

"Well, are we going?"

"No."

"How funny you are!" said Nekhlyudov. "Why don't you say you have no money. Take my ticket, if you want."

"And what about you?"

"He'll go in the box with his cousins," said Dubkov.

"No. I won't be going at all."

"Why not?"

"Because you know I don't like sitting in a box."

"Why?"

"I don't like it, I find it awkward."

"The same old story! I don't understand why you should feel awkward there, where everyone is happy to see you. It's ridiculous, *mon cher*."

"So what, *si je suis timide*!* I'm sure you've never blushed in your life and I do all the time, for the merest trifles!" he said, blushing as he spoke.

"*Savez-vous d'où vient votre timidité?... d'un excès d'amour-propre, mon cher,*"* said Dubkov in a patronizing tone.

"What has *excès d'amour-propre* to do with it!" replied Nekhlyudov, stung to the quick. "On the contrary, I am shy because I don't have sufficient *amour-propre*; I keep on thinking that I'm dull, unpleasant to be with... because of this..."

"Put your overcoat on, Volodya," said Dubkov, taking him by the shoulders and pulling off his jacket. "Ignat, help your master with his coat!"

"Because of this I often..." went on Nekhlyudov.

But Dubkov was no longer listening to him. "Trala-la, tra-la-la-la," he began to hum some kind of tune.

"You're not getting away with this," said Nekhlyudov. "I'll prove to you that shyness is not at all caused by self-esteem."

"You can prove it by coming with us."

"I've told you I'm not coming."

"Well, stay here then and prove it to the 'diplomat', and when we get back, he can tell us."

"I'll prove it," rebuffed Nekhlyudov with childish wilfulness, "only do come back soon."

"What do you think: am I proud?" he said, sitting down next to me.

Although I had made up my mind on that score, due to this unexpected appeal I lost my nerve to such an extent that I was unable to give him a quick reply.

"I do think so," I said, feeling my voice quiver and a blush covering my face at the thought that the moment had come for me to prove to him that I was clever, "I think that every person is proud and that everything a person does is out of pride."

"So, what is pride, in your opinion?" said Nekhlyudov, smiling, it seemed to me, somewhat scornfully.

"Pride," I said, "is the conviction of being better and cleverer than everyone else."

"And how can everyone be convinced of this?"

"I don't know whether this is right or not, but no one, except for me, will admit to it. I am convinced that I am cleverer than anyone else in the world and am sure that you are convinced of the same thing about yourself."

"No, I'll first speak for myself: I've met people whom I've recognized as cleverer than me," said Nekhlyudov.

"It can't be," I replied with conviction.

"Do you really think that way?" said Nekhlyudov, staring at me.

"I seriously do," I replied.

And suddenly an idea came to me, which I immediately expressed.

"I'll prove it to you. Why do we love ourselves more than we love others?... Because we consider ourselves better than others, more worthy of love. If we discovered others better than us, then we would love them more than ourselves, and that just never happens. And even if it does, I'm still right," I added with an involuntary smile of complacency.

Nekhlyudov remained silent for a moment.

"Well, I'd never thought you were so clever!" he said to me with such a good-natured, sweet smile that I suddenly felt extremely happy.

Praise has such a monumental effect on a person's feelings and on his mind that I felt myself becoming even cleverer under its pleasant influence, and one thought after another swarmed into my head with unusual speed. From pride we imperceptibly moved on to love and our conversation seemed inexhaustible on that topic. Although our discussions were so biased and obscure that they might have appeared completely meaningless to an outsider, they held a strong meaning for us. Our souls were in such happy harmony that the slightest chord struck in one found its echo in the other. We found pleasure precisely in the echoing sounds to the various chords we touched in conversation. We felt that we were running out of words and time to express to each other all of those ideas that were begging to be aired.

27

Beginning of a Friendship

FROM THEN ON a rather strange but extremely pleasant relationship was established between Dmitry Nekhlyudov and myself. He hardly took any notice of me when others were around, but as soon as we found ourselves alone, we would settle into a comfortable corner and begin our discussions, forgetting everything else and without noticing time flying by. We talked about the future, about art, government service, marriage, children's education, and it never once occurred to us that everything we said was the most dreadful nonsense. It did not occur to us, because the nonsense we spoke was clever and sweet nonsense, and when you are young, you still value and believe in the intellect. When you are young, all your inner striving is directed towards the future, and the future assumes such varied, lively and fascinating forms, influenced by a hope based not on past experience but on the imagined possibility of happiness, that at that age those shared and unspoken dreams of future life embody true happiness. During the metaphysical discussions that were one of our main areas of conversation, I loved that moment when thoughts followed one another faster and faster, growing more and more abstract, until they finally reached such a hazy stage that you could not see a way of expressing them and ended up saying something altogether different from what you initially intended. I loved that moment when you rose higher and higher into the realm of ideas and suddenly grasped all its immensity and realized the impossibility of going any further.

Once, during Shrovetide, Nekhlyudov was so busy with various pleasant activities that, although he came over to us several times a day, he did not talk to me once. I was so offended by this that I thought of him again as a proud unpleasant individual. I only waited for the chance to show him that I did not treasure his company at all and that I had no particular affection for him.

The first time he wanted to talk to me again after Shrovetide, I told him that I had lessons to prepare, and went upstairs, but fifteen minutes later someone opened the door to the schoolroom and Nekhlyudov came over to me.

"Am I disturbing you?" he asked.

"No," I replied, although I wanted to tell him that I indeed had things to do.

"Then why did you leave Volodya's room? It has been a long time since you and I had a talk. And I'm so used to that by now that it feels as though something is missing."

My annoyance disappeared in an instant and Dmitry became again that kind and dear person in my eyes.

"You probably know why I went out?" I said.

"Perhaps," he said, sitting next to me, "but even if I am guessing, it's not for me to tell you why; you can tell me," he said.

"I'll tell you: I went out because I was cross with you... not cross, but annoyed. It's simple: I'm always afraid that you look down on me because I'm still very young."

"Do you know why we have got along so well, you and I?" he said, responding to my confession with a kind, wise look. "Why I like you more than those people I know better and with whom I have more in common? I have just made up my mind: you have an amazingly rare quality – openness."

"Yes, I always say those things I am ashamed to admit to," I acknowledged, "but only to those I trust."

"Yes, but to trust someone you must be friends, and you and I are not yet friends, Nicolas; you remember, we spoke of friendship: to be true friends you must trust each other."

"Trust that you won't repeat to anyone what I tell you," I said. "Yet the most important and interesting thoughts are just those very ones we won't on any account tell each other."

"And what nasty thoughts! Such despicable thoughts that if we knew that we would have to confess to them, they would never even dare enter our heads. I have an idea, Nicolas," he added, getting up from his chair and rubbing his hands with a smile. "*Let's do it*, and you'll see how useful it will be for both of us: let's give our word that we'll confess everything to each other. We'll get to know each other and won't feel ashamed, and in order not to be afraid of others, let's give our word that we'll *never say anything about each other to anyone*. Let's do it."

"Let's," I said.

And we did indeed *do it*. I will recount later what came of it.

Karr* said that there are two sides in every attachment: one side loves, the other allows itself to be loved, one kisses, the other offers its cheek. That is very true. In our friendship I kissed and Dmitry offered his cheek, but he too was ready to kiss me. We loved each other evenly, because we both knew and valued each other, but this did not preclude his exerting an influence over me and my submitting to him.

It goes without saying that under Nekhlyudov's influence I instinctively adopted the same course as he did, which in essence consisted of a rapturous adoration of the ideal of virtue and the conviction that man's purpose is to constantly improve himself. To reform the whole of humanity and wipe out all vices and human misfortunes seemed easy to carry out then – it seemed very easy and simple to reform ourselves, to adopt all virtues and be happy...

Then again, God alone knows whether those noble youthful dreams were indeed ridiculous and whose fault it was that they did not come true...

Youth

1

What I Consider to Be the Beginning of My Youth

I HAVE SAID THAT my friendship with Dmitry opened up to me a new way of looking at life, its purpose and its implications. In essence this view consisted of a conviction that man's purpose is to strive for moral improvement and that such improvement is easy, is possible and would last for ever. So far, however, I had only enjoyed discovering new ideas flowing from this conviction, and making brilliant plans for a moral, active future, and my life continued on its same trivial, tangled and idle course.

Those virtuous thoughts, which I went over in my conversations with my adored friend Dmitry, "wonderful Mitya", as I sometimes called him under my breath, only appealed to my mind, not to my feelings. But the time came when these thoughts came into my head with all the renewed vigour of moral discovery and it frightened me to think of all the time I had wasted. I wanted immediately, that very instant, to apply those thoughts to life with the firm resolve never to betray them again.

I consider that moment to be the beginning of my *youth*.

I was nearly sixteen at the time. Tutors still came to teach me. Saint-Jérôme supervised my studies and, under pressure, I reluctantly prepared myself for university. Apart from my studies, my activities consisted of solitary rambling daydreams and reflections, of gymnastic exercises with the aim of becoming the strongest man in the world, of wandering without aim or thought from room to room and in particular along the maids' corridor and of looking at myself in the mirror, which always left me, however, with a painful feeling of dejection and even repulsion. I had convinced myself that I was not handsome and I could not even take comfort in the consolations that would be normal in such situations. I could not say that I had an expressive, intelligent or even noble face. There was nothing expressive about it – my features were most ordinary, coarse and ugly; my tiny grey eyes, particularly when I looked in the mirror, looked stupid rather than clever. There was even less manliness there: although I was tall and very strong for my age, all my features were soft, slack and undefined. There was nothing noble there either; on the contrary, my face was like that of a simple peasant, and so were my large hands and feet, and at that time this seemed very shameful to me.

2

Spring

IN THE YEAR I ENTERED UNIVERSITY, Holy Week fell rather late in April, so the entrance exams were fixed for the week following Easter Week; this meant that during Easter I had not only to fast for communion but also to make a final effort to revise for the exams.

After the sleet, which Karl Ivanych sometimes described as "the son following the father", the weather had been still, warm and clear for about three days. There was not a patch of snow left in the streets, dirty slush gave way to wet, glistening paving and swift-running streams. In the sun the last of the thawing snow was already dripping from the rooftops. In the front garden buds swelled on trees. In the yard the pathway was dry and by the stables past a frozen dung heap and in between the stones near the front porch mossy grass was showing green. It was that particular phase of spring which has the strongest effect on a person's soul: a bright if not yet hot sun shining everywhere, streams and thawed patches of earth, fragrant freshness in the air and a tender blue sky with long, transparent clouds. I do not know why, but it seems to me that this first period of spring, its birth, affects the soul even more strongly and palpably in the city – you see less, but you have a stronger premonition of it. I stood by the window and through its double-glazing the morning sun cast dusty beams across the floor of the schoolroom, which I was so unbearably tired of, and I was solving some long algebraic equation on the blackboard. I held the tattered, soft copy of Franker's *Algebra** in one hand and in the other a small piece of chalk with which I had already smudged my hands, my face and the elbows of my jacket. Nikolai, in his apron and rolled-up sleeves, was removing putty with pliers and bending back nails that held the frame of the window, which overlooked the front garden.* I was distracted by what he was doing and by the noise he made. And besides, I was in a very bad, disgruntled mood. Nothing was going right somehow; I had made a mistake at the beginning of my calculations so I had to start all over again; I had dropped the chalk twice and was aware that my face and hands were smudged; the sponge had disappeared somewhere and the tapping noise made by Nikolai was getting painfully on my nerves. I felt like getting cross and protesting; I threw down the chalk as well as the *Algebra* and began to pace up and down the room. But I remembered that it was Ash Wednesday and that we had to make our confessions on that day and had to refrain from all evil, and I suddenly went into a peculiar, gentle mood and walked over to Nikolai.

"Let me help you, Nikolai," I said, trying to sound very gentle, and the thought that I was behaving well by overcoming my annoyance and helping him reinforced that gentle mood even more.

The putty had been removed, the nails bent back, but the window frame would not budge, although Nikolai tugged at the crosspiece with all his might.

"If the frame comes out as soon as I begin to help him pull," I thought, "then it means that it would be a sin to study any more today." The frame gave way on one side and came off.

"Where shall I take it to?" I said.

"Please let me do it," replied Nikolai, visibly surprised and seemingly displeased with my efforts. "There must be no mistakes, and I put them away by number in the storeroom."

"I'll number it," I said, picking up the frame.

I believe that had the storeroom been about two versts away and had the frame weighed twice as much, I would still have been satisfied. I wanted to be worn out by performing this service for Nikolai. When I came back to the room, the small bricks and salt cones* had been moved to the window sill and Nikolai had swept sand and sleepy flies out of the open window with a feather. Fresh fragrant air had already come in and filled the room. From the window you could hear the city sounds and the twitter of sparrows in the front garden.

Every object was brightly lit and the room grew cheerful. A light spring breeze stirred the pages of my *Algebra* and the hairs on Nikolai's head. I went over to the window, sat on the ledge, leant over to the garden and was lost in thought.

A particularly strong and pleasant feeling that was new to me suddenly crept into my heart. The wet earth shot through here and there with bright-green blades of grass with tiny yellow stalks, the streams glistening in the sunshine with little bits of earth and wood winding their way along them, the reddening lilac twigs with swollen buds waving just below the window, the busy twitter of the birds stirring in that bush, the blackened fence wet from melting snow and above all that fragrant moist air and the joyful sun all spoke to me very clearly of something new and beautiful, which I cannot convey as it came to me, but which I will try to convey as I perceived it. It spoke of beauty, happiness and virtue, each of them easily accessible to me, that one could not exist without the other, and even of beauty, happiness and virtue being one and the same thing.

"How could I have failed to understand that? How bad I have been and how happy and good I could be and will be in the future!" I said to myself. "I must, as soon as possible, this very minute, become a different person and begin to live another way."

Yet in spite of all this, I remained seated on the ledge for a long time, idly dreaming away. Has it ever happened to you that you have taken a daytime nap in the summer when the weather is rainy and dull and, after waking up at sunset and opening your eyes, seen, through the widening quadrangle of the window, where the linen blind has filled out and knocks its rod against the window sill, the shady, lilac-tinted side of a lime-tree avenue wet from the rain, and a damp garden path, lit up by bright, slanting beams, and suddenly heard the chirpy bird life in the garden and seen the insects circling around the open window gleaming in the sunlight and absorbed the smell of the rain-washed air and thought: "How shameful to have missed out on such an evening," and leapt up hastily to go into the garden and rejoice in life? If that has happened to you, then it is a small token of that strong feeling I experienced at the time.

3

Daydreams

"Today I'll make my confession, I'll cleanse myself of all sins," I thought, "and I'll never again..." (at that point I remembered all those sins which troubled me most of all) "I'll go to church every Sunday without fail, and read the Gospel for a whole hour after that; then, when

I enter university, I'll definitely give the poor two and a half roubles (one tenth) of the twenty-five-rouble note I'll be receiving every month and I'll do it so that no one will know about it, and not just to the destitute, but I'll seek out those poor people, orphans and old women no one knows about.

"I'll have my own room (probably Saint-Jérôme's) and I'll tidy it up myself and keep it amazingly clean and I'll not make any servant do anything for me. They are just like me after all. Then I'll go to university each day on foot (and if they give me a *droshky** I'll sell it and put that money aside for the poor as well) and I'll carry out everything to the letter." (What "everything" was I could not have said then, but I felt it strongly and understood it as part of a judicious, moral and irreproachable life.) "I'll take notes at all the lectures and even study ahead of time so that I'll come top in the first course and will write my dissertation. I'll already know everything in advance for the second course and so they could transfer me straight away to the third course, so that by the time I'm eighteen I'll have completed the whole course as the top graduate with two gold medals. Then I'll obtain my Master's degree, my doctorate and I'll become Russia's leading academic... I could even be Europe's leading academic... And then?" I asked myself, but at that point I remembered that those dreams constituted the sin of pride, which I would have to tell the priest about that very evening, so I returned to the beginning of my reflections.

"To prepare for the lectures I'll go to Sparrow Hills* on foot; I'll find a place to sit under a tree and I'll read through the lectures. Sometimes I'll bring a snack, some cheese or a pie from Pedotti's,* or something else. I'll have a rest and then I'll read a good book or sketch some views or play some instrument (I'll certainly study the flute). Then *she*'ll also go walking on Sparrow Hills and at some stage *she*'ll walk up to me and ask me who I am. I'll look at her very sadly and tell her that I'm the son of a priest and that I can only be happy here when I'm completely and utterly alone. She'll give me her hand, say something and sit down beside me. And so we'll go there every day, we'll become friends and I'll kiss her... No, that's not good. On the contrary, from today onwards I'll no longer look at women. I'll never go near the maids' room, I'll even try not to walk past it, and in three years' time I'll be my own master and will definitely get married. I'll resolve to do as many exercises as possible, practise gymnastics every day so that when I'm twenty-five, I'll be stronger than Rappo.* On the first day I'll hold up a half-*pood* weight in my outstretched hand for five minutes, the next day twenty pounds, the third day twenty-two pounds and so on, so that I'll finally hold four *poods* in each hand and I'll be stronger than anyone in the household. And if someone suddenly takes it into his head to offend me or begins to speak disrespectfully of *her*, I'll just grab him by the chest and lift him up an *arshin* or two from the ground with one arm and hold him so that he can feel my strength and then let him go, but this is no good either; no, it's fine, I won't hurt him, I'll just show him that I..."

Let no one blame me if those dreams of my youth are as childish as those of my childhood and boyhood. I am convinced, if I am destined to live to a ripe old age and my story keeps up with the years, that as an old man of seventy my dreams will be just as impossible and childish as now. I will dream of some delightful Maria, who will fall in love with me, a toothless old man, as she fell in love with Mazepa.* I will dream of how my feeble-minded son suddenly becomes a minister because of some unusual coincidence, or how I will suddenly come to have lots of money. I am convinced that there is no human being of whatever age who does not have that beneficial, comforting ability to daydream. But leaving aside their common element – the impossible magic of daydreams – each person's dreams at different ages have their own distinctive character. In that period which I consider the end of my boyhood and the beginning of my youth, four feelings formed the basis of my dreams: love of *her*, the imaginary woman, whom I always dreamt about the same way and whom I expected to meet at any moment. She had a little of Sonyechka, a little of Masha, Vasily's wife, when doing some washing over the washtub, and a little of the woman with pearls around her white neck whom I once saw long ago in the box next to us at the theatre. The next feeling was love of love. I wanted everyone to know me and love me. I wanted to declare my name was Nikolai Irtenyev and have everyone, struck by this news, crowd around me and thank me for something or other. The third feeling was one of hope for a remarkable, glorious happiness – a hope so intense and strong that it verged on madness. I was so sure that very soon, following some unusual occurrence, I would suddenly become the wealthiest and most famous person in the world so that I found myself in a perpetual state of anxious expectation of something bewitchingly wonderful. I kept on waiting for *it to begin* and I would attain everything a person could wish for, and I would always hurry everywhere assuming that *it* was already *beginning* somewhere else without me. The fourth and most important feeling was one of self-loathing and remorse, but remorse mingled with hope for happiness to such a degree that in itself it held no sadness. It seemed to me so easy and natural to break away from the past, to alter, to forget everything that had been and to begin life anew in all respects, that the past was neither a burden nor a bind. I even wallowed in my aversion to the past and tried to see it in a gloomier light than it was. The darker the circle of past memories, the brighter and purer did the bright, pure moment of the present shine and the cheerful colours of the future unfold. That voice of remorse and passionate desire for perfection was the main new heartfelt feeling during that period of my development and it lay down new principles in the way I saw myself, other people and God's world. Blessed comforting voice, how many times since then, in those sad times when my soul has silently submitted to the power of life's falsehoods and corruption, have you suddenly risen against any untruth, furiously denouncing the past, pointing to and compelling me to love the clear moment of the present, and promising goodness and happiness in the future? Blessed comforting voice! Might you at some point in time fall silent?

4

Our Family Circle

PAPA WAS SELDOM AT HOME that spring. Yet whenever he was, he appeared extremely cheerful, strummed his favourite pieces on the piano, made sweet eyes at us and made up jokes about us and Mimi, such as the one where the Georgian Tsarevich had seen Mimi out riding and had fallen so deeply in love with her that he had submitted an application for a divorce to the synod, or the one where I had been made an assistant to the Viennese envoy – and he would put on a grave face when announcing those news items. He scared Katyenka with spiders, of which she was afraid; he was very affectionate with our friends Dubkov and Nekhlyudov, and was always telling visitors as well as us about his plans for the following year. Although those plans changed almost every day and contradicted one another, they were so fascinating that we listened spellbound and Lyubochka watched Papa's mouth without blinking for fear of missing a word. One plan was to leave us at university in Moscow and go to Italy with Lyubochka for two years. Another was to buy an estate in Crimea, on the southern shore, and go there every year; another to move to St Petersburg with the whole household, and so on. But besides particular high spirits there was another change in Papa that surprised me very much. He had a fashionable suit made for himself – an olive-coloured tailcoat, fashionable trousers with foot straps and a long winter coat which looked very good on him. There was often a whiff of lovely scent emanating from him as he set off to visit people, and one lady in particular, whom Mimi only mentioned with a sigh and such a face on which you could read, "Poor orphans! Unfortunate passion! Thank goodness *she* is no longer here," and so on. I heard from Nikolai, because Papa did not speak to us about his gambling, that he had had much luck that winter. He had won vast amounts, placed the money in a bank and that spring decided not to gamble any more. He probably wanted to go to the country as soon as possible because he feared not being able to maintain his resolve. He even decided not to wait for my entrance to university and to go to Petrovskoye with the girls straight after Easter. Volodya and I were to follow later.

All that winter and up to spring Volodya remained inseparable from Dubkov (they had begun to keep away from Dmitry). Their main pastimes, as far as I could make out from the conversations I overheard, consisted entirely in endlessly drinking champagne, sleigh riding below the window of a lady with whom they were apparently both in love, and dancing vis-à-vis, no longer at children's balls but at grown-up ones. Although Volodya and I loved each other, this last fact did much to draw us apart. We felt the difference was too big between the boy who had tutors coming to give him lessons and the man who danced at grand balls, to bring ourselves to confide our thoughts to one other. Katyenka was by now fully grown up. She read many novels and the thought that she might marry soon no longer seemed laughable to me. Although Volodya was now grown up too, they did not get along and even seemed to despise each other. On the whole, when Katyenka was alone at home, she did nothing besides read novels and was bored most of the time; when other men were present, however, she became very lively and amiable and made eyes at them and I could not in the slightest understand what she could mean by it. Only later, after hearing from her that a young girl's only permissible form of coquetry was with her eyes, could I explain to myself those odd unnatural eye contortions which others did not seem to find surprising at all. Lyubochka too began to wear practically full-length dresses, so that her goose-like legs were almost invisible, but she was just as much a cry-baby as before. She no longer dreamt of marrying a hussar but rather a singer or a musician and with that goal in mind she earnestly studied music. Saint-Jérôme, knowing that he was to remain with us only until the end of my exams, found himself a post with some count or other and since then looked upon our household with some kind of disdain. He was rarely at home, began to smoke cigarettes, which was at the time the height of dandyism, and constantly whistled some merry tune through a small piece of cardboard. Mimi became more and more embittered as each day went by and, from the time that we began to grow into adults, she seemed to expect nothing good from anyone or anything.

When I came into the dining room for dinner, I found only Mimi, Katyenka, Lyubochka and Saint-Jérôme there. Papa was not at home and Volodya was preparing for his exams with some friends in his room and had requested dinner to be brought up. On the whole it was Mimi who presided at the table most of the time and, as no one had much respect for her, dinnertime lost much of its appeal. Dinner no longer was, as with Maman or Grandmother, some kind of ritual which brought the whole family together at a set time and divided the day into two halves. Now we felt free to come in late, arrive for the second course, drink wine in tumblers (Saint-Jérôme himself had set the example), slouch on our chairs, get down before the end of the meal and similar liberties. From then on dinner stopped being, as before, a joyful daily family celebration. How different it had been in Petrovskoye, when at two o'clock everyone would sit in the drawing room, washed and dressed for dinner, happily chatting and waiting for the appointed time. At exactly that time, when the clock in the servant's room made a wheezing sound before striking two, Foka would come in softly, a napkin over his arm, with a dignified and somewhat stern face. "Dinner is served!" he would proclaim in a loud drawn-out voice and all, with happy, satisfied faces, the grown-ups first followed by the young ones, accompanied by the sound of starched skirts and the scraping of boots and shoes, would enter the dining room and, exchanging a few words in low voices, would take their customary places. Or in Moscow, when everyone, quietly chatting, would stand before the table set in the reception room waiting for Grandmother, to whom Gavrilo had already announced that dinner was served. Suddenly the door would open, there was the rustle of a dress and the shuffle of feet and Grandmother, bent sideways and wearing a bonnet with an unusual kind of lilac bow, either smiling or squinting sombrely (depending on her state of health), would come sailing out of her room. Gavrilo would rush over to her armchair, there would be some scraping of chairs and, feeling a kind of shiver running down my back (a sign of appetite), I would pick up my slightly damp, starched napkin, eat a tiny crust of bread and, rubbing my hands under the table with impatient and happy greed, I would glance at the steamy plates of soup the butler filled, as he took rank, age and Grandmother's intentions into account.

Now I no longer felt any joy or emotion as I came in to dinner.

The idle chatter coming from Mimi, Saint-Jérôme and the girls about the awful boots the Russian teacher wore, or how the Kornakov Princesses wore dresses with flounces and so on, their chatter, which had previously filled me with real contempt that I had not even attempted to conceal from Katyenka or Lyubochka, did not deflect me from my new virtuous frame of mind. I was unusually gentle; I listened to them very affectionately with a smile, respectfully asked them to pass me the *kvas* and agreed with Saint-Jérôme, when he corrected a phrase I used at dinner, saying that it was more attractive to say *je puis* than *je peux*.* I have to confess, however, that I was rather annoyed that no one paid any particular attention to my gentle and virtuous behaviour. After dinner Lyubochka showed me a piece of paper on which she had written down all her sins. I told her that I thought this a very good thing, but that it would be even better to make a note of all her sins within her soul and that "this was not quite right".

"Why not?"

"Well, it's all right anyway; you wouldn't understand me." And I went upstairs to my room, having told Saint-Jérôme that I was going to study, but in reality to write down before confession, which was due in about an hour and a half, a list of my responsibilities and tasks for my entire life, setting down on paper my life's goals and the rules by which I should always unfalteringly act.

5

Rules

I TOOK A SHEET OF PAPER and wanted first of all to start making a list of my tasks and responsibilities for the coming year. The paper needed ruling. But as I could not find a ruler, I used a Latin dictionary instead. It turned out that when I ran the pen along the edge of the dictionary and then removed it, I caused an oblong ink puddle to form on the paper instead of a line, besides which the dictionary was not long enough for the whole paper and the line curved down round its soft corner. I took another sheet of paper and by moving the dictionary I ruled it anyhow. After dividing my responsibilities into three categories: responsibility to myself, to my neighbour and to God, I began to write down the first few, but there turned out to be so many of them and so many kinds and subdivisions, that it was necessary to write down "Life Rules" first and then start the list. I took six sheets of paper, sewed them together to form a notebook and wrote on top: "Life Rules". Those two words were so skewed and unevenly written that I wondered at length whether I should rewrite them. I worried about it for quite a while, looking at the torn list and the distorted heading. Why was everything so beautifully clear in my soul and why did it come out so disgracefully on paper and in life in general, when I wanted to put some of my thoughts into practice?...

"The confessor has arrived; would you please come down to listen to the obligations," Nikolai came to tell me.

I hid the notebook in a drawer, looked in the mirror, brushed my hair upwards, which I believed gave me a pensive look, and went to the sitting room, where the table had already been prepared with the icon and burning wax candles. Papa came in from the other door at the same time as me. The confessor, a grey-haired monk with a stern old man's face, blessed Papa, who kissed his small broad cold hand. I did the same.

"Call Voldemar," said Papa. "Where is he? Oh no, don't; he's probably preparing for communion at university."

"He's studying with the Prince," said Katyenka and she looked at Lyubochka. Lyubochka suddenly blushed over something, made a face as if she were in some sort of pain and left the room. I followed her out.

She stopped in the drawing room and wrote something else down on her paper with a small pencil.

"What, have you committed another sin?" I asked her.

"No, it's fine," she replied with a blush.

Meanwhile Dmitry's voice could be heard in the entrance hall, saying goodbye to Volodya.

"See, everything's temptation for you," said Katyenka, coming into the room and addressing Lyubochka.

I could not understand what was going on with my sister; she was so disconcerted that tears came to her eyes and her confusion became such that it turned into annoyance with herself and Katyenka, who was clearly teasing her.

"Well, it's obvious that you are a foreigner" (nothing could be more insulting to Katyenka than being called a "foreigner", which was why Lyubochka used the term), "and before such a sacrament," she went on in a pompous voice, "and you upset me on purpose... you should understand... it isn't a joke at all..."

"Do you know, Nikolyenka, what she wrote down?" said Katyenka, offended at having been called a "foreigner", "she wrote—"

"I didn't expect you to be so spiteful," said Lyubochka, beginning to whimper as she moved away from us, "she leads me on purpose into sin at such a moment and indeed all the time. I don't pester you with your feelings and sufferings, do I?"

6

Confession

WITH THOSE and similar jumbled reflections I returned to the sitting room when everyone had gathered there and the confessor, having got to his feet, prepared to recite the prayer before confession. But as soon as the monk's stern expressive voice rang out in the overall silence, reciting the prayer, and particularly when he pronounced the words: "Reveal all your sins without shame, concealment or excuse, and your soul will be cleansed before God, but if you withhold anything, you will be committing a grave sin," the feeling of reverential awe I had experienced that morning when thinking about the forthcoming sacrament came back to me. I even found pleasure in the consciousness of that state and tried to hold on to it, stopping all other thoughts from coming into my head and making an effort to be fearful of something.

Papa was the first to go to confession. He stayed in Grandmother's room for a long time and meanwhile, in the sitting room, we remained silent or whispered the occasional word about who would go next. At last the monk's voice was heard through the door reciting a prayer, and then Papa's footsteps. The door creaked and he came in coughing and twitching his shoulder as usual and not looking at any of us.

"Now you go, Lyubochka, and make sure you tell all. You are my greatest sinner," said Papa cheerfully, pinching her cheek.

Lyubochka turned pale and then red, pulled out the little note from her apron pocket and then hid it again; then bowing her head and pulling in her neck somehow as though expecting a blow from above, she walked through the door. She was not in there long, but when she came out, her shoulders were shaking with sobs.

At last came my turn, after pretty Katyenka had come out smiling through the door. With that same dull fear and a wish to boost that feeling even more, I entered the half-lit room. The priest stood before the lectern and slowly turned to face me.

I spent no more than five minutes in Grandmother's room, but I came out of there happy and, as I believed then, completely pure, morally reborn and a new man. Despite the fact that I was unpleasantly struck by the same old environment, the same rooms, the same furniture, my own unchanged appearance (I would have liked everything on the outside to have changed the same way I felt I had changed on the inside) – despite all this, I remained in that happy mood until I went to bed.

I was already falling asleep, in my mind reviewing all the sins from which I had been cleansed, when I suddenly remembered one shameful sin I had withheld from confession. The words of the prayer before confession came back to me and rang relentlessly in my ears. All my peace of mind immediately vanished. I kept hearing the words: "But if you withhold something, you will be committing a grave sin…" and I saw myself as such an awful sinner that there was no fitting punishment for me. I tossed and turned for a long time, carefully thinking over my situation, expecting God's punishment at any moment and even sudden death, a thought that threw me into a state of indescribable horror. But all of a sudden a happy thought occurred to me: I would go on foot or ride to the monastery first thing in the morning and would visit the confessor and make another confession. With that I calmed down.

7

A Trip to the Monastery

I WOKE UP several times during the night, afraid that I might oversleep, and by six o'clock I was already up. There was hardly a glimmer of light through the windows. I put on my clothes and boots, which lay crumpled and dirty near my bed, because Nikolai had not had time to take them away, and without washing or saying my prayers, I went out alone for the first time in my life onto the street.

Across the street, behind the green roof of the big house, an icy, misty dawn was turning red. A fairly heavy spring-morning frost that had frozen the mud and streams crackled underfoot and stung my face and hands. There was not yet a single cab driver about in our side street and I had counted on one to travel quickly there and back. Only some carts slowly dragged along the Arbat* and a couple of bricklayers walked and chatted together on the pavement. About a thousand paces further along, I began to come across men and women going to market with small baskets and water carts being driven for water. A pieman came out at the crossroads; a *kalach** shop opened its doors, and I found a cab driver at the Arbat Gate, an old man who had been asleep, swaying slightly on his lightly sprung, shabby, patched-up bluish *droshky*. Still probably half asleep, he only asked for twenty copecks to get me to the monastery and back, but then he suddenly came to his senses and, as I was about to take a seat, he whipped his horse with the ends of the reins and began to drive away from me.

"I have to feed my horse! I can't take you, sir," he mumbled.

I talked him round with great difficulty, offering him forty copecks. He pulled up his horse, looked me over carefully and said: "Take a seat, sir."

I have to admit that I was a little frightened that he would take me to some back alley and rob me. Holding on to the collar of his tattered *armyak*, rather pitifully exposing his wrinkled neck above his badly hunched back, I climbed up to the wobbly, dented blue seat and we began to bump along down Vozdvizhenka Street. Along the way I was able to notice that the back of the *droshky* had been upholstered with a piece of the same greenish fabric the cab driver's *armyak* was made of and this reassured me for some reason; I was no longer afraid that the cab driver would take me to some back alley and rob me.

The sun had already risen quite high and brightly gilt the church domes as we approached the monastery. There was still some frost in the shade, but all along the road flowed swift murky streams and the horse sloshed through the thawing mud. Having entered the monastery enclosure, I asked the first person I saw where I could find the confessor.

"His cell is over there," said a passing monk, stopping for a moment and pointing to a small house with a small porch.

"I thank you kindly," I said.

But what could the monks have thought of me as they came out of church one by one and looked at me? I was neither a grown-up nor a child; my face was unwashed, my hair unbrushed, my clothes specked with fluff, my boots unpolished and still muddy. Among what class of people did the monks place me in their minds when they peered at me? And they were looking at me closely. I nevertheless went in the direction pointed out to me by the young monk.

An old man dressed in black, with bushy grey eyebrows, met me on the small narrow path leading to the cells and asked me what I wanted.

There was a moment when I wanted to say "Nothing", run back to the cab driver and go home, but despite his closely knit brows the old man's face inspired trust. I said that I needed to see the confessor, mentioning him by name.

"Let's go, young sir, I'll take you," he said, turning back and apparently at once guessing my situation. "Father is celebrating matins, but he'll soon be here."

He opened the door and led me through a neat little passageway and hall, over a clean linen mat, into the cell.

"Just wait here," he said with a kindly, reassuring look and went out.

The room I found myself in was very small and exceptionally neat and tidy. The furniture consisted of a small table covered with an oilcloth placed between two tiny casement windows with two geranium pots, a small stand holding icons and a little icon lamp hanging in front of them, one armchair and two ordinary chairs. In the corner hung a wall clock with flowers painted on its dial and with bronze weights held by chains; on a partition, joined to the ceiling by means of small whitewashed wooden sticks (and behind which probably stood a bed), hung two cassocks on nails.

The windows looked out onto a white wall, about two *arshins* away. Between the windows and the wall was a small lilac bush. Not a sound reached the room from outside, so that in that silence, the pleasant regular ticking of the pendulum sounded loud. As soon as I was alone in that quiet little corner, all my previous thoughts and recollections suddenly slipped from my mind as if they had never been there, and I sank into an inexpressibly pleasant state of contemplation. That yellowy cotton cassock with its worn lining, those old black leather book bindings with brass clasps, those dull-green flowers and carefully watered soil and washed leaves, and especially that monotonous staccato sound of the pendulum spoke to me clearly of some kind of new, hitherto unknown life, a life of solitude, prayer, of quiet peaceful happiness...

"Months go by, years go by," I thought. "He's always alone, always at peace and he always feels that his conscience is clear before God and his prayers have been heard." I remained seated on that chair for about half an hour, trying not to move or breathe loudly so as not to disrupt the harmony of sounds which said so much to me. And the pendulum kept on ticking, louder to the right, softer to the left.

8

A Second Confession

THE CONFESSOR'S FOOTSTEPS roused me from my contemplation.
"Good morning," he said, smoothing his grey hair with his hand. "What can I do for you?"

I asked him to give me his blessing and kissed his small yellowish hand with particular pleasure.

When I explained my request to him, he did not respond, but went up to the icons and began the confession ritual.

When that was over and I had told him, overcoming my shame, what was in my heart, he lay his hands on my head and pronounced with his soft ringing voice: "May the blessing of our heavenly Father be with you, preserve you for ever in faith, humility and submission. Amen."

I was completely happy. Tears of happiness rose in my throat; I kissed the pleat of his thin cloth cassock and raised my head. The monk's face was completely serene.

I enjoyed the feeling of being deeply moved and, fearful of somehow dispelling it, I quickly took leave of the confessor and, looking neither right nor left so as not to be distracted, I left the enclosure and sat down once more in the wobbly striped *droshky*. But the jolting of the carriage and the motley objects flashing before my eyes soon dispelled that feeling, and soon I was imagining how the confessor would probably now be thinking that he had never encountered in his life such a beautiful soul in a young man, nor would again, as no such others existed. I was convinced of it and that conviction filled me with a kind of elation that demanded to be shared with someone.

I dreadfully wanted to talk to someone, but since no one was at hand besides the cab driver, I turned to him.

"Was I away long?" I asked him.

"It was a long time and it's long past my horse's feeding time; you see, I'm a night driver," the little old cab driver replied, having clearly brightened up in the sunshine, compared with before.

"To me it felt I was away for just one minute," I said. "And do you know why I was at the monastery?" I added, moving to a dip in the *droshky* closer to the old driver.

"What's that got do with me? Where the passenger wants to go, there I'll take him," he replied.

"But all the same, what do you think?" I persisted

"Probably to bury someone, you went to buy a plot," he said.

"No, brother; do you know why I went?"

"I can't know, sir," he repeated.

The cab driver's voice seemed so kindly to me that for his edification I decided to tell him the reason for my trip and even the feeling I had experienced.

"Do you want me to tell you? You see…"

And I told him everything and described all of my beautiful feelings. I blush even now at the memory of it.

"Yes, sir," said the cab driver distrustfully.

And he remained silent and sat motionless for a long time after, only now and then adjusting his coat flap, which kept coming out from under his striped trouser leg bouncing inside the large boot on the *droshky*'s footboard. I was already thinking that he was having the same thoughts about me as the confessor: that there was not another young man so fine as me in the whole world, but he suddenly turned to me:

"Well, sir, yours is the Lord's business."

"What?" I asked.

"That business is the Lord's business," he repeated, mumbling between his toothless lips.

"He didn't understand me," I thought, and no longer spoke to him until we reached home.

Although the feeling of humility and of piety did not hold out all the way, the self-satisfaction from the experience did, despite the crowds that were out on the streets in the bright sunlight. But as soon as I arrived home, that feeling completely vanished. I did not have the forty copecks to pay the cab driver. Gavrilo the butler, to whom I was already in debt, would not lend me more. The cab driver, seeing that I had already run across the yard twice to get the money and probably guessing why I was running, leapt down from the *droshky*, and although he had seemed so kind to me, began to loudly hold forth, with the clear intention of riling me, about scoundrels who did not pay for the ride.

Everyone was still asleep at home so that, besides the servants, there was no one from whom I could borrow the forty copecks. Finally Vasily, to whom I gave my most solemn word, but who (I saw it in his face) did not believe me at all, paid the cab driver for me, because he loved me and remembered the good turn I had done him. So that feeling just vanished like smoke. As I began to dress for church to take communion together with everyone else, and it transpired that my outfit had not been altered and it was impossible to wear it, I committed a string of sins. After putting on another outfit, I went to communion in a strange state with thoughts whirling through my head and in complete mistrust of my fine disposition.

9

How I Prepare for My Exams

O N THE THURSDAY of Holy Week, Papa, my sister, Mimi and Katyenka all left for the country so that only Volodya, Saint-Jérôme and I remained in Grandmother's large house. The mood I had been in on the day of confession and on the day of my trip to the monastery had entirely gone; what remained was a hazy though pleasant memory gradually drowned out by the new impressions of a life of freedom.

The notebook headed "Life Rules" was hidden away with my rough exercise books. Although I liked the idea of being able to compile a set of rules for myself to deal with all of life's eventualities and of always being ruled by them, and it seemed to be an extremely simple idea as well as a great one, and although I fully intended to apply it to my life, I once again somehow forgot that I should do this immediately and kept on putting it off until another time. I was reassured, however, that each thought that now entered my head fitted into one of the subdivisions of my rules and responsibilities: whether relating to my neighbour, to myself or to God. "I'll put it down there as well as many more ideas that occur to me on the subject," I said to myself. Now I often ask myself: "When was I better and closer to being right? Was it when I believed in the omnipotence of the human intellect, or is it now, having lost the power for further growth, when I question its power and meaning?" And I can find no positive answer.

I felt so unsettled by the sense of freedom and that spring feeling of expectation I alluded to previously, that I could not control myself and prepared very poorly for the exams. Sometimes I might be studying in the schoolroom in the morning, knowing I had to work because I had to sit an exam the following day for which I still had not prepared two questions, when suddenly a spring fragrance would waft in through the window and it would seem as though there was something I had to remember urgently: my arms would automatically put the book down, my legs would automatically begin to move and pace up and down, but in my head it was as though someone had released a spring and set off a machine; various colourful happy dreams would begin to rush through my head with such lightness and so naturally and swiftly that I hardly managed to notice their blaze. And so one or two hours would pass unnoticed. Or I might be sitting with a book and somehow manage to focus all my attention on what I was reading, when I would suddenly hear a woman's footsteps and the swish of a dress in the corridor – and everything would leap out of my head and I could not possibly remain seated, although I knew full well that no one, besides Grandmother's old maid Gasha, could be walking along the corridor. "And what if it were *she*?" would cross my mind. "And what if *it is beginning* now and I miss it?" And I would dart out into the corridor and see that it was indeed Gasha, but I could not control my mind for a long time after. The spring had been released and there was a terrible commotion in my head again. Or in the evening I might be sitting alone with a tallow candle in my room; suddenly in the split second it took to snuff the candle or reposition myself on my chair, I would tear myself away from my book and see that it was dark in the doorway and the corners, and I would hear only silence throughout the house. It would again be impossible not to stop and listen to that silence and not to look at the blackness of the open doorway into the dark room and to stay in that motionless state for a very long time or to go down and wander through all the empty rooms. I also often sat unnoticed in the hall, listening to the sound of 'The Nightingale'* as played with two fingers on the piano by Gasha sitting alone by candlelight in the reception room. And by moonlight I would definitely have to get out of bed and lie on the window ledge overlooking the front garden and, watching the lit roof of the Shaposhnikov's house and the slender bell tower of our local church and the evening shadows the fence and shrubs cast across the garden path, I would have to stay there for so long that I would only wake up with difficulty at ten o'clock the next morning.

Therefore, had it not been for the tutors who continued to come to me, or for Saint-Jérôme, who reluctantly fanned my pride from time to time, and, most importantly, for the desire to show myself to be an able young man in the eyes of my friend Nekhlyudov by passing my exams with top marks, which he regarded as very important – had it not been for this, then spring and my freedom would have made me forget everything I actually did know and I would never have passed my exams.

10

The History Exam

O N 16TH APRIL I entered the large university hall for the first time, escorted by Saint-Jérôme. We went there in our rather dashing phaeton. I wore a tailcoat for the first time in my life, and all my clothes, down to the linen and the stockings, were the newest and the best. When the doorman relieved me of my overcoat downstairs and I appeared before him in all my finery, I even felt slightly embarrassed at being so dazzling. However, no sooner had I stepped into the bright parqueted hall full of people and seen hundreds of young men in grammar-school uniforms and in tailcoats, some of whom glanced at me with indifference, and self-important professors in the far corner casually walking by the tables or sitting in large armchairs, than I was instantly dashed in my hopes of attracting general attention. The expression on my face back home and even in the university entrance hall, that had denoted a kind of regret that I, against my will, should have such a noble and remarkable appearance, was soon replaced by an expression of overwhelming shyness and a certain despondency. I even went to the other extreme and was quite delighted to spot a sloppily dressed gentleman nearby, not yet old but almost entirely grey, sitting on a bench at the back, away from the others. I immediately sat down near him and began to scrutinize the other candidates and to draw my own conclusions about them. There were many varied figures and faces, but, going by my ideas at the time, they could easily be divided into three groups.

There were those who, like myself, had come to the exam accompanied by a tutor or a parent, and among them were the younger Ivin with the familiar Frost, and Ilyenka Grap with his elderly father. They were all similar with downy chins, displaying smart white shirts and sitting quietly, without opening the books or exercise books they had brought with them, watching the professors and the exam tables with obvious shyness. The second group of candidates were young people in grammar-school uniform, and many of them had already started shaving. They mostly knew each other, spoke loudly and called the professors by their names and patronymics.

They were getting ready for the exam questions, they passed each other exercise books, stepped over the benches, brought sandwiches and pies into the hall from the anteroom and ate them on the spot, bending their heads down only slightly to the level of the benches. And finally there was the third group and there were few of those; they were quite old, wearing tailcoats, but the majority wore frock coats and without any linen showing. They remained extremely serious, sat alone and looked very gloomy. The gentleman who had made me feel better by being certainly worse dressed than I belonged to that group. He sat reading a book, leaning his head on both hands with his unruly greyish hair poking out between his fingers; he only glanced briefly at me with his shining if not entirely friendly eyes, frowned gloomily and stuck his gleaming elbow in my direction to prevent me from moving closer to him. The grammar-school boys were on the contrary too sociable and I was a little wary of them. One of them, thrusting a book into my hand, said: "Pass that over to him." Another, passing by me, said: "Let me through, my dear fellow." A third leant onto my shoulder as he climbed over a bench as though I were a stool. I found all this very strange and unpleasant; I considered myself as being far above those grammar-school boys and thought that they should not allow themselves to be so familiar with me. The surnames began to be called out at last. The grammar-school boys boldly went up, answered well on the whole and came back in high spirits. Our group was a lot more timid and seemed not to answer as well. Of the older group, some answered very well and others very badly. When they called up Semyonov, my neighbour with the grey hair and shining eyes, he pushed me rudely aside as he clambered over my feet and went up to the table. He answered confidently and extremely well, as was plain from the professors' expressions. After returning to his place, he quietly picked up his exercise books and left the hall without finding out what mark he had been given. I had already shuddered several times at the sound of the surnames being called out, but it was not yet my turn, as it went in alphabetical order, although names beginning with K had already been called out. "Ikonin and Tenyev," someone suddenly shouted out from the professors' corner. An icy shiver ran along my back and up my hair.

"Who's been called? Who's Bartenyev?" people were saying around me.

"Ikonin, go on, they've called you, but who's Bartenyev, Mordenyev? I don't know, declare yourself," said a tall ruddy-faced grammar-school boy standing behind me.

"It's your turn," said Saint-Jérôme.

"My surname is Irtenyev," I said to the ruddy-faced schoolboy. "Did they call out Irtenyev?"

"Yes, they have; why aren't you going up? Look, what a dandy!" he added not loudly, but so that I heard his words as I left the bench. Ikonin went ahead of me: a tall young man of about twenty-five, belonging to the third group, the older ones. He wore a tight olive-coloured tailcoat, a dark-blue satin cravat, over which at the back lay long blond hair carefully brushed *à la muzhik*.* I had noticed his appearance before when we were sitting on the benches. He was not bad-looking, and was talkative and I was particularly struck by the strange red hair which he let grow on his throat, and an even stranger habit he had of continually unbuttoning his waistcoat and scratching his chest under his shirt.

Three professors sat behind the table which Ikonin and I approached; not one of them responded to our bows. A young professor shuffled the question slips like a pack of playing cards, a second professor with a star on his coat watched as a grammar-school boy was saying something very quickly about Charlemagne, adding "finally" to every word he said, and the third, an elderly man wearing glasses, had lowered his head and looked at us through his glasses pointing to the question slips. I felt that his glance was directed at both Ikonin and myself and that something about us displeased him (perhaps Ikonin's red hair), because, looking at both of us again, he gestured impatiently with his head for us to quickly pick up the slips. I was both annoyed and offended: firstly because none of them had responded to our bows, secondly for clearly linking me with Ikonin as being just another candidate and therefore being already prejudiced against me because of Ikonin's red hair. I confidently picked up a slip and was prepared to answer, but the Professor beckoned to Ikonin. I read my question: I knew the answer so, calmly waiting for my turn, I watched what was going on before me. Ikonin did not lose his nerve at all and even reached forwards over-confidently, twisting his body sideways to pick up a slip, shook his hair and briskly read what was written on his slip. He opened his mouth, apparently to give his answer, when the

Professor with the star, after dismissing the grammar-school boy with praise, suddenly looked at him. Ikonin seemed to remember something and stopped. There was complete silence for about two minutes.

"Well," said the Professor with the glasses.

Ikonin opened his mouth and again said nothing.

"Look, you are not the only one; are you prepared to answer or not?" said the young Professor, but Ikonin did not even look at him. He stared at his slip without uttering a word. The Professor in glasses looked at him through his glasses, over his glasses and without his glasses, as he managed in that time to take them off, wipe them and put them back on again. Ikonin did not utter a single word. Suddenly a smile lit up his face, he shook his hair, again swung sideways towards the table, put down the slip, looked at each professor in turn, then at me, turned round and, with a sprightly step and swinging arms, he returned to the benches. The professors exchanged glances.

"What a fine specimen!" said the young Professor. "And a fee-paying student* too!"

I moved closer to the table, but the professors continued to talk in a near-whisper among themselves as though none of them had even registered my presence. I was at that time firmly convinced that the question of whether I would pass and how well I would pass the exam was a matter of great importance in the professors' minds and that they were only pretending out of self-importance that they did not care at all about it and acting as though they had not noticed me.

When the Professor with the glasses turned to me half-heartedly, inviting me to answer the question, I looked him straight in the eye, feeling a little embarrassed on his behalf for putting on such an act in front of me; I stumbled a little at the beginning, but it became gradually easier and, as the question was about Russian history, which I knew perfectly, I ended brilliantly and became so worked up that, wanting to make the professors aware that I was not Ikonin and that we should not be confused with each other, I offered to pick up another slip. But the Professor, nodding his head, said: "That's fine," and made a note in his register. After returning to the benches, I immediately learnt from the grammar-school boys who, God knows how, found out everything, that I had been given a "five".

11

The Mathematics Exam

A T THE FOLLOWING EXAMS I had already made many new acquaint-ances, besides Grap, whose acquaintance I regarded as unworthy, and Ivin, who for some reason avoided me. Some of them were by now exchanging greetings with me. Ikonin was even glad to see me and in-formed me that he was to resit his history exam and that the history Professor had been cross with him ever since the previous year's exam, when he had, it seems, also "knocked him off his feet". Semyonov, who was joining the same faculty as me, the Faculty of Mathematics, kept away from everyone until the end of the exams. He sat alone in silence, leaning on his elbows and thrusting his fingers through his grey hair, and he gained top marks in his exams. He came second overall; a gram-mar-school boy from the top grammar school came first. The latter was tall and thin, with brown hair, extremely pale, with a black scarf wound round his cheek and a forehead covered in pimples. He had thin red hands with extremely long fingers and his nails were bitten down so badly that his fingertips seemed tied up in threads. To me this was all quite excellent and just as it should be with the top grammar-school boy. He talked to everybody just as everyone else did and even I made his acquaintance, but all the same I felt that there was something no-ticeably unusual, *magnetic* in his walk, in the movement of his lips and in his black eyes.

I arrived earlier than usual at the mathematics exam. I knew my subject quite well, but there were two algebra questions which I had somehow kept from my teacher and which I did not know at all. They were, as I remember, the theorems of combinations and Newton's binomial theorem. I sat on the benches at the back and looked at the two questions I had not prepared for, but the noisy environment, which I was not used to, and the awareness that time was short, prevented me from thoroughly taking in what I was reading.

"There he is, come here, Nekhlyudov," I heard Volodya's familiar voice behind me.

I turned round and saw my brother and Dmitry, who, with their frock coats unbuttoned and waving their arms, were making their way towards me in between the benches. It was instantly clear that they were second-year students, very much at home in the university. Their unbuttoned coats in themselves reflected disdain for those of us who were just on the threshold of university and instilled envy and respect in us. I felt very flattered to think that everyone around could see that I was acquainted with second-year students and I quickly stood up to meet them.

Volodya could just not resist expressing his feeling of superiority.

"Oh you, poor thing!" he said. "Have you not sat your exam yet?"

"No."

"What are you reading? Have you not prepared for this?"

"I have, but two questions not quite. I can't understand this one here."

"What? This one?" said Volodya and he began to explain Newton's binomial to me, but he did this so hurriedly and unintelligibly that he blushed when he read distrust of his knowledge in my eyes and in Dmitry's eyes too, no doubt, when he glanced at him, but he still went on saying something I did not understand.

"No, wait, Volodya, let me go over it with him if we can manage in time," said Dmitry, glancing over at the professors' corner and settling down next to me.

I immediately noticed that my friend was in that gentle self-assured mood he was always in when he was pleased with himself and which I particularly liked in him. As he was very good at mathematics and spoke clearly, he ran through the question so well that I remember it to this day. But he had hardly finished before Saint-Jérôme whispered loudly: "*À vous, Nicolas!*"* and I followed Ikonin from behind the bench without having had the chance to go over the other unprepared question. I went up to the table where two professors were sitting, with a grammar-school boy standing at a blackboard. The schoolboy was briskly writing out some formula, snapping off the chalk against the board, and went on writing although the Professor had already said, "That's enough," to him and had told us to pick out our question slips. "What if I get the theorem of combinations?" I thought, picking out a card from a soft pile of torn slips of paper with trembling fingers. Ikonin, with the same bold gesture as in the last exam, swinging his body completely sideways, just took the top slip without choosing, glanced at it and frowned crossly.

"I always get those same devilish ones!" he muttered.

I looked at mine.

Oh, horrors! It was the theorem of combinations!...

"And what have you got?" asked Ikonin.

I showed him.

"I know that one," he said.

"Do you want to swap?"

"No, I don't feel in the mood anyway." Ikonin hardly had time to whisper before the Professor summoned us to the blackboard.

"Well, it's hopeless!" I thought. "Instead of passing my exam brilliantly, as I expected to, I will be covered in shame for ever, worse than Ikonin." But all of a sudden Ikonin turned to me in front of the Professor, pulled the slip from my hand and gave me his. I glanced at the slip. It was Newton's binomial.

The Professor was not old and had a pleasant intelligent expression due mainly to the particularly bulging lower part of his forehead.

"What's this, gentlemen, are you exchanging slips?" he said.

"No, he just gave me his to look at, Professor," Ikonin came up with a quick answer and this time again the word "Professor" was the last word he uttered in that place; as he passed by me on his way back, he again glanced at the professors, then at me, smiled and shrugged his shoulders, as if to say, "It's all right, brother!" (I found out later that this was the third year Ikonin had presented himself at the entrance exams.)

I gave a perfect answer to the question I had only just gone over and the Professor even said that I had done better than required and gave me a "five".

12

The Latin Exam

E VERYTHING WENT PERFECTLY until the Latin exam. The grammar-school boy with the cravat round his cheek was in first position, Semyonov in second and I in third. I even began to feel proud and believe in earnest that, despite my youth, I should be taken seriously.

Ever since the first exam, everyone had spoken nervously about the Latin Professor, who was some kind of wild beast who took pleasure in the downfall of young men, especially fee-paying ones, and who apparently only spoke in Latin or Greek. Saint-Jérôme, who was my Latin teacher, tried to reassure me and indeed I felt as well prepared as anyone else, as I could translate Cicero and some of Horace's Odes without a dictionary, and I had excellent knowledge of Zumpt,* but things turned out differently. Throughout the morning all you heard were tales of the downfall of those who went up before me: he had given one a "zero", another a "one", he had berated and threatened to send away another, and so on and so forth. Only Semyonov and the top grammar-school boy went up as unruffled as usual and came back with a "five" each. I already had a premonition of disaster when Ikonin and I were called up together to the small table, behind which the terrifying Professor sat all alone. The terrifying Professor was a small, thin, sallow individual, with long greasy hair and a very absorbed look.

He gave Ikonin a book of Cicero's orations and told him to translate it.

To my huge amazement, Ikonin not only read but also translated several lines with the help of the Professor, who prompted him. Feeling my superiority before such a weak rival, I could not help smiling even a little scornfully when it came to parsing and Ikonin sank as before into an obviously hopeless silence. I wanted to please the Professor with my clever and slightly mocking smile, but it worked the other way.

"You clearly know this better, since you are smiling," the Professor said to me in bad Russian. "We'll see. Well, have your say."

I later found out that the Latin Professor was Ikonin's sponsor and that the latter even lived with him. I immediately answered the question on syntax that had been given to Ikonin, but the Professor pulled a glum face and turned away.

"Good, when it's your turn we'll see how much you know," he said without looking at me and began to explain to Ikonin what the question was about.

"You may go," he added, and I saw that he gave Ikonin a "four" in the register.

"Well," I thought, "he's not at all as strict as has been made out."

After Ikonin had gone, he spent probably five minutes, which seemed to me more like five hours, arranging his books and the question slips, blowing his nose, readjusting the armchair, lounging in it, looking all around the hall and everywhere except at me. All that pretence, however, was not enough for him and he opened a book and pretended to read as though I was not there at all. I moved nearer and coughed.

"Oh yes, you're still here? Well, translate something," he said, handing me a book. "No, this one's better." He leafed through Horace and turned to a page that I believed no one would ever be able to translate.

"I haven't prepared this one," I said.

"So you want to answer one that you learnt off by heart – that's a good one! No, you translate this one."

I somehow began to get to the gist of the passage, but the Professor shook his head each time I gave him an enquiring look and only said, "No," with a sigh. He finally shut the book with such nervous haste that he slammed his finger between its pages; he angrily pulled it out, gave me a grammar question slip and, leaning back in his armchair, he sank into the most ominous silence. I was about to answer, but the expression on his face froze my tongue and it seemed that anything I said was wrong anyway.

"It's not that at all, it's all wrong," he suddenly said with his vile accent, quickly changing position, leaning his elbow on the table and playing around with a gold ring which hung loose on the skinny finger of his left hand. "That's not the way, gentlemen, to prepare for entrance to a higher educational establishment; all you want is to wear a uniform with a dark-blue collar; you acquire a smattering of knowledge and you think that you can be students. No, gentlemen, you have to learn your subject thoroughly," and so on and so forth.

I looked blankly at his downcast eyes throughout his speech, delivered in mangled Russian. I was initially tormented by disappointment at not ending up third, then by fear of not passing the entrance exams at all, and to this was added a sense of unfairness, of wounded pride and undeserved humiliation, and to top all that, the scorn I felt for the Professor, because he was, to my mind, not *comme il faut** – I discovered this when I noticed his thick, short, round fingernails – inflamed me even more and turned all those feelings to poison. Having glanced at me and noticing my quivering lips and my tearful eyes, he probably read my distress as a plea to increase my mark and, as if taking pity on me, he said (and this in the presence of another Professor who had just joined us):

"Fine, I'll give you a pass mark" (which meant a "two"), "although you don't deserve it, and it is only in respect of your youth and in the hope that once at university you won't be so frivolous."

That last sentence, said in front of the other Professor, who looked at me as if to say, "Yes, now you see, young man!" completely disconcerted me. There was one moment when my eyes clouded over: the terrifying Professor seemed to be sitting with his table somewhere in the distance and a wild notion entered my head with terrible one-sided clarity: "And what if? What would happen if?..." But for some reason I did not do it. On the contrary, I bowed automatically and particularly respectfully to both professors and with a faint smile – probably the same kind of smile as Ikonin's – I moved away from the table.

That unfairness affected me so much at the time that, had I been able to act freely, I would not have continued with my exams. I lost all ambition (there was no point in thinking of coming third overall) and I sat the next exams without any effort or even emotion. My overall mark was just over "four", however, but even that no longer interested me. I decided and proved very clearly to myself that it was extremely stupid and even *mauvais genre** to try to come first; it was better to perform neither too badly nor too well, like Volodya. That was how I planned to work at university, although in that instance I differed for the first time from my friend.

By then I only thought of the uniform, the three-cornered hat, my own *droshky*, my own room and, most importantly, my own freedom.

13

I Am Grown Up

THEN AGAIN, those thoughts held their own charm.

On the 8th of May, on returning home from the final exam, which was Divinity, I found one of Rozanov's apprentices waiting there for me. I knew him from when he had brought over my uniform and frock coat made of glossy shot black cloth which had been hastily tacked together, and he had marked off the lapels with chalk. This time he brought me the whole new outfit, complete with shiny gold buttons wrapped in paper.

After putting it on and finding it splendid – although Saint-Jérôme declared that the back of the coat was wrinkled – I went downstairs with a self-satisfied grin that quite involuntarily spread all over my face, and proceeded to Volodya's room, aware, but pretending not to notice, that the servants were eagerly staring at me from the entrance hall and the corridor. Gavrilo the butler caught up with me in the hall, congratulated me with getting into university, handed me four twenty-five-rouble notes, on Papa's orders, and told me, equally on Papa's orders, that Kuzma the coachman, the open carriage and the bay horse Krasavchik would be entirely at my disposal from that day on. I was so overjoyed by this almost unexpected happy turn of events that I was quite unable to pretend indifference in front of Gavrilo; somewhat flustered and breathless, I said the first thing that came into my head – something to the effect that Krasavchik was a great trotter. Having glanced at the heads leaning out of the doors of the entrance hall and the corridor, and unable to hold out any longer, I dashed across the hall in my new frock coat with its shiny gold buttons. As I went into Volodya's room, I heard behind me the voices of Dubkov and Nekhlyudov, who had come to congratulate me and suggest that we go out to dinner somewhere and drink champagne in honour of my success. Dmitry said to me that although he did not like drinking champagne, he would come along to drink a toast to our using the familiar *ty* with each other. Dubkov said that I somehow really looked like a colonel. Volodya did not congratulate me and only said drily that we would now be able to go to the country the day after next. Although he was pleased that I had been admitted to university, it felt as though he was a little unhappy that I too was a grown-up like him. Saint-Jérôme, who had also come in, said very pompously that his responsibilities towards us were now over, that he did not know whether he had fulfilled them well or not, but that he had done all he could and that he would move to his count's household the next day. In response to everything that was being said, I felt my face lighting up against my will with a sweet, happy, slightly foolishly complacent smile and I noticed that this smile even communicated itself to everyone who spoke to me.

So there I was, with no tutor, with my own *droshky*, with my name on the students' list, I carried a sword in my sword belt, the policemen on duty might sometimes saluted me... I was grown up and was, it seemed, happy.

We decided to dine at Yar's after four o'clock, but as Volodya was going off to Dubkov's place and Dmitry as usual disappeared somewhere too, saying that he had something to do before dinner, I had two hours to spend any way I wished. For quite a long time I walked through all the rooms, looking at myself in all the mirrors, now with my coat buttoned up, now with all the buttons undone, now with only the top button done up, and it all looked perfect to me. Next, though I felt guilty at appearing too overjoyed, I could not resist visiting the stables and the coach house and looking at Krasavchik, Kuzma and the *droshky*. I then went indoors again and began to wander about all the rooms, looking in the mirrors and counting the money in my pocket, and I just kept on smiling happily. An hour had not gone by, however, before I began to feel slightly bored or to regret that no one could see me in such a splendid state and I felt the need for movement and activity. So I ordered the carriage to be harnessed and decided that I would do best to drive to Kuznetsky Bridge and do some shopping.

I remembered that, when Volodya had passed into university, he had bought himself some lithographs of horses by Victor Adam,* and some tobacco and a few pipes and I felt I had to do the same.

Under the general scrutiny and with my buttons, the cockade on my hat and my sword brightly lit up by the sun, I arrived on Kuznetsky Bridge and stopped by Datsiaro's picture shop.* Glancing around me on all sides, I went inside. I did not want to buy Adam's horses so as not to be accused of mimicking Volodya, but, embarrassed into making a quick decision by the trouble I was causing the helpful shop assistant, I chose a female head in gouache that was displayed in the window and paid twenty roubles for it. However, having paid the twenty roubles, I still felt embarrassed at having disturbed two smartly dressed shop assistants with such trifles, and I also thought that they were still looking at me rather too casually. Wanting to make them realize what kind of person I was, I turned my attention to a small silver object under glass and, discovering that it was a *porte-crayon** that cost eighteen roubles, I asked them to wrap it up for me. After paying for it and having also learnt that good pipes and tobacco could be found in a tobacco shop next door, I bowed politely to both shop assistants and went out into the street with the picture under my arm. In the next-door shop, which had a black man smoking a pipe painted on its sign, I bought – again not wanting to imitate anyone – Sultan's tobacco rather than Zhukov's,* a Turkish pipe and two lime-wood and rosewood pipe stems. As I left the shop on my way to the *droshky*, I caught sight of Semyonov in a civilian frock coat, keeping his head down as he sped along the pavement. I was annoyed that he did not recognize me. I said quite loudly: "Let's go!" and after getting into the *droshky*, I caught up with Semyonov.

"Good day, sir," I said to him.

"My respects," he replied, continuing on his way.

"How come you're not in uniform?" I asked him.

Semyonov stopped, screwed up his eyes and, baring his white teeth, as though it pained him to look into the sun, but actually to show me that he was unimpressed by my *droshky* or my uniform, looked silently at me and walked on.

From Kuznetsky Bridge I went on to a confectioner's shop on Tverskaya Street where, despite wanting to pretend that I was mainly interested in the newspapers in the shop, I could not refrain from eating one sweet pastry after another. Although I was embarrassed in front of a gentleman who was looking at me inquisitively from behind his newspaper, I very quickly finished off eight pastries of each kind on offer.

Back home I suffered slight heartburn, but I took no notice of this and began to inspect my purchases. Of these I took such a dislike to the picture that I neither put it in its frame nor hung it up in my room as Volodya had done, but I carefully hid it behind the chest of drawers where no one could see it. I did not like the *porte-crayon* either; I put it in a drawer, consoling myself with the thought that it was an important object made of silver and very useful for a student. But I did immediately decide to put the smoking accessories to the test.

I unsealed the quarter-pound packet, filled the pipe with reddish-yellow fine-cut Sultan tobacco and applied burning tinder to it. I took the stem in between my middle and third fingers (I particularly liked the position of my hand) and began to draw in the smoke.

The smell of tobacco was very pleasant, but I had a bitter taste in my mouth and the smoke caught my breath. However, I reluctantly continued to smoke for quite a long time, trying to blow smoke rings and to inhale. The room was soon filled with bluish clouds of smoke, the pipe began to wheeze, the hot tobacco to splutter and I could feel the bitterness in my mouth and a light dizziness in my head. I was ready to give up and just to take a look at myself with my pipe in the mirror, when to my amazement I began to sway on my feet; the room swirled and, after reaching the mirror with some difficulty, I saw that my face was as white as a sheet. I barely managed to drop down on the sofa before I was overcome by such nausea and felt so faint that I imagined the pipe to be fatal for me and thought I was dying. I was seriously alarmed and was prepared to call the servants and summon a doctor.

That fear, however, did not last long. I soon understood what had happened. Suffering from a terrible headache and feeling very weak, I lay on the sofa for a long time, gazing vacantly at the Bostanzhoglo coat of arms* displayed on the packet, at the pipe which had fallen on the floor and at the tobacco bits and remnants of the pastries. Saddened and disappointed, I thought: "I am apparently not grown up if I can't smoke like the others, and I'm clearly not destined to hold the pipe between the middle and third fingers like others do or inhale and blow the smoke out through a brown moustache."

Dmitry, who came to pick me up after four o'clock, found me in that unpleasant condition. I nearly recovered, however, after drinking a glass of water, and was ready to set off with him.

"And why this desire to smoke?" he said, looking at the traces of my smoking. "It is just foolishness and a waste of money. I promised myself not to smoke... Anyway, let's hurry, as we still have to pick up Dubkov."

14

What Volodya and Dubkov Were up to

A s soon as Dmitry came into my room, I realized from his face and his walk and from a characteristic gesture he made whenever he was in a bad mood – he blinked with one eye and pulled a face while twitching his head sideways as though adjusting his cravat – that he was in that cold stubborn mood which came over him when he was displeased with himself and which always had a cooling effect on my feelings for him. I had recently begun to observe and appraise my friend's character, but our friendship did not change in any way as a result of this; it was still such a new and strong friendship that from whatever angle I looked at Dmitry, I could not help seeing how perfect he was. He was two different people and both were wonderful in my eyes. One, whom I loved fiercely, was kind, affectionate, gentle, cheerful and conscious of those lovable qualities. When he was in that mood, his whole appearance, his voice and all his movements seemed to say: "I'm gentle and virtuous and, as you can all see, I enjoy being gentle and virtuous." The other person, whom I was just beginning to recognize and whose grandeur I admired, was aloof, strict with himself as well as with others, proud, religious to the point of fanaticism and pedantically moral. At this moment he was that second person.

After we had sat down in the *droshky*, I told him with the frankness that was an essential condition of our relationship that I was sad and pained to see him in such a sombre, unpleasant mood on what was such a happy day for me.

"I suppose something has upset you: why don't you tell me what it is?" I asked him.

"Nikolyenka!" he replied unhurriedly, nervously twisting his head sideways and blinking. "If I gave you my word not to conceal anything from you, then you have no reason to suspect me of being secretive. One can't always be in the same mood and if something has upset me then I cannot account for it myself."

"What a remarkably open, honest character he has," I thought and did not say another word to him.

We arrived at Dubkov's place in silence. Dubkov's apartment was unusually attractive, or at least so it appeared to me. There were rugs everywhere, and pictures, curtains, colourful wallpaper, portraits, curved armchairs, Voltairean armchairs and on the walls hung rifles, pistols, tobacco pouches and some cardboard wild-animal heads. Seeing that study, I understood whom it was that Volodya had imitated when arranging his own room. We found Dubkov and Volodya playing cards. Some unfamiliar gentleman (probably insignificant judging by his meek demeanour) sat near the table attentively following the game. Dubkov himself wore a silk dressing gown and soft shoes. Volodya sat opposite him on the sofa without a coat and, judging by his reddened face and the disgruntled cursory glance he threw us as he tore himself away from his cards for a split second, was very absorbed in the game. When he saw me, he blushed even more.

207

"Well, it's your turn to deal," he said to Dubkov. I understood that he was not pleased that I had found out that he played cards. But his expression did not betray embarrassment and seemed to say to me: "Yes, I play cards and you're surprised at this because you are still young. But it isn't bad and it's even essential at our age."

I instantly felt and understood this.

Dubkov did not, however, start dealing the cards, but got to his feet, shook hands with us, gave us a seat and offered us pipes, which we refused.

"So here he is, our diplomat, the guest of honour," said Dubkov. "My goodness, he does look awfully like a colonel."

"Hm!" I mumbled, feeling my face once again dissolving into a foolishly self-satisfied smile.

I respected Dubkov as only a sixteen-year-old boy can respect a twenty-seven-year-old aide-de-camp whom all the grown-ups declared to be an exceptionally respectable young man who danced perfectly, spoke French, and who deep down despised my youth, but clearly tried to conceal this.

During the whole time I knew him and despite the respect I felt for him, God knows why, I found it hard and awkward to look him in the eye. I have since noticed that I find it awkward to look three kinds of people in the eye: those who are far worse than I am, those who are a lot better and those with whom we mutually agree not to mention things we both know to be true. Dubkov may have been better or worse than I, but he often lied and would not admit to it, and I had noticed that weakness in him and, of course, could not bring myself to tell him about it.

"Let's play one more hand," said Volodya, twitching his shoulder like Papa and shuffling the cards.

"How he insists!" said Dubkov. "We'll finish later. Oh well, let's just play one more hand then."

I watched their hands while they played. Volodya had a large attractive hand. When he held the cards, part of his thumb and the arch of his other fingers looked so much like Papa's hand that I even thought at one point that Volodya held his hand like that on purpose to look like a grown-up, but when you glanced at his face it was quite clear that he thought of nothing but the game. Dubkov, on the contrary, had small, chubby hands turned inwards, extremely nimble and with soft fingers, just the kind of hands that wear rings and belong to people who are good with their hands and who like to possess beautiful things.

Volodya must have lost, because the gentleman, after looking at his cards, remarked that he had terribly bad luck, and Dubkov took out a small notebook, wrote something down and said, after showing Volodya what he had written: "Is this right?"

"Quite right!" said Volodya, looking at the notebook with feigned absent-mindedness. "Now let's go."

Volodya drove Dubkov and Dmitry took me in his phaeton.

"What game were they playing?" I asked Dmitry.

"Piquet. It's a stupid game, and card games are generally stupid."

"And are they playing for a lot of money?"

"Not a lot, but it's bad anyway."

"Don't you play?"

"No, I gave my word not to play, but Dubkov always has to beat someone."

"That's not good on his part," I said. "I suppose Volodya doesn't play as well as he does?"

"Of course it's not good, but there is nothing particularly bad about it. Dubkov loves playing and is good at it and is still an excellent person."

"I wasn't at all thinking—"

"And you shouldn't think badly of him at all, because he's really a wonderful person. And I love him very much, despite his weaknesses."

I somehow felt that the reason Dmitry stood up so heatedly for Dubkov was because he no longer liked or respected him; yet he would not acknowledge this out of stubbornness and in order never to be accused of inconstancy. He was one of those people who love their friends for life, not so much because they continue to find them so lovable but because once they have grown fond of someone, even mistakenly, they consider it dishonourable to stop loving that person.

15

I Am Being Celebrated

DUBKOV AND VOLODYA knew everyone at Yar's by name, and everyone, from the doorkeeper to the landlord, showed them much respect. We were immediately led away to a private room and offered an amazing meal, chosen by Dubkov from the French menu. A bottle of champagne on ice, which I tried to look at as casually as possible, was ready for us. Dinner proceeded very pleasantly and cheerfully, although Dubkov as usual told the strangest stories, claiming they were true – one of them being about his grandmother being attacked by three robbers and killing them with a musketoon* (I blushed and, lowering my eyes, turned away from him) – and also despite the fact that Volodya visibly flinched every time I began to say something, which was totally unnecessary because as far as I remember I did not say anything disgraceful. When the champagne was passed round, everyone congratulated me and I crossed arms with Dubkov and then with Dmitry, drinking to our friendship and addressing each other with the familiar *ty*.* I did not know who had provided the champagne (I was later told that everyone had contributed) and I wanted to treat my friends with my own money, which I kept on fingering inside my pocket. I stealthily got hold of a ten-rouble note, called the waiter, gave him the money and said to him in a whisper, yet loud enough for everyone to hear, because they were silently looking at me, to bring us "another half-bottle of champagne please". Volodya blushed so brightly and was so twitchy as he gave me and the others an alarmed look that I felt I had made a mistake. But a bottle was brought over and we drank it all up with great pleasure. It all continued to feel very cheerful. Dubkov kept on making up new stories and Volodya also told some funny anecdotes and did it very well, which I had not at all expected from him, and we laughed a lot. The nature of Volodya's and Dubkov's humour lay in imitating and reinforcing a well-used joke: "So, have you been abroad?" one would say. "No, I've not been abroad," the other would reply, "but my brother plays the violin." They both reached such heights of perfection with this kind of nonsensical humour that they told the same anecdote, changing it to: "My brother has never played the violin either." They replied to each question in the same vein and sometimes tried to link two of the most unrelated things without even asking a question. They uttered this nonsense with such serious faces that the result was very funny. I began to understand how it worked and also wanted to say something funny, but they all looked at me nervously or tried to avoid looking at me while I spoke and the joke fell flat. Dubkov said, "You're all in a tangle, brother diplomat," but I felt so happy after the champagne and in the company of grown-ups that this remark barely touched me.

Only Dmitry, though he drank as much as we did, remained strictly serious, which somewhat checked the general merriment.

"Well, listen to me, gentlemen," said Dubkov, "after dinner we have to take our diplomat in hand. Why don't we go to Auntie's, and we can deal with him there."

"But Nekhlyudov won't go," said Volodya.

"What an insufferable drip! You are an insufferable drip!" said Dubkov, addressing him. "Come with us and you'll see what a lovely lady Auntie is."

"Not only will I not go, but I won't let him go with you either," replied Nekhlyudov, blushing.

"Who's that? The diplomat? Do you want to go, diplomat? Look, he has even begun to glow all over as soon as we mentioned Auntie."

"It's not that I won't let him," went on Nekhlyudov as he got to his feet and began to pace up and down without looking at me, "I'm advising him against it and do not wish him to go. He's still a child and if he wants to he can go by himself, without you. And you should be ashamed, Dubkov; what you're doing is wrong and you want others to do likewise."

"What's wrong with it?" said Dubkov, winking at Volodya. "That I should invite you all to have tea at Auntie's? But if you don't like us going, do as you wish. Volodya and I will go. Volodya, are you coming?"

"Hm!" agreed Volodya. "Let's drive over there and go back to my place afterwards and continue our game of piquet."

"Well, do you want to go with them or not?" said Dmitry, coming up to me.

"No," I replied, moving aside on the sofa to make room for him, and he sat down next to me. "I simply don't want to, and if you advise me not to, then I wouldn't go for the world. No," I added, "I'm telling a lie when I say I don't want to go, but I'm glad I'm not going."

"That's excellent," he said, "live according to your own rules and, best of all, don't dance to anyone else's tune."

That short argument did nothing to spoil our enjoyment at all and even added to it. Dmitry was suddenly in that gentle mood I loved most. As I later noticed more than once, the consciousness of having acted well had that effect on him. He was pleased with himself for having held me back. He cheered up enormously, asked for another

211

bottle of champagne (which was against his principles), invited a perfect stranger into our room and began to pour him a drink. He sang *Gaudeamus igitur*,* asked everyone to join in and suggested we go for a drive in the Sokolniki Gardens, whereupon Dubkov remarked that that was just too sentimental.

"Let's enjoy ourselves today," said Dmitry, smiling, "I'll get drunk for the first time in honour of his entrance to university, and so be it."

Those high spirits became him rather oddly. He was like a tutor or a kind father who is pleased with his children and has let himself go to amuse them and to prove at the same time that it is possible to have a good time in an honest and decent way. All the same, the others and myself were infected by those unexpected high spirits, especially as we had almost another half-bottle of champagne each.

It was in this pleasant frame of mind that I went out into the main room to have a cigarette that Dubkov had given me.

As I stood up I noticed that my head was spinning a little and that I had to concentrate very hard to get my legs to move and my arms to behave naturally. Otherwise, my legs would bear to one side and my arms would make all sorts of gestures. I directed all my attention on those limbs, ordered my arms to lift themselves up and button up my coat and flatten my hair (somehow my elbows were thrown up terribly high), and I ordered my feet to walk to the door, which they did, but they trod either very hard or too softly, particularly my left foot, which kept on standing on tiptoe. A voice called out: "Where are you off to? They'll bring you a candle." I guessed that the voice was Volodya's and I felt pleased at the thought that I had guessed right, but only smiled faintly in reply and walked on.

16

A Quarrel

IN THE MAIN ROOM, a short, stocky gentleman with a red moustache and dressed in civilian clothes sat eating something at a small table. Next to him sat a tall, brown-haired, clean-shaven gentleman. They were speaking French. I was embarrassed when they looked at me but still resolved to light my cigarette at the candle in front of them. Glancing away so as not to catch their eyes, I walked up to the table and began lighting my cigarette. Once it was lit, I could not help taking a look at the gentleman who was dining. His grey eyes were fixed on me malevolently. I wanted to turn away, when his red moustache began to twitch and he said in French:

"I don't like people smoking when I'm having dinner, dear sir."

I muttered something incomprehensible.

"No sir, I don't like it," the gentleman with the moustache went on sternly, giving the clean-shaven gentleman a hasty glance as though inviting him to admire the way he was about to deal with me. "And, dear sir, I don't like people who are rude enough to smoke right under my nose."

I figured out at once that the gentleman was telling me off and I initially believed that I had indeed done him some great wrong.

"I didn't think that it would disturb you," I said.

"Ah, you didn't see yourself as a boor, but I did," the gentleman shouted.

"What right have you to shout?" I said, feeling that he was being offensive and beginning to get angry myself.

"The right not to allow anyone to be rude to me, and I'll always teach lads like you a lesson. What is your surname, dear sir? And where do you live?"

I was incensed, my lips were trembling and I had difficulty catching my breath. But I still felt guilty, probably because I had drunk a lot of champagne. So I was not at all rude to the gentleman and, on the contrary, my lips very meekly spelt out my name and our address.

"My surname is Kolpikov, dear sir, and make sure you are more polite in future. We'll be seeing each other, *vous aurez de mes nouvelles*,"* he concluded, and in fact the whole conversation had been in French.

I only said: "Delighted," trying to make my voice sound firm, turned round and went back to our private room with my cigarette, which had by then gone out.

I did not tell my brother or the others what had happened, particularly as they seemed to be embroiled in some heated argument, and I sat down on my own in a corner, going over the strange incident. The words "you are a boor, dear sir" (*un mal élevé, monsieur*) kept on ringing in my ears, increasingly troubling me. I had completely sobered up. When I turned over in my mind how I had behaved in this affair, the terrible thought suddenly occurred to me that I had behaved like a coward. "What right did he have to attack me? Why did he not simply say that I was in his way? Was he guilty, in that case? When he called me a boor, why did I not say to him: 'A boor, dear sir, is the one who takes the liberty of being rude himself.' Or why did I not simply shout, 'Hold your tongue!' at him? It would have been perfect. Why did I not challenge him to a duel? No! I did none of those things and just swallowed the insult like a despicable coward."

"You are a boor, dear sir" rang more and more irritatingly in my ears. "No, it can't be left at that," I thought and rose to my feet with the firm intention to go up to that gentleman again and say something horrible, or even, if needs be, to hit him across the head with a candle-holder. I dreamt of doing the latter with the greatest pleasure, but went back very apprehensively into the main room. Fortunately Mr Kolpikov was no longer there and there was only a waiter in the room, clearing the table. I was tempted to tell the waiter about the incident and explain to him that I was not to blame in the least, but for some reason I reconsidered and returned to our room in a very sombre mood.

"What's happened to our diplomat?" said Dubkov. "Perhaps he's deciding the fate of Europe."

"Oh, just leave me alone," I said sullenly, turning away. And as I paced up and down the room, I began to reflect that Dubkov was not a good person at all. "As for those constant jokes of his and the nickname 'diplomat': there's nothing amiable about that. All he wants is to beat Volodya at cards and then go to some Auntie or other... There's nothing nice about him. Everything he says is a lie or some banality and he constantly wants to pour ridicule on everything. I think he's simply a stupid or even a bad person." I spent about five minutes with these thoughts in mind, for some reason feeling increasingly hostile towards Dubkov. The latter was not paying attention to me, which angered me further. I was even annoyed with Volodya and Dmitry for talking to him.

"You know what, gentlemen? We need to pour water over the 'diplomat'," said Dubkov suddenly, looking at me with a smile which to me seemed mocking and even treacherous. "He's in a bad way! My God, he's in a bad way!"

"You too need to have water poured over you, as you are in a bad way yourself," I replied, smiling spitefully.

That reply must have surprised Dubkov, but he turned away indifferently and went on talking to Volodya and Dmitry.

I would have tried to join in their conversation, but I felt absolutely unable to put on an act, and moved away to my corner again, where I remained until our departure.

When we had settled the bill and began to put on our overcoats, Dubkov turned to Dmitry:

"Well, where are Orestes and Pylades* off to? Home probably to converse about love; while we will be calling on sweet Auntie, and that's better than your sour friendship."

"How dare you speak so and laugh at us?" I suddenly said, going up very close to him and waving my arms about. "How dare you laugh at feelings that you are unable to understand. I won't let you. Hold your tongue!" I shouted and then stopped, not knowing what to say next and breathless with emotion. Dubkov was surprised at first; then he tried to smile and take it as a joke, but in the end, to my utter amazement, he took fright and lowered his eyes.

"I'm not at all laughing at you nor at your feelings; I just talk like that," he said meekly.

"Exactly!" I shouted, but at the same time I began to feel ashamed and also sorry for Dubkov, whose troubled red face expressed genuine distress.

"What's the matter with you?" Volodya and Dmitry both asked. "No one was trying to offend you."

"Yes, he did want to offend me."

"That's your reckless brother for you," said Dubkov, as he was leaving the room to avoid hearing what I was about to say.

I might have been inclined to rush after him and make more rude remarks, but just then that same waiter who had witnessed my incident with Kolpikov handed me my coat and I instantly calmed down. I pretended to be angry still in front of Dmitry so that my sudden change of heart would not appear odd. The next day Dubkov and I met at Volodya's and did not mention what had happened, but we addressed each other formally and it became even harder to look each other in the eye.

The memory of my quarrel with Kolpikov, whom I did not hear from the next day or any day after, remained for many years horribly vivid and painful to me. I squirmed and screamed inwardly for five years afterwards every time I remembered the unavenged insult and consoled myself when I remembered with self-satisfaction how well I had dealt with Dubkov instead. It was only much later that I began to look at the matter very differently: I recalled the quarrel with Kolpikov with amusement and was sorry about the undeserved insult I had inflicted on that "kind fellow" Dubkov.

When that same evening I told Dmitry about my adventure with Kolpikov and I described his appearance in detail, he was extremely surprised.

"That's the very man!" he said. "Just imagine, that Kolpikov is a well-known scoundrel and a cheat and above all a coward. He was expelled from his regiment by his comrades because someone slapped him in the face and he refused to fight. Where does he get the energy from?" he added, looking at me with a kind smile. "Did he not say anything besides 'boor'?"

"No," I replied, blushing.

"That's bad, but not a tragedy!" Dmitry comforted me.

It was very much later, when I calmly reflected on the incident, that I came to the conclusion that Kolpikov had probably after many years felt justified in attacking me in the presence of the clean-shaven gentleman, as a revenge for having been slapped in the face, just as I had taken my revenge for being called a "boor" on the innocent Dubkov.

17

I Prepare to Pay Some Visits

THE FIRST THOUGHT that came to me when I woke up the next morning was the incident with Kolpikov. I began to rush around the room again, muttering to myself, but there was nothing to be done. This was also my last day in Moscow and, at Papa's bidding, I had to pay certain calls which he had listed in writing for me. On Papa's part this was not so much concern for our morals or our education as for our maintaining the right social connections. In his hurried, uneven handwriting Papa had written on the paper that I should visit: 1) Prince Ivan Ivanovich *without fail*, 2) the Ivins *without fail*, 3) Prince

Michael, 4) Princess Nekhlyudova and the Valakhins if there was time and of course also the university administrator, rector and professors.

Dmitry advised me against making those last calls, saying that not only were they unnecessary but even rather inappropriate, but the rest all had to be done that day. I was particularly apprehensive about the first two visits, next to which Papa had written "without fail". Prince Ivan Ivanych was an elderly full general, and he was wealthy and lived alone. Accordingly I, a sixteen-year-old student, would have to meet him on direct terms and I foresaw that this would not reflect well on me. The Ivins were also wealthy and their father was some important general in the civil service* who had visited us only once while Grandmother was still alive. After Grandmother's death I noticed that the youngest Ivin avoided us and seemed to give himself airs. The older brother, as I heard on the grape vine, had already finished his course on jurisprudence and had a position in St Petersburg; the second brother, Sergei, whom I once adored, was a big stout cadet in the *Corps des Pages*,* also in St Petersburg.

In my youth I not only disliked having to associate with people who considered themselves above me, but I found such relationships unbearably painful because of a constant fear of being insulted and having to exert all my mental powers to prove my independence to them. However, if I was not going to follow Papa's last order, then I would have to make amends by fulfilling the first ones on the list. I was walking around the room examining my clothes, hat and sword, laid out on chairs, and was about to get ready to leave when the old man Grap called in to congratulate me, bringing along his son Ilyenka. Grap the father was a Russified German, unbearably cloying and ingratiating and very often drunk. He mostly came to us with some request and Papa sometimes received him in his study, but he was never invited to dine with us. The way he begged and abased himself went so well with his superficial good nature and familiarity in our house that everyone gave him great credit for his apparent devotion to us, but for some reason I did not like him and I always felt ashamed for him when he spoke.

I was very put out by the arrival of these visitors and did not attempt to hide my displeasure. I was so used to looking down on Ilyenka and he was so used to considering it our right to do so that I was not too pleased that he was now a student like myself. It seemed to me that he even felt a little ashamed in front of me at finding us on an equal footing. I greeted them coldly and did not offer them a seat because I was embarrassed to do so, believing that they could have sat down without my invitation, and I ordered my carriage to be prepared. Ilyenka was a kind, very honest young man and far from stupid, but he was one of those prone to extreme moods seemingly without reason, when he would either be very tearful or burst out laughing or take offence at the slightest triviality, and this time he appeared to be in that latter frame of mind. He did not utter a word, gave his father and me a surly look and it was only when addressed that he smiled the constrained, resigned smile with which he had become accustomed to covering up his feelings, and in particular the sense of shame for his father that he must have experienced in our presence.

"So, Nikolai Petrovich," said the old man, following me round the room as I was getting dressed, and slowly and deferentially turning a silver snuffbox, a gift from Grandmother, between his thick fingers. "As soon as I heard from my son that you had passed your exams with such excellent results – indeed your intellect is known to us all – I immediately ran over here to congratulate you. I used to carry you on my shoulders, and God sees how I love you like my own, and my Ilyenka wanted to come over so much. He too feels quite at home here."

Meanwhile Ilyenka sat silently by the window as though examining my three-cornered hat and, barely audibly, muttered something under his breath.

"Well, I wanted to ask you, Nikolai Petrovich," the old man went on, "did my Ilyenka pass his exams well? He told me that he'll be following the same course as you; so please do not abandon him and do keep an eye on him and give him advice."

"He passed his exams very well indeed," I replied, glancing at Ilyenka, who stopped moving his lips and blushed when he felt my eyes on him.

"And could he spend the day with you?" said the old man with such a timid smile, as though he was afraid of me. He kept so close to me all the time that wherever I moved to, I could not get away even for an instant from the wine and tobacco fumes which he oozed. I was annoyed at him for putting me in such a false position with his son and for taking my mind away from my very important task just then, that of getting dressed, and above all the smell of alcohol which followed me disturbed me so much that I very coldly said to him that I could not spend time with Ilyenka because I would be out all day.

"But you wanted to go to your sister's, Father," said Ilyenka, smiling but not looking at me, "and I have things to attend to as well."

I felt even more annoyed and embarrassed, and to make amends for my refusal I hastened to explain that I would not be at home because I had to pay a visit to *Prince* Ivan Ivanych, and to *Princess* Kornakova, and to Ivin, the one who held such an important post, and that I would most probably dine at *Princess* Nekhlyudova's. I thought that once they realized how important the people I was planning to visit were, they could no longer lay claims on me. As they prepared to leave, I invited Ilyenka to call in another time, but he just mumbled something and smiled stiffly. It was clear that he would never set foot in my house again.

After they left, I set off on my visits. Volodya, whom that morning I had asked to go with me so that I would not feel so awkward alone, had refused, on the pretext that it would be just too sentimental to have two "brothers" travelling together in "one small carriage".

18

The Valakhins

S O I SET OFF ON MY OWN. I first visited the Valakhins as they lived closest, on the Sivtsev Vrazhek.* I had not seen Sonyechka for about three years, and of course my love for her had gone long before, but a vivid and poignant memory of that former childhood love survived in my heart. During those three years, I had sometimes happened to remember her with such force and clarity that I would shed tears and feel myself in love again, but that would only last a few minutes and did not often recur.

I knew that Sonyechka had lived abroad with her mother for about two years and the story went that they had been involved in a stagecoach accident when it overturned, that Sonyechka's face had been cut by glass from the carriage and that she had apparently lost much of her beauty as a result. On the way to their house I vividly remembered the Sonyechka I had known and wondered how I would find her now. After her two-year stay abroad I imagined her to be extremely tall for some reason, with a beautiful figure, and to be serious and dignified, but also uncommonly charming. My imagination refused to picture her face disfigured by scars; on the contrary, having heard of a passionate lover who stayed true to his love despite some disfiguring pockmarks, I tried to think of myself as in love with Sonyechka so that I would be able to stay true to her despite her scars. As I drove up to the Valakhins, I was in fact not in love at all but, having stirred up old loving memories, I was well prepared to fall in love and very much wanted to, all the more so since I had long felt embarrassed that I had fallen so behind my friends, all of whom were in love.

The Valakhins lived in a small, neat little wooden house that you entered from the courtyard. At the ring of a little bell, which at the time was quite a rarity in Moscow, a very small, well-dressed boy opened the door. He was either unable or did not want to tell me whether the family was at home and, leaving me to stand alone in the dark entrance hall, he ran off into an even darker corridor.

I remained alone for a long time in the dark hall, which had another closed door, besides the front door and the one leading to the corridor. Part of me was surprised at the gloomy aspect of the house and part of me supposed that it had to be so with people who had been abroad. After about five minutes, the door to the reception room was opened from inside by the same boy, who led me to a neat but modest drawing room, into which Sonyechka came in after me.

She was seventeen. She was very short and very thin with a sallow, unhealthy complexion. There were no signs of facial scars, but her lovely prominent eyes and her bright, good-natured, cheerful smile were the same I had known and loved in my childhood. I had not at all expected her to be like this and could therefore not immediately give vent to those feelings I had prepared on the road. She offered me her hand the English way and that was as rare at the time as the little doorbell, and she openly squeezed my hand and made me sit next to her on the sofa.

"Oh, I'm so happy to see you, dear Nicolas," she said, looking into my face with such a genuine expression of pleasure that in the words "dear Nicolas" I read only a friendly tone rather than a patronizing one. To my surprise she was, since having been abroad, even more natural, sweet and warm in her manner than before. I noticed two small scars near her nose and on her eyebrow, but her wonderful eyes and her smile were completely true to my memories and sparkled as before.

"How you have changed!" she said. "You have really grown up. Well, and I, how do you find me?"

"Oh, I would not have recognized you," I replied, although at that very moment I thought that I would have recognized her anywhere. I was in that carefree, happy mood of five years ago, when I had danced the *Grossvater* with her at Grandmother's ball.

"So, have I become a lot less attractive?" she asked, shaking her head.

"No, not at all; you've grown a little, you've become older," I hastily replied. "On the contrary… and even—"

"Well, it doesn't matter a bit, and do you remember our dances and our games, Saint-Jérôme and Madame Dorat?" (I did not remember any Madame Dorat; she was evidently carried away and confused by the pleasure of childhood memories.) "Oh, it was a glorious time," she went on, and that same smile, even sweeter than the one I had carried in my head, and those same eyes sparkled before me. While she was talking, I managed to fully absorb the situation I was in at that very moment and decided that in that very moment I was in love. And the instant I came to that conclusion, my happy, carefree mood vanished, a kind of mist cloaked everything before me, even her eyes and her smile, and I became embarrassed, blushed and lost my power of speech.

"Now times have altered," she went on, sighing and raising her eyebrows a little, "everything has considerably changed for the worse, and so have we, don't you think, Nicolas?"

I could not reply and looked at her speechless.

"Where are the Ivins now, the ones we knew then, and the Kornakovs? Do you remember?" she continued, looking a little curiously at my frightened, blushing face. "What a glorious time that was."

I still could not respond.

I was for the moment drawn out of that painful situation by the entrance into the room of Valakhina, Sonyechka's mother. I rose to my feet, bowed and my speech came back to me. But with the arrival of her mother a strange change came over Sonyechka. Suddenly all her cheerfulness and her warmth disappeared, even her smile changed and, except for her height, she suddenly became that young lady whom I had expected to find in the first place, just returned from abroad.

That change seemed to come from nowhere; her mother smiled as pleasantly as in the past and her gestures expressed the same gentleness as before. Valakhina sat on a large armchair and pointed to the seat next to her. She said something in English to her daughter and the latter immediately left the room, which was an even greater relief to me. Valakhina asked me about my family, my brother, my father, then she told me about her grief – the loss of her husband – and finally, when she felt that there was nothing more to talk about, she looked at me silently, as if to say, "If you get up now and bow and leave then you will do very well, my dear," but a strange thing happened to me. Sonyechka returned with some needlework, went to sit in the other corner of the room and I felt her looking at me. While Valakhina told me about the loss of her husband, I remembered again that I was in love and thought that her mother had probably guessed as much, I was once more prey to an attack of timidity so severe that I did not feel capable of moving a single limb naturally. I knew that in order to get up and leave the room I would need to think about where to place my foot, what to do with my head, with my hand, in short, I felt almost the same way I had the previous day after drinking half a bottle of champagne. I felt that I could not cope with all that and would not be able to get to my feet, and indeed I was physically incapable of doing so. Valakhina was no doubt amazed when she saw my bright-red face and total immobility, but I decided that it was better to remain seated in that stupid position than to risk getting up and leaving looking somewhat ridiculous. So I sat for quite a long time waiting for some unforeseen opportunity to get me out of the situation. This presented itself in the person of an insignificant young man who came into the room as would a servant and bowed politely to me. Valakhina got up and excused herself, saying that she needed to talk to her *homme d'affaires*,* and looked at me with a puzzled expression, as if to say: "If you want to stay sitting for ever, I won't drive you out." I somehow made a huge effort and got to my feet, but I was not able to bow and, as I walked out accompanied by the commiserating glances of mother and daughter, I tripped over a chair that was not at all in my way, and did so simply because all my attention was focused on not tripping over the rug under my feet. Once in the fresh air however – after fidgeting and mumbling so loudly that even Kuzma enquired several times whether I wanted something – that feeling soon vanished. I began to reflect quite calmly on my love for Sonyechka and about her relationship with her mother, which had appeared odd to me. When I later told my father how I had noticed that Valakhina's relationship with her daughter was not a good one, he said:

"Yes, she torments her, poor thing, with her terrible stinginess. And it's strange," he added with a rather stronger feeling than you would simply show for a relative, "what a charming, dear, wonderful woman she used to be! I can't understand why she has changed so much. Did you see some kind of secretary of hers, when you were there? What a strange thing for a Russian lady to have a secretary," he said angrily moving away.

"Yes, I did see him," I said.

"Is he at least good-looking?"

"No, not at all."

"Incomprehensible," said Papa and he twitched his shoulder angrily and coughed.

"So now I am in love," I thought as I rode on in my *droshky*.

19

The Kornakovs

THE SECOND VISIT EN ROUTE was to the Kornakovs. They lived on the first floor of a large house on the Arbat. The staircase was extremely grand and in good trim, but not sumptuous. Thin striped rugs lay everywhere, held down by very well-burnished brass rods, but there were no flowers or mirrors anywhere. The reception room with its brightly polished floor, which I crossed to get to the drawing room, was also starkly and neatly decorated. Everything was gleaming and looked solid, though not quite new, and there were no pictures or curtains, and not a single ornament anywhere to be seen. Some of the princesses were in the drawing room: they sat so stiffly and with empty hands that it was instantly noticeable that they must sit very differently when they had no visitors.

"Maman will soon be here," the eldest Princess said, coming to sit by me. For a quarter of an hour that Princess chatted with me so freely and easily that the conversation never flagged for an instant. It was all too obvious that she was entertaining me and I did not like her for that reason. She told me among other things that their brother Stepan, whom they called "Étienne" and who had been sent to the Junker School,* had already been promoted to officer. When she spoke about her brother and particularly when she said that he had joined the hussars against his mother's will, she pulled a frightened face and all the younger princesses who were sitting silently also pulled frightened faces. When she spoke of Grandmother's death, she pulled a sad face and all the younger princesses did the same. When she recalled how I had struck Saint-Jérôme and how they had led me out of the room, she laughed, showing her bad teeth and all the princesses began to laugh, showing their bad teeth.

Their mother came in. She was the same small, wizened woman with darting eyes and a habit of looking round at others while talking to you. She took hold of my hand and raised her own hand to my lips for me to kiss her, something I would not have done, assuming it to be unnecessary.

"How glad I am to see you," she said in her usual garrulous manner, looking round at her daughters. "Oh, how he looks like his Maman, don't you think so, Lise?"

Lise agreed, although I knew that there was not the slightest likeness between my mother and me.

"And how grown up you've become! And my Étienne, you remember him, he's your second cousin… no, not second, how does it go, Lise? My mother was Varvara Dmitriyevna, the daughter of Dmitry Nikolayich, and your grandmother was Natalya Nikolayevna."

"So he's a third cousin, Maman," said the eldest Princess.

"Oh, you're mixing everything up," her mother shouted angrily at her, "not a third cousin at all, but *issu de germains*,* that's your relationship with my little Étienne. He's already an officer, did you know? The only bad thing is that he has too much freedom. You young people still need to be kept in hand, that's certain! You won't get angry with me, your old aunt, will you, for telling you the truth. I was very strict with Étienne and I feel that that's what's needed.

"Now, this is how we're related," she went on, "Prince Ivan Ivanych is my uncle and he was your mother's uncle. So it follows that your mother and I were first cousins, no, second cousins. Yes, that's it. Now tell me: have you been to see Prince Ivan Ivanych?"

I told her that I had not yet been, but was planning to go that same day.

"Oh, how is it possible!" she exclaimed. "That should have been your first visit. You do know that Prince Ivan is like a father to you. He has no children, so you and my children are his only heirs. You must show him respect for his age and his position in society and everything else. I know that you young people of this generation don't think much of kinship and you don't like old people, but you listen to me, your old aunt, because I love you and I loved your mother and I also loved and respected your grandmother very very much. Yes, do go to him without fail."

I said that I would go without fail, and as the visit had lasted quite long enough for me, I got to my feet and wanted to leave, but she held me back.

"No, wait a moment. Where is your father, Lise? Do ask him to come here; he will be so glad to see you," she went on, turning to me.

Prince Mikhailo did indeed come in within a couple of minutes. He was a short, stocky gentleman, very scruffily dressed, unshaven and with such a kind of uninterested expression on his face that it made him almost look stupid. He was not glad to see me at all, at least he gave no semblance of being so. But his wife, of whom he was apparently very much afraid, said to him:

"Isn't it true that Voldemar" (she had clearly forgotten my name) "is so like his Maman?" and she made such a sign with her eyes that the Prince, probably guessing what she was after, came up to me and, with the most impassive and even discontented look, offered me his unshaven cheek, which I had to kiss.

"You're not even dressed yet and you need to go out," the Princess began to say immediately afterwards with an angry tone she was clearly in the habit of using with members of her household. "You'll make people cross with you again and once again have them turn against you."

"I'm going, I'm going, my dear," said Prince Mikhailo and left the room. I bowed and also left.

This was the first time I had heard that we were Prince Ivan Ivanych's heirs, and I was unpleasantly affected by that news.

20

The Ivins

I FOUND IT EVEN HARDER to think of the next unavoidable visit. But on the way to the Prince I had to call in at the Ivins. They lived on Tverskaya Street, in a very large attractive house. It was not without some apprehension that I went in at the main entrance, where a doorman stood with a mace.

I asked him whether anybody was at home.

"Who do you need to see? The General's son is at home," the doorman said.

"And the General himself?" I asked boldly.

"I'll have to announce you. Who should I say is calling?" said the doorman, and he rang a bell. A pair of footman's legs in gaiters appeared on the stairs. I felt so shy for some reason that I told the footman not to announce me, since I would first go and see the General's son. As I walked up the large staircase, I felt that I had become terribly small (not in the metaphorical sense, but in the real sense of the word). I had experienced the same feeling when my carriage reached the main gate, as though the *droshky*, the horse and the coachman had become tiny. When I came into his room, the General's son was lying asleep on the sofa with an open book before him. His tutor, Herr Frost, who still lived with them, followed me into the room with his showy step and woke his pupil up. Ivin did not give any sign of particular joy at seeing me and I noticed that he looked at my eyebrows when he talked to me. Although he was very civil, I felt that he was entertaining me the same way the Princess had done and that he was not particularly drawn to me. He had no need for my acquaintance, as he probably had his own circle of friends. I mostly imagined all this because he looked at my eyebrows. In short, he treated me, as unpleasant as it is for me to acknowledge it, in almost the same way that I had treated Ilyenka. I became rather irritated and was quick to catch any glance of Ivin's; when he caught Frost's eye, I interpreted it as: "Why has he come to see us?"

After a brief chat, Ivin told me that his father and mother were home and asked me whether I wanted to go and see them with him.

"I'll get dressed right away," he added, going into the next room, although he was well dressed as it was in a new frock coat and white waistcoat. A few minutes later he came in wearing his uniform, buttoned up all the way, and we went downstairs together. The front rooms we passed through were extremely large, with high ceilings, and sumptuously decorated; there was marble and gold, there were things wrapped in muslin and others made of glass. At the same moment that we entered a small room past the drawing room, Ivina, the lady of the house, came in through another door. She greeted me in a very friendly and warm manner, offered me a seat beside her and asked after all the members of my family with interest.

I had only seen her about twice before in passing, and now looked at her carefully and liked her very much. She was tall, thin, very white and looked constantly doleful and worn out. She had a sad but extremely kindly smile; her large tired eyes were slightly crossed, which gave her an even sadder and more appealing expression. Although she was not hunched up when sitting down, her whole body seemed to sag, and all her movements flowed downwards. She spoke listlessly, but the sound of her voice and her indistinct pronunciation of her Rs and Ls were very pleasing. She did not try to entertain me. She clearly found a melancholy interest in my answers concerning my family, as though, when listening to me, she sadly remembered better times. Her son went off somewhere, and she silently looked at me for a minute or two before suddenly bursting into tears. I sat in front of her and could not imagine what I should say or do. She continued to cry without looking at me. At first I felt sorry for her, and then I thought: "Should I comfort her and how should I go about this?" and I finally became annoyed at her for putting me into such an awkward position. "Do I really look so pathetic?" I thought. "Or is she doing this on purpose to find out how I would react in such a situation? It would be awkward to leave now, as though I was running away from her tears," I went on thinking. I turned on my chair to remind her at least of my presence.

"Oh, how foolish I am!" she said, glancing at me and attempting a smile. "There are days like this one when you cry for no reason."

She began to look for a handkerchief near her on the sofa and suddenly began to cry even harder.

"Oh my God! How ridiculous this constant crying is. I loved your mother so, we were such friends... and..."

She found a handkerchief, covered her face with it and went on crying. And so I found myself once more in an awkward situation, and this went on for rather a long time. I was annoyed and even more sorry for her. Her tears seemed sincere and I kept on thinking that she was crying not so much about my mother as because she was not happy right now, and those former times had been much better. I do not know how all this would have ended had young Ivin not come in to say that her husband had asked for her. She got to her feet and was about to leave, when her husband himself came in. He was a small, sturdy gentleman with bushy black eyebrows and a complete head of short-cut grey hair and an extremely stern, firm set to his mouth.

I got up and bowed to him, but Ivin, who wore three stars on his green tailcoat, not only ignored my bow but also hardly looked at me; I suddenly felt that I was not a person but some object unworthy of attention – an armchair or a small window – or if I was a person, then that I was one completely indistinguishable from a chair or a window.

"You have still not written to the Countess, my dear," he said to his wife in French with an impassive but firm look on his face.

"Goodbye, Monsieur Irtenyev," said his wife, suddenly nodding her head haughtily and looking at my eyebrows as her son had done. I bowed to her once more and to her husband, and again my bow made no more impact on old Ivin than a small window being opened or shut. The student Ivin accompanied me to the door, however, and told me on the way that he was transferring to St Petersburg University, because his father had been offered a position there (he named some very important position).

"Well, whatever Papa wants," I muttered to myself as I took a seat in the *droshky*, "but I will never set foot here again. That cry-baby weeps when she sets eyes on me as if I were some unfortunate creature and that swine Ivin does not bow back; I'll give him…" What I would give him, I really did not know, but it sounded good.

Later I would often have to endure Papa urging me that it was essential to cultivate their acquaintance and that I could not expect that a man of Ivin's position would have anything to do with a mere boy like me. But for a long time I stood firm in my resolve.

21

Prince Ivan Ivanych

"NOW TO NIKITSKAYA STREET for our last visit," I said to Kuzma, and we drove off to Prince Ivan Ivanych's house.

Having just gone through the ordeal of several visits, I would normally have gained some self-confidence and would have driven up to the Prince's house feeling quite calm, but I suddenly recalled Princess Kornakova's words declaring that I was his heir, and when I spotted two carriages by the front porch, I felt my former shyness return.

I thought that the old doorman who opened the door for me and the footman who took my coat and the three ladies and two gentlemen whom I found in the drawing room, and above all Prince Ivan Ivanych himself, who sat on the sofa in civilian dress – I thought that they all looked at me as an heir and therefore with some hostility. The Prince showed great affection towards me and kissed me, that is to say he put his thin soft cold lips against my cheek for just a second. He asked after my studies, my plans, he joked with me, asking if I still wrote verses like those I had written for Grandmother's name day, and added that I should stay for dinner. But the more affectionate he was the more I felt he was only trying to be kind to cover up the fact that he disliked my being his heir. He had a habit, resulting from having a mouth full of false teeth, of raising his upper lip towards his nose after speaking, making a slight wheezing sound as though drawing his lip into his nostrils. When he did this, I kept on thinking that he was saying to himself: "Little boy, little boy, I don't need you to tell me that you are my heir, my heir," and so on.

As children we used to call Prince Ivan Ivanych "Grandfather", but now, as his heir, my tongue refused to say Grandfather to him. Yet to say "Your Excellency", as did one of the other gentlemen there, felt humiliating and as a result I tried not to call him anything throughout the conversation. But I was most disturbed by an elderly Princess who was also an heiress and who lived in his house. Throughout dinner, when I sat next to her, I assumed that she did not speak to me because she hated me for also being the Prince's heir and that the Prince ignored our side of the table because the Princess and I, as his heirs, were both equally repulsive to him.

"You won't believe how unpleasant I found it," I said to Dmitry that same evening, wanting to boast to him about my feeling of revulsion at being an heir (I felt it was a noble sentiment), "how unpleasant it was to spend two whole hours with the Prince. He is an excellent man and he was very affectionate towards me," I said, wishing equally to convince my friend that everything I was saying was not because I had felt humbled before the Prince. "But," I went on, "the thought that I might be seen in the same way as the Princess, who lives with him and who plays up to him, is a terrible thought. He's a wonderful old gentleman and extremely kind and sensitive with everyone and it is painful to watch him *mistreat* the Princess. That wretched money spoils all relationships! You know, I think that it would be much better to simply have it out with the Prince," I said, "tell him that I respect him as a man, but that I have no thoughts of inheritance, beg him not to leave me anything and say that I will only visit him under those circumstances."

Dmitry did not burst out laughing when I said this; on the contrary, he became quite thoughtful and remained silent for a few minutes; then he said to me:

"You know what? You're wrong. Either you mustn't in any way assume that they think of you in the same way as they do that Princess of yours, or, if you must, then go further: assume that you know what they think of you and that those thoughts are so alien to you that you despise them, and on that basis you'll do nothing. You assume that they assume that you assume… in a word," he added, feeling that he was getting entangled in his own argument, "it would be far better not to assume any of this."

My friend was absolutely right. Only much later did I become convinced from experience how harmful it was to think and even worse to say lots of things which may seem noble but which should be concealed for ever in a person's heart. I was also convinced that noble words were rarely compatible with noble deeds. I am sure that once an intention has been put into words it is difficult and for the most part impossible to carry it out. But how do you resist giving way to such self-satisfied youthful outbursts? You remember them and only much later regret them in the same way that you regret not having resisted plucking an unopened flower and seeing it later withered and trampled upon on the ground.

Having just told my friend Dmitry that money spoils relationships, I promptly borrowed twenty-five roubles in notes from him for the journey, which he offered me before our departure for the country the following morning, when it transpired that I had squandered all my money on various pictures and Turkish pipes. I remained in his debt for a very long time afterwards.

22

An Intimate Conversation with My Friend

THIS CONVERSATION took place in the phaeton on our way to Kuntsevo. Dmitry had dissuaded me from going to visit his mother in the morning, but came to pick me up after dinner to go and spend all evening, and even overnight, at his dacha where his family were staying. It was only when we left town behind us, when the mud-patched streets and the intolerable deafening sound of the main road were replaced by wide views of fields and the soft squeaking of wheels on the dusty road, and as the spring fragrance in the air and the wide expanses embraced me on all sides, only then did I come to my senses a little, after two days of complete confusion brought on by the wide variety of new impressions and the sensation of freedom. Dmitry was communicative and gentle. He did not adjust his cravat or twitch nervously or frown. I was pleased at having expressed those noble feelings and assumed that because of them he had forgiven me wholeheartedly for that shameful business with Kolpikov and that he did not despise me for it. So we chatted happily together about many intimate matters, which you cannot talk about at just any time. Dmitry told me about his family, whom I did not yet know, about his mother, his aunt, his sister and the one Volodya and Dubkov regarded as my friend's flame and called "the redhead". He spoke of his mother with some kind of cold solemn praise, as though to forestall any further comment on that subject. He spoke ecstatically, if with slight condescension, about his aunt. He said very little about his sister, as though he was ashamed of mentioning her to me, but he spoke with animation about the "redhead", who was in fact called Lyubov Sergeyevna and who was a rather older spinster who lived in the Nekhlyudov household through some family connection.

"Yes, she is an amazing young woman," he said, blushing with embarrassment and at the same time looking me boldly in the eye, "she's not actually young, even rather old, and not at all pretty, but it is such stupidity, such nonsense, to love beauty! I can't understand it, it is so stupid" (he said this as though he had just discovered the newest and most remarkable truth) "and what a soul she has, and a heart as well as principles... I'm sure there is not another woman like her in the world today." I don't know from whom Dmitry had taken over the habit of saying that "rarely could anything good be found in the world today", but he loved repeating that phrase and somehow it suited him.

"I only fear," he went on calmly, having thus completely demolished anyone who would be stupid enough to love beauty, "I fear that you'll not understand her or get to know her quickly enough: she is modest and even reticent and she doesn't like showing off her wonderful amazing qualities. My mother, for instance, whom you'll see is a splendid, clever woman, has known Lyubov Sergeyevna for several years and yet she cannot and does not want to try to understand her. Even yesterday... I'll tell you why I was not in a good mood when you asked me. The day before yesterday Lyubov Sergeyevna wanted me to go with her to visit Ivan Yakovlevich* – you've probably heard of Ivan Yakovlevich, who appears to be insane, but is in fact a remarkable man. I have to tell you that Lyubov Sergeyevna is extremely religious and she understands Ivan Yakovlevich perfectly. She often goes to see him, chats with him and gives him money for the poor, which she herself has earned. You'll see, she's an amazing woman. So I went with her to visit Ivan Yakovlevich, and was very grateful to her that I had the chance to see that remarkable man. But my mother doesn't want to understand and regards all this as superstition. And last night I quarrelled with Mother for the first time in my life and it was rather heated," he concluded, fitfully twitching his neck, as though remembering what the quarrel had felt like.

"Well, and what do you think? I mean, when you imagine what's ahead... or perhaps you talk to her about how things will turn out, what the outcome will be of your love or friendship?" I asked him, wanting to distract him from the unpleasant memory.

"You mean if I'm thinking of marrying her?" he asked, blushing again, but boldly facing me as he turned to me.

"This is perfectly fine," I thought, trying to calm down, "we are *grown-ups*, two friends travelling in a phaeton discussing our future. Anyone would enjoy overhearing and looking at us."

"Why not?" he went on after I had said yes. "You see, my aim in life, as it is for every sensible person, is to be happy and as good as possible, and if she were willing, when I'm quite independent, I'll be happier and a better person with her than with the greatest beauty in the world."

Immersed in these conversations, we did not notice that we had arrived in Kuntsevo nor that the sky had clouded over and it was going to rain. The sun was already quite low to the right above the old trees of the Kuntsevo garden. Half of its bright-red circle was hidden by a grey, faintly translucent storm cloud; from the other half sprays of splintered fiery rays burst forth, which with startling brightness lit up the old trees in the garden whose thick green crowns gleamed motionless against a brightly lit patch of light-blue sky. The glow from that part of the sky sharply contrasted with the heavy purple storm cloud lying low just in front of us, above a young birch grove visible on the horizon.

A little further to the right, behind trees and shrubs, you could already spot different-coloured roofs of small dachas, some of which reflected the glowing sun rays and others which assumed the gloomy character of the other half of the sky. To the left a still, deep-blue pond appeared, surrounded by small, pale-green crack willows darkly reflected in its lustreless, seemingly swollen surface. Halfway up a hill, beyond the pond, stretched dark fallow land, and the straight line of a bright-green boundary strip, cutting right across it, disappeared into the distance running into the thundery leaden horizon. On either side of the soft road, along which the phaeton rocked evenly to and fro, juicy tufts of rye grew sharp green, here and there beginning to form stalks. The air was completely still and smelt fresh; the green of the leaves, trees and rye was unmoving and extraordinarily fresh and bright. It seemed as though each leaf and each grass shoot lived its own individual full and happy life. I noticed a dark path near the road winding its way through dark-green rye that had already grown to more than a quarter of its full size. For some reason that path reminded me very strongly of our country village and, following some strange train of thought, my mind went from the country to a strong image of Sonyechka and to the fact that I was in love with her.

In spite of my great friendship for Dmitry and the pleasure his openness gave me, I no longer wanted to know anything about his feelings or intentions towards Lyubov Sergeyevna, but very much wished to tell him about my love for Sonyechka, which seemed to me to be on a much higher plane. But for some reason I could not bring myself to tell him my plans: how nice it would be when, having married Sonyechka, I would live in the country, how I would have little children crawling on the floor who would call me Papa and how happy I would be when he, with his wife Lyubov Sergeyevna, came to visit in their travelling clothes... Instead of which I pointed at the setting sun and said: "Dmitry, look, how delightful!"

Dmitry did not respond, clearly displeased that in answer to his confession, one he had probably found difficult to make, I drew his attention to nature, which on the whole left him rather indifferent. Nature made a very different impact on him than on me; it was not its beauty that impressed him as much as its being a diversion. He liked it more with his mind than with his heart.

"I'm very happy," I said to him next, without taking any notice of the fact that he was clearly preoccupied with his own thoughts and totally oblivious to what I might say. "I must have told you about a young lady I was in love with when still a child; I saw her today," I went on enthusiastically, "and now I'm definitely in love with her..."

And I told him about my love and all my plans for my future wedded bliss, although he continued to look uninterested. And strangely, no sooner had I told him in detail about the full strength of my feeling than I felt that feeling beginning to diminish.

A shower caught up with us as we were turning into the birch avenue leading up to the dacha. But we did not get wet. I only noticed that it was raining because several drops fell on my nose and hands and because something plashed on the young sticky birches which, hanging their curling branches without stirring, seemed delighted to receive those fresh clear drops, a delight they expressed by exuding a strong scent that filled the avenue. We climbed out of the carriage to run quickly across the garden to the house, but right at the entrance to the house we ran into four ladies. Two of them carried some needlework, one had a book and another a dog and they arrived with hasty steps from the opposite direction. Dmitry introduced me at once to his mother, sister, auntie and Lyubov Sergeyevna. They stopped for a moment, but the shower was turning into a steady drizzle.

"Let's go to the veranda and you can introduce him to us again," said the one whom I took to be Dmitry's mother, and we went up the stairs with the ladies.

23

The Nekhlyudovs

OUT OF ALL OF THAT COMPANY I was initially most struck by Lyubov Sergeyevna, who climbed the stairs behind the others, carrying a fluffy little white lapdog in her arms and wearing thick knitted slippers. She stopped a couple of times and turned to look at me closely and straight away after that she kissed her little dog. She was not pretty at all. She had red hair and was thin, short and a little lopsided. What made her ugly face even uglier was her strange hairstyle, with a parting to one side (one of those hairdos bald women devise for themselves). As much as I tried for my friend's sake, I could not find a single attractive feature in her. Even her brown eyes, although they had a kindly look, were too small and insipid and definitely not attractive; even her hands – always a telling feature – though neither large nor badly shaped, were red and rough.

When I followed them to the terrace, each of the ladies – with the exception of Varyenka, Dmitry's sister, who only looked at me closely with big dark-grey eyes – said a few words to me before taking up their needlework again, and Varyenka began to read aloud from a book she held on her lap, marking her place with her finger.

Dmitry's mother, Princess Marya Ivanovna, was a tall svelte woman of about forty. She could have appeared older with her greying curls, openly displayed beneath her bonnet, but her fresh, extremely delicate, almost wrinkle-free face and the lively, cheerful gleam of her large eyes made her seem much younger. She had wide brown eyes; her lips were too thin and somewhat stern; her nose was fairly straight if slightly bent to the left. She wore no rings on her hands, which were large, almost masculine, with beautiful long fingers. She wore a dark-blue high-necked dress tightly hugging her slender, still youthful waist, which she clearly liked to show off. She sat extremely upright sewing some garment. When I came onto the veranda, she took my hand

and drew me to her as though wishing to look me over more closely; glancing at me with that same slightly cool and frank look her son had, she said that she had long known me from Dmitry's stories, and invited me to stay overnight and into the next day to become better acquainted with everybody.

"Do whatever you like, don't be shy with us and we won't be with you either; go for walks, read, listen or sleep, if that's what you fancy," she added.

Sofya Ivanovna was an old spinster and the Princess's younger sister, although she looked older. She had that particular bulging type of physique that you encounter only in short, very stout old spinsters wearing corsets as though her robust good health strained upwards with such force that it threatened any moment to choke her. Her short podgy little arms were not able to meet below the waist where the bodice curved outwards, and she could not even see that overstretched curve itself.

There was a strong family likeness between the sisters, although Princess Marya Ivanovna had dark hair and dark eyes while Sofya Ivanovna was blonde and had big blue eyes that were lively and at the same time (which is very rare) serene. They had the same expression, the same nose, the same lips; only Sofya Ivanovna's nose and lips were slightly thicker and slanted to the right when she smiled, whilst her sister's slanted to the left. Sofya Ivanovna, judging by her clothes and her hairstyle, was still trying to appear younger than her age and would not have put her grey curls on display had she had any. Her glance and her manner with me seemed very haughty at first and this unsettled me, whereas I felt, on the contrary, completely relaxed with the Princess. It was perhaps her corpulence, and a certain likeness to the portrait of Catherine the Great which had struck me, that gave her that haughty look in my eyes. I completely lost my nerve when she stared at me saying, "The friends of our friends are our friends." When, after uttering those words, she fell silent and, opening her mouth, gave a heavy sigh, I calmed down and suddenly changed my mind about her completely. It was probably her stoutness that caused her to sigh heavily after uttering only a few words, slightly opening her mouth and rolling her big blue eyes a little. In this way she expressed such a sweet, good nature that, after that sigh, I lost all fear of her and even liked her very much. She had beautiful eyes, a pleasant, ringing voice and even those rounded curves, in that time of my youth, did not seem without beauty.

It was Lyubov Sergeyevna's turn, as a friend of a friend (I assumed), to say something very friendly and heartfelt, and she even looked at me for quite a long time in silence as though undecided whether what she was planning to say would perhaps sound too friendly. She interrupted that silence only to ask me what faculty I was in. Then she stared at me again for quite a long time, clearly wavering over whether to say or not to say those heartfelt friendly words; I, noticing her hesitation, willed her with my eyes to speak out, but all she said was: "Apparently there is little interest these days in studying the sciences at university," and she called her little dog Suzette to her.

That entire evening, Lyubov Sergeyevna said things that on the whole had no bearing on the subject in hand, nor on each other, but I had such faith in Dmitry and he looked so solicitously now at me, now at her, all evening with an expression of: "Well, and what do you think?" that although in my heart convinced that there was nothing special about Lyubov Sergeyevna, I was, as often happens, still extremely far from putting that thought into words, even to myself.

Finally the last member of that family, Varyenka, was a very chubby young girl of about sixteen.

Large dark-grey eyes expressing a combination of good spirits and calm consideration, very similar to her aunt's, a very long light-brown plait and extremely delicate pretty hands were her only attractive features.

"I imagine it's boring for you to have to listen from the middle of the book," said Sofya Ivanovna to me with her good-natured sigh, as she turned over some bits of a dress she was sewing.

The reading session had meanwhile stopped because Dmitry had left the room to go somewhere.

"Or perhaps you have already read *Rob Roy*?"

At that time and with people I knew little, I considered it my duty, as one who wore a student uniform, to be sure to give a very "clever and original" answer to even the simplest question, and I thought it shameful to give short, clear answers such as "yes", "no", "it's boring", "it's fun" and others like that. Glancing at my new fashionable trousers and shiny coat buttons, I replied that I had not read *Rob Roy*, but that I would be very interested to hear it because I preferred to read a book from the middle than from the beginning.

"It's twice as interesting: you can guess what came before as well as what will come next," I added, smiling complacently.

The Princess burst out laughing with what seemed an unnatural laugh (later I noticed that she had no other laugh).

"Well, that must be true," she said. "And will you stay here for a while, Nicolas? You won't be offended that I don't say *monsieur* to you? When will you be leaving?"

"I don't know; perhaps tomorrow or perhaps we'll stay a little longer," I replied for some reason, although we most likely had to leave the next day.

"I would wish you to stay, for your sake and for my Dmitry's sake," remarked the Princess, staring somewhere into the distance. "At your age friendship is a wonderful thing."

I felt everyone looking at me and waiting to hear what I would say, although Varyenka pretended to be looking at her aunt's needlework. I felt that I was being examined in some way and that I had to prove myself as favourably as possible.

"Yes, Dmitry's friendship is helpful to me," I said, "but I can't be of much help to him: he's a thousand times better than I." (Dmitry was not there to hear what I was saying, otherwise I would have been afraid that he would have sensed the insincerity of those words.)

The Princess laughed again with that unnatural, but to her natural, laugh.

"Well, if you listened to him," she said, "then *c'est vous qui êtes un petit monstre de perfection.*"*

"*Monstre de perfection* – that's excellent, I must remember that," I thought.

"But then, without mentioning you, he's a master at that," she went on, lowering her voice (which especially pleased me) and looking towards Lyubov Sergeyevna. "He discovered in that *poor auntie* (that's what they called Lyubov Sergeyevna), whom I've known for twenty years with her Suzetka, such qualities I had never suspected in her... Varya, ask them to bring me a glass of water," she added, looking once more into the distance, probably finding it too soon or even unnecessary to let me in on family matters, "or no, let *him* go. *He* isn't doing anything and you go on reading. Go, my dear, straight through the door and stop after taking fifteen steps, then call out in a loud voice: 'Pyotr, bring Marya Ivanovna a glass

238

of water with ice'," she said to me and again laughed a little with her unnatural laugh.

"She probably wants to talk about me," I thought, leaving the room, "she probably wants to say that she has noticed that I'm an extremely clever young man." I had hardly gone fifteen steps before plump Sofya Ivanovna, panting but with light hasty steps, caught up with me.

"*Merci, mon cher*,"* she said, "I'm going there myself, so I'll tell him."

24

Love

SOFYA IVANOVNA, as I later found out, was one of those rare middle-aged women born for family life but denied that happiness by Fate. As a result they suddenly decide to pour out on a chosen few all those reserves of love for a husband and children that have been stored and grown and strengthened for so long. And those reserves are so inexhaustible in older spinsters of that kind that, though the chosen are many, plenty of love remains to pour out on all those people around them, on everyone good and bad with whom they come into contact in their lives.

There are three kinds of love:
1) Aesthetic love
2) Self-sacrificing love and
3) Active love

I am not speaking of the love of a young man for a young girl and vice versa. I fear those displays of affection and have been unfortunate enough in my life never to have seen a glimmer of truth in that kind of love but only lies, where sensuality, marital relations, money, the desire to tie or untie one's hands have so muddled the feeling itself that it defies understanding. I am speaking of love for another person, a love that focuses on one, or a few, or many, depending on how strong your heart is: love for one's mother, father, brother, children, friend – male or female – a fellow countryman, love for another human being.

Aesthetic love is love for the beauty of the feeling itself and its expression. To people who love this way, the beloved object is only lovable in so far as he or she arouses that pleasant sensation, the consciousness and expression of which is their delight. People who love this way are not much concerned with their love being reciprocated, as it has no bearing on the beauty or pleasure of the feeling. They often change the objects of their love, because all they want is to keep the pleasant sensation of love constantly stimulated. In order to sustain that pleasant sensation, they never stop speaking of their love, using the most elegant expressions, addressing the object of their love itself and everyone else, even those who have nothing to do with it. In our country people of a certain class, lovers of *beauty*, not only tell everyone of their love, but they always declare it in French. It may be a ridiculous and odd thing to say, but I am sure that there have been many people and that there are plenty now from that particular class, especially women, whose love for their friends, husbands and children would instantly be crushed, were they forbidden to speak about it in French.

The second kind of love – *self-sacrificing love* – consists in loving the actual process of sacrificing oneself for the beloved object, regardless of whether he or she derives any benefit from that sacrifice. "There is not a single unpleasantness I would not undergo to prove my devotion to the whole world and to *him* or to *her*." Such is that love's formula. People who love this way never believe in reciprocal love (because it is even more deserving to sacrifice yourself for someone who does not understand you). They are always sickly, which also adds to the significance of the sacrifice. They are on the whole constant, because they would find it hard to waste those sacrifices they have made for their loved one, and they are always prepared to die to prove their total devotion to *him* or *her*. Yet they disregard those small daily tokens of love that do not need particular bursts of selflessness. They do not care whether you have eaten well, or slept well, whether you are in good spirits or healthy, and they do nothing to procure you those comforts, even were it in their power to do so. But to stand in the firing line, brave fire or water, or to waste away for love is something they are always ready to do, should the opportunity arise. In addition, people who are inclined to selfless love are always proud of it. They are exacting, jealous, distrustful and, strangely, they wish the objects of their love to be in some danger so that they might rescue them, or to suffer misfortunes so that they might comfort them, and even to have faults in order to reform them.

You live alone in the country with your wife, who loves you selflessly. You are healthy and at peace and you keep busy and enjoy what you do. Your loving wife is so weak that she cannot take care of the household, a task that has been passed on to the servants, nor of the children, who are in the care of nannies, nor in fact of anything she may have liked, because she loves nothing but you. She is *clearly* ill, but, not wishing to upset you, she does not want to talk about it. She is *clearly* bored, but for you she is prepared to be bored all her life. The fact that you are intently involved in what you are doing (whatever it may be: hunting, books, farming, government service) *clearly* kills her; she sees that those occupations will be the death of you, but she suffers in silence. Then you are taken ill, and your loving wife forgets her own illness and constantly sits by your bedside, despite your entreaties not to upset herself for nothing. Every second you feel her look of commiseration fixed on you saying, "I told you so, but it doesn't matter, I'll not leave you anyway." In the morning you feel a little better and you go into the room next door. It has not been heated or cleaned: soup, which is all you can eat, has not been ordered from the cook, medicine has not been sent for, but, exhausted by the night's vigil, your loving wife still watches you with her commiserating look and walks around on tiptoe whispering unfamiliar and obscure orders to the servants. You want to read and your loving wife sighs and says she knows you will not listen to her, that you will get cross, but that she is used to it, but that it would be better for you not to read. You want to walk around the room, but it would be better if you did not do that either. You want to talk to a friend who has come by, and again are told it would be best not to talk. During the night the fever recurs and you want to doze off, but your loving wife, skinny and pale, hardly breathing, sits opposite you in the armchair in the dim glow of the night light and you get annoyed and fretful at the slightest movement or noise. You have a servant you are used to and with whom you have already lived twenty years; he serves you willingly and very well, because he has had a good sleep and gets paid for his service, but she will not let him look after you. She does everything herself with her weak, inexperienced fingers and you cannot help but watch with suppressed anger as those white fingers vainly try to uncork the bottle, snuff the candle, pour the medicine or squeamishly* touch you. If you are an impatient, hot-tempered man and you ask her to leave the room, your ears will be irritably and painfully on the alert to her

241

resigned sighs behind the door, and to her crying and to some nonsense she whispers to your servant. Finally, if you have not died, your loving wife, who has not slept for twenty nights during your illness (which she constantly reminds you of), is taken ill herself, fades away, suffers, becomes even more incapable of performing any task and, when you are back to normal, she expresses her selfless love with a humble boredom she involuntarily communicates to you and to all those around her.

The third kind, *active love*, consists of attempting to satisfy every need, every wish, every whim and even every vice of the beloved one. People who love this way love for life, because the more they love, the better they know the beloved one and the easier it is to love him or her, or indeed to satisfy all his or her wishes. Their love is rarely expressed in words, and even if it is then not in an elegant, self-satisfied way, but rather with embarrassment and awkwardness because they are always afraid that they do not love enough. These people even love their beloved's vices because it offers them the opportunity to satisfy yet more desires. They seek reciprocal love and, willing even to deceive themselves, they believe in it and are happy if they find it. Even if it turns out otherwise, they continue to love the same way: not only do they wish for the happiness of the beloved one, but they constantly try to obtain it by all the spiritual and material means, big or small, at their disposal.

And it was that active love for her nephew, niece, sister and Lyubov Sergeyevna, and now even for me, because Dmitry loved me, that shone in Sofya Ivanovna's eyes, and in every word and gesture of hers.

It was only very much later that I fully appreciated Sofya Ivanovna, but the question arose even before as to why Dmitry, who tried to perceive love in a very different way from other young people, and who always had sweet loving Sofya Ivanovna in front of him, why he suddenly fell passionately in love with the enigmatic Lyubov Sergeyevna and yet would only concede that his aunt possessed some good qualities too. Clearly the saying: "A prophet is not without honour save in his own country" is correct. It is either one or the other: either there really is more bad than good in every individual or a person is more susceptible to the bad than to the good. He had only recently known Lyubov Sergeyevna, but had experienced his aunt's love since he was born.

25

I Become Better Acquainted

WHEN I RETURNED TO THE VERANDA, they were not talking about me at all, as I had assumed, but Varyenka was no longer reading and had put her book aside. She was having a heated argument with Dmitry, who was pacing to and fro while adjusting his cravat and frowning. The argument seemed to be about Ivan Yakovlevich and superstition, but it was too passionate for its underlying meaning not to be another one, much closer to home. The Princess and Lyubov Sergeyevna sat in silence listening to every word, clearly wanting to participate at times, but holding back and leaving the two to speak for them: Varyenka for one and Dmitry for the other. When I came in, Varyenka glanced at me with such indifference that it was clear that she was deeply absorbed in the argument and did not care whether I heard what she said or not. The Princess also had that expression on her face and was clearly on Varyenka's side. But Dmitry began to argue even more heatedly in front of me, and Lyubov Sergeyevna seemed very alarmed at my return and said to no one in particular:

"Older people rightly say, '*Si jeunesse savait, si vieillesse pouvait.*'"*

That saying did not cut the argument short, but it led me to think that Lyubov Sergeyevna and my friend were in the wrong. Although I felt somewhat guilty at witnessing a minor family argument, I was also pleased to see the real relationships within the family exposed as a result of the quarrel and to feel that my presence there did not prevent them from being exposed.

It can often occur that for years you see a family covered by the same false veil of respectability and true relationships between its members remain a secret to you. (I have even noticed that the more impenetrable and therefore more beautiful the veil, the uglier the actual relationships that are kept hidden from us!) But then quite unexpectedly what may sometimes seem an innocuous question crops up within the family circle, about some blonde or a visit made on the husband's horses, and the argument becomes more and more bitter without any obvious reason, and it begins to feel too cramped beneath the veil to examine the issue further: suddenly, to the horror of those involved in the argument and the amazement of the bystanders, all the real, nasty relationships jump to the fore and the veil no longer covers anything, dangles between the warring parties and merely reminds you of how long you have been deceived. It is often less painful to knock your head very hard against the lintel of a door than to touch a sensitive sore spot ever so lightly. There is such a sensitive sore spot in almost every family. In the Nekhlyudov household that sore spot was Dmitry's strange love for Lyubov Sergeyevna, which awoke in his mother and sister if not a feeling of jealousy, then one of hurt family pride. That is why the quarrel about Ivan Yakovlevich and superstition was of such great consequence to them.

"You always try to see something in things others laugh at and despise," said Varyenka in her ringing voice and pronouncing every letter very distinctly. "You're really trying to find something unusually good in all this."

"In the first place, only the most frivolous person could speak of despising such a remarkable man as Ivan Yakovlevich," replied Dmitry, fitfully twisting his head away from his sister, "and secondly, it is you who, on the contrary, are trying not to see the good which is staring you in the face."

Sofya Ivanovna, having just returned, looked apprehensively at her niece, her nephew and at me in turn and, opening her mouth, she twice sighed heavily, as though she had just said something in her head.

"Please, Varya, do read on," she said, handing her the book and tenderly patting her hand, "I really want to know whether he found her again or not." (I don't think there was anything about finding someone in the novel or the conversation.) "And you, Mitya, you should bandage that cheek, my dearest, it is getting chilly and your teeth will start hurting again," she said to her nephew, despite the disgruntled look he threw her, probably because she had interrupted the logical thread of his argument. The reading resumed.

That small argument in no way disturbed the general peace and judicious harmony, with which that female circle was imbued.

The nature of that circle, which clearly took its direction and character from Princess Marya Ivanovna, was completely new and appealing to me: it combined logic with simplicity and elegance. This was reflected for me in the beauty, purity and solidity of the objects – a little bell, a book binding, an armchair, a table – and in the upright, corseted posture of the Princess, her grey curls put on display, her way of simply calling me Nicolas on first acquaintance, in their tasks, their reading and dressmaking, and in the unusual whiteness of the ladies' hands. (They all had a common family trait, which was that the fleshy part of their palms was red and was separated by a sharp straight line from the unusually white skin of the upper part of their hands.) But the character of that circle was above all reflected in the way all three spoke excellent Russian and French and pronounced each letter distinctly, ending each word and sentence with pedantic precision. All this and, in particular, the fact that they treated me simply and seriously like a grown-up, giving me their opinions and listening to mine, meant that I did not feel the slightest reserve in their company, and I was so unaccustomed to this that, despite my shiny buttons and blue cuffs, I kept on fearing that they would suddenly say to me: "Do you really think we are holding a serious conversation with you? Off to your studies." So I got up, moved from place to place and talked boldly to everyone, except Varyenka, as I thought it was improper and even for some reason forbidden to talk to her on my first visit.

I listened to her pleasant, ringing voice while she was reading, and glanced either at her or at the sandy path in the flower garden, where darkening round spots of rain were appearing, and at the lime trees, on whose leaves occasional raindrops continued to splash down from the pale blue-streaked edge of the storm cloud which had caught us out before. Then I looked at her again, or at the last crimson rays of the setting sun, lighting up the thick old birches wet with rain, then again at Varyenka and I thought that she was actually not as unattractive as she had seemed to me before.

"What a pity that I'm already in love," I thought, "and that Varyenka isn't Sonyechka. How good it would be to suddenly become a member of this family: I would suddenly have a mother and an aunt and a wife." As I thought this, I stared at Varyenka while she read, and decided to hypnotize her and make her look up at me. Varyenka raised her head from her book, glanced at me and, meeting my eyes, turned away.

"It has not stopped raining yet," she said.

And I suddenly had a strange feeling: I remembered that everything that was happening to me now was a repeat of what had happened to me once before. Fine rain had also fallen then and the sun had set behind the birches and I had looked at her and she had read and I had hypnotized her and she had looked up and I even remembered that that had happened another time before that.

"Could it be she... *she*?" I thought. "Is *it* perhaps *beginning*?" But I soon concluded that it was not *she* and that it was not *beginning*. "Firstly, she is not pretty," I thought, "and she is simply a young lady I have met in the most ordinary manner. The one that I'll meet somewhere in an exceptional place will be exceptional. And the reason I like this family so much is that I've not yet seen anything," I reflected, "and there will most likely always be such families and I'll come across many more in my life."

26

I Show My Best Side

THE READING STOPPED AT TEATIME and the ladies began to chat amongst themselves about people and circumstances unfamiliar to me; they did this, so I thought, to make me feel the difference there was between us in years and social position, despite their warm welcome. However, in the course of a more general conversation in which I was able to take part, I tried, in order to make up for my previous silence, to display my exceptional intellect and originality, which my uniform seemed to expressly require of me. When the conversation turned to dachas, I suddenly told them that Prince Ivan Ivanych had a dacha near Moscow, that people came from London and Paris to see it and that it had a railing that cost 380,000 roubles. I also said that Prince Ivan Ivanych was a very close relative of mine, that I had dined with him that day and that he had urged me to come and spend all summer with him at his dacha, but that I had refused because, having been there several times before, I knew the dacha well, that all those railings and bridges were of no interest to me because I could not stand luxury, especially in the country, as I liked the country to be just that, the country... Having told this awful, convoluted lie, I became confused and blushed so that everyone probably noticed that I was lying. Varyenka passed me a cup of tea and Sofya Ivanovna watched me as I spoke, then both turned away and began to chat about something else with an expression which I later often saw in kind-hearted people when a very young man clearly begins to lie to their face, an expression which implies: "We know he's lying, so why does he do it, poor devil!"

I told them that Ivan Ivanych had a dacha because I saw no other way of introducing the subject of my kinship with Prince Ivan Ivanych or of telling them that I had dined with him that day, but why I mentioned a railing costing 380,000 roubles and about my often having been there, when I never had nor could have been, as Prince Ivan Ivanych only lived in Moscow and Naples – a fact the Nekhlyudovs were well aware of – why I said all this I really cannot explain. Neither in my childhood nor boyhood nor in my more mature years was I aware of being a liar. On the contrary, I was rather too truthful and outspoken. Yet in that first phase of youth I was often drawn by the strange desire to tell lies in the most reckless fashion for no obvious reason. I use the phrase "in the most reckless fashion" because I lied about things on which it was very easy to catch me out. I think that my overweening desire to show myself to be different than I was, together with the vain hope of telling lies without being caught out, were the main reasons for that strange tendency.

After tea, as the rain had passed and the weather at sunset was calm and clear, the Princess suggested we go for a walk to the lower garden and admire her favourite spot. True to my principle of remaining original at all times, and considering that clever people like the Princess and myself should stand above ceremony, I replied that I could not bear walking aimlessly and that if I felt like walking I would do so on my own. I did not in any way think that this was simply rude, because I felt then that since there was nothing more shameful than platitudes, there was nothing more endearing and original than some degree of insolent outspokenness. And feeling very satisfied with my reply, I went for a walk with the rest of the company anyway.

The Princess's favourite spot was in the most overgrown part of the garden, at the very bottom, on a small bridge thrown across a narrow little swamp. The view from there was very restricted, yet very inspiring and stylish. We are so accustomed to mixing art with nature that natural phenomena we have never encountered in art very often seem unnatural to us, as though nature could be artificial, and vice versa: those phenomena which are too often repeated in paintings appear trite to us, and some views, which are too loaded with one single idea or feeling, appear fanciful when encountered in reality. The view from the Princess's favourite spot was of this kind. It consisted of a small pond overgrown around the edges and a steep hill right behind it, covered with huge old trees and bushes with many shades of green often interweaved. At the bottom of the hill was an old birch suspended over the water, which, clinging with part of its thick roots to the damp edge of the pond, was leaning with its crown against a tall graceful aspen and hanging its curling branches over the smooth surface of the pond, which reflected both the branches and the surrounding greenery.

"How charming!" said the Princess, with a slight toss of her head and not addressing anyone in particular.

"Yes, it's wonderful, but it does look terribly like a stage set," I said, wishing to show that I had my own opinion on everything.

As though she had not heard my remark, the Princess went on admiring the view and, turning to her sister and Lyubov Sergeyevna, she pointed out a detail she especially liked: an overhanging crooked branch and its reflection. Sofya Ivanovna said that it was all very pretty and that her sister liked to spend many hours there, but it was clear that she only said this to please the Princess. I have noticed that people who have the capacity of *loving actively* are rarely susceptible to the beauties of nature. Lyubov Sergeyevna was also enchanted and asked among other things: "How does that birch manage to hold on? Can it stay that way for long?" and she kept a constant eye on her Suzetka, who, wagging her fluffy tail, ran to and fro on her short crooked legs across the bridge and looked so restless it was as if it was the first time in her life she found herself out of doors. Dmitry began to argue very logically with his mother about how a view with a restricted horizon could in no way be beautiful. Varyenka said nothing. When I glanced back at her, she was leaning on the railing of the bridge and gazing ahead, with her profile towards me. Something seemed to be strongly engaging her attention and even affecting her, because she was lost in thought and was oblivious of herself and of anyone watching her. Her large eyes expressed such rapt attention and calm clear thought and her pose such ease and even, despite her small size, such presence that I was again struck by what seemed like a memory of her and again I asked myself: "Is *it* beginning?" And again I replied to myself that I was already in love with Sonyechka and that Varyenka was simply a young lady, my friend's sister. But I did like her at that moment and therefore felt a vague urge to do or say something slightly unpleasant to her.

"Do you know, Dmitry," I said to my friend, moving closer to Varyenka so that she should hear what I was about to say, "I find that even without mosquitoes there would be nothing pleasant about this place, but now," I added, flicking at my forehead and actually squashing a mosquito, "it is really awful."

"You don't seem to take an interest in nature?" said Varyenka without turning her head.

"I find it an idle, useless pursuit," I replied, very pleased to have made a slightly unpleasant remark and an original one at that. Varyenka lifted her eyebrows very faintly for an instant with an expression of pity and went on gazing ahead as serenely as before.

I became annoyed with her, but, irrespective of that, the bridge's grey railing she leant against, with its faded paintwork, the reflection in the dark pond of the suspended birch's hanging branch – a reflection that seemed to want to join with other overhanging branches – the smell of the swamp, the sensation left on my forehead by the squashed mosquito and Varyenka's concentrated look and dignified pose, all this would often quite unexpectedly spring up in my imagination later on.

27

Dmitry

WHEN WE RETURNED HOME AFTER OUR WALK, Varyenka did not want to sing as she usually did in the evenings and I was presumptuous enough to assume that this was on my account, because of what I had said on the bridge. The Nekhlyudovs did not eat supper and usually retired early to their rooms, but on that day Dmitry did indeed have a toothache, as Sofya Ivanovna had predicted, and we went to his room earlier than usual. Believing that I had done everything the blue collar and the buttons of my uniform had required of me and that everybody was very taken with me, I was in a happy, contented mood. Dmitry, on the other hand, after the quarrel, and suffering from his toothache, was taciturn and sombre. He sat down at the table, got hold of his notebooks – a diary and an exercise book in which he was in the habit of writing down every evening what he had done and any future tasks he would undertake – and he wrote for quite a long time, continually frowning and touching his cheek with his hand.

"Oh, leave me alone," he shouted at the maid sent by Sofya Ivanovna to enquire about his teeth and whether he wanted to apply a poultice. Then saying that my bed would soon be made up and that he would be back right away, he went to see Lyubov Sergeyevna.

"What a pity Varyenka isn't pretty and that she isn't Sonyechka," I fantasized, left alone in the room. "How good it would be to come here after finishing university and propose to her. I would say: 'Princess, I'm no longer young, and so cannot love with passion, but I will love you always like a dear sister. I've always respected you,' I would say to her mother, 'and you, Sofya Ivanovna, please believe that I hold you in high esteem.' And again to Varyenka: 'So simply tell me straight: will you be my wife?' 'Yes.' And she will give me her hand and I will squeeze it and say: 'My love consists not of words but of deeds.' And what if," it occurred to me, "if suddenly Dmitry fell in love with Lyubochka – Lyubochka is in love with him after all – and wanted to marry her? Then one of us would not be allowed to marry.* And that would be excellent. This is what I'd do. I would notice at once what was going on, but not say anything and then go to Dmitry and say: 'It would be useless to attempt to conceal things from one another: you know that my love for your sister will only end with my death. And I know everything that's going on: you have deprived me of my fondest hope and have caused my unhappiness. But do you know how Nikolai Irtenyev is repaying you for causing him unhappiness for the rest of his life? Here is my sister,' and I would give him Lyubochka's hand. And he would say: 'No, not for anything!' and I would say: 'Prince Nekhlyudov! It is pointless trying to be more magnanimous than Nikolai Irtenyev. There is no one in the world more magnanimous than he.' I would bow and leave the room. Dmitry and Lyubochka would run after me in tears begging me to accept their sacrifice. And I might agree and could be extremely happy if only I were in love with Varyenka…" Those daydreams were so pleasant that I wanted to share them with my friend, but despite our vow of mutual frankness, I somehow felt that it was physically impossible to tell him.

Dmitry came back from Lyubov Sergeyevna with drops for his toothache which she had given him; he was in even greater pain and even more sombre as a result. My bed had not yet been made, and a boy, Dmitry's servant, came to ask where I was to sleep.

"Go to hell!" screamed Dmitry, stamping his foot. "Vaska! Vaska! Vaska!" he shouted the instant the boy had gone out, and shouting louder with every word. "Vaska, make my bed up here on the floor."

"No, it's better if I lie on the floor," I said.

"Well, it doesn't matter, make the bed up anywhere," went on Dmitry with the same angry tone of voice. "Vaska! Why are you not making the bed up?"

But Vaska clearly did not understand what was expected of him and stood motionless.

"Well, what's the matter with you? Get on with it, make the bed! Vaska! Vaska!" screamed Dmitry, suddenly flying into some kind of mad fury.

But Vaska still did not understand and, having lost his nerve, did not move.

"So you've sworn to destr… to drive me mad?"

Dmitry leapt off his chair, rushed over to the boy and hit him over the head with his fist several times with all his might; Vaska ran headlong out of the room. Having stopped at the door, Dmitry glanced round at me and his mad, cruel expression, which had been there just an instant before, changed to such a gentle, remorseful and loving childlike look that I felt sorry for him and as much as I wanted to turn away I could not do so. He did not say anything to me, but for a long time paced up and down the room wordlessly, now and then looking up at me with the same expression begging for forgiveness. Then he took his exercise book from the table, wrote something in it, took off his coat, folded it carefully, went up to the corner with the icon, folded his big white hands across his chest and began to pray. He prayed for so long that Vaska managed to bring a mattress in and make a bed on the floor, as I told him in whispers what to do. I undressed and lay down on the bed on the floor and Dmitry still continued praying. When I glanced at his slightly stooped back and saw the soles of his feet rather humbly displayed in front of me when he bowed down all the way to the ground, I loved him more than ever and kept on thinking: "Should I tell him or not that I was dreaming about our sisters?" After finishing his prayers, Dmitry lay down on my bed and, leaning on his elbow, he looked at me silently with a tender, chastened look. It was clearly painful for him, but he seemed to be punishing himself. I smiled as I looked at him. He smiled too.

"Why don't you tell me," he said, "that I behaved vilely? Were you not, after all, thinking that?"

251

"Yes," I replied, although I had been thinking of something else, but it seemed to me that I had indeed thought that. "Yes, it was very bad, I didn't expect it of you," I said, feeling particular satisfaction right then at having addressed him with the familiar *ty*. "And how is your toothache?" I added.

"It's gone. Oh, Nikolyenka, my friend!" Dmitry said this so tenderly that there seemed to be tears in his shining eyes. "I know and feel how wicked I am and God sees how much I wish to be a better person and how I beg him to help me, but what can I do if I have such an unfortunate and loathsome character? What can I do? I try to restrain myself, to mend my ways, but it is impossible to do so in one go and certainly to do it on my own. I need someone to support and help me. So there is Lyubov Sergeyevna who understands me and has been a great help. I know from my notes that I have improved a lot in one year. Oh, Nikolyenka, my dear friend!" he went on with particular and unexpected tenderness and with a calmer tone of voice after this confession. "How much the influence of such a woman can mean! My God, how good it could be, once I'm independent, to be with such a friend as she! I'm a completely different person when I'm with her."

And after this Dmitry began to unfold his plans for marriage, a country life and constant work to improve himself.

"I'll be living in the country and you will come to visit me and perhaps you will be married to Sonyechka," he said, "and our children will play together. All this may seem ridiculous and foolish, but it could happen."

"And how! It very well could," I said, smiling and meanwhile thinking how it might be even better if I married his sister.

"You know what I'm going to say?" he said after a brief pause. "You're probably only imagining that you're in love with Sonyechka, but as I see it, it is all nonsense and you don't yet know what the real feeling is like."

I did not object because I partly agreed with him. We remained silent for a while.

"You've probably noticed that I was in a vile mood again today and had a nasty quarrel with Varyenka. I was terribly upset about it afterwards, especially since it happened with you there. Although she doesn't always think the way she should about things, she is a lovely, very good girl; you've not really known her long enough."

I was extremely glad that he had moved the conversation from my not being in love to singing his sister's praises, and this made me blush, but I still did not tell him about his sister and we went on talking of other things.

And so we chatted on until the cock crowed a second time, and the pale dawn was already peeping in at the window when Dmitry went back to his bed and snuffed the candle.

"Well, now for some sleep," he said.

"Yes," I replied, "just one more thing."

"Go ahead."

"Is it wonderful to be alive in this world?"

"Yes, it is," he replied with such a voice that I felt I could see the expression of his joyful, tender eyes and his childlike smile in the dark.

28

In the Country

THE NEXT DAY Volodya and I travelled to the country by post-chaise. As I ran various Moscow memories through my mind along the way, I did think of Sonyechka Valakhina, but only in the evening, when we had already passed five staging posts. "It's rather strange," I thought, "that I'm in love and have completely forgotten about it; I must think of her." And I began to think of her in a rambling sort of way, as one does when travelling, but also vividly to the extent that after our arrival in the country I deemed it somehow necessary to appear sad and pensive for two days in front of the whole household and especially in front of Katyenka, whom I considered an expert in those matters and to whom I had given a hint as to the state of my heart. Yet, despite all my attempts at putting on an act for others and myself and deliberately assimilating all the symptoms I had noticed in others who were in love, I remembered that I was in love for only two days, and even then not all the time, but mainly in the evenings, and in the end, as soon as I had settled into the new country routine and pursuits, I completely forgot about my love for Sonyechka.

We reached Petrovskoye by night and I was so soundly asleep that I did not see our house or the birch avenue or any of the servants, who had already gone to bed and been asleep long since. Stooped old Foka, on bare feet, wearing some kind of quilted jacket of his wife's and holding a candle, unbolted the door for us. When he saw us, he began to shake with joy, kissing us each on the shoulder, and he quickly tidied away his felt bedding and began to dress. I walked through the anteroom and up the stairs, not yet fully awake, but once in the entrance hall, the door lock and bolt, the slanting floorboard, the chest, the old candlestick covered in dripping tallow as usual, the shadows from the crooked, cold tallow candle, whose wick had just been lit, the inner window, dusty as ever, that was never removed, behind which, as I remembered, grew a rowan tree – all this was so familiar, so full of memories, so many things in harmony with each other as though connected by one thought, that I suddenly felt the dear old house's warm caress. I instinctively asked myself: "How could the house and I have survived so long without each other?" and hurrying onwards, I ran to see whether all the other rooms had remained unchanged. Everything was the same, only smaller and lower, and I seemed to have grown taller, heavier and coarser, but the house joyfully enfolded me in its embrace, just the way I was, and every floorboard, every window, each step of the stairs, every sound conjured up a host of images, sensations and events from an irretrievable, happy past. We went into our childhood bedroom: the same childish horrors lurked in the dark corners and doorways; we crossed the drawing room: the same serene, tender mother's love poured over all the objects in the room; we went through the reception hall: a noisy, carefree, childish joyfulness seemed to have settled in that room and was just waiting to be brought to life again. In the sitting room where Foka took us and where he had made up some beds for us, everything – the mirror, the screens, the old wooden icon, every irregularity in the white papered wall – spoke of suffering, of death, of what would never be again.

We lay down and Foka left us after saying goodnight.

"Is this the room Maman died in?" said Volodya.

I did not answer him and pretended to be asleep. Had I spoken, I would have burst into tears. When I woke up next morning, Papa, not yet dressed, in soft shoes and dressing gown and with a cigar between his teeth, was sitting on Volodya's bed, chatting and laughing with him. He jumped up with a merry twitch of his shoulder, came over to me and slapped my back with his big hand, offered me his cheek and pressed it against my lips.

"Excellent, thank you, diplomat," he said in his own particular jokingly affectionate way and looked at me with his small shining eyes. "Volodya tells me that you passed your exams well, good fellow, that's splendid. You too are my good boy when you decide not to fool around. Thank you, my friend. We'll settle very well down here for now and perhaps move to St Petersburg in the winter. It's only a pity that the hunting season is over, otherwise I would have entertained you that way. Can you hunt with a gun, Voldemar? There are lots of game birds and I may go with you some day. And in winter, God willing, we'll move to St Petersburg, where you'll meet people and make connections. You are now grown-up boys and as I was just saying to Voldemar: 'You are now standing on the road and my task is over; you can go onwards by yourselves and if you want to seek my advice, do. I'm no longer looking after you but am your friend, or at least I would like to be your friend, companion and adviser where possible and nothing more. How does that fit in with your philosophy, Koko? Well? Is it good or bad? Well?"

Of course I said that it was excellent and indeed thought so. Papa had a particularly personable, cheerful and happy expression that day and that new relationship with him, as an equal and a friend, made me love him even more.

"Well, tell me, did you visit all your relatives? The Ivins? Did you see the old man? What did he say to you?" he went on questioning me. "Did you go and see Prince Ivan Ivanych?"

And we went on chatting for so long before getting dressed that the sun had already begun to move away from the sitting-room window and Yakov (who seemed just as old as ever and twirled his fingers behind his back and said "but then again" just as before) came into the room and announced to Papa that the small carriage was ready.

"Where are you going?" I asked Papa.

"Oh, I almost forgot," said Papa with a resentful twitch and a slight cough, "I promised to go to the Epifanovs today. Do you remember Epifanova, *la belle Flamande*? She used to visit your mother. They are splendid people." And Papa, bashfully twitching his shoulder – or so it seemed to me – left the room.

Lyubochka had already come to the door several times and asked if she could come in, and each time Papa had called out to her through the door: "Absolutely not, we're not dressed."

"So what! Have I not seen you in your dressing gown before?"

"You can't see your brothers without their *unmentionables*," he had shouted to her, "now each one will knock on the door, is that good enough for you? Go on, knock. Even talking to you in such a state of undress is indecent."

"Oh, how impossible you are! Do at least come as soon as possible to the drawing room; Mimi so wants to see you," Lyubochka had shouted from behind the door.

As soon as Papa had gone, I briskly put on my student coat and went to the drawing room. Volodya did not hurry, however, and remained upstairs for a long time, chatting to Yakov about the whereabouts of the great and the common snipe. As I have already mentioned, nothing in the world scared him off more than shows of affection from his little brother and baby sister or his dear Papa – as he expressed it – and, avoiding all manifestation of feeling, he would go to the other extreme, coolly distancing himself, which often deeply offended people who did not know where it came from. I ran into Papa in the entrance hall as he walked over to his carriage with small swift steps. He wore his fashionable new Moscow frock coat and smelt of perfume. When he saw me, he cheerfully nodded his head as if to say: "See how nice I look?" and I was struck again by the happy expression in his eyes, which I had noticed that morning.

The drawing room was just the same, a bright, high-ceilinged room with a yellowy English piano and large open windows through which green trees and reddish-yellow garden paths joyfully looked in. After kissing Mimi and Lyubochka and going over to Katyenka, it suddenly occurred to me that it would no longer be proper to kiss her and I stopped in my tracks without a word and blushed. Katyenka, without any trace of confusion, put out her white hand and congratulated me on getting into university. The same thing happened when Volodya came in and he greeted Katyenka. It was indeed difficult to decide, having grown up together and seen each other every day for all that time, how we should now greet each other after our first separation. Katyenka blushed much more than any of us. Volodya showed no embarrassment and, bowing lightly to her, he went over to Lyubochka and, after exchanging a few words, he went off for a walk somewhere on his own.

29

Our Relationship with the Girls

VOLODYA HAD SUCH A STRANGE ATTITUDE towards the girls that he would be concerned about whether they had eaten enough, slept well, were dressed appropriately, about whether they made mistakes in French which could embarrass him in front of others, but he would not concede that they could think or feel like human beings and even less admit the possibility of discussing anything with them. When they turned to him with a serious question (and they did try to avoid doing this), if they asked for his opinion about some novel or about his university studies, he would pull a face at them and leave the room without a word or answer with some mispronounced French phrase: *come si tri joli** or such like, or else he would pull a serious, deliberately stupid face and would utter some nonsensical word that had no bearing on the question at all; he might say, his eyes glazing over, the words "bread roll", or "let's go", or "cabbage" or something else in that vein. When I happened to repeat to him something Lyubochka or Katyenka had said, he always said to me:

"Hm! So you still discuss things with them? No, I can see that you are still not much good."

And you had to hear and see him in those moments to appreciate the deep, unfailing contempt expressed in that phrase. Volodya had been a grown-up for two years by then and he kept falling in love with every beautiful woman he met; yet, although he saw Katyenka every day and she too had worn long dresses for two years and was growing prettier every day, the possibility that he could fall in love with her never occurred to him. Whether this was because prosaic childhood memories – the wagonnette, bed sheets, capricious behaviour – were still too fresh in his mind, or from an aversion common in very young people to everything connected to home, or from general human weakness circumventing the first pretty and good thing encountered on their path and saying to themselves: "Oh! I'll encounter much more of this in life"; whatever the reason, Volodya had not up till then looked at Katyenka as a woman.

It was clear all that summer that Volodya was bored. His boredom came from his contempt for us, which, as I mentioned, he did not try to hide. The expression on his face would constantly announce: "Ugh! Such boredom and no one to talk to!" He might set off in the morning on his own, go out with his gun to hunt, or he might stay in his room reading a book and not get dressed until dinner time. If Papa was not at home, he would come down to dinner with a book, go on reading it and not talk to any of us, which made us all feel somehow guilty before him. And then in the evenings too he would stretch his legs out on the sofa in the drawing room and sleep leaning on his arm or else he would make up the most terrible nonsense with a serious face, some of it not always appropriate, which made Mimi get cross and come out in red blotches and made us die of laughter, but he never deigned to hold a serious conversation with any member of our family except with Papa and occasionally with me. I quite unconsciously copied my brother in my attitude towards the girls, although, unlike him, I was not afraid of showing affection and my contempt for them was not as firmly rooted. During that summer I sometimes even tried, out of boredom, to draw closer to Lyubochka and Katyenka and chat with them, but each time I encountered such a lack of logical thought in them and such an ignorance of the simplest everyday things, such as, for example, the meaning of money, what one studied at university, the meaning of war, and so on, and also such indifference to the explanations of all these things, that such attempts only reinforced my poor opinion of them.

I remember Lyubochka one evening repeating some unbearably tedious piece on the piano for the hundredth time and Volodya dozing on the sofa in the drawing room and once in a while muttering with cruel irony, without addressing anyone in particular: "Oh, there she goes, pounding away... our little musician... *Beethoven*!..." (this he pronounced with particular irony) "Fantastic... there she goes again... why not... that's the way!" and so on. Katyenka and I stayed at the tea table and I do not remember how Katyenka brought the conversation round to her favourite subject – love. I was in a mood for philosophizing and began patronizingly to define love as a desire to acquire from another that which you lack yourself, and so on. But Katyenka replied that on the contrary it was no longer love if a young girl thought of marrying a rich man and that in her opinion fortune was the most hollow thing and that true love was the only love that could withstand separation (I understood from this that she was alluding to her love for

Dubkov). Volodya, who must have heard our conversation, suddenly raised himself on his elbow and shouted out questioningly:

"*Katyenka! Russians?*"

"Your eternal nonsense!" said Katyenka.

"*In the pepper pot?*" went on Volodya, stressing every vowel. And I had to agree that he was absolutely right.

Apart from the general, intellectual, emotional and artistic faculties developed in people to a greater or lesser degree, there is a specific capacity – which I shall call *understanding* – which exists within various circles of society and especially within families, also developed to a greater or lesser degree. The essence of this capacity consists of an agreed sense of proportion and an agreed, shared view of things. Two people from the same circle or family who possess this understanding will allow an expression of feeling up to a certain point, after which they will both see only words; they can both see at the same moment where praise ends and irony begins, where enthusiasm ends and pretence begins, which for people with a different understanding may seem utterly different. People with the same understanding are struck in the same way by every object seen by them essentially from a funny or pretty or unappealing angle. To facilitate this mutual understanding people of the same circle or family establish their own language, their own turns of phrase, even their own words which define those shades of understanding that do not exist for others. In our family Papa and we brothers had developed such an understanding to the highest degree. Dubkov too somehow fitted well in our circle and *understood*, but Dmitry, despite being much cleverer, did not. But only with Volodya, having grown up with him under the same conditions, was I able to bring this capacity to such a pitch of refinement. Even Papa had long fallen behind and much that was as clear to us as twice two is four was incomprehensible to him. Volodya and I, for example, had established (God only knows how) the following words with their corresponding meanings: "raisins" meant wishing to show off you had money, a "cone" (and with this we had to join our fingers and put particular stress on the o) meant something fresh, healthy, elegant, but not dandyish; a noun used in the plural meant an unreasonable passion for that object and so on. Then again, the meaning depended more on facial expressions and on the general topic of conversation so that, whatever new expression one of us thought up for a given nuance, the other with just one hint would immediately catch on. The girls were not in on our understanding and that was the main reason for our mental disconnection from them and the contempt we felt for them.

Perhaps they had their own *understanding*, but it was so alien to ours that where we saw just words they saw a feeling, our irony for them was truth and so on. But at the time I did not understand that this was not their fault and that the lack of this common understanding did not stop them from being lovely clever girls, and so I despised them. Besides, once I had come up with the idea of frankness, taking that notion to extremes for myself, I accused Lyubochka's calm trusting nature of secretiveness and pretence, just because she saw no need to unearth and analyse all her thoughts and inner fancies. For instance, the fact that Lyubochka made the sign of the cross over Papa every night, or that Katyenka and she cried in the chapel when they went to say prayers for Mother, or that Katyenka sighed and rolled up her eyes when she played the piano – all this seemed to me utter pretence and I asked myself: "When had they learnt to pretend like grown-ups do and why were they not ashamed of doing so?"

30

My Occupations

DESPITE ALL THIS, I drew closer to our young ladies that summer than in previous years because of my newly found passion for music. In the spring a young man, a neighbour, called in to introduce himself to us in the country, and as soon as he came into the drawing room, he kept staring at the piano and imperceptibly edging his chair towards it, all the while chatting with Mimi and Katyenka. Having talked about the weather and the delights of country life, he had skilfully led the conversation round to a piano tuner, to music, to the piano, and had finally announced that he could play, and then he very quickly played three waltzes while Lyubochka, Mimi and Katyenka stood near the piano watching him. That young man never came to visit us again, but I was very much taken with his playing: the way he sat at the piano and tossed his hair and particularly the way he played the octaves with his left hand, swiftly stretching his little finger and thumb over the whole width of the octave and then slowly drawing them back together and quickly stretching them out once more. This graceful movement, his casual pose, the tossing of his hair and the interest our ladies accorded his talent gave me the idea of playing the piano. And so, convinced that I had talent and a passion for music, I began to learn how to play. In that respect I went about it in the same way millions of the male and particularly the female sex learnt, without a good teacher, without a true calling and without the slightest understanding of what art had to offer and what should be done to gain something from it. For me music, or rather piano-playing, was a way of charming the girls with my sensitivity. After learning the notes with Katyenka's help and exercising my thick fingers a little, which, by the way, took me about two months of great effort to manage – and I even worked on my rebellious fourth finger on my knee at dinner and on my pillow in bed – I straight away began to play piano pieces, and played them of course soulfully, *avec âme*, as even Katyenka acknowledged, but entirely without keeping time.

My choice of piano pieces was predictable – waltzes, gallops, romances and so on. All of them were by those pleasing composers, a small pile of whose works anyone with a modicum of taste, choosing from stacks of excellent pieces in a music shop, would select and say, "These are the pieces you should *not* play, because nothing worse, more tasteless or senseless was ever written on music scores." And, probably for that very reason, you will find them on every Russian young lady's piano. Of course at home we also had those unfortunate pieces forever mangled by young girls: Beethoven's *Sonata Pathétique* and 'Sonatas in C Minor', which Lyubochka played in Maman's memory, and some other good pieces set by her Moscow teacher, but there were some compositions by that same teacher, absurd marches and gallops, which Lyubochka also played. Katyenka and I did not like serious things and mostly preferred '*Le Fou*'* and 'The Nightingale', which Katyenka played in a way that made you lose sight of her fingers, and I myself was beginning to play quite loudly and fluently. I adopted the gestures of the young man and was often sorry that there were no outsiders to watch me play. But soon Liszt and Kalkbrenner seemed beyond my powers and I saw that it was impossible to catch up with Katyenka. So, imagining classical music to be easier and also partly to be original, I suddenly decided that I loved German classical music and went into raptures when Lyubochka played the *Sonata Pathétique*, although it was true to say that I had found that sonata extremely hateful for a long time, and I began to play Beethoven myself, pronouncing him the German way. Through all this nonsense and pretence, as I now remember it, I did have some kind of talent, because music often moved me to tears and I could somehow pick out by ear the notes on the piano for those pieces I liked. Had someone at the time taught me to regard music as a goal, as a pleasure in itself and not as a means to charm young girls with the speed and sensitivity of my playing, I might perhaps indeed have become a decent musician.

Another occupation of mine that summer was reading French novels, and Volodya had brought many of them with him. At the time *Monte-Cristo* and various "Mysteries" had begun to appear and I became engrossed in the novels of Sue, Dumas and Paul de Kock.* The most unnatural characters and events were totally real to me. I could not begin to suspect the author of lying; in fact the author did not exist for me and real live people and events materialized before me from the printed page. Even if I had never encountered characters like those I read about, I did not for a moment doubt that *in the future they would exist*.

I discovered in myself all the passions described in each novel and an affinity with all the characters, whether heroes or villains, in the same way a hypochondriac finds the symptoms of all possible diseases in himself when reading a medical book. I liked the crafty ideas in those novels, the ardent feelings, the magical events and the one-dimensional characters: if someone was good then he was totally good, when bad then totally bad – just like I imagined people to be in my early youth. I very much liked the fact that this was all in French and that I could memorize noble words uttered by noble heroes to be referred to in some noble situation. How many French phrases did I not think up with the help of those novels that I could say to Kolpikov, were I ever to meet him, and to *her* when I would finally meet and declare my love for her. I prepared myself to say *such things* that they would have perished on the spot on hearing me. I even established new ideals of moral virtues I wished to attain based on those novels. First of all I wanted to be *noble* in all my dealings and actions (I use the French *noble* and not its Russian equivalent, because the French *noble* has another nuance; this was understood by the Germans, who took the word *nobel* to differentiate it from *ehrlich*).* Then I wanted to be *passionate* and finally to be as much as possible *comme il faut*, and I was inclined to this already. I even tried to look and act like the heroes who had some of these qualities. I remember that in one of the novels, from the hundreds I read, there was one particularly passionate character with bushy eyebrows and I so wanted to be like him in appearance (I felt that I was exactly like him inside) that, looking at my eyebrows in the mirror, I thought of trimming them lightly so that they would grow thicker, but once I began to cut them, I found that I had clipped more in one place and that I needed to even them out, so that by the end, to my horror, I saw myself in the mirror with no eyebrows and very ugly as a result. However, hoping that I would soon grow bushy eyebrows like my passionate hero, I calmed down and worried only about how I would explain it to my family when they saw me without eyebrows. I took some of Volodya's gunpowder, rubbed it on my eyebrows and lit it. Although the powder did not explode, I looked sufficiently seared and no one discovered my ruse, and I did indeed grow much thicker eyebrows long after my passionate hero had been forgotten.

31

Comme Il Faut

I N THE COURSE OF THIS STORY I have already alluded several times to the concept that corresponds with this French heading and I now feel the need to dedicate an entire chapter to this notion, which was one of the most pernicious, deceitful notions in my life, instilled in me by society and my upbringing.

Mankind can be divided into a multitude of categories – rich and poor, good and bad, military and civilian, clever and stupid and so on, but each person is bound to have his favourite and main subdivision according to which he instinctively classes each new individual he meets. My favourite and main subdivision at the time I write about was between people who were *comme il faut* and those who were not *comme il faut*. This second category was in addition divided between people not strictly *comme il faut* and common people. I respected people who were *comme il faut* and considered them worthy of being on equal terms with me. I pretended to scorn the second group, but I actually hated them, nurturing some kind of sense of personal insult in relation to them. The third group did not exist for me: I totally despised them. My *comme il faut* consisted first and foremost in having excellent knowledge of French and its pronunciation in particular. A person who pronounced French badly immediately provoked a feeling of hatred in me. "Why do you want to talk like us when you don't know how?" I would mentally ask him with vicious mockery. The second condition of *comme il faut* was fingernails, which had to be long, well cared for and clean; the third was an ability to bow, dance and converse; the fourth, a very important one, was indifference to everything and a constant air of elegant, scornful boredom. Besides all this, there were some general signs that would lead me to decide in which category someone I had not even spoken to belonged. The foremost sign, apart from the furniture in his room, his seal, his handwriting and his carriage, were his legs. The way his boots looked in relation to his trousers instantly established a person's situation in my eyes. Boots without a heel, an angular toe and narrow trouser ends without foot straps were just *common*. A boot with a round, narrow toe and a heel and narrow trouser ends with straps fitted over the foot or wide trousers with straps overlapping the toe like a canopy denoted a person of *mauvais genre*, and so on.

It is strange that this concept caught on with me as it did, when I was so completely incapable of being *comme il faut* myself. Or perhaps it grew so powerfully in me for the very reason that it took such huge effort for me to acquire this *comme il faut* myself. It is terrible to remember how much of the best and invaluable time in my sixteen-year-old life I wasted on acquiring that quality. It seemed to come easily to all those I imitated – Volodya, Dubkov and the majority of my acquaintances. I looked at them with envy and I worked surreptitiously on my French, on the way to bow without looking at the person you bow to, on my conversation, my dancing and on cultivating that air of indifference and boredom towards everything, on my fingernails, which I cut down to the quick with scissors. Yet I still felt that much more effort was needed to reach my goal. And I was never able to arrange my room, my desk or my carriage to be *comme il faut*, although I tried to deal with all of this despite my dislike of practical things. To others it all just seemed to happen perfectly and effortlessly as though it could not be otherwise. I remember how once, after much useless effort on my nails, I asked

Dubkov, whose nails were amazingly attractive, whether they had been so for long and how he did it. Dubkov replied: "Ever since I remember, I have never done anything to make them look like this and I can't understand how a respectable man's nails could be otherwise." That reply upset me deeply. I did not know then that one of the main conditions of being *comme il faut* was secretiveness regarding the efforts needed to be *comme il faut*. For me *comme il faut* was not only an important merit, a wonderful quality, a perfection which I wanted to attain, but it was also a necessary condition of life without which there could be no happiness, fame nor anything good on earth. I would not have respected a famous artist or scholar or a benefactor of mankind, unless he was *comme il faut*. A person who was *comme il faut* would stand higher than them, even beyond comparison with them; he would leave them to paint pictures, write music and books, do good, and even praised them for it – why not praise good wherever it may be – but he could not be on a level with them: he was *comme il faut*, and they were not, and that was enough. It even seems to me that if I had had a brother, a mother or a father who were not *comme il faut*, I would have said that it was a misfortune, but that there could not be anything in common between us. But it was not the loss of precious time wasted on constant attention at keeping up with those difficult conditions of *comme il faut* which excluded any serious passion, nor the hatred and scorn for nine-tenths of mankind, nor the lack of attention for everything beautiful accomplished outside the circle of *comme il faut* that was the worst evil resulting from that notion. The main evil lay in the conviction that being *comme il faut* meant having an independent standing in society, that a man did not even need to look to being a civil servant, a soldier, a coach-builder or a scholar when he was *comme il faut*; that having reached that state, he had fulfilled his purpose and was even above the majority of people.

Every man usually finds himself at a particular period in his youth, after many mistakes and passions, having to take an active part in society. He chooses some occupation and devotes himself to it. But this seldom happens to a person who is *comme il faut*. I have known and still know very many older people, proud, smug and sharp in their judgements, who, were they to be asked in the next world: "What are you? And what have you done?" would not be able to reply other than with: "*Je fus un homme très comme il faut.*"*

That was what was in store for me.

32

Youth

D ESPITE THE JUMBLE OF NOTIONS going on in my head that summer, I was young, innocent, free and therefore almost happy.

Sometimes, and indeed quite often, I would get up early. (I slept in the open air on the veranda and was woken up by the bright slanting rays of the morning sun.) I quickly got dressed, took a towel and a French novel under my arm and went to bathe in the river, in the shade of a birch grove about half a verst from home. There I lay on the grass in the shade and read, now and then looking up from my book to glance at the surface of the river, purple in the shade and beginning to ripple with the morning breeze, at the field of yellowing rye on the further bank, at the bright-red morning sunlight that tinted the white birch trunks that hid one behind the other, receding from me into the deep forest, and I delighted in feeling the very same fresh young life force in myself that nature exuded all around me. When there were small grey morning clouds in the sky and I froze after my swim, I often went wandering off the paths through fields and woods, joyfully getting my feet wet right through my boots with fresh dew. At such times I would dream enthusiastically about the heroes of the last novel I had read and would imagine myself either a military leader or a minister or an unusually strong man, or a passionate individual, and I would constantly look around me with some trepidation, hoping to suddenly meet *her* in a clearing or behind a tree. When during such wanderings I came across peasant men and women at work, although "common people" did not exist for me, I involuntarily always felt deeply embarrassed and tried to avoid being seen by them. When it grew hot and our ladies had not yet come down for tea, I often went to the vegetable garden or the garden itself to eat any vegetables and fruit that were ripe. And doing that was one of my greatest pleasures.

You steal into the orchard to the very heart of a tall overgrown thick raspberry patch. Above you is the bright, hot sky and around you are the pale-green prickly leaves of the raspberry bushes mixed in with weeds. Dark-green nettles with slender flowering tops surge gracefully upwards; palm-leafed burdocks with their unusual purple burrs push rudely above the raspberries and above your head; together they reach up in places as high as the spreading pale-green branches of the old apple trees, where at the top, gleaming like bone, round green apples ripen with the help of the hot sun. Below is a young raspberry bush, practically dry, leafless and twisted, reaching up for the sun; green needle-like grass shoots and young burdocks, breaking through last year's leaves still damp with dew, turn green and juicy in the constant shade, as though unconscious of the sun playing brightly on the leaves of the apple tree.

It is always damp in this thicket. It smells of perpetual dense shade, of cobwebs, of fallen apples that turn black and are scattered on the mouldy earth, of raspberries, or sometimes of little bugs, which you unwittingly swallow with a berry, and then you quickly eat another. As you step forwards, you frighten off the sparrows who always live in those thickets; you hear their hurried twittering and the beating of their swift little wings against the branches; in one spot you hear the buzzing of a bee and somewhere along the path the footsteps of the gardener Akim, the idiot, and his perpetual humming under his breath. You think to yourself: "No! No one on earth can find me here, not even him…" and with both hands you pluck the juicy berries left and right off their little white conical stalks and you swallow them with delight one by one. Your legs are already soaked through well above the knee, some awful nonsense goes on in your head (you mentally repeat thousands of times: a-a-and by twent-ie-ie-ies a-a-and by se-se-sevens), your arms – and your legs through your soaking trousers – are stung by nettles, the perpendicular sunbeams begin to scorch your head as they pierce through the thicket, you are not hungry at all by now, yet you remain sitting there; you look round, listen out, think and mechanically tear off and swallow the best berries.

I usually go to the drawing room after ten o'clock, mostly after tea, when the ladies are already involved in various tasks. By the first window with its unbleached canvas blind lowered against the sun, through whose chinks the bright sun drops such dazzling fiery circles everywhere it lands that it hurts the eyes to look at them, stands the embroidery frame with flies wandering noiselessly along its white linen. Behind the frame sits Mimi, crossly shaking her head all the time and moving from place to place away from the sun, which suddenly bursts out somewhere and lands a fiery stripe here and there, on her face or on her hand. The light through the other three windows shaded by their frames forms solid bright squares; on one of those squares on the unpainted floor of the drawing room lies Milka, out of old habit; she pricks up her ears and glances at the flies wandering across the bright square. Katyenka knits or reads on the sofa and impatiently brushes the flies away with her small white hands that look transparent in the bright light or else she frowns or tosses her head to get rid of a fly entangled in her thick golden hair and struggling to get free. Lyubochka either paces up and down the room with her hands behind her back, waiting to go into the garden, or plays some piece on the piano every note of which is long familiar to me. I sit down somewhere, listen to the music or the reading and wait for the moment when I can sit at the piano myself. After dinner I sometimes deign to go riding with the girls (I considered going for walks incompatible with my age and my position in society). And those rides when I accompany them to unusual places and near ravines are very pleasant. Sometimes we get caught up in an adventure when I can show myself at my best and the ladies praise my mount and my courage and regard me as their protector. In the evening, if there are no guests, and after tea, which we have on the shady veranda, and after a walk with Papa round the estate, I lie in my old place in the Voltairean armchair and listen to Katyenka's or Lyubochka's music-making and I read and dream as I used to. Sometimes I remain alone in the drawing room with Lyubochka playing some old piece and I just abandon my book and gaze through the open balcony door at the curling branches of the tall birch trees over which the evening shadows are already passing, and at the clear sky where, if you look intently, a dusty yellowy spot suddenly appears and then disappears. And as I listen to the sound of music coming from the reception room and the creaking of the gates and the peasant women's voices and the herds returning to the village, I suddenly vividly remember Natalya Savishna and Maman and Karl Ivanych and for a moment I feel sad. But my soul is so full of life and hope at the time that the memory only brushes me like a wing and flies on.

After supper and an occasional night stroll in the garden with someone else – I was frightened of roaming the dark avenues on my own – I would go off to sleep on my own on the veranda floor, which gave me great pleasure, despite being devoured by millions of mosquitoes. By full moon I often spent whole nights sitting on my mattress, peering at the light and shadows, listening carefully to the stillness and the sounds, dreaming of different things, mainly of a poetic and sensual happiness, which then seemed to me to be the greatest form of happiness in life, and saddened by the fact that so far I had only been able to imagine it. At times, as soon as everyone had retired for the night and the candles from the drawing room had moved to the rooms upstairs, from where the sound of women's voices and the banging of windows being opened and shut could be heard, I would make my way to the veranda, where I walked up and down, avidly listening out for all the sounds of the house on the edge of sleep. So long as there was a tiny unfounded hope of realizing even a part of that happiness I dreamt about, I could not build an imaginary happiness for myself.

At every sound of bare feet, of coughs or sighs, the thud of a small window, the rustle of a dress, I would leap up from my bed, listen out furtively, watch out and for no obvious reason become very excited. But the lights would disappear from the upstairs windows, the sounds of footsteps and chatter were replaced by snores, the nightwatchman began his nightly beating of the gong, the garden looked both gloomier and brighter as soon as the strips of red light disappeared from the windows, the last light moved from the storeroom to the hall, throwing a strip of lighting on the dewy garden, and I could see Foka's bent figure through the window, as he went to his bed in his shirt, holding a candle in his hand. I would often get a great thrill from creeping through the wet grass in the dark shadow of the house, and when I reached the hall window I would hold my breath to listen to the young servant's snores and Foka's groans when he thought that no one could hear him, and to the sound of his old man's voice reciting his prayers for a very long time. Finally his last candle was snuffed, the window slammed shut and I remained completely alone, timidly looking on all sides in case a white lady emerged by the flower bed or by my bed, and then I would rush back to the veranda. And so when I lay down on my bed facing the garden and had covered myself up as much as possible against mosquitoes and bats, I looked into the garden, listened to the sounds of the night and dreamt of love and happiness.

Then everything took on a different meaning for me: the sight of the old birches with their curling branches shining in the moonlight on one side and on the other gloomily obscuring the bushes and the road with their black shadows; the still, luscious sheen on the pond swelling steadily like sound; the moonlight shimmer of dew drops on the flowers in front of the veranda, as they also cast their graceful shadows across the grey flower bed; the cry of a quail beyond the pond and a man's voice on the main road, and the quiet, barely audible creaking of two old birches one against the other; the buzzing of a mosquito above my ear under the blanket; an apple, caught by a branch, as it fell on dry leaves; the hopping of frogs who sometimes made it to the terrace steps, their greenish backs somehow glistening mysteriously in the moonlight, all this took on a strange meaning, a sense of an overabundance of beauty and of incomplete happiness. And then *she* would appear, with a long black plait and full bosom, always sad and beautiful, with bare arms and sensual embraces. She loved me and I sacrificed my whole life for one moment of her love. But the moon rose higher and higher and brighter and brighter in the sky, the luscious sheen on the pond steadily intensifying like sound turned clearer and clearer, the shadows grew darker and darker, the light turned more and more transparent, and when I looked and heard all this, something told me that even *she* with her bare arms and ardent embraces was a long way from being the only happiness and that love for her was a long way from being the only bliss. And the more I looked up at the risen full moon, the higher and purer and nearer true beauty and bliss seemed to Him, the source of all beauty and bliss, and tears of an unsatisfied yet stirring joy welled up in my eyes.

And still I was alone, and still it seemed to me that nature in its grandeur was secretly drawing the bright circle of the moon to her, and that the moon itself, which for some reason had stopped at a high indeterminate spot in the pale-blue sky, was also everywhere, as though filling every part of the vast expanse, and that I was an insignificant worm, already defiled by all petty pathetic human passions, but with an immense power of imagination and love, and so it seemed to me in such moments as though nature, the moon and I were all one and the same.

33

Neighbours

I WAS VERY SURPRISED WHEN, on the first day after our arrival, Papa called our neighbours the Epifanovs splendid people, and even more surprised that he went to visit them. For a long time there had been ongoing litigation between us and the Epifanovs about some land. As a child I had heard Papa more than once rage about the litigation, berating the Epifanovs and appealing to various people in order to protect himself, as I understood it, from them, and I had heard Yakov calling them our enemies and "black people". I also remember that Maman had even asked for them not be mentioned in her house or in her presence.

With those facts in hand I had formed in my childhood a firm, clear notion that the Epifanovs were our enemies, prepared to knife or strangle not only Papa but his son too if he fell into their hands, and that they were literally "black people", so that when I saw Avdotya Vasilyevna Epifanovna, *la belle Flamande*, looking after Mother the year she died, I had difficulty believing that she came from a family of "black people". And yet I still retained the lowest opinion of that family. Although we often saw each other this summer, I continued to be strangely biased against them all. In essence the family consisted of the mother, a fifty-year-old widow, still a youthful and spirited old lady, and her beautiful daughter, Avdotya Vasilyevna, and a son who stuttered, Pyotr Vasilyevich, a retired lieutenant and a bachelor with a very serious disposition.

Anna Dmitriyevna Epifanova had lived apart from her husband for about twenty years before his death. She sometimes stayed in St Petersburg, where she had relatives, but mainly lived in her own country estate of Mytishcha, which was just over three versts away from us. Such horrors were spread in the neighbourhood about her lifestyle that they made Messalina seem an innocent child in comparison.* That was why Mother had requested that the name Epifanov should not be mentioned in her house. But not even one tenth of the most evil kinds of gossip – that between country neighbours – should ever be believed, and I mean this without any attempt at irony. At the time I knew Anna Dmitriyevna, there was nothing of the sort going on despite the continued rumours, though she had brought one of her serfs into her house, the clerk Mityusha, who, with his pomaded curls and Circassian-style frock coat, would stand behind Anna Dmitriyevna's chair during dinner and she would often invite her guests in French and in his presence to admire his beautiful eyes and mouth. It seemed that for the last ten years, ever since she had recalled her dutiful son Pyotr from the army and asked him to come and live with her, she had in fact completely changed her lifestyle. Anna Dmitriyevna's estate was small, counting about one hundred souls,* but her expenses in her merry times had been many, so that ten years before, her property, which had of course been mortgaged to the hilt, was overdue for repayment and inevitably had to be put up for auction. In those extreme circumstances, judging that the trusteeship, the property inventory, the court case and other such nuisances were caused not so much by unpaid interest as by her being a woman, Anna Dmitriyevna wrote to her son in his regiment asking him to return to save his mother in her situation. Although Pyotr Vasilyevich's service in the army had been going so well that he was soon hoping to earn his own keep, he threw it all aside, went into retirement and, like a dutiful son who considers it his first duty to comfort his mother in her old age (and he quite sincerely communicated this to her in his letters), he came to the country.

Pyotr Vasilyevich, despite his unattractive face, clumsiness and stammer, was a man of extremely firm principles and a remarkably practical mind. In one way or another, with small loans, delaying tactics, pleas and promises, he kept hold of the property. Having become a landowner, Pyotr Vasilyevich put on his father's winter overcoat which had been stored away, got rid of the carriages and the horses and dissuaded visitors from coming to Mytishcha. He dug drains, increased arable land, decreased peasant land, had his trees cut down by his own men and profitably sold the wood and so put things right. Pyotr Vasilyevich gave his word that until all debts were repaid he would only wear his father's overcoat and a canvas coat which he had sewed himself, and would only go out in a cart using peasant horses – and he kept his word. He tried to spread that stoic lifestyle to the whole family in so far as his servile respect for his mother, which he regarded as his duty, would permit. In the drawing room he stammered and grovelled in front of his mother, fulfilled all her wishes, scolded the servants if they did not do what Anna Dmitriyevna had ordered them to do. But in his own study and in the office he took the servants sternly to task for bringing duck to the table without his own orders, or for sending, at Anna Dmitriyevna's request, a peasant to enquire about a neighbour's health, or for sending the peasant girls to gather raspberries in the woods instead of getting them to weed the vegetable plot.

Within about four years the debts were all repaid and Pyotr Vasilyevich went off to Moscow and returned with a new outfit and a *tarantass*.* Yet, despite the flourishing state of his affairs, he still kept to his stoical ways, in which he seemed to take glum pride, in front of his family and outsiders, and he often stammered that, "Whoever genuinely wants to see me will be happy to see me in a sheepskin coat and will eat my cabbage soup and my porridge. I eat them myself after all," he would add. Each word and gesture of his was full of pride, based on the consciousness of having sacrificed himself for his mother and having redeemed the property, and scorn for others who had done nothing like it.

The mother and daughter were very different characters and also very unlike each other in many ways. The mother was one of those women who were always pleasant and good-naturedly cheerful in society. She found pleasure in everything sweet and fun. She even had the ability to enjoy to the utmost the sight of young people enjoying themselves, a trait encountered only in the most good-natured older people. Her daughter, Avdotya Vasilyevna, had, on the other hand, a serious nature, or rather she had that peculiar casually distracted demeanour and quite unwarranted haughtiness usually found in unmarried beauties. When she wanted to be cheerful, her cheerfulness was expressed rather oddly – it was unclear whether she was laughing at herself, or at the person she was talking to or even at the whole world, which she probably did not intend. I was often surprised and asked myself what she meant to say when she uttered phrases such as: "Yes, I'm terribly beautiful; well of course everyone is in love with me," and so on. Anna Dmitriyevna was always doing something. She had a passion for arranging her little house and garden, for flowers, canaries and nice little things. Her little rooms and little garden were small and modest, but everything was arranged so neatly and tidily and bore so much the general character of light-hearted cheerfulness expressed by a pleasant waltz or a polka that the words "like a little doll's", often used in praise by visitors, suited Anna Dmitriyevna's little rooms and garden very well. Anna Dmitriyevna was herself like a little doll – small, thin, with a fresh complexion, nice little hands, always in good spirits and becomingly dressed. Only the slightly too prominent dark-purple veins on her small hands upset that general impression. Avdotya Vasilyevna, on the other hand, hardly ever did anything, and not only did not like occupying herself with small things or flowers but also took very little care of herself; she would invariably rush off to get dressed as visitors were arriving. But once dressed and back in the room, she looked unusually pretty, except for a distant fixed expression in her eyes and smile, common to all very beautiful individuals. Her sternly regular beautiful face and her slender figure seemed to constantly tell us: "Feel free to look at me."

Yet, notwithstanding the mother's lively character and the daughter's distracted appearance, something told you that the former had neither then nor now ever loved anything but what was nice and fun and that Avdotya Vasilyevna was one of those people who, once they love, will sacrifice their whole lives for the one they love.

34

Father's Marriage

FATHER WAS FORTY-EIGHT YEARS OLD when he married again, taking Avdotya Vasilyevna Epifanova for his wife.

When he came to the country alone with the girls that spring, I imagine that Papa had been in that particular exhilarated and sociable frame of mind which gamblers usually find themselves in when they stop playing after huge winnings. He felt that he had much unspent luck in him, which, if he no longer wanted to use it on cards, he could on the whole use towards success in life. And also it was spring, he had an unexpectedly large sum of money at his disposal, he was completely alone and was bored. As he chatted with Yakov about his affairs and recalled the ongoing litigation with the Epifanovs and the beautiful Avdotya Vasilyevna, whom he had not seen for a long time, I can imagine him saying to Yakov: "Do you know, Yakov, how we should deal with that litigation? I think we should just let them have that confounded land; what do you think?"

I imagine Yakov's fingers twirling in disagreement behind his back at such a question and him pointing out, "*But then again*, we have right on our side, Pyotr Alexandrovich."

But Papa ordered his carriage to be prepared, put on his fashionable olive overcoat, brushed what hair he had left, sprinkled his handkerchief with scent and, in the happiest of spirits, caused by his conviction that he was acting like a gentleman and mostly in the hope of seeing a pretty woman, drove over to his neighbours.

I only know that on his first visit Papa did not find Pyotr Vasilyevich at home, as the latter was out on his land, and that he spent about two hours with the ladies. I imagine how he showered them with compliments, how he charmed them, tapping the floor with his soft boot, lisping slightly and throwing them sweet looks. I also imagine how the cheerful old lady suddenly took a tender liking to him and how her cold beautiful daughter perked up.

When the housemaid came running, out of breath, to tell Pyotr Vasilyevich that old Irtenyev himself had arrived, I can imagine him crossly replying, "Well, and what if he has arrived?" and that as a result he would have walked home as slowly as possible and perhaps, after returning to his study, he would deliberately have put on his dirtiest coat and sent a message to the cook that on no account should anything be added to dinner even if the ladies were to order him to do so.

I often later saw Papa with Pyotr Vasilyevich, which is why I can vividly picture that first meeting. I can imagine Pyotr Vasilyevich being sullen, even with Papa offering to end the litigation peacefully, and angry that he had sacrificed his career for his mother while Papa had done nothing of the kind, which did not surprise him, and how Papa, pretending not to notice his sullenness, would have been playful and spirited and would have treated him as being remarkably funny, and at times Pyotr Vasilyevich would have been offended by this and at others he would have gone along with it despite himself. Papa, with his penchant for making a joke out of everything, for some reason called Pyotr Vasilyevich a colonel and although the latter once, with me there, remarked, stuttering worse than ever and blushing with annoyance, that he was not a co-co-lonel but a lieu-lieu-tenant, five minutes later Papa called him a colonel again.

Lyubochka told me that before our arrival in the country they had met up with the Epifanovs every day and that it had been a lot of fun. Papa, with his flair for organizing everything in an original, humorous and at the same time simple and elegant way, arranged hunting and fishing expeditions and firework displays, at all of which the Epifanovs had been present. "And it would have been even more fun had it not been for that unbearable Pyotr Vasilyevich, who grumbled, stammered and upset everything," Lyubochka had said.

Since our arrival, the Epifanovs had only visited us twice and we all drove over to them once. After St Peter's day, when, as it was Papa's name day, they were there as well as a whole lot of other guests, our relations with the Epifanovs ended completely for whatever reason and only Papa continued to visit them on his own.

In that short period in which I saw Papa with Dunyechka, as her mother used to call Avdotya Vasilyevna, I managed to observe the following. Papa was all the time in that happy mood which had struck me on the day of our arrival. He was so cheerful, young, full of life and happiness that the glow of that happiness radiated to everyone around, unconsciously imparting the same mood to all of us. He would not leave Avdotya Vasilyevna's side when she was in the room, constantly paid her such sugary compliments that I felt embarrassed for him, or else he would watch her silently, twitching his shoulder and coughing slightly in a passionate, self-satisfied sort of way. Sometimes he even whispered to her, but he did this with an expression of it all being a joke somehow, which was his way even in the most serious matters.

Avdotya Vasilyevna had picked up, it seemed, Papa's expression of happiness which at that time shone almost constantly in her large blue eyes, except in those moments when she would suddenly be seized by such shyness that I felt sorry and pained looking at her, as I knew the feeling well. At such moments she was manifestly afraid of every glance or gesture, felt as though everyone was looking at her and thinking only about her, finding everything about her unseemly. She would look round at everybody, continually turn red or pale and would begin to talk nonsense loudly and boldly, aware of doing so and feeling that everyone including Papa could hear it and then she would blush even more. But on those occasions Papa did not even notice the silly things she said and, coughing slightly, he would continue to look at her just as passionately and ecstatically as ever. I noticed that although those fits of shyness came over Avdotya Vasilyevna without reason, they sometimes followed immediately after some beautiful young woman had been mentioned in Papa's presence. Her frequent switching over from pensiveness to that strange awkward cheerfulness I spoke of earlier, the way she would repeat Papa's favourite words and turns of phrase or continue with others conversations begun with Papa, all that would have explained Papa's relationship with Avdotya Vasilyevna, had the main character not been my father and had I been older. But at the time I suspected nothing even when Papa became very upset, in front of me, after receiving a letter from Pyotr Vasilyevich, and stopped visiting the Epifanovs until the end of August.

At the end of August Papa began to go over to the neighbours again and, the day before Volodya's and my departure for Moscow, he announced to us that he was to marry Avdotya Vasilyevna Epifanova.

35

How We Took the News

T HE DAY BEFORE THE OFFICIAL ANNOUNCEMENT, everyone in the house already knew about it and judged the situation in different ways. Mimi did not leave her room all day and cried. Katyenka sat with her and only came out for dinner with a somewhat outraged expression, clearly borrowed from her mother. Lyubochka on the contrary was very cheerful and told us at dinner that she knew a wonderful secret that she, however, would tell no one.

"There is nothing wonderful about your secret," Volodya said to her, not sharing her enthusiasm, "if you could but take anything seriously, you would understand that it is, on the contrary, very bad."

Lyubochka stared at him in surprise and kept silent.

After dinner Volodya wanted to take me by the arm but, probably afraid that it might look like a sign of affection, he just touched my elbow and motioned me to the reception room.

"Do you know what secret Lyubochka was talking about?" he said to me after reassuring himself that we were by ourselves.

Volodya and I rarely talked to each other face to face about anything serious, which is why, when it happened, we felt a kind of mutual awkwardness and "little spots would begin to leap in our eyes", as Volodya put it. But this time, in response to the confusion reflected in my eyes, he continued to stare at me in earnest with a look that said, "There is nothing to be confused about here; we are brothers after all and we have to consult each other on a serious family matter." I understood him and he went on:

"Papa is going to marry Avdotya Epifanova, did you know that?"

I nodded because I had already heard the news.

"This is actually very bad," Volodya continued.

"Why?"

"Why?" he replied, annoyed. "How pleasant will it be to have this stutterer, this colonel and all the others for relatives? And she may appear kind now, but who knows what she'll be like. For us it may be of no consequence, but Lyubochka is soon to come out in society. And with such a *belle-mère** it won't be very pleasant; she doesn't even speak French properly and what manners could she teach her? She's a fishwife – nothing more, and even accepting she's kind, she's still a fishwife," concluded Volodya, obviously very pleased with the appellation "fishwife".

Although it was strange for me to hear Volodya thus calmly judging Papa's choice, I did feel that he was right.

"Why is Papa getting married?"

"It's a murky affair, God only knows. I know only that Pyotr Vasilyevich persuaded him to marry her, insisted upon it, although Papa didn't want to. Then he had this fantasy, a chivalrous gesture – it's a murky affair. I have only now begun to understand Father," continued Volodya (the fact that he called him Father and not Papa caused me a sudden sharp pang), "he's an excellent man, kind and clever, but so frivolous and changeable... it's amazing! He cannot look at a woman and keep cool. You know that he falls in love with every woman he meets. Even Mimi, you know."

"What are you saying?"

"I'm telling you; I've only found out recently that he was in love with Mimi when she was still young, he wrote her poetry and something happened between them. Mimi is still suffering now." And Volodya burst out laughing.

"It can't be!" I said in amazement.

"But the main thing is," continued Volodya, serious again and suddenly beginning to speak in French, "will our relatives be pleased with such a marriage? And she'll probably have children."

I was so struck by Volodya's common sense and foresight that I did not know what to reply.

Lyubochka came in at that point.

"So you know?" she asked with a joyful expression.

"Yes," said Volodya, "only I'm surprised, Lyubochka: you are no longer a babe in arms, so how can you be happy that Papa is going to marry some piece of trash?"

Lyubocha suddenly looked serious and hesitated.

"Volodya! Why trash? How dare you speak like that about Avdotya Vasilyevna? If Papa is going to marry her, then she can't be trash."

"Fine then, not trash, I was just saying, but all the same—"

"There's no 'all the same' about it," interrupted Lyobochka, getting worked up, "I have not called that lady you are in love with trash; so how can you speak this way about Papa and that wonderful woman? You may be my elder brother, but you mustn't say such things to me, you mustn't."

"Why should we not discuss—"

"It's wrong to," Lyubochka interrupted him again, "it's wrong to discuss a father like ours. Mimi is allowed to, but not you, my elder brother."

"You still don't understand anything," said Volodya scornfully, "now get this: is it good that some Epifanova, Dunyechka, should take the place of your late Maman?"

Lyubochka was silent for a moment and suddenly tears welled up in her eyes.

"I knew that you were arrogant, but I didn't think that you were so nasty," she said and left us.

"*To the bread roll,*" said Volodya, pulling a half serious, half comic face and making his eyes look glazed. "So you try to reason with them," he continued in self-reproach for having forgotten himself to the point of condescending to having a conversation with Lyubochka.

The next day the weather was bad and neither Papa nor the ladies had yet come down for tea by the time I went into the drawing room. During the night there had been a cold autumn rain. What was left of the rain cloud that had caused the night's downpour rushed across the sky and the bright circle of the sun, already quite high, shone dimly through it. It was windy, damp and grey. The door to the garden was open and on the veranda floor, blackened by moisture, the puddles from the overnight rain were drying up. The open door was shaking on its iron hook in the wind; the paths were damp and muddy; the old birches with their bare white branches, the shrubs and grass, nettles, currant bushes and elders with the pale side of their leaves twisted outwards tossed about on the spot, seemingly trying to tear themselves away from their roots. Round yellow leaves, twirling and chasing each other, flew up from the lime-tree avenue and, getting soaked, settled on the wet path and the wet aftermath* of the meadow. My thoughts were taken up with my father's impending marriage, looking at it from Volodya's point of view. The future seemed to hold nothing good for my sister, for us brothers or even for Father. I was troubled by the thought that an outsider, a stranger and above all a *young* woman with no rights whatsoever would in many respects take the place of – of whom? – that an ordinary *young* lady would take the place of our dead mother! I felt sad and Father seemed to me more and more to blame. Just then I heard him and Volodya talking in the pantry. I did not want to see my father right then, and moved away from the door, but Lyubochka came in and said that Papa was asking for me.

He stood in the drawing room leaning his hand on the piano and he looked impatiently as well as solemnly in my direction. His face had already lost that youthful, happy expression I had noticed in him lately. He was sad. Volodya was pacing up and down the room with a pipe in his hand. I went up to Father and greeted him.

"Well, my friends," he said determinedly, raising his head and speaking in that particularly hasty tone used by people when things that are obviously unpleasant and which are already beyond discussion have to be said, "I think you know that I'm to marry Avdotya Vasilyevna." He paused for a short while. "I never wanted to remarry after your Maman, but…" he stopped for a moment, "but… it must be fate. Dunyechka is a kind, sweet girl, no longer very young; I hope you will learn to love her, children, and she already loves you with all her heart; she is a good person. As for you," he said, turning to Volodya and me as though in a hurry to speak before we could manage to interrupt him. "It is already time for you to leave, but I shall stay here until the new year and then I'll come to Moscow," and again he stopped short, "with my wife and Lyubochka." I began to feel pained seeing my Father somehow shy and guilty before us and I moved closer to him, but Volodya, continuing to smoke and keeping his head down, went on pacing across the room.

"So you see, my friends, what your old man has been up to," concluded Papa, blushing, coughing slightly and putting his hand out to Volodya and me. He had tears in his eyes as he said this and his hand, held out to Volodya, who was at the other end of the room, shook a little. The sight of that shaking hand struck me painfully and a strange thought occurred to me which affected me even more – it occurred to me that Papa had served in the 1812 campaign and had, as was well known, been a brave officer. I held back his large veined hand and kissed it. He pressed my hand hard and suddenly, with a sob, took Lyubochka's dark little head in both his hands and began to kiss her on the eyes. Volodya pretended he had dropped his pipe and, bending down, he stealthily wiped his eyes with his fist and, trying to remain unnoticed, left the room.

36

University

THE WEDDING WAS TO TAKE PLACE in two weeks' time, but our lectures were starting and Volodya and I went off to Moscow at the beginning of September. The Nekhlyudovs also came back from the country. Dmitry (when we had parted, we had given our word to write to each other, and of course never did) came to see me straight away and we decided that he would accompany me to the university the next day for my first lectures.

It was a bright sunny day.

As soon as I entered the lecture hall, I felt my own identity disappear in that crowd of young, happy individuals, who swung noisily to and fro through all the doors and corridors in the bright sunlight streaming through the large windows. It was very pleasant to feel part of this huge company. But only few out of so many were familiar to me, and even encounters with those were restricted to nods and the words: "Good morning, Irtenyev!" All around me people shook hands and jostled each other, and words of friendship, smiles, goodwill, jokes, flew about. I felt the bond that united all this youthful company everywhere and felt with sadness that the bond somehow passed me by. But that was only a momentary impression. Following this and the annoyance it produced in me, I soon discovered that it was very good not to belong to any particular group and that I should have my own circle of respectable people. I sat down on the third bench where Count B., Baron Z., Prince R., Ivin and other gentlemen of that ilk were seated. Of those I only knew Ivin and Count B. But even those gentlemen looked at me in a way that made me feel that I did not entirely belong to their group either. I began to watch everything that went on around me. Semyonov, with his tousled grey hair and white teeth, and his frock coat unbuttoned, sat not far away from me and, leaning on his elbow, nibbled at his quill pen. The grammar-school boy who had come first in the examinations sat on the first bench, still wearing a black cravat wound around his cheeks, and he was playing around with a silver watch key hanging from his satin waistcoat. Ikonin, who did make it to university after all, sat on a higher bench in pale-blue braided trousers that covered his boots completely, and he laughed loudly and called out that he was in Parnassus. Ilyenka, who to my surprise not only bowed to me coldly but even with contempt, as though he wished to remind me that here we were all equals, sat in front of me, placed his skinny legs rather casually on the bench (I felt this to be on my account) and chatted to another student while occasionally glancing at me. Ivin's group next to me spoke in French. Those gentlemen appeared particularly stupid to me. Every word I overheard from their conversation not only seemed to me to be meaningless but even incorrect, simply not French ("*Ce n'est pas français*,"* I said to myself), and the attitude, conversation and the actions of Semyonov and Ilyenka and others seemed to me undignified, improper, just not *comme il faut*.

I did not belong to any group and, feeling alone and unable to make contact, became bad-tempered. One student on the bench in front of me bit his nails, leaving the skin around them all raw, and this seemed to me so disgusting that I moved to a seat further from him. I remember that my heart felt very heavy that first day.

When the Professor came in and everyone, after shuffling about in their seats, stopped talking, I remember that I even extended my satirical glance to the Professor and was struck that he began his lecture with an introductory phrase that in my opinion made no sense at all. I wanted the lecture to be so clever from start to finish that it would be impossible to discard or even add one single word. Feeling disappointed, I immediately, under the heading *First Lecture*, began to sketch eighteen profiles joined in a circle in the shape of a flower in the beautifully bound exercise book I had brought with me. I occasionally moved my hand on the paper to lead the Professor (who I was sure took great interest in me) to believe that I was taking notes. Having decided at that first lecture that noting down everything every Professor said would be unnecessary and even stupid, I kept to that principle to the end of the course.

At the following lectures I no longer felt so alone. I met many other students, shook hands, chatted, but for some reason a real rapprochement did not happen between us and I still often felt sad inside and just put on an act. I could not become intimate with the company of Ivin and the aristocrats, as everyone called them, because, as I now remember, I was shy and rude to them and bowed to them only after they had bowed to me, and they evidently had very little interest in knowing me. With most of the students, however, this inability to get closer happened for a very different reason. As soon as I felt someone I knew begin to be well disposed towards me, I would immediately give him to understand that I was in the habit of dining with Prince Ivan Ivanych and that I had my own *droshky*. I only said all this to show myself to my best advantage and so that my friend would like me even more. But on the contrary, almost every time I mentioned my kinship with Prince Ivan Ivanych and my *droshky*, my new friend would suddenly, to my amazement, become haughty and distant with me.

There was among us a state-aided student called Operov. He was a modest, very able and diligent young man, who always held out his hand like a plank, without bending his fingers and not moving it at all, so that some friends would offer him their hand the same way as a joke and call it shaking hands "plank-like". I nearly always sat next to him and often talked to him. I particularly liked Operov for his free and easy opinions when he spoke his mind about the professors. He defined the qualities and shortcomings in the way each professor taught very clearly and precisely and sometimes even poked fun at them, which had a particularly strange and startling effect on me when he said it in a quiet voice, coming out of his tiny little mouth. Despite all this, however, he carefully noted down all the lectures without exception in his small handwriting. We were becoming friends and had decided to prepare together for the exams, and his small, myopic grey eyes already turned happily towards me when I came to sit down in my place next to him. But I once found it necessary to explain to him in conversation that my dying mother had begged my father not to send us to a state institution and that I had since become convinced that all state schoolboys might indeed be very clever but that for me... they were not at all the thing, *ce ne sont pas des gens comme il faut** and in saying this I became flustered and felt myself blush for some reason.

Operov said nothing, but at the next lectures he did not greet me first, did not offer me his plank-like hand and did not speak to me; when I sat at my place, he bent his head sideways very close to his exercise books and pretended to be looking inside them. I was surprised at Operov's sudden unwarranted coolness. But *pour un jeune homme de bonne maison** I considered it improper to try and ingratiate myself with Operov, the state-educated student, and left him alone, although I confess that his coolness saddened me. Once I arrived before him and as the lecture, to be given by a popular professor, was attended by students who were not in the habit of coming to all the lectures and all the seats were taken, I sat down in Operov's place, set my exercise books down on the desk and went off. When I returned to the lecture hall, I saw that my exercise books had been moved to a bench further back and that Operov was sitting in his usual place. I pointed out to him that I had put my books there.

"I don't know," he replied, suddenly blushing and not looking at me.

"I am telling you that I put my books there," I said, beginning to get excited on purpose, thinking that I would frighten him off with my boldness. "Everyone saw it," I added, looking round at the students, but although many looked at me with curiosity, no one replied.

"Seats can't be bought here and whoever comes first sits down," said Operov, straightening himself angrily on his seat and for an instant looking at me indignantly.

"This means you're a boor," I said.

It looked as though Operov muttered something, it even seemed that he muttered: "And you're a stupid little boy," but I certainly did not hear that. And what would have been the use if I had heard it? Quarrelling like some *manants,** nothing more? (I liked the word *manant* very much, and it was the answer and solution to many tangled relationships.) I might have said something else, but at that moment the door slammed and the Professor in a dark-blue tailcoat bowed and quickly walked up to the rostrum.

Before the exam, however, when I was in need of notes, Operov, remembering his promise, offered me his and invited me to study together with him.

37

Matters of the Heart

MATTERS OF THE HEART took up a lot of my time that winter. I was in love three times. The first time I fell passionately in love with a very stout lady who used to ride in my presence at the Freitag Riding School, and so every Tuesday and Friday – the days she rode – I would go to the riding school to gaze at her. But each time I was afraid she would see me and so I would invariably stand so far away from her and rush off so hastily from the place she was about to pass and turn away in such an offhand manner whenever she looked in my direction, that I never even managed to see her properly and to this day do not know whether she really was pretty or not.

Dubkov, who knew this lady, once found me at the riding school hiding behind the footmen and the fur coats they were holding. He had heard about my infatuation from Dmitry and put such fear into me with an offer to introduce me to the Amazon that I rushed headlong out of the riding school, and the very thought that he would tell her about me meant that I no longer dared to go there, even as far as the footmen, for fear of meeting her.

When I was in love with women I did not know and especially married women, I would be overwhelmed by shyness a thousand times worse than the shyness I had felt with Sonyechka. What I feared most of all in the world was that the object of my love should find out about my feelings and even about my existence. I thought that if she found out about my feelings she would find it such an insult that she would never be able to forgive me. And indeed, had that Amazon known in detail how, gazing at her from behind the footmen, I imagined myself abducting her and carrying her off to the country, and fancied how we would live there together and what I would do with her, she would have had every right to be insulted. But I could not grasp clearly that her knowing me did not mean she could suddenly find out all my thoughts about her and that there was therefore nothing embarrassing in simply being introduced to her.

The second instance was when I fell in love with Sonyechka after seeing her at my sister's. My second infatuation for her had long gone, but I fell in love with her for the third time after Lyubochka gave me a notebook of verses copied by Sonyechka in which many bleak love passages from Lermontov's* *The Demon* had been underlined in red ink and covered with little flowers. Remembering how the previous year Volodya had kissed his young lady's purse, I tried to do the same, and indeed in the evening when I was on my own, I began to dream, looking at one of the flowers, and to press it to my lips, which put me in some kind of pleasant weepy mood, and I was in love again for several days, or so I supposed.

Finally, the third instance that winter was when I fell in love with a young lady Volodya was in love with and who came to visit us. As I now recall, there was absolutely nothing good-looking about that young lady, especially not the kind of good looks that usually appealed to me. She was the daughter of a Moscow lady well known for her intelligence and learning. She was small, skinny, with long, light-brown, English-style ringlets and a delicate profile. Everyone said that the young lady was cleverer and more learned than her mother, but I simply could not be the judge of that as I nurtured some kind of abject fear at the very thought of her intelligence and learning and so only spoke to her once and even then with inexplicable trepidation. But Volodya's rapturous feelings – he was never shy of expressing his rapture in front of those present – communicated itself so powerfully to me that I too fell passionately in love with the young lady. I did not tell him about my love, as I felt that Volodya would not like hearing about two brothers being in love with the same girl. On the contrary, the thought that pleased me most about it was that our love was so pure that, despite the object of our love being one and the same charming creature, we would remain friends and be prepared, if needs be, to sacrifice ourselves for one another. As regards self-sacrifice, however, Volodya apparently did not quite share my views: he was so passionately in love that he was prepared to slap the face of a real diplomat who – rumour had it – was to marry her, and to challenge him to a duel. I would have been very pleased to sacrifice my own feelings, probably because it would not have required great effort given that I had rather fancifully spoken to that young lady only once, about the merits of classical music, and my love, as much as I tried to nurture it, had vanished by the following week.

38

Society

THE WORLDLY PLEASURES I dreamt of indulging in upon entering university, in imitation of my brother, were an utter disappointment to me that winter. Volodya danced a great deal and Papa went to balls too with his young wife, but they must still have considered me either too young or too inept for those pleasures, for no one introduced me to those homes where balls were held. I told no one about my wish to go to balls – not even Dmitry, despite my promise of being open with him – and not about how painful and annoying it was that I was forgotten and was evidently looked upon as some kind of philosopher, which as a result I pretended to be.

But that winter there was an evening party at Princess Kornakova's house. She personally invited us all, including me, and for the first time I was to go to a ball. Before starting off, Volodya came into my room and wished to see what I was wearing. I was very surprised and taken aback by that gesture on his part. I thought that the desire to be well dressed was a shameful one and should be kept hidden; he, on the other hand, considered that desire so natural and essential that he quite openly said that he was concerned that I might disgrace myself. He told me to be sure to wear patent-leather boots, was horrified when I wanted to wear suede gloves, arranged my watch on me in a particular fashion and took me to the hairdresser's on Kuznetsky Bridge. They curled my hair. Volodya moved back and looked at me from a distance.

"That looks good, but is there no way of flattening those tufts?" he said, addressing the hairdresser.

But however much Monsieur Charles oiled my tufts with some sticky essence, they still stood up when I put my hat on, and on the whole my curly look seemed to me to make matters much worse than before. My only salvation was affecting an air of casualness. Only in that way did my appearance amount to something.

Volodya appeared to be of the same opinion, because he asked me to get rid of my curls, and when I had done that and it still did not look right, he stopped looking at me and was silent and gloomy all the way to the Kornakovs.

I stepped into the Kornakov's house boldly together with Volodya, but when the Princess invited me to dance, I for some reason told her I did not dance, even though my sole purpose in coming had been to dance a great deal; after this I lost my nerve and, ending up alone among strangers, lapsed into my usual insurmountable and ever growing shyness. I stood in silence in the same spot all evening.

One of the Princesses came up to me during a waltz and, with the formal courtesy common to the whole family, asked me why I was not dancing. I remember how shy I became with that question and how at the same time, quite involuntarily, a complacent smile spread across my face, and I began to speak such nonsense in French, using the most pompous language, with parentheses, that now, even after dozens of years, I am ashamed to remember it. The music must have had that effect on me, tingling my nerves and drowning, I believed, the not altogether intelligible part of my speech. I said something about high society, about the shallowness of men and women, and finally became so entangled in lies that I stopped in the middle of a word in some sentence that could not be completed anyway.

Even the Princess, a woman of society, was embarrassed and looked at me reproachfully. I smiled. At that critical moment Volodya noticed that I was speaking heatedly and probably wanted to know what I was saying to make amends for not dancing and so he came towards us together with Dubkov. He saw my smiling face and the frightened look on the Princess's face and, when he heard the awful nonsense with which I ended, he blushed and turned away. The Princess got to her feet and left me. I continued smiling, but suffered so intensely at that moment from the consciousness of my stupidity that I was ready to sink through the floor and felt the need to move and say something at any price in order to somehow alter my situation. I went over to Dubkov and asked him whether he had danced many waltzes with *her*. I was pretending to be playful and cheerful, but in reality I was begging for help from that same Dubkov to whom I had shouted: "Hold your tongue!" when we had dinner at Yar's. Dubkov pretended not to hear me and turned the other way. I moved towards Volodya and, with great effort and trying to give my voice a joking tone, said, "Well, Volodya, are you tired out?" But Volodya looked at me as if to say: "You don't talk to me this way when we are alone," and silently moved away from me, evidently afraid that I might somehow latch on to him.

"Dear God, even my own brother deserts me!" I thought.

However, for some reason, I did not have the strength to leave. I spent the rest of the evening gloomily in one spot, and only when everyone was leaving and crowding the corridor and the footman who was helping me into my overcoat caught the edge of my hat and made it tip up did I burst out into painful tearful laughter and, not addressing anyone in particular, said: "*Comme c'est gracieux.*"*

39

The Drinking Party

EVEN THOUGH under Dmitry's influence I had not yet indulged in the common student amusement known as *kutyozh* or drinking spree, that winter I did once take part in such merry-making and came away from it with a less than agreeable feeling. This is how it came about. At a lecture at the beginning of the year, Baron Z., a tall fair-haired young man with an extremely serious expression and regular features, invited us all to his place for an evening among friends. All of us meant all those friends from our course who were more or less *comme il faut*, which of course did not include Grap or Semyonov or Operov, or any other less acceptable gentlemen. Volodya smiled scornfully when he heard that I was going to a first-year drinking party, but I anticipated rare and great enjoyment from a pastime that was as yet completely unknown to me, and so arrived punctually at the appointed time of eight o'clock at Baron Z.'s house.

Baron Z., in an unbuttoned frock coat and white waistcoat, received his guests in the brightly lit reception and drawing rooms of the small house where his parents lived. They had let him have the main reception rooms for that evening's festivities. You could catch glimpses of the heads and dresses of inquisitive housemaids in the corridor and once a lady's dress flashed past in the refreshment room, which I took to be the Baroness herself. There were about twenty guests, all of them students except for Herr Frost, who had come with Ivin, and a tall red-faced gentleman in civilian clothes, who was in charge of the feast and who was introduced to everyone as a relative of the Baron and a former student of Derpt University. The rather bright lighting and customary formal furnishings of the main rooms had a sobering effect at first on that young crowd; they all instinctively stood along the walls except for some bold spirits and the Derpt student, who had undone his waistcoat and seemed to be in every room at once as well as in every corner of every room, filling the whole space with his pleasant, loud and persistent tenor voice. The others, however, mainly remained silent or spoke modestly about professors, studies, exams: on the whole about serious and uninteresting subjects. All without exception looked towards the door to the refreshment room and, although they tried to conceal it, their expressions seemed to say, "Well, it's time to begin." I too felt it was time to begin and awaited the *beginning* with impatient delight.

After tea, which the footmen passed round to the guests, the Derpt student asked Frost in Russian:

"Can you make a punch, Frost?"

"*O ja!*" replied Frost, wiggling his calves, but the Derpt student said to him, again in Russian:

"Then take the matter in hand." (They were on familiar terms, using *ty*, as they were both from Derpt University.) And Frost, striding across with his bent, muscular legs, began to go to and fro between the drawing room and the refreshment room, and soon a large soup tureen appeared on the table with a ten-pound sugar loaf* suspended above it held up by three students' crossed swords. Baron Z. meanwhile kept on going up to all the guests who were gathered in the drawing room gazing at the soup tureen, and saying almost the same thing to everyone with a serious face throughout: "Come on, gentlemen, let's drink this cup student style to *Brüderschaft*, otherwise there is no comradeship at all on our course. Do unbutton your coats and even take them off like he has." And indeed the Derpt student had taken off his coat, rolled up his shirtsleeves above his white elbows and, resolutely planting his legs apart, had already set fire to the rum in the soup tureen.

"Gentlemen! Turn off the lights," the Derpt student suddenly shouted, with such authority and so loudly as one would shout only if everyone else had been shouting too. We, however, all looked silently at the soup tureen and at the Derpt student's white shirt and we all felt that the festive moment had arrived.

"*Löschen sie die Lichter aus, Frost!*"* the Derpt student shouted out again, in German this time, probably because he was overexcited. Frost and the rest of us went to extinguish the candles. It grew dark in the room; only the white sleeves and hands supporting the sugar loaf on the swords were lit by a bluish flame. The Derpt student's loud tenor was no longer the only voice, for there was chatter and laughter in every corner of the room. Many took off their coats (particularly those who wore fine freshly laundered shirts): I did the same and understood that it *had begun*. Although there was nothing exciting going on, yet I was very sure that it would turn out excellently once we had each had a glassful of the drink that was being prepared.

The drink was ready. The Derpt student poured out the punch into glasses, badly staining the table, and shouted: "Well, gentlemen, let us begin." When each of us had taken hold of a full, sticky glass, the Derpt student and Frost began to sing a German song in which the exclamation "*Juchhe!*"* was repeated several times. We all burst into song, joining in rather discordantly, and began to clink glasses, call out, praise the punch and cross arms or just drink the sweet and potent liquid. There was no longer anything to wait for, the party was in full swing. I had finished one whole glass of punch and another was poured out; my temples were throbbing, the flames looked crimson, all around me there was shouting and laughter, but even so not only did it not feel cheerful but I was even convinced that I, as well as everyone else, was finding this dull and that I and everyone else for some reason considered it necessary to pretend that we were having fun. The only one who was perhaps not pretending was the Derpt student. He turned redder and redder and was everywhere at once; he filled up everyone's empty glass and spilt more and more over the table, which became sugary and sticky all over. I do not remember in what order things happened, but I do remember that I desperately loved the Derpt student and Frost that evening, that I learnt the German song by heart and that I kissed them both on their sugary lips. I also remember that I hated the Derpt student that evening and wanted to hurl a chair at him, but that I stopped myself. I remember that, besides the feeling that all my limbs were uncontrollable, as I had experienced that time I had dinner at Yar's, my head hurt so badly that evening and I was so dizzy that I was terribly frightened of dying that very moment. And I remember that we all sat down on the floor for some reason and waved our arms about imitating a paddling movement, that we all sang 'Down along the Mother Volga' and that I thought at the time that it was totally unnecessary to do so. I remember that, lying on the floor with my legs interlocked, I wrestled gypsy-like, that I dislocated someone's neck and that I thought that this would not have happened had he not been drunk. I remember also that we had supper and drank something else, that I went outside to get some fresh air, and that my head felt cold and that when I drove off it was terribly dark, that the open carriage's running board was slanting and slippery and that there was no use holding on to Kuzma because he had come over all weak and swung around like a rag. But the main thing I remember is that throughout the whole evening I constantly felt that I was acting very stupidly by pretending that I was having a lot of fun, that I loved drinking a lot and did not consider myself drunk. I also constantly felt that the others were also acting stupidly by pretending likewise. I thought that it was as unpleasant for each one individually as it was for me, but that each one supposed that he was the only one feeling like that and so felt obliged to pretend to be happy in order not to upset the general fun, and besides, strange as it may sound, I regarded myself obliged to pretend because three bottles of champagne at ten roubles each and ten bottles of rum at four roubles each had been poured into the soup tureen, which added up to seventy roubles without counting supper. I was so convinced of all this that the next day at lectures I was amazed that my friends who had attended Baron Z.'s party were not only unashamed when recounting what they had done there, but that they spoke of the evening so that other students could hear. They said that it had been a most excellent party, that the Derpt men were great at those things and that forty bottles of rum had been imbibed by twenty people and that many had been left for dead under the table. I could not understand why they told these things and even less why they lied about themselves.

40

My Friendship with the Nekhlyudovs

THAT WINTER I not only very frequently saw Dmitry, who often came to our house, but also the rest of his family, with whom I had begun to grow closer.

The Nekhlyudovs – mother, aunt and daughter – spent every evening at home, and the Princess liked to have young people come and visit, men of the kind who, in her own words, were able to spend an entire evening without playing cards or dancing. But there must have been few of those, because I, who went over to them nearly every evening, rarely met other visitors there. I had become used to the members of that family, to their different moods, and had already gained a clear understanding of their mutual relationships. I had grown used to the rooms and the furniture and, when there were no other visitors, felt completely relaxed, except for those occasions when I was left alone in the room with Varyenka. I kept on thinking that, as she was not a very pretty girl, she would badly want me to fall in love with her. But even that feeling of embarrassment began to pass. She demonstrated so naturally that it was all the same to her whether she spoke to me or her brother or Lyubov Sergeyevna, that I took to seeing her simply as a person whose company I could visibly enjoy without it being a shameful or dangerous thing. During the whole time we knew each other, she would some days seem very unattractive and on others not too bad-looking, but I did not even ask myself once whether I was in love with her or not. At times I would speak directly to her, but more often I would chat to her while addressing myself to Lyubov Sergeyevna or Dmitry, and I particularly liked doing this. I derived great pleasure in talking in her presence and listening to her singing and generally being aware of her in the same room as me, but any thought as to the consequences of my relationship with Varyenka or dreams of sacrificing myself for my friend if he were to fall in love with my sister rarely came into my head now. If such dreams and thoughts did appear, I unconsciously pushed aside any thought of the future, feeling satisfied with the present.

Despite this closer relationship I continued to consider myself fully obliged to conceal my real feelings and inclinations from all the Nekhlyudovs and particularly from Varyenka, and I tried to show myself to be a completely different young man, and even one that could not possibly have existed, from the one I was in reality. I tried to appear passionate; I went into raptures, sighed, made impassioned gestures when something seemed to please me enormously, or I tried to pretend indifference to anything unusual I might see or was told about. I tried to be wickedly sarcastic, holding nothing sacred, and at the same time sharply observant. I tried to appear logical in all my actions and precise and efficient in my life and at the same time scornful of all material things. I can boldly assert that in reality I was much nicer than the strange creature I tried to pass myself off as. Nevertheless the Nekhlyudovs loved me even with all that pretence and seemed fortunately not to believe in it. Only Lyubov Sergeyevna, who considered me a hugely selfish, godless and sarcastic young man, seemed not to like me, and often argued with me. She would get angry and take me aback with her fragmented, incoherent phrases. But Dmitry continued to maintain those strange relations with her, relations that went beyond friendship, and said that no one understood her and that she did him an extraordinary amount of good. Just the same, his friendship with her continued to grieve the whole family.

Once Varyenka talked about that bond, which was incomprehensible to us all, and explained it this way:

"Dmitry is vain. He is too proud and despite his intellect he loves praise and admiration. He loves always to be first and as for *auntie*, she admires him in the innocence of her soul and does not have the discretion to conceal this admiration from him; so she ends up flattering him, but she does not do this in pretence but in all sincerity."

These comments stayed with me and, examining them later, I had to accept that Varyenka was very clever and as a result was delighted to raise her higher in my estimation. Although I was pleased to think highly of her on discovering her good mind and her other moral qualities, I remained strictly moderate and never went into raptures about her, which would have been exaltation to the extreme. So when Sofya Ivanovna, who talked incessantly about her niece, told me how four years ago in the country Varyenka, when still a child, had given all her dresses and shoes away to peasant children without asking permission so that they had to be taken back afterwards, I did not immediately consider that fact as worthy of my raised opinion of her and even mentally mocked her for having such an impractical view of things.

When the Nekhlyudovs had visitors, and sometimes Volodya and Dubkov were among them, I would retire smugly to the background with the calm consciousness of my strength in being part of the household, and I would not talk, but just listen to what the others were saying. And I found everything the others said so incredibly stupid that I was inwardly amazed that the Princess, such a clever logical woman, and her whole logical family could listen to such inanities and respond to them. Had it occurred to me at the time to compare what the others said to what I said myself when I was alone with them, I should probably not have been surprised at all. And I would have been even less surprised had I believed that the women in our own household – Avdotya Vasilyevna, Lyubochka and Katyenka – were just like any other women and in no way inferior, and had I remembered what things Dubkov, Katyenka and Avdotya Vasilyevna spoke about with happy smiles for whole evenings or how Dubkov seized almost every opportunity to read with feeling the verses: "*Au banquet de la vie, infortuné convive…*"* or excerpts from *The Demon*, and on the whole what nonsense they uttered with great delight for hours on end.

It goes without saying that when there were visitors Varyenka took less notice of me than when we were alone, and there was none of the reading or music which I loved to hear. When she spoke to her visitors, she lost what for me was her main charm – her quiet good sense and simplicity. I remember how her conversations with my brother Volodya about the theatre and the weather affected me strangely. I knew that Volodya avoided and despised banal conversation more than anything, and that Varyenka too always laughed at so-called absorbing conversations about the weather and so on. So why did they constantly, when they got together, utter the most unbearable rubbish and did this as though they were embarrassed for each other? Every time after those conversations I secretly resented Varyenka and on the following day made fun of the visitors, but I was more than ever pleased to be alone in the Nekhlyudov family circle.

At all events, I began to find greater pleasure in being with Dmitry in his mother's drawing room than with him alone, face to face.

41

My Friendship with Dmitry

JUST AT THIS TIME my friendship with Dmitry was hanging by a thread. I had been judging him for too long not to have found some faults in him. Yet in our first youth we love only passionately and therefore only love those who are perfect. But once the fog of passion gradually begins to dissipate or the clear light of reason begins to pierce spontaneously through it, we see the object of our passion in its true colours, with both virtues and shortcomings, and it is the shortcomings alone which, taking us by surprise, strike us with clarity and that are magnified. Our attraction to novelty and the hope that perfection in another person is not an impossibility prompt us not only to act coolly towards the one who was formerly the object of our passion but even to feel repulsed by him, and so we cast him aside without regret and rush onwards to find some new perfection. If this is not what happened to me with regards to Dmitry, I owe it entirely to his persistent, pedantic, more rational than heartfelt attachment, which I would have felt too ashamed to betray. Moreover, we were bound by our strange rule of frankness. We were too afraid, if we separated, to leave all the guilty moral secrets we had confessed to each other in the other's power. In fact, as we were well aware, we had not adhered to the rule of frankness for a long time: it often inhibited us and caused us to be on strange terms.

Nearly every time I went to Dmitry's place that winter, I would find Bezobyedov there, a fellow student with whom he studied. Bezobyedov was a small, pockmarked, skinny little man with tiny freckled hands and a big mop of unkempt red hair; he was always ragged, dirty, uncouth and was not even good at his studies. Dmitry's relationship with him was incomprehensible to me, as was the one with Lyubov Sergeyevna. The only reason he could have had for choosing him amongst all the other fellow students and becoming friends with him was that there was no one who looked worse than him in the whole university. It must have been for that very reason that Dmitry had wanted to offer him his friendship in defiance of everyone else. In his whole relationship with this student he expressed the following proud sentiment: "I don't care who you are, you're all the same to me and if I like him he must be all right."

I wondered how he did not seem to find it hard to have constantly to put up a front and how the unfortunate Bezobyedov could stand his own awkward position. I really did not like their friendship.

I once arrived at Dmitry's to spend the evening with him in his mother's drawing room and to chat and listen to Varyenka reading or singing. But Bezobyedov was upstairs and Dmitry sharply replied that he could not come down because, as I could see, he had a guest.

"What's the fun down there?" he added. "It's much better to sit up here and chat." Although I was not at all drawn to the idea of spending a couple of hours with Bezobyedov, I could not decide to go down to the drawing room on my own and so, annoyed at my friend's strange behaviour, I sat down in the rocking chair and began to rock in silence. I was really annoyed with Dmitry and Bezobyedov for depriving me of the pleasure of being downstairs; I waited to see if Bezobyedov would leave early, and felt angry with him and with Dmitry as I silently listened to their conversation. "What a pleasant guest to sit with!" I thought when the footman came in bringing tea, and Dmitry had to ask Bezobyedov about five times to take a glass because the bashful guest had felt obliged to refuse the first and second glasses and to say: "Do have some yourself." Dmitry with obvious effort kept his guest entertained with conversation and several times tried to draw me into it. I preserved a gloomy silence.

"There's no point making that 'no one could suspect that I'm bored' face," I mentally told Dmitry as I silently rocked back and forth in my chair. I inwardly whipped up, with some pleasure, an ever growing feeling of quiet hatred for my friend: "What a fool he is," I thought, "he could have been spending a pleasant evening with his dear family, but no, he is sitting here instead with that beast and now time is going by and it will be too late to go to the drawing room," and I glanced from behind the edge of my chair at my friend. And his hand, his posture, his neck and especially the back of his head and his knees appeared so loathsome and offensive to me that I would gladly at that moment have done something very unpleasant to him.

Bezobyedov got to his feet at last, but Dmitry could not immediately let such a pleasant guest leave and asked if he would like to stay the night; Bezobyedov fortunately refused, and left.

After seeing him off, Dmitry came back smiling somewhat smugly and rubbing his hands – probably because he had kept his side up so well and had finally rid himself of boredom – and he began to pace up and down the room glancing at me from time to time. He was more loathsome than ever to me. "How dare he walk around and smile?" I thought.

"Why are you angry?" he suddenly said, stopping in front of me.

"I'm not angry at all," I replied, as everyone does in such circumstances, "it only annoys me that you are putting on an act for me and Bezobyedov and yourself."

"What nonsense! I never put on an act for anyone."

"I'm not forgetting our rule of frankness, I'm telling you straight. I'm convinced that you find Bezobyedov as unbearable as I do, because he is stupid and God knows what else, but you enjoy giving yourself airs in front of him."

"I do not! Firstly, Bezobyedov is an excellent person—"

"And I tell you, you do; I'll even tell you that your friendship with Lyubov Sergeyevna is also based on the fact that she regards you as a god."

"And I tell you that's not so."

"And I tell you it is, because I know it by my own experience," I replied with the heat of restrained vexation and hoping to disarm him with my frankness, "I've told you and I'll tell you again that I always seem to like those people who say nice things to me, but when I really look into it then I see that there is no real attachment."

"No," continued Dmitry, adjusting his cravat with an angry gesture, "when I love, then neither praise nor abuse can change that feeling."

"That's not true; I once confessed to you that when Papa called me a good-for-nothing, I hated him for a while and wished him dead; just like you—"

"Speak for yourself. It's very sad if you are like that—"

"On the contrary," I shouted, jumping up from my chair and looking at him in the eyes, bold with despair. "What you're saying is not nice. Did you perhaps not tell me about my brother – I won't bring it up because it would be unfair – did you perhaps not tell me… and I'll tell you how I see you now."

And, trying to hurt him even more than he had me, I began to prove to him that he did not love anyone and also to express everything I felt I had the right to reproach him for. I was very pleased that I had my say, completely forgetting that its only possible purpose was to make him admit to the faults I was exposing in him, which could not be achieved at that time when he was so worked up. I never said those things to him when in a quieter mood he might have confessed.

The argument was turning into a row, when Dmitry suddenly stopped talking and went off to the other room. I was about to follow him, continuing to talk, but he did not reply. I knew that on his list of defects there was hot temper and that he was now overcoming it. I cursed all his lists.

That is where our rule had led us to, the rule of *telling each other everything we felt and never telling a third person anything we had said to each other*. In our enthusiasm for openness we sometimes came to make the most shameless confessions, passing off, to our shame, a simple intention or a dream as a distinct wish and a feeling, as for example I had just done when I said those things to him. And those confessions were no longer able to tighten the bond between us, but dried up the feeling itself and separated us. All of a sudden his pride would now not allow him even the most trivial admission and in the heat of our quarrel we used those weapons we had previously given each other and which dealt us very painful blows.

42

Our Stepmother

ALTHOUGH PAPA HAD ONLY WANTED to come to Moscow with his wife after the New Year, he actually arrived in October, in the autumn, when the season of hunting with hounds was still in full swing. Papa said that he had changed his mind because his case was to be heard in the Senate, but Mimi told us that Avdotya Vasilyevna had been so bored in the country, had so often mentioned Moscow and feigned ill-health that Papa decided to go along with her wish.

"Because she never loved him and only kept droning on about her love because she wanted to marry a wealthy man," added Mimi, sighing thoughtfully as though saying: "That's not how *some people* would have acted had he only been able to appreciate them."

Some people were being unfair towards Avdotya Vasilyevna. Her love for Papa, her passionate, devoted, selfless love was evident in every word, look and gesture. But such a love did not prevent her in any way, together with her wish not to be separated from her adored husband, from wishing for an exceptional bonnet from Madame Annette's, or a hat with an exceptional blue ostrich feather, or a dress made of dark-blue Venetian velvet, which would skilfully reveal her graceful white bosom and arms not yet seen by anyone except her husband and her maids. Katyenka was of course on her mother's side. Between our stepmother and us some strange, facetious relationship was established from the day of her arrival. The moment she stepped down from the carriage, Volodya, with a serious face and glazed eyes, went up bowing and scraping to take her hand and said as though announcing someone:

"I have the honour to congratulate dear Mama on her arrival and to kiss her little hand."

"Oh, my dear son!" said Avdotya Vasilyevna, smiling her beautiful fixed smile.

"And don't forget your second son," I said as I too came up to her hand and instinctively tried to imitate Volodya's facial expression and voice.

If, together with our stepmother, we had been sure of our mutual affection, that expression might have signified contempt for public expressions of love. If we had already been ill disposed towards each other, it could have indicated irony, or disdain for pretence, or a wish to conceal our true relationship from our father who was present, or many other such thoughts and feelings. But in this case that expression, which suited Avdotya Vasilyevna very well, meant nothing and only concealed a lack of any feeling. I have often subsequently noticed such facetious, false relationships in other families, when its members have a premonition that real relations would not be very good, and such was the kind of relationship that was established between Avdotya Vasilyevna and ourselves. We rarely deviated from it, were always unctuously courteous to her, spoke French, bowed and scraped and called her *chère Maman*, to which she would reply with similar jests and her beautiful fixed smile. Only Lyubochka the cry-baby with her goose-like legs and artless conversation grew very fond of her stepmother and she, sometimes rather naively and at times clumsily, tried to bring her closer to the rest of the family, but then, besides her passionate love for Papa, the only person in the world for whom Avdotya Vasilyevna had even a grain of affection was Lyubochka. She even displayed, much to my amazement, some kind of rapturous admiration and timid respect for her.

At first, Avdotya Vasilyevna, when calling herself stepmother, often liked to point out how children and servants always saw a stepmother in an unfair and bad light and how difficult her own position was as a result. But, foreseeing the whole unpleasantness of that situation, she did nothing to avoid it, such as being nice to one, giving a present to another, or not being grumpy, which would have come easily to her because she was undemanding and very kind by nature. Not only did she do nothing of the sort but, on the contrary, foreseeing the whole unpleasantness of the situation, she prepared to defend herself even before being attacked and, assuming that all the servants would use all possible means to be nasty and offensive to her, saw evil intentions in everything and considered that the best way forwards was to suffer in silence; so of course doing nothing, she did not win love but only dislike. Moreover she lacked that capacity of *understanding* that was, as I mentioned before, so strongly developed in our home, and her habits were so opposed to those embedded in our house that this by itself did not play in her favour. She always lived in our neatly organized household as though she had just arrived: she got up and went to bed sometimes early, sometimes late; sometimes she came down for dinner, sometimes she did not; one day she had supper, another day she did not. When there were no visitors she nearly always walked around half-dressed and was not embarrassed in front of us or even the servants to show herself in a white slip and a shawl thrown over it, exposing her bare arms. At first I liked that simple attitude but very soon that very simplicity made me lose any respect I still had for her. It was even stranger for us that there were two completely different women in her, depending on whether there were visitors or not. One, in the presence of guests, was a young, healthy, cold beauty, sumptuously dressed, neither stupid nor clever, but cheerful; the other, when there were no visitors, was an exhausted, languishing woman, no longer that young, who, although loving, was slovenly and bored. I often looked at her when, smiling and rosy from the winter cold and happy in the knowledge of her beauty, she would return from her visits and, after taking off her hat, would go and look at herself in the mirror, or when, rustling her sumptuous low-necked ball dress and both embarrassed and proud in front of the servants, she would walk over to her carriage, or else when we had small soirées at home and she wore a high-necked silk dress with some thin lace round her delicate neck, and would beam at everyone with her beautiful fixed smile – I looked at her and thought of what those who were captivated by her would say if they saw her as I did on those evenings when she stayed at home, waiting up after midnight for her husband to return home from the club, wearing some kind of housecoat, her hair unkempt, and wandering like a shadow through the dimly lit rooms. She would either go up to the piano and play the only waltz she knew, knitting her brow with the strain of it, or she would pick up a novel and, after reading a few lines from the middle, would throw it aside, or, so as not to wake up the servants, she would go to the pantry and get herself a gherkin and some cold veal and eat them standing by the pantry window, or, tired and depressed, she would drag herself once more aimlessly from room to room. But what distanced her most of all from us was her lack of understanding, which expressed itself in the way she indulgently paid attention when you spoke to her about things which were incomprehensible to her. It was not her fault that she had gained the unconscious habit of smiling faintly only with her lips and bending her head when she was told things that were of little interest to her (and besides herself and her husband, nothing interested her), but that smile and the bent head, often repeated, were unbearably off-putting. Her cheerfulness, as though making fun of herself, of you and the whole world, was also awkward and not contagious, and her sensitiveness was too cloying. And above all she was not embarrassed to speak incessantly of her love for Papa. Although she was not in the least bit lying when she said that her love for her husband was her whole life, and although she proved it throughout her life, such constant brazen emphasis on her love was revolting and we were even more embarrassed for her when she mentioned it in front of outsiders than when she made mistakes in French.

She loved her husband more than anything in the world and her husband loved her, particularly at first and when he saw that she was not attractive to him alone. Her only purpose in life was gaining his love, but she seemed to do everything that might displease him on purpose and all that to prove to him the strength of her love and her readiness for self-sacrifice.

She liked fine clothes and Father liked to see her in society as a beauty attracting praise and admiration; yet she sacrificed her passion for fine attires for Father's sake and she became more and more accustomed to sitting at home in a grey blouse. Papa always regarded freedom and equality as necessary conditions within family relationships and hoped that his favourite Lyubochka and his kind-hearted young wife would become sincere friends, but Avdotya Vasilyevna sacrificed herself and found it necessary to display unbecoming respect towards "the real mistress of the house", as she used to call Lyubochka, painfully offending Papa as a result. He gambled a great deal that winter and lost considerably, and as always, not wishing to mix his gambling with family life, he hid his gambling affairs from the whole household. Avdotya Vasilyevna sacrificed herself and, sometimes when she was ill, and even towards the end of the winter when she was pregnant, she felt obliged to stay up for Papa, even until four or five in the morning, and she would be there swaying with exhaustion in her grey blouse and with her hair dishevelled, when he came back from the club, at times tired after losing money and ashamed after his eighth fine.* She absent-mindedly asked him if he had been lucky at cards and with indulgent attention, smiling and nodding her head, she would listen to what he told her about what he did at the club and as for the hundredth time he begged her never to wait up for him. Yet although winning or losing at cards, on which Papa's fortune depended, were not of the slightest interest to her, she was still the first to meet him every night when he came back from the club. And this was motivated, apart from her passion for self-sacrifice, by a suppressed jealousy which caused her the greatest pain. Nothing in the world could convince her that Papa returned that late from the club and not from some mistress. She tried to read the love secrets on Papa's face and, not finding anything there, she would sigh, rather wallowing in her grief and giving herself over to contemplating her unhappiness.

As a result of these and endless other sacrifices, in the last months of that winter during which Papa lost a good deal of money and was therefore in bad spirits, a feeling of *silent hatred* began to be periodically noticeable in his relations with his wife: that suppressed aversion for the object of one's affections that is expressed by an instinctive urge to cause that object all sorts of petty aggravations.

43

New Friends

WINTER WENT BY LARGELY UNNOTICED and by now it had begun to thaw and the exam timetable had already been posted in the university, when I suddenly remembered that I would have to give answers in eighteen subjects I had attended lectures on, even though I had not listened or taken down notes or done any preparations. It is strange that a plain question such as: "How will I sit my exams?" had not occurred to me before. But I was in such a daze that winter from the delight of being grown up and *comme il faut* that when I thought of sitting my exams I compared myself to my fellow students and thought: "They will sit and the majority of them are not *comme il faut*, so I must have an advantage over them and I'm bound to pass the exam." I went to lectures only because I was used to doing so and because Papa sent me out of the house. And I also knew many students and often enjoyed myself at university. I liked the noise, the chatter, the laughter in the lecture hall. During a lecture I liked to sit on a bench at the back and to dream about something or other to the even sound of the Professor's voice or to watch my fellow students. At times I liked to run off with someone to Matern's for a glass of vodka and a bite and, knowing that I could be told off for it, cautiously opening the door with a creak, come back into the hall after the Professor. I liked taking part in student pranks when everyone from every course crowded into the corridor with much laughter. It was all very enjoyable.

When everyone began to attend lectures more regularly and the Professor of Physics completed his course and took leave until the exams, the students began to gather their notebooks and prepare themselves in groups and I thought that I should get ready too. Operov, with whom I was on very cold terms as I mentioned previously, although we still bowed to each other, not only offered to share his notes but invited me to come over to his place and prepare for the exams together with him and other students. I thanked him and accepted, and hoped that by doing him this honour, our previous misunderstanding would be fully smoothed out. I did ask, however, that we should all gather at my place every time, as I had very nice rooms.

I was told that they would study at different places in turn, now here, now there, wherever was closest. We gathered at Zukhin's the first time. It was a small room behind a partition in a large house on Trubny Boulevard. On the first day I came late and arrived when they had already begun reading. The small room was filled with smoke from low-grade tobacco, used by Zukhin. On the table stood a bottle of vodka, a wineglass, some bread, salt and a mutton bone.

Zukhin, without getting up, invited me to drink some vodka and to take off my coat.

"You are not used to this sort of refreshment, I believe," he added.

Everyone was in dirty cotton undershirts and false shirt fronts. Attempting not to show my contempt for them, I took off my coat and stretched out on the sofa in a companionable way. Zukhin read out, consulting his notebooks from time to time; others stopped him with questions and he gave concise, clever and accurate explanations. I began to listen carefully, but understood little, because I had not heard what had gone on before, and I put a question to him.

"Oh, dear fellow, you shouldn't be listening if you don't know that," said Zukhin. "I'll pass you my notebooks and you can go through them for tomorrow; there's no use explaining anything now."

I began to feel embarrassed at my ignorance and, acknowledging the fairness of Zukhin's remark, I stopped listening and began to observe those new friends. When categorizing people as *comme il faut* and not *comme il faut*, they obviously belonged to the second group and therefore inspired in me not only contempt but also some kind of personal hatred for them because, though not *comme il faut*, they seemed to consider me not only their equal but even patronized me in a good-natured way. It was their legs and their dirty hands with bitten-off nails and one long fingernail growing on Operov's little finger and the pink shirts and shirt fronts that provoked this feeling in me, as well as the swear words they used as terms of affection with each other, and the dirty room and Zukhin's habit of constantly sniffling by pressing one nostril with his thumb, and particularly the way they spoke, their use of certain words and their intonation. For example, they used the words "oaf" instead of "fool", "as though" instead of "as if", "magnificent" instead of "wonderful" and so on, which sounded bookish and horribly inappropriate. But I was even more incensed by the way they accented certain Russian words, and in particular foreign words: they said *mach*ine instead of mach*ine*, *act*ivity instead of act*ivity*, *on* purpose instead of on *pur*pose, fire*place* instead of *fire*place, Shake*speare* instead of *Shake*speare, and so on and so on.

I felt attracted to them, however, despite their appearance, which was indefinably repulsive to me at the time, sensing something good in those people and envying them their cheerful comradeship, and I wanted to grow closer to them, however difficult that would be for me. I already knew the gentle and honest Operov. Now I liked the brisk, remarkably clever Zukhin very much, who evidently dominated this little group. He was a small, stocky, brown-haired young man with a somewhat puffy and invariably shiny face, but with an extremely clever, lively and independent expression. His low, prominent forehead over his deep dark eyes, and his bristly short hair and thick black beard that seemed permanently unshaven, gave him that look. He did not seem to think about himself (I always liked this in people), but it was evident that his brain never stopped working. He had one of those expressive faces that suddenly change completely in your eyes a few hours after seeing them for the first time. That is what happened to me with Zukhin's face by the end of the evening. Suddenly new lines appeared on it, his eyes sank deeper, his smile looked different and his whole face changed so much that I would have had difficulty recognizing him.

When they had finished reading, Zukhin, the other students and I, to prove my wish to be friends, drank a glass of vodka each, so that there was hardly any left in the bottle. Zukhin asked if anyone had a twenty-five-copeck piece so that he could send an old woman who looked after him to get some more vodka. I wanted to offer my money, but Zukhin turned to Operov as though he had not heard me and the latter took out a small bead purse and gave him the required sum.

"Watch you don't drink too much," said Operov, who did not drink himself.

"Don't worry," replied Zukhin, sucking the marrow from the mutton bone (I remember thinking that he was so clever because he ate marrow).

"Don't worry," went on Zukhin, smiling slightly, and his smile was one of those you could not help but notice and feel grateful for, "and even if I do drink too much, that's not a disaster. Now, brother, let's see who does better, him or me. It's all ready, in there," he added, boastfully knocking his forehead. "But Semyonov could fail; he has taken to drinking rather heavily."

And indeed, that same Semyonov with the grey hair, who had pleased me so much at the first exam because he looked worse than me and who had come second in the entrance examination and had attended every lecture during the first month at university, had started to drink heavily even before the preliminary tests and by the end of the course had not appeared at university at all.

"Where is he?" someone asked.

"I have lost sight of him by now," went on Zukhin, "the last time we were together we smashed up the Lisbon.* We had a magnificent evening. Afterwards there was some incident, they say... There's a good head! What fire in that man! What an intellect! It's a shame if he falls by the wayside. But he will do so no doubt: with those outbursts he's not the kind of fellow to remain at university."

After some more conversation, everyone got up to leave, agreeing to meet up at Zukhin's again the following day, because his place was the nearest to get to for everyone. When we were all outside, I felt somewhat ashamed that they were all on foot and I was the only one to go by *droshky* and in my embarrassment I offered to take Operov home. Zukhin came out with us and, borrowing one rouble from Operov, he went off to visit some friends somewhere for the whole night. On the way Operov told me a lot about Zukhin's character and lifestyle and, after I got home, I did not sleep for a long time, thinking about those people I had newly met. I wavered for a long time as I lay awake between a feeling of respect for them on the one hand, to which their knowledge, simplicity, honesty, youthful poetry and audacity inclined me, and on the other hand a repulsion caused by their unseemly appearance. Despite very much wanting to, it was literally impossible for me to become close friends with them at that time. Our understanding of things was totally different. There were innumerable nuances that represented for me the whole charm and meaning of life that were completely incomprehensible to them and vice versa. But my frock coat made of fabric that cost twenty roubles, my *droshky* and my Dutch shirt were the main reason that made closeness impossible. That reason was particularly important to me: I felt that I was unwittingly offending them by the outward signs of my prosperity. I felt guilty before them, and now resigning myself, now rebelling against this unwarranted resignation and switching over to arrogance, I could not join them on equal, sincere terms. The crude, depraved side of Zukhin's character was to such an extent overshadowed by that strong poetic audacity I sensed in him that it did not have a bad effect on me at all.

I went over to study at Zukhin's nearly every evening for about two weeks. I studied very little because, as I have said, I lagged behind the rest and, not having the will-power to study on my own to catch up, I only pretended that I listened and understood what they read. I think that my companions guessed at my pretence and I often noticed that they skipped passages they knew and never questioned me.

Every day I found more and more excuses for that circle's lack of manners and I was drawn to their lifestyle, finding much poetry in it. It was only the promise I had given Dmitry that I would not go drinking with them anywhere that stopped me from longing to join them in their pastimes.

I once wanted to boast to them about my knowledge of literature, especially French literature, and I led the conversation to that topic. It turned out to my surprise that, although they pronounced foreign titles the Russian way, they had read much more than I, and they knew and appreciated English and even Spanish writers, and Lesage,* whom I had never even heard of. For them Pushkin and Zhukovsky were literature (not, as they were to me, little yellow-bound books which I had read and learnt as a child). They despised Dumas, Sue and Féval, and I had to admit that their appraisal of literature, and Zukhin's especially, was much better and clearer than mine. I equally held no advantage over them in their knowledge of music. And to my even greater surprise, Operov played the violin, another one of the students in our study group played the cello and the piano, and they both played in the university orchestra, appreciated good music and knew a good deal about music in general. In a word, everything I had wanted to boast to them about they knew better, except for French and German pronunciation, yet they never took any pride in this. I could have boasted of my status in society, but in that respect I was not like Volodya. So what were those heights from which I looked down upon them? Was it that I knew Prince Ivan Ivanych? Or my French accent? My carriage? My Dutch shirt? My fingernails? And was that not all nonsense? These were thoughts that would at times come vaguely into my head prompted by a feeling of envy for the comradeship and good-hearted youthful high spirits I saw before me. They were all on familiar terms, using *ty* with one another. The ease of their manner with each other reached a point of crudeness, but beneath those rough exteriors you could perceive a fear of even slightly offending each other. The words "scoundrel", "swine", used by them as terms of endearment, only grated on me and gave me the excuse to laugh at them inwardly, but those words did not offend them and did not stand in the way of their being on the most genuine friendly terms with each other. They were as careful and sensitive with one another as only very poor and very young people can be. But above all I sensed something expansive and wild in Zukhin's character and his adventures in the Lisbon. I had a feeling that those drinking sprees were quite different from the pretence with the burning rum and champagne I had participated in at Baron Z.'s place.

44

Zukhin and Semyonov

I DO NOT KNOW what social class Zukhin belonged to, but I do know that he had been to S. Grammar School, had no fortune and apparently did not belong to the gentry. He was about eighteen years old at the time, though he looked much older. He was exceptionally intelligent and especially quick on the uptake: he found it easier to take in a whole complex subject in one go, foresee all its details and conclusions, than to consider consciously the laws that brought about those conclusions. He knew he was clever and was proud of it and, in consequence, was equally easy and good-natured with everyone. He had undoubtedly gone through much in life. His ardent, receptive nature had managed to draw love, friendship, business and money to himself. There was nothing he had experienced, even in small measure and even among the lower echelons of society, for which he did not feel contempt or indifference or lack of consideration, because of the great ease with which everything came his way. He undertook everything new with such fervour, only to despise what he had achieved once he had attained his goal, and with his gifted nature he invariably attained his goal and the right to despise it. It was the same when it came to his studies: he studied little, took no notes, had perfect knowledge of mathematics and was not boasting when he said he could beat his professor. He thought that there was a lot of rubbish in the lectures, but with his own brand of instinctive practical trickery he immediately made himself into what a professor required of him, and all the professors liked him very much. He was direct in his dealings with the authorities and they respected him in turn. He neither respected nor loved learning and he even despised those who were seriously studying that which came so easily to him. Learning, as he saw it, did not use up one tenth of his aptitude. Life as a student was not something he could give himself over to completely: his ardent, active nature, as he called it, demanded life and he threw himself into drinking sprees as far as his means would allow and gave himself up to them with passionate ardour and a desire to extend himself "to the limits of my strength". Now, before the exams, Operov's prediction came true. Zukhin had disappeared for about two weeks, and lately we had been studying at another student's place. But at the first exam he appeared in the hall, looking pale and jaded, his hands trembling, and passed brilliantly into the second year.

There had been about eight young men in the band of revellers since the start of the course, with Zukhin at the head. Ikonin and Semyonov had initially been part of the group, but the former left them because he could not endure the frenzied debauchery they gave themselves up to at the beginning of the year and the latter left because he thought there was not enough of it. During the first period of our course we watched them with some horror and told each other their exploits.

The main heroes of those exploits were Zukhin and, by the end of the course, Semyonov. Latterly Semyonov had been looked at with some kind of horror, and whenever he came to a lecture, which happened quite rarely, there was excitement in the lecture hall.

Before the exams themselves, Semyonov ended his drinking spree in the most original and vigorous fashion, and thanks to Zukhin, I was a witness to this. This is how it happened. One evening, after we had just got together at Zukhin's, and Operov, his head pressed to his notebooks and having put a tallow candle in a bottle next to him as well as another candle in a holder, had begun reading his finely annotated physics notebooks in his thin little voice, when the landlady came into the room and announced to Zukhin that someone had come with a note for him.

Zukhin went out and swiftly returned with his head bowed and a pensive face, holding an opened note in grey wrapping paper and two ten-rouble notes in his hand.

"Gentlemen! There's been an extraordinary event," he said, raising his head and giving us a sort of grave solemn look.

"Well, have you received money for private tutoring?" said Operov, leafing through his notebook.

"Come on, let's read on," said someone.

"No, gentlemen! I'm not reading any more," went on Zukhin in the same tone. "I'm telling you, an incomprehensible event! Semyonov has just sent me, via a soldier, twenty roubles which he once borrowed and he writes that if I want to see him I should go to the barracks. Do you know what this means?" he added, looking round at us all. We all kept silent. "I'm going to him right now," went on Zukhin, "let's go, whoever wants to come along."

We immediately put on our coats and prepared to go over to see Semyonov.

"Won't it be somewhat awkward," said Operov with his thin little voice, "that we should all go to look at him as though at some kind of oddity?"

I was fully in agreement with Operov's remark, especially in my case as I knew Semyonov very little, but I was so pleased to find myself taking part in a general comradely event and I so wanted to see Semyonov himself, that I did not say anything in response to that remark.

"Nonsense!" said Zukhin. "What's awkward about the fact that we're all going to bid farewell to a friend, wherever he is. Rubbish! Whoever wants to should go."

We got hold of some cab drivers, took the soldier with us and set off. The duty non-commissioned officer would not let us into the barracks, but Zukhin somehow talked him round, and that same soldier who had come with the note accompanied us to a large room, almost dark, only dimly lit by a few night lights, where on both sides recruits in grey overcoats and with their heads shaven sat or lay on bunks. After entering the barracks, I was struck by a particular oppressive smell and the sound of a few hundred people snoring, and, walking through with our guide and Zukhin, who strode firmly ahead between the bunks, I looked at each recruit with trepidation and applied to each one what memory I still had of Semyonov's worn-out, sinewy figure with his long, tousled, partly grey hair, his white teeth and sombre, shining eyes. At the furthest corner of the barrack by the last clay pot, filled with black oil, over which a suspended, burning wick was smoking, Zukhin hastened his step and suddenly stopped.

"Splendid, Semyonov," he said to a recruit with a shaved head similar to the others, who sat in a thick soldier's shirt and a grey overcoat thrown over it, with his feet on his bunk, eating something while chatting to another recruit. It was *he*, with closely cropped grey hair, a

311

bluish, shaven forehead* and his usual sombre and lively expression. I feared that my glance might offend him and so I turned away. Operov too, who seemed to share my opinion, stood behind us all. But the sound of Semyonov's voice, when he greeted Zukhin and the others in his usual curt way, reassured us completely and we hurried forwards to offer, in my case, my hand, and Operov his "plank-like" hand. But Semyonov stretched out his big dark hand ahead of us, saving us from the unpleasant feeling of somehow doing him the honour. He spoke as always reluctantly and quietly:

"Greetings, Zukhin. Thank you for coming. Oh, gentlemen, do sit down. Just allow me, Kudryashka," he turned to the recruit with whom he had been chatting and eating, "we'll finish our conversation later. Do sit down. Well? Did I surprise you, Zukhin? Well?"

"Nothing has ever surprised me coming from you," replied Zukhin, settling down next to him on the bunk, a little like a doctor who sits on a patient's bed. "I would have been surprised if you had turned up at the exams, that's for sure. So tell me where you disappeared to and what happened?"

"Where I disappeared to?" he replied in his deep, strong voice. "I disappeared into taverns, inns, generally into establishments. Do sit down, gentlemen, there's plenty of room. Pull in your legs, you," he shouted authoritatively, showing his white teeth for an instant at a recruit who lay on the left of him on his bunk with his head resting on his arm and who was watching us with idle curiosity. "Well, I lived it up. It was both bad and good," he went on, the expression on his lively face changing with every abrupt sentence. "You know that business with the merchant: well, the rascal died. They wanted to drive me out. Whatever money I had I squandered. And even that would not have been that important. But I had a huge amount of debts left, nasty ones. I had nothing to pay them off with. Well, that's all."

"And how did you end up with this idea," said Zukhin.

"This is how: I was drinking in the Yaroslav, you know, on the Stozhenka. I was drinking with some kind of merchant boss. He was a recruiting agent. I said: 'Give me one thousand roubles and I'll go.' And I went."

"But how can you – a nobleman?" said Zukhin.

"Nonsense! Kirill Ivanov arranged everything."

"Who is Kirill Ivanov?"

"The one who bought me." (His eyes shone in a particular strangely funny, mocking way and it was as though he smiled.) "Permission was given in the Senate. I lived it up some more, paid off my debts and went. That's it. So what, they can't flog me... I have five roubles... And perhaps there'll be a war..."

Then he began to tell Zukhin his strange, incomprehensible adventures, the expression on his lively face constantly changing, his eyes shining sombrely.

When we could no longer stay in the barracks, we began to say our goodbyes to him. He offered us each his hand, pressed ours firmly and, without getting up to see us off, he said:

"Come again some time, gentlemen; they say we won't be sent off before next month," and again he seemed to smile.

Zukhin, however, having taken a few steps, turned back again. I wanted to see them say goodbye to each other and so stopped as well. I saw Zukhin take some money out of his pocket and give it to him and Semyonov push his hand away. Then I saw them kiss one another and I heard how Zukhin, going towards him again, shouted out quite loudly:

"Farewell, brains! You will probably be an officer and I won't have finished my course."

In response to this Semyonov, who never laughed, burst into unexpected resounding laughter, which struck me very painfully. We went outside.

Zukhin remained silent the whole way home, which we took on foot. He continually sniffled, pressing his thumb against one nostril, then the other. When we got home, he immediately left us and from that day on went on a drinking spree right up to the exams.

45

I Fail

THE FIRST EXAM CAME AT LAST – Differential and Integral Calculus – but I was still in some kind of strange haze and was not really aware of what lay ahead. In the evenings, after being in the company of Zukhin and the other friends, the thought that there was something not quite right and not good with some of my convictions and that I should change them somehow did cross my mind, but by morning in the sunlight I became *comme il faut* again and was perfectly satisfied with that and did not look to change anything in myself.

Such was my frame of mind when I arrived at the first exam. I sat on a bench on the same side as the princes, counts and barons, began to speak to them in French and (strange as it may seem) it did not even occur to me that I would soon have to answer questions on a subject I knew nothing about. I calmly watched those who went up to be examined and even allowed myself to make fun of some of them.

"Well, Grap," I said to Ilyenka when he came back from his examination, "were you scared?"

"Let's see how you get on," said Ilyenka, who, ever since he had entered university, had completely rebelled against my influence, did not smile when I spoke to him and was hostile towards me.

I smiled scornfully at Ilyenka's reply, although the doubt he expressed gave me a sudden fright. But the haze clouded that feeling again and I remained absent-minded and indifferent to the point of promising to go and have a bite at Matern's with Baron Z. as soon as I had been examined (as though to me that was the most trivial of things). When I was called up together with Ikonin, I adjusted the coat tails of my uniform and with complete composure walked up to the examination table.

A slight shiver of fear ran across my spine only when the young Professor, the same one who had examined me at the entrance exam, looked me straight in the face and I reached for the notepaper on which the questions were written. Ikonin, although he took the question slip with the same swinging movement of his whole body as in previous exams, did somehow give an answer, although a very bad one, but I did the same thing he had done in the first exams, or even worse, because I took a second slip and gave no answer at all. The Professor looked me in the face with pity and in a quiet firm voice said:

"You will not pass into the second year, Mr Irtenyev. It's best not to sit any further exams. We need to clean up the faculty. The same goes for you, Ikonin," he added.

Ikonin asked, as though begging for alms, to be allowed to retake the exam, but the Professor replied that he would not be able to achieve in two days what he had not done during the course of a year and that there was no way he would pass. Ikonin plaintively and abjectly implored him again, but the Professor refused once more.

"You may go, gentlemen," he said in the same soft firm voice.

Only then did I bring myself to walk away from the table and I felt ashamed that by my silent presence I had seemed to associate myself with Ikonin's humiliating entreaties. I do not remember how I crossed the hall past the other students, how I replied to their questions, how I reached the anteroom and made it home. I was offended and humiliated and genuinely miserable.

I did not come out of my room for three days, saw no one and, as in childhood, found solace in tears and cried a lot. I looked for pistols to kill myself with should I feel a strong urge to do so. I thought that Ilyenka Grap would spit in my face when he met me and that he would be justified in doing so; that Operov would be rejoicing in my misfortune and would tell everyone about it; that Kolpikov had been completely right to shame me at Yar's; that my stupid conversations with Princess Kornakova could have had no other consequences, and so on and so on. One by one all the painful moments in my life that had tormented my pride came into my head. I tried to blame someone else for my misery: I thought that someone had done all this on purpose; I invented a whole intrigue against myself and I grumbled about the professors, my friends, Volodya, Dmitry, even Papa for sending me to university; I grumbled about Providence letting me live to suffer such a disgrace. At last, feeling that I was ultimately ruined in the eyes of everybody who knew me, I asked Papa to let me join the hussars or go to the Caucasus. Papa was not pleased with me, but, seeing my terrible distress, consoled me by saying that however bad the situation was, things could be put right if I transferred to another faculty. Volodya did not see anything terrible in my misfortune either, and said that in another faculty I would at least not feel ashamed in front of new fellow students.

The ladies did not understand at all, and did not wish to or could not understand what an exam actually meant or what it meant not to pass one and they felt sorry for me only because they saw my grief.

Dmitry came over to see me every day and was extremely affectionate and gentle, but that was exactly what made me think that he had cooled off towards me. I always found it painful and humiliating when he came to see me upstairs and sat close next to me in silence, with an expression similar to that of a doctor's who sits on a very sick patient's bed. Sofya Ivanovna and Varyenka sent me, via Dmitry, some books that I had previously wanted to have, and wished me to go and visit them, but in that attention alone I saw a proud, humiliating condescension towards a person who had already fallen too low. After about three days, I calmed down a little, but I did not leave the house until our departure for the country and, sunk in my grief, I idly wandered from room to room, trying to avoid any member of the household.

I thought and thought, and finally, late one evening, sitting downstairs on my own and listening to Avdotya Vasilyevna's waltz, I suddenly leapt up, ran upstairs, got hold of the notebook where I had written down the 'Life Rules', opened it and went through a moment of remorse and moral impulse. I cried, but the tears were no longer ones of despair. I recovered and decided to write the 'Life Rules' again and I was firmly convinced that I would never again do anything bad, nor idle away even one minute and that I would never betray those rules.

Whether this moral impulse went on for a long time and what it consisted of and what new beginnings it brought in my spiritual development I will tell you in the next, happier half of my youth.*

24th September, Yasnaya Polyana

Note on the Text

This translation is based on *Detstvo, Otrochestvo, Yunost'* (Moscow: Izdatel'stvo Khudozhestvennaya Literatura, 1966).

Notes

p. 5, *Auf, Kinder, auf... s'ist Zeit. Die Mutter ist schon im Saal*: "Get up, children, get up! It's time. Your mother is in the drawing room" (German).

p. 5, *Nu, nun, Faulenzer*: "Well, well, lazy-bones" (German).

p. 6, *Ach, lassen sie, Karl Ivanych*: "Oh, let me be, Karl Ivanych" (German).

p. 6, *Dyadka*: This diminutive of *dyadya* (uncle) was a term often used for serfs or servants looking after children.

p. 7, *Sind sie bald fertig*: "Are you nearly ready" (German).

p. 7, *Histoire des Voyages*: *A History of Travel*, published in Paris in nineteen volumes (1746–70).

p. 7, *Northern Bee*: A political and literary newspaper, which appeared in 1825–64 and 1869–70.

p. 8, *Lieber Karl Ivanych*: "Dear Karl Ivanych" (German).

p. 10, *Clementi's*: Muzio Clementi (1752–1832), Italian composer and pianist, who performed in Russia.

p. 10, *Marya Ivanovna*: Marya Ivanovna is the name and patronymic of Mimi, the girls' governess.

p. 10, *Ich danke, lieber Karl Ivanych*: "I thank you, dear Karl Ivanych" (German).

p. 12, *poods*: A *pood* was an old Russian measure of weight, equivalent to 16.38 kilograms.

p. 15, *Wo kommen sie her*: "Where have you come from" (German).

p. 15, *Ich komme vom Kaffee Haus*: "I've come from the coffee shop" (German).

p. 15, *Haben sie die Zeitung nicht gelesen*: "Have you not read the newspaper"(German).

p. 17, *Von al-len Lei-den-schaf-tent... haben sie geschrieben*: "Of all the sins the worst is... have you written this down" (German).

p. 17, *Die grausamste ist die Un-dank-bar-heit... Ein grosses U*: "The worst is ingratitude... a capital U" (German).

p. 17, *Punctum*: "Full stop"(German).

p. 17, *dinner*: Dinner (*obyed*) was the main meal of the day, usually around two o'clock.

p. 18, *holy fool*: The holy fool or *yurodivy* features throughout Russian literature. Holy fools were usually dressed in rags, were homeless, spoke in riddles and were believed by many to be clairvoyant. They held a particular status, particularly with the tsars, and were often believed to be divinely inspired.

p. 19, *Parlez donc français*: "Do speak French" (French).

p. 19, *Mangez donc avec du pain*: "Do eat this with some bread" (French).

p. 19, *Comment est-ce que vous tenez votre fourchette*: "How are you holding your fork" (French).

p. 20, *bolshak*: That's how he always addressed men. (TOLSTOY'S NOTE) Literally: elder, head of the family.

p. 21, *je suis payée pour y croire*: "I have good cause to believe in them" (French).

p. 22, *klepper*: Small German breed of horse.

p. 23, *borzois*: Russian wolfhounds, similar to greyhounds.

p. 24, *armyak*: Peasant's long wide coat made from heavy cloth.

p. 25, *the spot… gathered*: The term for the actual gathering of hounds in readiness for being unleashed is *ostrov*, literally meaning "island", a particular hunters' term.

p. 28, *Robinson suisse*: French title of *Der Schweizerische Robinson* (*The Swiss Family Robinson*), the 1812 novel by the Swiss writer Johann David Wyss (1743–1818).

p. 29, *C'est un geste de femme de chambre*: "It's the gesture of a chambermaid" (French).

p. 30, *à bonnes fortunes*: "Successful" (French).

p. 31, *his friend A.*: A.A. Alyabyev (1787–1851) composed the well-known 'Nightingale' and other popular romances.

p. 31, *Don't Wake… Semyonova… Tanyusha*: Lyrical songs popular in the beginning of the nineteenth century; a reference to the opera singer N.S. Semyonova (1787–1876).

p. 32, *Field*: John Field (1782–1837) Irish composer and pianist. From 1802 he lived in Russia, where he gave music lessons in aristocratic homes in St Petersburg and Moscow.

p. 33, *britzka*: An open four-wheeled carriage with a folding top.

p. 33, *et puis au fond c'est un très bon diable*: "And he's basically a very kind old devil"(French).

p. 33, *the note*: This note is written in very poor Russian.

p. 38, *she granted her her freedom*: This was before the Emancipation of the Serfs (1861).

p. 39, *incense from Ochakov... there*: Tolstoy mentioned this in his *Recollections* (1903–06). According to family legend, Tolstoy's grandfather, Prince N.S. Bolkonsky, brought back incense from Ochakov. During the Russo-Turkish War (1787–92) the Ochakov fortress was captured by storm by Russian soldiers.

p. 39, *kvas*: Russian fermented drink made from rye.

p. 41, *everyone had gathered... facing*: It was customary in Russia (and still is now to some extent) to sit together in silence for a few minutes before setting off on a long journey.

p. 41, *chuika*: Knee-length cloth jacket.

p. 43, *sazhen*: An old Russian measure of length, equivalent to 2.13 metres.

p. 43, *verst*: An old Russian measure of length equivalent to approximately 1.06 kilometres.

p. 46, *name day*: The day of the saint after whom someone was named.

p. 47, *lesson slip*: A slip of paper which the visiting tutor would eventually hand in to receive payment.

p. 47, *Dmitriev nor Derzhavin*: Russian poets, I.I. Dmitriev (1760–1837) and G.R. Derzhavin (1743–1816).

p. 51, *Charmant*: "Charming" (French).

p. 52, *ma bonne tante*: "My dear aunt" (French).

p. 52, *un garçon qui promet*: "A promising boy" (French).

p. 53, *je vous demande un peu*: "I ask you" (French).

p. 55, *Bonjour, chère cousine*: "Good morning dear cousin" (French).

p. 56, *Ségur*: Louis-Philippe, Comte de Ségur (1753–1830) author of *Histoire universelle ancienne et moderne* (published in Brussels in 1822). A copy of this was kept at Yasnaya Polyana, Tolstoy's family home.

p. 58, *ma bonne amie*: "My dear friend" (French).

p. 58, *un parfait honnête homme*: "A perfect gentleman" (French).

p. 61, *Tatishchev's dictionaries*: A Complete French-Russian Dictionary in three volumes compiled by I.I. Tatishchev.

p. 65, *Quelle charmante enfant*: "What a charming child" (French).

p. 66, *the formal or the familiar "you"*: There is a distinction in Russian between the formal and informal you: *vy* (*vous* in French) is the formal way of address and *ty* (*tu* in French) is informal and used only within the family and very close friends. Being asked to use *ty* instead of *vy* can be very significant. See chapter 23, when Sonyechka suggests they use the familiar *ty*.

p. 68, *Voyez, ma chère… votre fille*: "Look my dear… Look how this young man has dressed up to dance with your daughter" (French).

p. 69, *chaîne*: This and the following terms in French are various dance steps.

p. 69, *The Danube Maiden: Das Donauweibchen*. Opera composed by F. Kauer (1751–1831), based on a Viennese play by K.F. Hensler.

p. 69, *Vous êtes une habitante de Moscou*: "Are you an inhabitant of Moscow" (French).

p. 69, *Et moi, je n'ai encore jamais fréquenté la capitale*: "And I have never frequented the capital yet" (French).

p. 70, *vis-à-vis*: Dancing opposite each other.

p. 70, *pas de Basques*: An old mazurka step.

p. 71, *Rose ou ortie*: "Rose or nettle" (French).

p. 72, *Il ne fallait pas danser si vous ne saviez pas*: "You shouldn't have danced if you didn't know how to" (French).

p. 73, *Grossvater*: An old-fashioned German dance.

p. 78, *La belle Flamande*: "The beautiful Flemish woman" (French).

p. 83, *Hoffman's Drops*: Friedrich Hoffmann (1660–1742), German physician and chemist, introduced several new drugs, among which were Hoffmann's drops, which were spirit of ether.

p. 84, *Maman died in terrible agony*: Tolstoy's own mother died when he was two and so he had no recollection of her. His father died when he was nine. A year later his grandmother died, followed in 1841 by the death of his aunt Alexandra, who had looked after the orphans.

p. 85, *the band on her forehead*: A strip of paper on which is written a hymn, which is put on the forehead of the deceased.

p. 85, *for a prank*: The Russian text for this translation has the word pity rather than prank. The difference lies in one letter (*zhalost'* (pity) versus *shalost'* (prank). The version on Lib.Ru/Klassika has the word prank, and I feel that there must be a misprint in my text, as the word prank fits in so much better than the word pity in this context.

p. 87, *white trimming*: It was customary to wear white trimming for mourning.

p. 89, *Nasha*: "Ours" (Russian).

p. 91, *pounds*: Pound here refers to an obsolete Russian measure of weight equivalent to 409.5 grams.

p. 91, *kutya*: Dish made of rice, raisins and sugar served at a Russian Orthodox funeral.

p. 99, *Vasily... servant*: Vasily had been paying rent for land on his landlord's estate and has now been made a house servant and freed from this obligation (*obrok*).

p. 99, *we are using our own horses and carriages*: As opposed to going by stagecoach.

p. 101, *onuchas*: Socks or cloth worn in boot or bast shoe.

p. 102, *arshin*: An old Russian measurement equivalent to seventy-one centimetres.

p. 102, *shaft bow... withers*: A shaft bow is part of a harness: it is an arc over the horse's withers (base of neck above the shoulders) that is attached to the front of the shafts of a horse-drawn vehicle.

p. 104, *barankas*: Ring-shaped rolls like bagels.

p. 112, *dyadka*: Like the servant Nikolai. See second note to p. 6.

p. 119, *Voldemar*: Another way Volodya was sometimes called, mainly by his father.

p. 120, *gouverneur*: "Tutor" (French).

p. 120, *des enfants de bonne maison*: "Children from a good family" (French).

p. 122, *Geselle*: "Associate" (German).

p. 122, *Lose*: "Lots" (German).

p. 122, *Soldat*: "Soldier" (German).

p. 122, *Bierkrug*: "Mug of beer" (German).

p. 123, *aber der Franzose warf sein Gewehr und rief Pardon*: "But the Frenchman threw over his rifle and begged for mercy" (German).

p. 123, *thalers*: An obsolete German silver coin.

p. 124, *vedro*: Old Russian liquid measure equivalent to approximately twelve litres.

p. 124, *auf und ab*: "To and fro" (German).

p. 124, *'Qui vive?' sagte er auf einmal*: "Who goes there?" (French) "He suddenly said" (German).

p. 124, *sagte er zum zweiten Mal*: "He said the second time" (German).

p. 124, *sagte er zum dritten Mal*: "He said the third time" (German).

p. 126, *Armee*: "Army" (German).

p. 126, *Jäger*: Light infantry.

p. 126, *sagte auf einmal mein Vater*: "Said my father suddenly" (German).

p. 127, *Mutter... die Arme*: "'Mama!' I said, 'I'm your son, your Karl!' And she threw herself into my arms" (German).

p. 127, *Überrock*: "Frock coat" (German).

p. 127, *Nachtwächter*: "Nightwatchman" (German).

p. 127, *Macht auf*: "Open up" (German).

p. 127, *Macht auf im Namen des Gesetzes*: "Open up in the name of the law" (German).

p. 127, *Ich gab ein Hieb*: "I gave him a blow" (German).

p. 127, *Ich kam nach Ems*: "I reached Ems" (German).

p. 128, *Lundi... Géographie*: "Monday, two to three, History and Geography master" (French).

p. 128, *Smaragdov's textbook*: S.N. Smaragdov (1805–45) wrote a series of history textbooks for secondary schools.

p. 128, *Kaidanov's book*: I.K. Kaidanov (1782–1845), author of *A Universal and Russian History*.

p. 129, *two... mark book*: In the Russian marking system you can obtain five marks, five being a perfect mark, one being the lowest.

p. 130, *lesson slip*: See first note to p. 47.

p. 130, *St Louis's Crusade*: Louis IX, commonly known as St Louis (1214–70), led a crusade to Palestine in 1249. His mother was Blanche of Castile.

p. 130, *Bulanka*: A nickname for a dun-coloured horse.

p. 132, *Voyons, messieurs... Faites vos toilettes et descendons*: "Well, gentlemen! Go and freshen up and let's go down" (French)

p. 132, *bonbonnière*: "Candy box" (French).

p. 134, *petits jeux*: "Games" (French).

p. 134, *Lange Nase*: "Long Nose" (German).

p. 136, *C'est bien*: "That's fine" (French).

p. 137, *violette*: "Violet" (French).

p. 139, *Oh mon père... soit faite*: "Oh, my Father, oh my benefactor, give me your blessing for the last time and God's will be done" (French).

p. 139, *à genoux*: "On your knees" (French).

p. 141, *all's well that ends well*: The saying here actually translates as: "Keep on grinding and there will be flour".

p. 141, *rozanchiki*: Sweet, rose-shaped pastries.

p. 142, *C'est ainsi… à genoux*: "Is this how you obey your second mother; is this how you pay her back for her kindness? On your knees!" (French).

p. 142, *Tranquillisez-vous… comtesse*: "For God's sake, do calm down, Countess"(French).

p. 145, *fouetter*: "Flog" (French).

p. 145, *accents circonflexes*: "Circumflex accents" (French).

p. 145, *mauvais sujet, vilain garnement*: "Scoundrel, evil rascal" (French).

p. 145, *À genoux, mauvais sujet*: "On your knees, you scoundrel" (French).

p. 147, *stove bench*: A shelf running along the side of a Russian stove on which it is possible to sleep.

p. 148, *Agafya Mikhailovna*: Gasha's Christian name and patronymic.

p. 152, *Schelling*: Friedrich Wilhelm Schelling (1775–1854), German philosopher. He expounded a theory whereby the surrounding world is only seen through "the intellectual intuition" of the object.

p. 154, *le fond de la bouteille*: "The bottom of the bottle" (French).

p. 157, *jeu perlé*: "Brilliant piece" (French).

p. 159, *chuikas*: See second note to p. 41.

p. 160, *Votre grand-mère est morte*: "Your grandmother has died" (French).

p. 160, *who they will go to*: The servants, as serfs, would become someone else's property.

p. 162, *un homme comme il faut*: "A respectable man" (French).

p. 164, *à la coq*: "Crest-like" (French).

p. 165, *si je suis timide*: "If I'm shy" (French).

p. 165, *Savez-vous… mon cher*: "Do you know what causes your shyness?… An excess of pride, my dear" (French).

p. 168, *Karr*: The French author Jean Alphonse Karr (1808–90), whose works L. Tolstoy read in the summer of 1854.

p. 174, *Franker's Algebra*: *The Complete Pure Mathematics Course* by Louis Franker (1773–1849), published in Russian in the 1830s and 1840s in two volumes.

p. 174, *removing... front garden*: In spring the inner window was removed, to be put back in winter to keep out the cold.

p. 175, *salt cones*: Little cones of salt and small bricks are placed between the double windows to absorb the humidity.

p. 177, *droshky*: A low four-wheeled open carriage.

p. 177, *Sparrow Hills*: One of the highest points in Moscow, near Moscow State University, known as the Lenin Hills in Soviet times.

p. 177, *Pedotti's*: The delicatessen shop Pedotti's was on the Kuznetsky Bridge from 1840 to 1860.

p. 178, *Rappo*: Karl Rappo (born Karl von Rapp) was a famous strongman and juggler, nicknamed the Northern Hercules. He performed in Moscow in 1839.

p. 178, *Mazepa*: Ivan Mazepa (or Mazeppa) (1639–1709) Ukrainian hetman, fighting for the separation of Ukraine from Russia. Maria's love for Mazepa forms the central theme of A.S. Pushkin's poem *Poltava* (1828–29).

p. 182, *je puis... je peux*: Two forms of "I can" in French, *je puis* being used more formally.

p. 186, *Arbat*: The Arbat is a street right in the historical centre of Moscow, about eight hundred metres from the walls of the Kremlin. The Arbat Gate on Arbat Square is the site of one of the ten gates of the old city wall. The Arbat is one of the oldest surviving streets in Moscow, dating from the fifteenth century. Nowadays it is pedestrianized.

p. 186, *kalach*: A white, round bread roll.

p. 192, *The Nightingale*: A popular song (1827) by A.A. Alyabyev from the poem *A Russian Song* (1825–26) by A.A. Delvig (1798–1831).

p. 195, *à la muzhik*: Peasant style, cut square all round.

p. 196, *fee-paying student*: Fee-paying as opposed to those students supported by the state.

p. 198, *À vous, Nicolas*: "It's your turn, Nikolai" (French).

p. 200, *Zumpt*: Karl Gottlob Zumpt (1792–1849) German philologist, author of *A Short Latin Grammar*, which was published five times in Russia, from 1832.

p. 201, *comme il faut*: Literally meaning "as is expected/as it should be done", the nearest translation in English would be "proper/conforming to society's expectations".

p. 202, *mauvais genre*: "In bad taste/bad form". In other words: not *comme il faut* (French).

p. 204, *Victor Adam*: Victor Adam (1801–66), a French painter and lithographer.

p. 204, *Datsiaro's picture shop*: A famous art publishing house founded by Giuseppe Datsiaro (Dazziaro).

p. 204, *porte-crayon*: "Pencil holder" (French).

p. 204–5, *Sultan's… Zhukov's*: "Zhukovsky" tobacco was named after the owner of a St Petersburg tobacco factory, V.G. Zhukov; Sultan's tobacco was Turkish tobacco.

p. 206, *Bostanzhoglo coat of arms*: The tobacco factory of Bostan-zhoglo was situated in Moscow on Staraya Basmannaya Street.

p. 210, *musketoon*: A shorter barrelled version of the musket.

p. 210, *crossed arms… ty*: In the ceremony known as drinking *Brüder-schaft* (from the German *Brüderschaft trinken*) the two participants interlock their right arms, drain their glasses, kiss each other and ever afterwards address each other as "brothers" with the familiar *ty*.

p. 212, *Gaudeamus igitur*: "Let's rejoice" (Latin). The first line of the students' hymn.

p. 213, *vous aurez de mes nouvelles*: "You'll hear from me" (French).

p. 215, *Orestes and Pylades*: Ancient Greek heroes regarded as the perfect example of true friendship.

p. 217, *general in the civil service*: The title of general in Tsarist Russia could also denote the status of a member of the first four grades of the civil service.

p. 217, *Corps des Pages*: Name of a military school in St Petersburg.

p. 219, *Sivtsev Vrazhek*: A side street not far from the Arbat. The name literally means Sivka Stream and refers to a historical stream now locked in an underground sewer.

p. 222, *homme d'affaires*: In this case business adviser or just secretary (French).

p. 224, *Junker School*: Junker Schools prepared low-rank military for officer rank.

p. 224, *issu de germains*: "Second cousin" (French).

p. 232, *Ivan Yakovlevich*: Ivan Yakovlevich Koreisha (1780–1861), a famous Moscow "holy fool" with a reputation for being able to foretell the future.

p. 238, *c'est vous qui êtes un petit monstre de perfection*: "It's you who are a little monster of perfection" (French).

p. 239, *Merci, mon cher*: "Thank you, my dear" (French).

p. 241, *squeamishly*: This is another instance where one letter possibly misprinted in my text gives this word an entirely different meaning. In my text *bryuzglivo* means "grumbling/peevish" while *brezglivo* means "squeamish", which is more appropriate here. In a recent edition published by Eksmo, Moscow, the word is *brezglivo*: squeamish.

p. 243, *Si jeunesse savait, si vieillesse pouvait*: "If youth but knew, if old age could" (French).

p. 250, *one of us... marry*: It was illegal in Russia for a brother-in-law to marry a sister-in-law.

p. 257, *come si tri joli*: A distortion of *comme c'est très joli*: "How pretty it is" (French).

p. 261, *Le Fou*: 'The Madman' by the German composer Friedrich Kalkbrenner (1785–1849).

p. 262, *the novels of Sue, Dumas and Paul de Kock*: The historical and social novels of the French writers Alexandre Dumas (1802–70) – *The Three Musketeers* and *The Count of Monte Cristo* – and of Eugène Sue (1804–57) – *Les Mystères de Paris* – were very popular in Russia in the 1840s. Sue's novel *The Paris Mysteries* gave rise to many imitations (Paul Féval's *The Mysteries of London* (1845) and the anonymous *Berlin Mysteries*) and many others. The novels of Paul de Kock (1793–1871) were also popular in Russia, dealing with the more frivolous side of Parisian life.

p. 262, *noble... ehrlich*: *Noble*, besides meaning of noble birth, also means "noble/dignified", as opposed to the Russian *blagorodny*, which has the sense of "well born/honourable". *Ehrlich* means "honest/honourable" in German.

p. 265, *Je fus un homme très comme il faut*: "I was a very respectable man" (French).

p. 271, *Messalina... comparison*: The famously promiscuous Messalina was the third wife of the Roman Emperor Claudius.

p. 272, *souls*: "Souls" here means the number of serfs owned by the landowner.

p. 272, *tarantass*: Four-wheeled, springless, horse-drawn Russian carriage.

p. 278, *belle-mère*: "Stepmother" (French).

p. 280, *aftermath*: New grass after mowing, also known as aftergrass.

p. 282, *Ce n'est pas français*: "This is not French" (French).

p. 283, *ce ne sont pas des gens comme il faut*: "They are not respectable people" (French).

p. 284, *pour un jeune homme de bonne maison*: "For a young man from a good family" (French).

p. 284, *manants*: "Louts" (French).

p. 286, *Lermontov's*: Mikhail Yuryevich Lermontov (1814–41) famous for his romantic poetry and his novel *A Hero of Our Time*.

p. 289, *Comme c'est gracieux*: "How elegant"(French).

p. 290, *sugar loaf*: A conical moulded mass of sugar which was the traditional form in which refined sugar was produced and sold until late in the nineteenth century.

p. 290, *Löschen sie die Lichter aus, Frost*: "Turn off the lights, Frost" (German).

p. 291, *Juchhe*: "Hurrah" (German).

p. 295, *Au banquet de la vie, infortuné convive*: "Come to the banquet of life, unfortunate table companion" (French). From the *Odes Written in Imitation of Many Psalms*, by the French poet Nicolas Gilbert (1751–80).

p. 303, *fine*: At that time in Russia you were fined for staying at the gambling club after midnight.

p. 307, *the Lisbon*: A Moscow public house.

p. 308, *Lesage*: French writer Alain-René Lesage (1668–1747), author of *Le Diable boiteux* and *Gil Blas de Santillane*.

p. 312, *shaven forehead*: All recruits had their foreheads shaved.

p. 316, *the next... youth*: Despite his intention to write this second part, Tolstoy never did.

Extra Material

on

Leo Tolstoy's

Childhood, Boyhood, Youth

Leo Tolstoy's Life

Leo Nikolayevich Tolstoy was born in 1828, and died in 1910; his life began when Russia was still almost entirely an agrarian and feudal country ruled by an autocrat, and ended just seven years before the overthrow of the Tsar in 1917 and the inauguration of a period of huge industrialization by the Soviet regime. His earliest publication appeared in 1852, when he was twenty-four, and from that moment until very near to his death almost sixty years later, obsessed and tormented by questions as to the meaning and purpose of life, he poured out novels, novellas, short stories, plays, essays and pamphlets on a vast range of moral, social and philosophical problems, such as how humanity should live ethically, how society should be reformed and organized, the aims and means of education, religion, art and culture, the futility of war and of violent protest against one's living conditions, and the imperative need to adopt peaceful non-resistance to evil, springing from the supremacy of love over everything else. In addition he kept a diary and notebooks for most of his adult life, besides writing over 8,500 letters. His collected works run to ninety volumes, and therefore it is impossible to give more than a cursory overview here of his life and of his major and most characteristic works.

Birth and Early Life

His father's family came from a long line of highly distinguished nobles who moved in court circles, but his grandfather and his father Nikolai had brought the family almost to total destitution with their extravagant lifestyle and gambling habits. In 1822, Nikolai married Maria Volkonskaya, who possessed a large fortune and the massive estate of Yasnaya Polyana (Clear Glade, or, possibly, Ash Tree Glade) some 130 miles south-west of Moscow, with eight hundred serfs. She soon gave birth to four sons, Nikolai, Sergei, Dmitry and then, finally, Leo, on 28th August 1828 (Old Style). (Russian dates in the nineteenth century were twelve days behind the western calendar, and thirteen days behind from 1900–18. All dates in this section are given in Old Style.) However, just before Leo was two, his mother died giving birth to a daughter, Maria, and from then on much of the care of the children passed to "Aunt" Tatyana, his father's second cousin, who lived at Yasnaya Polyana, a gentle and warm person whose love Tolstoy remembered throughout his life. The boys were taught, as was the custom, by a German tutor, and were brought up bilingual in French and Russian. Leo also acquired a good reading knowledge of German and English. He listened enthralled while his eldest brother Nikolai invented stories, including that of the existence of an all-encompassing secret behind life which, when discovered, would enable the whole human race to live in peace and harmony. That secret, Nikolai told them, was inscribed on a "green stick" which was buried in a wood on the estate.

In 1836, when Leo was eight, the family moved to Moscow so that the children could gain a broader education, but within a few months, in early 1837, their father died suddenly, and their devoutly religious aunt, their father's sister Countess Alexandra, became their legal guardian. Day-to-day care of the children now passed fully into the hands of "Aunt" Tatyana, who seems in many ways to have taken the place of the children's dead mother.

Death in the Family Shortly afterwards, the children's grandmother died, followed in 1841 by their guardian Alexandra. All this left Tolstoy at a very early age with a questioning and painful awareness of the inevitability of death.

Experience in the Brothel Following their guardian's death, the family once again moved – this time, when Leo was just thirteen, to the distant town of Kazan, to the estate of another aunt who was married to a wealthy local landowner. Leo began to study for the entrance exams to Kazan University, but by now was being distracted by his burgeoning sexuality. When he was sixteen, his brothers finally took him to a brothel, and after the experience he stood by the lady's bed weeping, then started dreaming regularly of an ideal woman whom he could marry and live with in perfect happiness, and not have physical contact with in this animal manner. Many of his much later works, both fiction and non-fiction, display a revulsion to sex, even in marriage, and the roots of this may have been in his experience in the brothel.

He failed the university entrance exams in spring 1844, *Entering University* but retook them successfully in the autumn. He entered the Department of Oriental Languages intending to become a diplomat, but then decided at the start of the next academic year to study law instead. He began a diary which he kept up with only brief interruptions for the rest of his life, and he drew up an arduous programme of mental and physical self-improvement which was intended to include daily physical exercise and a course of intensive reading, including the Russian classics, French and English novels, the New Testament and works by philosophers such as Hegel and Voltaire. He especially made a profound study of the French philosopher Jean-Jacques Rousseau, arguably the thinker who influenced him most throughout his life, with his ideas of the corrupting influence of civilization on the original, noble, innate human nature.

Despite these attempts at self-improvement, Tolstoy more than once had to spend periods in hospital at this time as a result of venereal disease contracted during visits to brothels.

Tolstoy was now losing interest in his legal studies, and just *Moving Back to* at this time he gained control of Yasnaya Polyana as his part *Yasnaya Polyana* of the legal settlement of the parents' goods after his father's death, so in May 1847 he dropped out of university, returned to his estate, and attempted to improve it and make conditions better for the serfs – leading to great perplexity on their part. He then moved on to sample the high life of Moscow and Petersburg, where he lost large amounts at gambling. In Petersburg he contemplated joining the local elite-guards unit, but finally returned to Yasnaya Polyana to continue his efforts as an enlightened rural landowner. He also spent a great deal of time there studying music and playing the piano. He loved music his entire life, and his favourite composers included Glinka, Tchaikovsky, Weber, Mozart, Haydn, Schumann, Schubert and Bach; he also had a great liking for folk and gypsy music.

In 1851, he returned to Moscow briefly, and made more gambling losses, but began to write; various ideas for stories are recorded in his diaries, although only unfinished fragments remain from this period.

The Caucasus   Tolstoy's eldest brother Nikolai was by now an officer in an army unit which was stationed in the Caucasus, at the time Russia's southern frontier, where Russian troops were still involved in skirmishes with local tribespeople. In April 1851, Leo set off with Nikolai to the Caucasus for a change of scenery, and possibly to try to find a meaning to his somewhat dissolute and unfocused life.

Publication of   While there Tolstoy read widely, including Laurence Sterne's
Childhood   *Sentimental Journey* in English, part of which he translated into Russian, and began to write his first published work, a semi-fictionalized autobiography, *Childhood*, based on his recollections of his infancy. Finally he enlisted in the Russian artillery in the Caucasus as a "bombardier fourth class" – a junior rank – and conducted himself very bravely, on more than one occasion almost being killed in the action. During this period of army service, he continued his writing, finishing *Childhood* and starting on a short story, 'The Raid', drawn from his military experiences. In November 1852, when Tolstoy was twenty-four, *Childhood* was published, to great acclaim in the press and from established writers such as Turgenev and Dostoevsky. He was now recommended for promotion but, resolving to become a full-time writer, sent in his resignation from the army – however, this was turned down until the end of the Russo-Turkish War.

He now began work on *Young Manhood* (the first variant of what was to become *The Cossacks*), also based on his military experiences, although the final version of this tale was not to be finished until 1862. He carried on reading voraciously, especially the works of Lermontov, Pushkin, Goethe, Schiller and many others, including Dickens. He later acknowledged that Dickens's narrative technique in *David Copperfield* had influenced him deeply in the writing of *Childhood*, its sequel *Boyhood* and the volume which completed this trilogy of early reminiscences, *Youth*.

Tolstoy's regiment now transferred to central Europe, and he took part with them in numerous campaigns against the Turks. By this time he had been promoted to the rank of warrant officer, and he requested to be sent to the most dangerous theatre of the war, the Crimea.

He was accordingly moved to Sebastopol, and joined in the heroic defence of that city when it underwent a year-long siege from October 1854 to October 1855. In that same year

Boyhood was published, to more positive reviews. He carried *Sebastopol* on his intensive reading, including, from the British classics, Thackeray's *Vanity Fair*, *Henry Esmond* and *Pendennis*. He was now also working on *Youth*, the continuation of his *Childhood* and *Boyhood*. Prefiguring his religious transformation of the late 1870s, he was already by March 1855 noting in his diary his plans to found a new religion, based on the teachings of Christ – principally the Sermon on the Mount – but with no supernatural or mystical elements, and promising not bliss in an afterlife in heaven, but here and now on earth. He also jotted down plans for military reform.

During 1855 and 1856 Tolstoy published three *Sebastopol Stories*, depicting his experiences of the combat, and already expressing his contempt for the senseless slaughter of war. Although heavily censored, they too created a great impression among the public, and Tsar Alexander II was so affected that he issued orders that the young author should not in future be sent to dangerous battle zones.

Incidentally, these *Sebastopol Stories* were the first works to be published under Tolstoy's full name; his previous writings had all appeared with simply the initials "L.N." on the cover and title page – although the author's identity was no great secret.

Following the end of the Russo-Turkish War, Tolstoy's regiment moved to barracks in Petersburg in November 1855, and he found himself regarded by the literati as the best up-and-coming young author of the day, for his literary style, eye for detail and psychological insight. While in Petersburg he began once again to gamble away large amounts of money, and to have mistresses. However, he was still writing, publishing short stories such as *Two Hussars* and *The Snowstorm*, and becoming more and more dissatisfied with his aimless social life. In February 1856 his brother Dmitry died of tuberculosis, exacerbating his growing preoccupation with death.

Although promoted to second lieutenant in March 1856 for *Resignation* "outstanding bravery" at Sebastopol, he now decided the army *from the Army* was definitely not for him, and he resubmitted his resignation, which was accepted, becoming effective from the beginning of 1857.

When he officially re-entered civilian life, he went on a tour, from January to July of 1857, of France, Switzerland, Italy and Germany, and was horrified when he witnessed an execution by guillotine in Paris. He now wrote to a friend that human law was nonsense, government was a plot to exploit and corrupt people, and that he would from now on never serve any government anywhere.

In 1857 *Youth* was published, to lukewarm reviews. He started rereading the gospels and, although still living a rather dissolute life, he was already beginning to alter his views on the way society was organized. This young owner of an enormous estate with 800 serfs signed a manifesto calling for all serfs to be freed, with each being given his own private plot of land.

Return to
Yasnaya Polyana
Back at Yasnaya Polyana, Tolstoy continued to exercise his landowner's rights over the young female serfs, who worked both on his land and as house servants. His numerous liaisons included a passionate affair with a peasant woman, Axinya Bazykina, who bore him a son who became a servant on the estate for the rest of Tolstoy's life.

While there he continued to read the latest artistic works both from home and abroad, including George Eliot's *Scenes of Clerical Life* and *Adam Bede*, both of which he admired enormously. He pursued his own writing too, and in 1859 published the novella *Family Happiness*, which received rather poor reviews.

He now commenced thinking about the aims and means of education, and set up a school for local peasant children at Yasnaya Polyana, free of charge, and based on non-coercive principles, where, rather like the experiments of some twentieth-century educationalists such as A.S. Neill at Summerhill, children would not attend lessons if they did not want to, or could suggest changes to the curriculum if they did not like certain subjects or the way something was being taught. Learning would not be by rote, as it was in most other schools throughout Russia and Europe at the time, but by trying to catch the pupils' genuine interest so that they would learn spontaneously. The children could argue with the teacher with no fear of punishment, and most of the assistant teachers were recruited from the ranks of young men who had dropped out of university as Tolstoy had, or been expelled from university for participating in radical student activity.

Travels Abroad
In July 1860, Tolstoy travelled to Western Europe to study modern educational methods. He remained there until April 1861. His beloved eldest brother Nikolai, who was now

seriously ill from tuberculosis, came with him to spend time at a sanatorium. However, his condition rapidly worsened and he died in Leo's arms, intensifying the writer's gloominess and bewilderment at the inevitability of death. He wrote in his diary: "Why? It's not long before I go there. Where? Nowhere… Nikolenka's death has been the most powerful impression of my life…"

While abroad, Tolstoy visited schools in Germany, France, Belgium, Italy and England. In London, where he spent two weeks from early 1861, he met Matthew Arnold, then an Inspector of Education, who arranged a visit for him to a school. Tolstoy was disappointed to find the same rote learning there as everywhere else.

On his return to Yasnaya Polyana, Tolstoy began once again *Back Home* to throw himself into writing in earnest, working on *The Cossacks*, and experimenting with numerous literary projects, including stories of ordinary peasant life, none of which were finished.

In May 1861, he was appointed Justice of the Peace, to resolve disputes in his local region between former serfs, who had been emancipated recently by imperial order, and their previous masters over the land settlements the old serfs were now meant to receive. Tolstoy received a torrent of vilification from local landowners, because he had arranged very generous terms with his own freed serfs, and was considered too partisan to the newly emancipated peasants in general and not to have the interests of his own class at heart. He finally resigned in disgust in May 1862.

In February of the same year, Tolstoy had once again lost heavily at cards, but this was the last episode of this kind. He now hastened to complete *The Cossacks* to pay his debts off.

In July 1862, while he was absent, the secret police searched his school looking for evidence that the teachers had been sowing sedition among their pupils and the local peasants. Nothing was found. Tolstoy protested violently, and considered emigration, probably to England.

That summer, at the age of thirty-four, Tolstoy fell in love *Marriage* with the eighteen-year-old daughter of a local landowner, Sofya (Sonya) Behrs, and they married on 23rd September. Tolstoy insisted, before they married, that she read his diaries, which, among other things, detailed his previous sexual exploits and affairs, and although they were at first very happy, the seeds of doubt had already been planted in Sofya's mind as to her husband's general conduct.

The couple, in spite of numerous quarrels, did in fact live harmoniously together for the first fifteen years or so of their marriage, until Tolstoy's religious conversion, when they started to drift apart. In all, they had thirteen children, of whom eight survived until maturity.

The peasant school at Yasnaya Polyana was closed because of Tolstoy's new literary and family commitments, but whenever time permitted, he would continue till old age to teach peasant children on his estate, and wrote a number of simple reading primers for both peasant children and illiterate adults.

War and Peace In 1863, he at last published *The Cossacks*, which received mixed reviews. During this year he also began to work on *War and Peace*, and Sofya copied and recopied the whole vast manuscript for him, which underwent many revisions. It took six years to complete. On 6th October 1863 he wrote in his diary: "I'm happy with her [Sofya], but terribly dissatisfied with myself. I'm sliding down towards death and I barely feel the strength in myself to stop. I don't want death, though, I want and love immortality… There's no use choosing. The choice was made long ago. Literature, art, pedagogy, family."

By 1867, Tolstoy had published the first three volumes of *War and Peace* in instalments, and the last three volumes were issued in 1868 and 1869.

When not involved in writing, Tolstoy still pondered deeply about educational aims and means, and studied how to improve his farm, taking a deep practical interest in this – he planted an apple orchard and took up beekeeping. He still maintained a programme of intensive physical exercises such as weight-training and gymnastics, and kept up his reading, including Dickens's *Our Mutual Friend* and Trollope's *The Bertrams*. In 1868 he had begun to read the works of the philosopher Schopenhauer, and was enthusiastic about his ideas. Schopenhauer became the thinker who had the most influence on Tolstoy after Rousseau.

When *War and Peace* had been published in full, critical opinion was generally very positive; what negative comments there were came from those who disagreed with his view of history expressed in the novel – that great events are predetermined, and are caused by the virtually infinite number of actions of ordinary people through the ages, rather than being produced by the great rulers and leaders whom history concentrates on.

He was also, at this period, starting to work out his philosophy of the purpose of art, to attack the notion of private property and to extol the peasant commune, although these views only achieved full expression later on.

Around this time he had two experiences which shook him considerably. Firstly, in 1866, he tried unsuccessfully to defend a mentally disturbed soldier for having struck an officer; in the end, the man was executed. The second incident was in September 1869 in the town of Arzamas in the Penza Province, which he was visiting with the intention of buying property. In a hotel he was overcome by a strange need to escape from an unknown force, and he felt utterly helpless in the face of death. Prayers did not help, and Tolstoy fled the town immediately, terrified, full of "anguish, fear and horror".

In 1870 he took up an intensive study of ancient Greek, and within three months was reading Plato, Xenophon and Homer in the original. He also started to work out his ideas for his next large novel, *Anna Karenina*, although he only began to write it in March 1873; it too was issued in instalments, and it was finally published in full only in 1878, to very favourable reviews, although the sexual content did evoke some scandalized reactions in the more puritanical sections of the press. Though Tolstoy's profound spiritual and psychological crisis and abrupt reorientation in life is conventionally dated as beginning around 1878, after his completion of *Anna Karenina*, it had commenced several years earlier, leading him to feel profound distaste for the earlier drafts of the novel, and to change his intentions drastically several times during the writing of it.

His beloved "Auntie" Tatyana, who had taken the place of his mother early in his life after the death of his mother, died in June 1874; in February 1875, his baby son Nikolai died in agony of meningitis, and at the end of that year a prematurely born daughter, who was never named, died almost immediately after birth. It was now that Tolstoy underwent his fundamental psychological and spiritual transformation.

As well as reworking *Anna Karenina* time and time again as his views on the meaning of life were darkened by these tragedies, Tolstoy reverted to his interest in education, and around this time published five volumes for the teaching of

Anna Karenina

reading to adults and children consisting of simple and vivid stories written in the style of folk tales. He planned to open what he termed a "university in bast sandals" on his estate to train peasant teachers, but there were too few applicants, so the project never came to fruition.

Ill Health and Religious *Conversion* The year 1877 saw the onset of the ill health and depression which was now to affect Tolstoy for most of the rest of his life, and he pondered more and more as to whether religion might be of any use. Accordingly he visited church services and monasteries and kept the fasts of the Orthodox Church, but gradually became repelled by what he saw as the irrelevance of all this to Christ's true teaching. In October 1879 he began to write his *Confession*, chronicling his spiritual and philosophical searches for an answer to the meaning of life. Over these years he read extensively in the sciences and philosophy, and in various non-Christian religious systems, including those of Islam and Buddhism, but came to the conclusion that these too were dead ends. Turning away from established religion, he immersed himself intensively, as many other educated members of his own class were doing at the time, in what was perceived as the simple, devout wisdom of the peasants. He started work on *A Translation and Harmonization of the Gospels*, in which he attempted to synthesize the gospels and purge them of all accretions and metaphysical and miraculous elements and get back to the basic practical teachings of Christ. The *Confession* was completed by 1882, and was promptly banned – but, like many of Tolstoy's works from now on, circulated unofficially and was later published abroad.

In March 1881 Tsar Alexander II was assassinated by terror-ists, and Tolstoy wrote a letter to the new Tsar, Alexander III, asking that the six assassins should be pardoned and spared the death penalty as an act of Christian forgiveness. Not surprisingly, the Tsar refused. Tolstoy began to write more and more on social, religious and political questions, taking on all of them almost an anarchist position based on peace and love. He was now being kept under constant surveillance by the Tsarist Police.

In 1882 Tolstoy bought a large house with grounds in Moscow, Khamovniki, and from then till the end of his life divided his time between his country estate and Moscow. In the city he undertook an assiduous study of Hebrew with a rabbi.

During 1883 he worked intensively on *What I Believe*, inveighing against personal profit and private property and urging a return to the original message of Christ. Tolstoy's behaviour was becoming more and more erratic and he was repeatedly threatening to leave his home and family to live the simple life of a peasant or even an itinerant pilgrim. He started to wear peasant garb and to try to learn how to become proficient at various types of manual labour and handicrafts, such as making his own shoes.

In October 1883 he met Vladimir Chertkov, a twenty-nine-year-old wealthy nobleman and fanatical Tolstoy disciple, who had resigned his position as Captain of Horse Guards to live on his own estate improving the lot of the local peasants.

In 1884 Chertkov suggested that Tolstoy should set up The Intermediary (Posrednik) Publishing House to disseminate not only those of Tolstoy's works that had not been banned, but good literature in general at very low prices. During its first four years, The Intermediary sold over twelve million books. Chertkov laboured to have published abroad the works of Tolstoy which were suppressed or censored in Russia, and Tolstoy worked on translating and editing works for publication in his own country. He now became a vegetarian, and gave up alcohol, hunting and smoking. More and more "disciples" were appearing at Yasnaya Polyana, both from Russia and abroad, and many went back to their own areas to set up communes based on Tolstoyan principles.

However, his wife detested Chertkov's fanaticism and increasing influence over her husband, and Chertkov returned her animosity. Tolstoy and his family drifted further and further apart. In June 1884 he actually walked out on them, but returned shortly afterwards. By this time, he had seriously alarmed the government and church, was under police surveillance, and many of his old acquaintances feared he was mad.

In 1885, interestingly for British readers, he recommended for publication by The Intermediary all the works of Dickens, and George Eliot's *Felix Holt*, which he described as "outstanding"; he also claimed that Matthew Arnold's *Literature and Dogma* agreed with many of his own principles.

In addition to his polemical writings, Tolstoy also at this time wrote a certain amount of fiction, mainly novellas, such as *The Death of Ivan Ilyich* and *The Kreutzer Sonata*, all of which, although extremely powerful, were still written to make points in agreement with Tolstoy's new world view. *The Kreutzer Sonata* was at first banned because it advocated sexual abstinence even in marriage, and was only finally published in 1891 following a personal interview by Sofya with the Tsar.

Tolstoy began his last full-length novel, *Resurrection*, in 1889, which was completed only in 1899, when it was published in full volume form after being issued in instalments.

In 1890 Tolstoy criticized the recent persecution of the Jews in Russia, and continued to attract hundreds of idealistic disciples from home and abroad. He was now world-famous as a spiritual leader and social critic. The following year he renounced the rights to most of his works published after 1881, although he still retained the royalties from works issued before this date to maintain his family. He also distributed his wealth (580,000 roubles) in ten lots among Sofya and his nine living children.

In 1892, along with other writers and artists, such as Chekhov, he worked hard to alleviate conditions for those suffering from the catastrophic famine in central Russia, although he had already expressed a belief that organized charity merely perpetuated the division between rich and poor. The government tried to suppress news of the disaster, and were outraged to such a degree at Tolstoy's efforts to spread awareness of the tragedy abroad that there was a real possibility that the elderly writer would at last be imprisoned or exiled.

Among Tolstoy's other thunderous denunciations of these years was *The Kingdom of God is within You*, published in Berlin in 1894, which excoriated both church and state for crushing the masses, and advocated mass passive non-resistance to these oppressive powers to achieve change.

Another one of Tolstoy's children, Ivan, died in February 1895 from scarlet fever, driving Sofya into temporary insanity and almost to suicide. She developed an infatuation at this period with the much younger composer Sergei Taneyev, which continued till 1904, although there is no clear evidence as to how intimate their relationship became. Tolstoy, not surprisingly, was furious and threatened more and more often to leave.

At this period he began to advocate land reform, rejecting the notions of private ownership and centralized government, and extolling the rural village commune as a model for social organization.

In 1895 he undertook a vigorous campaign for the peasant religious sect of the Dukhobors to be allowed to emigrate from Russia. They were being persecuted for refusing to serve in the army and pay taxes and, although not basing their ideas on Tolstoy's teachings, in their way of life they had much in common with what he was propounding. Tolstoy suggested that the authorities persecute him instead, but they refused, believing this would make a martyr out of him. However, Chertkov and other prominent Tolstoyans who supported the Dukhobors were exiled for five years. Finally, in 1897, the Dukhobors were allowed to emigrate to Canada, with funds raised by Tolstoy, including the advance for his novel *Resurrection*. He was by now claiming publicly that patriotism was evil, that the Tsar lacked all authority and should abdicate, and that all states are illegitimate and should be dissolved.

He now also began to write on the purpose and aim of art. *What Is Art?* He commenced *What Is Art?* in 1896, and finished it in early 1898, when it was published simultaneously in Russia – in a heavily censored version – and in Britain, in English.

The book attracted both praise and censure, and sparked intense debate in the press. In this essay Tolstoy repudiated most of his own early work previous to his new polemical and didactic phase, and derided Shakespeare's *Hamlet* and Beethoven's *Ninth Symphony*. He attacked existing art as elitist and corrupting, and expounded the view that art must be produced to appeal to the masses and to create a brotherhood of humanity. In this work he claimed that Dickens was the greatest novelist of the nineteenth century because of his vivid and accessible style, and descriptions of the social conditions of the poor of the time.

In that year, he visited an exhibition of Impressionist paintings in Moscow and criticized them for lacking any central idea. Around the same time he wrote that Anton Chekhov wrote like a decadent and Impressionist – possibly a criticism of Chekhov's lack of a social position in his writing.

Tolstoy now laboured extremely hard to finish *Resurrection*, *Ill Health* which he decided to sell at a greater price than that of the cheap editions of his previous works, so that the profits could be donated to the Dukhobors to finance their continuing emigration. Despite being heavily altered by the censor, the novel was still perceived as mocking the Orthodox Church when it was published in full volume form in 1901, and Tolstoy was promptly excommunicated by an edict accusing him of numerous heresies and urging him to repent – which he refused adamantly to do. Letters of sympathy poured in from all over the world. He then wrote a letter to the Tsar calling for human rights and religious freedom – a demand which was of course ignored. He was still regularly feeling the temptation to leave home, although he did not do so because he was afraid Sofya would commit suicide. Although up until this point he had been very fit and active for his age – now over seventy – and had still done gymnastics and weight-training and played tennis in summer, his health now began to decline following a serious bout of malaria which almost killed him. He drew up a will, in which he stipulated that almost all of the proceeds from his previous works were to be devoted to social causes, and to his publishing company, to further his teachings. Sofya and his children were outraged, and a protracted and bitter struggle over his will began. Tolstoy went down to the Crimea to recover from his illness, and was visited by Gorky and Chekhov, whose most recent plays he disliked, although he admired some of his stories. Tolstoy now suffered in quick succession from typhoid fever and pneumonia, which once again brought him close to death.

He remained in the Crimea from September 1901 to June 1902, and despite his weakness while there, he wrote a long essay entitled 'What Is Religion?', and sent a letter beginning "Dear Brother" to Tsar Nicholas II, urging social reforms, and warning him that oppression by church and state had brought the masses near to insurrection.

Tolstoy continued to produce essays and pamphlets on social questions. In January 1903, he protested vehemently against the massacre of Jews in Kishinyov and wrote three stories to be published for the victims' financial benefit.

He was now gradually becoming frailer, and his output declined, but he still managed to finish a short novel, *Hadji Murat*, set in the Caucasus, and in 1904 published his notorious essay 'Shakespeare and the Drama', in which he questioned the reputation of *King Lear* and many of Shakespeare's other plays, prompting two extremely critical letters to him by George Bernard Shaw.

EXTRA MATERIAL

During this time the Russo-Japanese War broke out and, in 1905, insurrections flared up all over Russia, which were brutally suppressed. Tolstoy issued several articles condemning the use of violence by both sides in the war, and asserting that, although the insurrections were inevitable, the participants should try to achieve results by adopting his own doctrine of non-resistance to evil.

After the upheavals, the Tsar granted a limited amount of civil rights, but Tolstoy was contemptuous, claiming that there was nothing in these reforms for the common masses. He criticized not only violent revolutionaries, but even peaceful social democrats aiming for a liberal democracy, since he believed that all forms of government were evil: he was now in his writings coming to reject civilization altogether, in all its manifestations, and advocating a return to the simple life of the peasantry, with social organization based on the democratic village peasant commune, where everybody had a say. He wrote to influential Russian statesmen urging the abolition of private property, the abandonment of industrialization and city life, and a return to agriculture and rural crafts.

In 1906, Sofya was operated on for a large tumour; the surgery was successful, although it left her debilitated. Tolstoy's love for her resurfaced, and he looked after her devotedly, in so far as his own weak condition would allow. But in November 1906 his daughter Maria died suddenly of pneumonia, and a few months later his brother-in-law was murdered during a strike in St Petersburg.

This only deepened Tolstoy's depression, and he renewed his interest in oriental thought. Sofya's behaviour became erratic, and the arguments over his will increasingly savage. Chertkov had now moved back to Russia from exile, and Sofya accused Tolstoy of having a homosexual relationship with him. The writer began to suffer frequent dizzy spells, and he grew weaker and weaker. In September 1909, he received an admiring letter from Mohandas (later Mahatma) Gandhi, who throughout his life was profoundly influenced by Tolstoy's social theories and his promotion of peaceful non-resistance to evil. A correspondence began between them which continued till Tolstoy's death.

In 1909 Tolstoy revised his will, leaving control of his writings after his death to his daughter Alexandra, now twenty-five, who was to supervise their publication along with Chertkov. This was kept secret from Sofya.

Flight from Home
and Death

In 1910, at three o'clock on the morning of 28th October, Tolstoy awoke to hear his wife going through his papers, in search of his latest will. He wrote her a letter thanking her for forty-eight years of marriage, and begging forgiveness, woke his daughter Alexandra and his personal doctor, who helped him pack, and then finally, at the age of eighty-two, dressed in the garb of a wandering pilgrim, he left home, as he had threatened to do for so many years. Leaving the house in secret, he spent a couple of days in a nearby convent where his sister was a nun, but after his whereabouts had been discovered, he took a train on 31st October heading towards Rostov on Don. Later that day he developed a high temperature, and at Astapovo station was carried into the station master's cottage. The station master immediately moved a bedstead into the living room, and did his best to make the world-famous writer comfortable. The house was soon besieged by dozens of journalists, who sent off hourly bulletins round the world on the electric telegraph, reporting on Tolstoy's condition. Thousands of his disciples and idle onlookers turned up there too, though Tolstoy, in his declining state, seemed to be largely unaware of them. Sofya arrived on a privately chartered train, but by the time she saw him he was too ill to recognize her.

On 7th November he died of pneumonia, and his body was buried at Yasnaya Polyana, as he had requested, in the wood where, according to the story told by his brother Nikolai in their childhood, a stick was buried inscribed with the secret of world peace and harmony.

Sofya survived him by almost exactly nine years, dying on 4th November 1919.

Leo Tolstoy's Works

Tolstoy's collected works run to ninety volumes, comprising both fiction and a vast amount of non-fiction in the form of books, essays, articles and pamphlets on his ideas for reform in all areas of human existence. This short survey will deal with only a few of his major and most characteristic works, both as a writer of fiction and as a polemicist.

Tolstoy's fiction covers three main subject areas: in the earliest work, semi-fictionalized autobiography; then, in the later writings, marriage and sexual relationships, and the happiness or misery they can produce; parallel to this latter theme in many of his short stories runs the necessity of a moral reorientation and turning away from the false values of civilization, and the adoption of the life of simple country folk, in order to regain an idea of the meaning of life.

One of Tolstoy's major techniques throughout his career as a fiction-writer is what has been called "making strange" – he describes everyday experiences and events, not as if they are commonplace, but as if they are being perceived and undergone for the first time; in conjunction with this, he frequently gives an account not simply of an episode as it occurs in the outside world, but also describes in intense and almost hypnotic detail, from within the mind of an observer, the mental states, with all their fluctuations, associated with the episode. He stated on a number of occasions that one of his aims was to lead readers to experience what he was describing with the same vivid sensations that he had undergone when first encountering it himself.

The fictional works described in this section are divided into novels and novellas, although it is occasionally difficult to decide whether some of them are short novels or long short stories.

The *Childhood, Boyhood, Youth* series was the first major work of prose published by Tolstoy. These three titles, although now always printed together and considered to be one work, were written and issued separately: *Childhood* was published in 1852, *Boyhood* in 1854 and *Youth* in 1857. The trilogy (originally conceived as a tetralogy, to contain a fourth volume, *Young Manhood*) forms a semi-fictionalized autobiography of Tolstoy's own memories from the age of ten to his entry into university, when he becomes involved with a dissolute and cynical group of new young male friends; the work concludes with the realization of the futility and meaninglessness of this kind of life. During the period he was writing the three sections of the trilogy, he read Dickens's *David Copperfield* at least twice, and he later acknowledged his debt to Dickens's narrative technique, and his manner of incorporating autobiographical details into his fictional works. *Childhood, Boyhood, Youth*

He began to write *Childhood* in 1851, when he first arrived in the Caucasus with his brother Nikolai; he then enlisted in the Russian army, and completed the story during intervals between engaging in skirmishes with the local tribespeople. *Childhood*

The work is written, not from the point of view of an adult looking back, but from the point of view of the child's own experiences at the time; Tolstoy projects himself back into his own earlier mind, and recreates the intensity with which the child – in the book named Nikolai Irtenyev – experiences something for the first time, and then mentally processes the resulting perceptions and sensations.

We are given descriptions of the child's German tutor, his father, mother, household servants, the half-mad wandering pilgrims who visited the house and the family's games, parties and dances, both at home and at neighbours'. This first volume concludes with the end of this age of blissful innocence following the death of the narrator's mother. It will be remembered that Tolstoy's own mother had died before he was two years old, which was surely too early for him to remember; the recreation in *Childhood*, from the boy's point of view, of his mother's death and burial, and the intense emotions accompanying these, is a reminder that the volume is not entirely autobiographical, but that even when Tolstoy was inventing events and emotions, both here and in other novels, he possessed an extraordinary capacity to "become" the character he was describing, and to recreate vividly any experience these characters were going through.

The story met with great public and critical acclaim for its eye for minute detail, and its depth of psychological insight.

Boyhood   Tolstoy wrote *Boyhood*, the continuation of *Childhood*, between 1852 and 1854, in the little leisure time left to him from military campaigns in the Russo-Turkish war. It was published in 1854, once again to great acclaim in the Russian press. The book follows the family's move to Moscow after their mother's death, in order for the children to broaden their education. We are given once again sensations throughout as experienced from the young narrator's point of view, including: his impressions of sights seen en route to Moscow, his life in Moscow, his first becoming aware of sexual desires and his broadening of his circle of acquaintances. The boy listens admiringly to the grown-up talk of his elder brother, now at Moscow University. At the end of this second part of the trilogy, the narrator, who is by now himself preparing for university entrance, strikes up a friendship with a young man named Dmitry Nekhlyudov, with whom he has ardent conversations about art, education, the future and possible ways of reforming and perfecting humanity and society. The character of Nekhlyudov appears in passing in several of Tolstoy's later short stories, and finally re-emerges as the central figure of Tolstoy's last novel, *Resurrection*, prompting speculation that, in his interest in reform in the earlier book, and his moral "resurrection" in the novel of that name, he is a portrait of Tolstoy himself.

Tolstoy began work on the final volume of the trilogy in 1855, shortly after taking part in the defence of Sebastopol against the Turkish siege; it was published in 1857, and met with mixed reviews. In *Youth*, we are told how the narrator's friendship with Nekhlyudov deepened, and how, under the latter's influence, he embarked – as did the author himself – on a programme of self-perfection, which entailed drawing up a list of rules to live by. A brief description is given of the lackadaisical way the narrator prepared himself for the university entrance exams. He then takes us through several of these exams, and his feelings while sitting them. His father remarries, and the narrator enters university. *Youth*

But he fails his first-year exams disastrously, and is refused entry to the second year; he even briefly contemplates suicide. He falls into a state of profound moral questioning, and asks his father for permission to enter a Hussar regiment. The very last sentence of the entire trilogy promises us a continuation detailing the next, "happier" part of the narrator's youth.

However, the nearest we have to this is *The Cossacks*, published in 1863, which is told in the third person and whose central character is different from the narrator of the earlier trilogy. *The Cossacks*

The original version of this, first entitled *Young Manhood*, then *The Fugitive*, was begun in 1852; the initial drafts were conceived as forming the final volume of *Childhood, Boyhood, Youth*.

The novel opens with a brief chapter set in a fashionable restaurant in Moscow late at night; a wealthy and privileged young nobleman, Dmitry Olenin, is carousing for the last time with his old chums – although, like Tolstoy, he has begun to question this whole way of life, and is preparing to travel down to the Caucasus to join the Russian army there.

Some time later, he and his regiment are billeted in a small Cossack village in the far south of Russia. These Cossacks have been there for centuries, and form part of the barrier against encroaching local Chechen tribespeople, who are trying to shake off Russian domination.

The disenchanted Olenin, searching for an aim in life, believes he has found it in the simple life of the Cossacks, and he falls in love with a young village girl, Marianka, who has been tacitly assumed by everybody in the village for quite some time to be the intended bride of one of the young Cossacks, Luka.

Olenin makes numerous acquaintances in the village, including an elderly man called Yeroshka, who earns his living hunting, and seems full of the old country wisdom that Olenin believes is the answer to life's problems. Olenin assumes therefore that he has penetrated into the heart of these people and will be able to live their life. Resolving to forsake civilization and become one of the locals, he finally prepares to propose marriage to Marianka. But, at this moment, the Chechens stage a raid; Luka is seriously wounded, possibly on the point of death – though we are never told whether he actually dies or not. Marianka undertakes the nursing of Luka, and angrily tells Olenin to get out of her life, because she wants nothing to do with him. Mortified, Olenin asks his commanding officer for a transfer away from the village back to regional headquarters, and this is granted.

As he is driven out of the village by his servant coachman, neither Marianka nor Yeroshka even bother to give him a backward glance. It becomes apparent that his success in penetrating into the life of the "simple people" was just an illusion.

War and Peace   *War and Peace*, Tolstoy's first major novel, is generally considered to be his masterpiece. He began working on the story in 1863 and completed it in 1869. It was published in volume form, after having been serialized, with the early instalments considerably revised, in 1869, and was reprinted immediately. He was at first contemplating the title of *All's Well that Ends Well* for the entire work; "War and Peace" as a possible title is found in his papers for the first time in 1867.

The novel was widely praised for its combination of historical sweep and the eye for detail and psychological insight that had typified earlier works such as *Childhood*.

Tolstoy wrote at this time that, since he envisioned the whole work as a great epic set against the backdrop of authentic history, he had not created an elaborate plot, nor provided a definitive ending for the story, for life and history continue after it has finished.

The work begins in the year 1805, in the high society of Moscow and St Petersburg, when a war against Napoleon and his forces was becoming increasingly likely. The narrative of events during both war and peace is continued until 1812, and the major body of the novel concludes with Napoleon's invasion of Russia, his defeat and retreat.

The story is interspersed throughout with essays giving us Tolstoy's philosophy of life and history; the author believed, as mentioned above, that although history is taught in schools and universities as being directed by rulers and great individuals, it is in fact created by the interweaving of a virtually infinite number of human actions performed by the entire mass of people stretching back to the beginning of time; the people nominally in charge, such as rulers and generals, are at the mercy, at any instant, of the sum total of unforeseen vicissitudes resulting from these past actions. Retrospectively, a successful leader seems to have been in control of what was happening from the beginning; however, this is simply because he has adjusted adroitly to unexpected occurrences and turned them to his advantage.

War and Peace contains some 580 characters, from Napoleon, Tsar Alexander I and the General of the Russian forces, Prince Kutuzov, right down to common soldiers, peasants, priests and urban labourers. Tolstoy had carried out considerable historical research beforehand, including talking to many elderly people who had been alive during the period described in his novel.

The major protagonists, however, are the numerous members of five aristocratic families, the Bolkonskys, Bezukhovs, Rostovs, Koragins and Drubetskoys: their lives and family histories become progressively more intertwined in the years of war and peace between 1805 and 1812. There are several intermarriages, and we are given long and detailed accounts of the lives of these families in peacetime, at their country estates and town mansions. At the same time, we are taken through the long and tense build-up to hostilities, and given depictions of the fighting, principally the battles of Smolensk and Borodino, Napoleon's laying siege to and burning of Moscow, and his final defeat and retreat from

Russia – all as seen from the personal view of the common soldiers on both sides, who do not have a clue what is happening on the battlefield, surrounded as they are by smoke, noise and confusion. The senseless savagery of war is chronicled unflinchingly.

The final section contains two epilogues. The first epilogue takes us up to 1820, giving us the characters' reflections on the events described in the main body of the novel, and telling us how their lives are now progressing. The second epilogue deals with Tolstoy's deterministic philosophy of history.

Anna Karenina

Anna Karenina, voted the greatest novel ever in a poll by *Time Magazine* in 2007, was written by Tolstoy between 1873 and 1877. Like *War and Peace*, it was published in instalments from 1875 onwards, to critical acclaim, although some of the more conservative magazines had reservations about its morality and sexual content. The last instalment, number seven, was rejected by the editor because of its stance against the Russo-Turkish war. Accordingly, Tolstoy published the book in novel form, including the final section, in 1878.

Tolstoy considered this his first true novel – as noted above, he'd viewed *War and Peace* as more of an "epic", and he commented that, whereas *War and Peace*'s theme had been the "nation", *Anna Karenina*'s was the "family".

In fact, it more specifically concerns adultery, and the disgrace this would bring on the guilty couple – although, of course, moral vilification would be directed at this period far more against the woman than the man.

Anna Karenina is the attractive and charismatic wife of the boring senior civil servant Alexei Karenin, and mother to their son Sergei. She lives with them in St Petersburg. At the beginning of the story she is visiting her brother Stepan Oblonsky in Moscow, where she encounters Count Alexei Vronsky, who immediately falls in love with her. Both he and a rural landowner, Konstantin Levin, loosely based on Tolstoy himself, are suitors for Stepan's young sister-in-law, Kitty.

Levin proposes marriage to Kitty, but she rejects him, as she is expecting a proposal from Vronsky. However, at a ball Vronsky flirts and dances with Anna, and Kitty is devastated.

On her way back to her family in Petersburg, Anna realizes that she is falling in love with Vronsky. On arriving home, she finds that, in comparison with Vronsky, she is beginning to find her husband repulsive.

Vronsky visits St Petersburg more and more frequently to try to enter into a relationship with Anna, and although at first she rejects him, she finally succumbs. Karenin warns them that their behaviour has been noticed, and is giving rise to gossip in public.

Anna becomes pregnant, presumably by Vronsky. Karenin contemplates a divorce, and threatens to take legal custody of their son if Anna's illicit relationship continues.

Anna gives birth to a daughter, and Karenin at first forgives Vronsky, following which the latter, overcome with remorse, attempts suicide, but merely succeeds in seriously injuring himself. Meanwhile, the landowner Levin has once again proposed to Kitty, and she has accepted him.

Anna now leaves Karenin and her son to live with Vronsky, but many of their old friends snub them because of their situation. They leave urban high society to try to settle down together on Vronsky's country estate. But Anna is now approaching a mental breakdown: she grows more and more jealous of Vronsky, even if he merely goes out for short walks. She writes to Karenin insisting on a divorce so that she can regularize her situation; he refuses and obtains legal custody of her baby daughter. Her increasing strain and distress mean she is now constantly arguing with Vronsky. She contemplates suicide and, on a visit by the couple to Moscow, throws herself in front of a train and dies.

Vronsky, devastated, goes to Serbia to fight on the side of the Russian troops and volunteers supporting that country in its uprising against the ruling Turks.

Tolstoy's last full-length novel, *Resurrection*, was begun in *Resurrection* 1889, completed in 1899, and issued throughout this period in instalments. It was finally published in full book form in 1901. The novel was written at the period when Tolstoy had become a polemicist and social and moral reformer, and had come to believe that all art should further such reform; therefore, in the view of almost all commentators when it first appeared and since, after an excellent opening two thirds of the novel, it gradually turns into a tract on the need for human beings to undergo a moral and spiritual regeneration.

The anti-hero who undergoes the major moral "resurrection" of the title is Prince Dmitry Nekhlyudov, whom we first encountered in *Childhood, Boyhood, Youth* as one of the narrator's closest, most idealistic and wisest friends.

353

In the book, Katerina Maslova, an illegitimate child of a farm worker on a country estate, is brought up by two elderly spinsters, the owners of the estate.

Prince Nekhlyudov, their nephew, visits them, seduces Katerina, then leaves and forgets her. She becomes pregnant, which leads her elderly female guardians to throw her out. She turns to prostitution, and one day she is falsely accused of murdering a client. At the trial Nekhlyudov is one of the jury members and, recognizing the girl as one of his early conquests, he realizes that her present condition is a result of his youthful, callous attitude towards her. She is found guilty, despite all the evidence being for her innocence, and she is sentenced to labour in Siberia, followed by lifelong exile there. Nekhlyudov sells all his property to accompany her to Siberia, intending, once her labour sentence is completed, to marry her, give her a decent life and so make amends to her. However, she refuses him, and consequently his attention turns towards helping out all the prisoners, who live in appalling conditions. As the novel turns into a polemic, we are told, in typical Tolstoyan fashion, that the society which condemns these people consists of individuals just as corrupt as them, and therefore not only the criminal system, but society as a whole needs to be reformed radically as well.

The final chapter depicts Nekhlyudov's full moral and spiritual rehabilitation when he by chance starts reading the Bible. This chapter consists almost entirely of quotations from the New Testament book of St Matthew, leading Nekhlyudov to conclude the novel by expounding at length Tolstoy's views about how human beings should live.

Family Happiness   Along with his major full-length novels, there are many examples of Tolstoy's shorter fiction worth mentioning. An early example of this is *Family Happiness*, begun in 1858 and completed and published in 1859.

Katya, a seventeen-year-old orphan, marries a much older guardian, their neighbour Sergei. She has for years viewed him with love and esteem. But when she marries him and moves to his country estate, she finds that she no longer goes to balls, or glittering social engagements, since her husband is concerned with managing his land, and very rarely visits neighbours or the big cities. She becomes bored and depressed. After a time they discuss a separation. They move for some time to St Petersburg so that she can try to regain some interest in life, but her husband grows more and more alienated from Petersburg life, and wishes to return to the country.

On the couple's resettling at the estate, Katya begins to adapt to her new life and, following the births of children, gradually realizes that, although she no longer has her old girlish passion for her husband, she now feels a new kind of love for him and for her rural family existence, which will last their whole lives.

The story received lukewarm reviews, and Tolstoy himself repudiated it shortly afterwards as false and insincere in its depiction of family life.

Many of Tolstoy's most famous tales, though extremely powerful, were written after his change of direction from being an artist to a polemicist in the mid-to-late 1870s, and therefore are all designed to make a point in line with Tolstoy's beliefs.

The Death of Ivan Ilyich was begun in 1882, and finished and published in 1886.

The Death of Ivan Ilyich

Ivan Ilyich has done all the things that one is meant to do to have a happy and successful life: he has a senior civil service job, is married with a couple of children and entertains friends.

However, in middle age, he begins to feel progressively more and more ill; we are never told what he is suffering from, but the symptoms seem to be those of cancer. As he approaches death, he starts to wonder what the real point of his existence has been.

In the last few months of his life, when he is incapable even of moving about by himself, and has to be wheeled or carried everywhere, and looked after twenty-four hours a day, he establishes a friendship with his young, patient, gentle, never-complaining servant Gerasim, who was originally a peasant. It is Gerasim upon whom the entire responsibility of caring for his master now falls. Ivan Ilyich realizes that his existence has been based on false values, and that the meaning of life is to be found in Gerasim's true love for humanity and his peasant wisdom.

Ivan Ilyich loses his fear of death, his pain disappears, and for the last couple of hours of his life he is mentally and spiritually at peace: as he dies, all anguish and terror is replaced by a vision of light.

The Kreutzer Sonata was begun in 1887, completed in 1889 and published in 1891.

The Kreutzer Sonata

An unnamed narrator tells us how he is on a train and is joined in his carriage by a strange individual who begins to tell him about his married life; we are never quite certain whether this new passenger is mad, and whether the tale is true or not. His entire story is a rant about the wiles of women, and how they use their sexuality to entice men into marriage. He tells the narrator that his relationship with his wife became more and more troubled as he started to sense he was trapped and to feel a deep revulsion towards sex. His wife began to have music lessons, and the stranger tells how he suspected her of having an affair with her teacher. Finally, the passenger describes how he returned one day to his house unexpectedly early with the intention of finding them *in flagrante delicto*, although it appeared when he entered the room nothing improper had been going on at all. In a fit of jealousy, he killed his wife with a dagger, and the piano teacher fled. The stranger, then realizing what he had done, left by train after his wife's funeral to begin a new life. The question arises: if his story was true, why didn't the narrator immediately summon the police, and have him arrested?

Master and Man *Master and Man* was begun in 1894, and published in 1895. A rich merchant, although pleasant and kind, has spent most of his life making money and doing what one should do in the eyes of the world. One evening he sets off on a journey out of town in his carriage driven by his peasant coachman. They are caught in a violent snowstorm, and can make no further progress. The merchant has no fear of freezing to death, since he is wearing a thick and expensive fur coat. However, he now realizes that the coachman is not so well dressed, and there is no space for him in the carriage, so he will almost certainly die of cold. The merchant leaves the vehicle and lies next to the man, trying to enfold both of them in his fur coat. The rich man dies, having achieved total peace and seen the meaning of life. The coachman, because of his strong working-class constitution, survives, and lives for another twenty years.

Finally, it is worth highlighting some of Tolstoy's non-fiction.

Confession Following the death of two of his children in 1875, and the onset shortly afterwards of ill health and depression, Tolstoy underwent a profound psychological transformation which was to turn him from a creative artist into a polemicist for the rest of his career.

The major expression of his change of direction in this period is his *Confession*. In this book he describes his progressive alienation from the things which people of his class seemed to consider so necessary for life, such as possessions, a prominent position in work and society, and the usual round of carousing and pleasure. People of his own class, he tells us, claim they believe in Christianity, but in fact they are full of lust, pride and anger, and their religion seems to be something extraneous to their way of life.

Educated people, including writers and artists – most of them cynical and dissolute – seem to believe they have access to some higher truth denied to those without education, and are convinced they have a kind of divine right to attempt to perfect humanity with their works.

Tolstoy tells us how he started searching for a meaning to life through studying religious teachings and philosophy. In *Confession* he quotes numerous authorities such as Socrates, Buddha Shakyamuni, Schopenhauer and the Old Testament Book of Ecclesiastes as testimony to the emptiness and meaninglessness of what most people view as the important things in their lives. But he comes to the conclusion that either these teachings are irrelevant or provide no real solution.

Tolstoy also wrote scores of other works which made much the same points. The most important of these – in chronological order – are: *What I Believe* (1881–84), published in Russia in 1884, banned by the censor, and then issued abroad in several western European countries; *What then Must We Do?*, begun in 1885, and intended for serial publication; the first instalment, however, was immediately banned in Russia, and the full volume was published for the first time in Switzerland only in 1889; *The Kingdom of God Is within You* (1890–93), which was also banned, then published in Berlin in 1894; *What Is Religion?* (1901–02), banned in Russia but published in Russian in Britain in 1902.

Tolstoy's numerous writings on the subject of art are exemplified by this short volume, *What Is Art?*, written from 1896 to 1898, and published in 1898.

What Is Art?

He tells us here that art is a universal activity, not just restricted to a few, and that its essence consists in conveying to others precisely what the feelings of the creator are when producing it, consequently inspiring, ennobling and deepening those who experience it. Art should always be accessible to the masses and prompt the recipients to try to perfect themselves morally and spiritually, leading to a total transformation of society. Abstruse music and literature – such as, for instance, the works of Beethoven and Shakespeare – are incomprehensible to the masses, and therefore should be abandoned by humanity as not being true art. In other publications Tolstoy criticized in a similar vein the works of Symbolist and "Decadent" writers and the Impressionist school of painters, while at the same time extolling the works of such writers as Dickens and George Eliot for what he perceived as their realistic depiction of everyday life.

Translator's Note

Leo Tolstoy began writing *Childhood* in 1851 in the Caucasus, when he was in his early twenties. His idea was to write a work of autobiographical fiction in four parts, the result of which is *Childhood, Boyhood, Youth*; the planned fourth part – which he refers to at the end of *Youth* as the second "happier half of my youth" – was never written. *Childhood* met with instant success when Nikolai Nekrasov published it in the literary journal *The Contemporary* in November 1852. *Boyhood* was published in 1854, followed by *Youth* in 1857. In later years Tolstoy became very critical of this early work, declaring it an incoherent jumble of events from his own and his friends' childhoods, and claiming it was insincerely written. But for all its flaws, inconsistencies and sentimental outpourings, *Childhood, Boyhood, Youth* is not only of immense biographical interest to us, but also a fascinating precursor to Tolstoy's later work.

To the translator the work presents a series of interesting challenges. Tolstoy is known for his straightforward, simple language and his love of repetition: the same word may often be repeated several times in a single paragraph or reoccur each time a person or type of landscape is mentioned. He uses repetition for emphasis or characterization – Nikolyenka's father has a shoulder twitch, for example, Lyubochka has goose-like legs, birch trees have curling branches – and for the most part I have remained true to his style, at the cost of seeming unadventurous.

The length of his sentences can also be problematic, with long strings of words punctuated by numerous commas and semi-colons. Again I have largely stuck close to his style, but in places felt it preferable to break up particularly unwieldy sentences to allow the reader to catch his breath.

At times Tolstoy switches from the past to the present tense and back again to the past in a relatively short space of time, intending to carry the reader into the immediacy of a scene. Although this can be very effective, it can occasionally be confusing, and in a few cases I have found it necessary to avoid the switch. Likewise his sudden changes in person, the authorial voice speaking one minute in the first person singular and referring to himself in the second person singular in the next. In most cases I have left it as it is. Once or twice, however, where the shift seemed rather abrupt or disconcerting, I have avoided it, maintaining the first person instead, for clarity of reading.

Lastly a note on names. Notoriously confusing in many Russian novels, the names used in *Childhood, Boyhood, Youth* are thankfully fairly straightforward. It is customary in Russian to address people by their Christian names and patronymics, with the exception of family, close friends and children, for whom diminutives are the norm. On the occasions when the Christian name and patronymic appear together when a diminutive had previously been used, I have included a footnote to clarify to whom they refer.

Select Bibliography

Standard Edition:
Tolstoy, Leo, *Detstvo, Otrochestvo, Yunost'* (Moscow: Izdatel'stvo Khudozhestvennaya Literatura, 1966).

Biographies:
Maude, Aylmer, *The Life of Tolstoy* (Oxford: OUP, 1987)
Shklovsky, Viktor, *Lev Tolstoy*, translated from Russian by Olga Shartse (Moscow: Progress, 1978)
Simmons, E.J., *Leo Tolstoy* (London: Routledge and Kegan Paul, 1973)
Troyat, Henri, *Tolstoy*, translated from French by Nancy Amphoux (Harmondsworth: Penguin, 1970)
Wilson, A.N., *Tolstoy* (Harmondsworth: Penguin, 1989)

Additional Background Material:

Bayley, John, *Tolstoy and the Novel* (London: Chatto and Windus, 1966)

Bayley, John, *Leo Tolstoy* (Plymouth: Northcote House, 1997)

Berlin, Isaiah, 'The Hedgehog and the Fox: An Essay on Tolstoy's View of History', in Berlin's *Russian Thinkers* (Harmondsworth: Penguin, 1979)

Bloom, Harold, ed., *Leo Tolstoy: Modern Critical Views* (New York: Chelsea House, 1986)

Christian, R.F., *Tolstoy: A Critical Introduction* (Cambridge: CUP, 1969)

Gifford, Henry, ed., *Leo Tolstoy: A Critical Anthology* (Harmondsworth: Penguin, 1971)

Gifford, Henry, *Tolstoy* (Oxford: OUP, 1982)

Knowles, A.V., ed., *Tolstoy: the Critical Heritage* (London: Routledge and Kegan Paul, 1978)

Matlaw, Ralph E., ed., *Tolstoy: A Collection of Critical Essays* (Englewood Cliffs, New Jersey: Prentice-Hall, 1967)

Silbajoris Rimvydas, *Tolstoy's Aesthetics and his Art* (Columbus, Ohio: Slavica, 1991)

Steiner, George, *Tolstoy or Dostoevsky: An Essay in the Old Criticism* (Harmondsworth: Penguin, 1967)

The Diaries of Sofia Tolstoy, transl. Cathy Porter (Surrey: Alma Books, 2010)

Tolstoy's Diaries, trans. and ed. by R.F. Christian, 2 vols, (London: Athlone Press, 1985, and abridged in one volume, London: Flamingo, 1994)

Tolstoy's Letters, transl., ed. and introduced by R.F. Christian, 2 vols (London: Athlone Press, 1978)

Tussing Orwin, Donna, ed., *The Cambridge Companion to Tolstoy* (Cambridge: CUP, 2002)

Wasiolek, Edward, *Tolstoy's Major Fiction* (Chicago and London: Chicago University Press, 1978)

Wasiolek, Edward, ed., *Critical Essays on Tolstoy* (Boston: G.K. Hall, 1986)

On the Web:
www.utoronto.ca/tolstoy

Appendix

Early Reviews of Childhood, Boyhood, Youth

Russian Reviews:

The poet and author Nikolai Nekrasov (1821–77) was editor and owner of the leading literary journal of his time, *The Contemporary* (*Sovremennik*). Tolstoy sent him his manuscript of *Childhood* signed only with his initials L.N., on 3rd July 1852, and an accompanying letter claiming it was the first part of a projected tetralogy.

Nekrasov replied, in a letter that is undated but must relate to mid-August that year:

> I have read your manuscript. It contains so much of interest that I am publishing it. Without knowing how it continues, I cannot speak with any certainty, but I think the author has talent. At any rate, the author's method and the simplicity and reality of the content form the undoubted value of the work. If in the following parts, as is to be expected, there is more liveliness and action, then it will be a good novel. Please send me the sequel. Both your novel and your talent have caught my interest.

And on the sequel to the above, *Boyhood*, he wrote to Tolstoy on 17th Feb 1855:

> Your *Boyhood* has had what is termed an "effect", that is, people in St Petersburg are all talking about it. As for literary circles, all honest people are unanimous in finding it full of poetry, original and artistically written.

Nikolai Chernyshevsky (1828–89), the leading radical literary critic of the time wrote a long review of *Childhood*, *Boyhood* and some of the short stories Tolstoy had written by this time, in *The Contemporary*, 1856, no. 12; this review finishes with an assessment of Tolstoy's method and style which may serve for his artistic works throughout his career:

Count Tolstoy's special talent lies in the fact that he does not limit himself to a description of the results of the psychic process; he is interested in the process itself; the scarcely perceptible manifestations of this inner life, changing from one into another with great speed and an inexhaustible variety, are described by Count Tolstoy in masterly fashion. There are painters who are famous for their art in capturing the flickering reflections of the sun's rays on the fast-rolling waves, the shimmering light on rustling leaves, and the play of colours on the changing shapes of clouds; it is generally said of them that they can capture the life of nature. Count Tolstoy does something similar with the secret movement of the psychic life. It seems to us that it is in this that the completely original character of his talent lies.

English-language Reviews:

Anonymous review of *Childhood and Youth* (sic – *Boyhood* is not mentioned in the title) – the first review of any Tolstoy work in English – in *Saturday Review*, 29th March 1862. The author was given on the tile page as "Count Nicola Tolstoy", leading to the assumption for some years in the English-speaking world that the novel had been written by Lev's elder brother Nikolai.

The translation was by Malwida von Meysenbug, who does not seem to have been a native English speaker, since it is often stiff and unidiomatic.

[The volume] is at the best a very thin narration of the early life of an affectionate and sensitive boy, and the whole production is insipid. He is not, we think, justified in telling his family history in this way, and in probing the failings of parents in order that he may have the satisfaction of sketching his own childhood.

Review of the same translation in *Athenaeum*, 16th August 1862:

This is a very clever and lifelike story of childhood and boyhood. It gives a well-described picture of Russian daily life. Story it can scarcely be called, for it is the rambling recollections of a child and youth. But it gives an insight into the thoughts, perverseness and sorrows of a child.

Acknowledgements

It would have been impossible for me to complete this translation without the support of several people. First and foremost I wish to thank Anthony Bales for his constant encouragement and support, for all the time he has dedicated to reading the drafts and his willingness to discuss many challenging word or phrase issues over recent months. Next I would like to thank my daughter Fiona O'Brien for her inspired editing skills and again for spending so much time reading through the work. Other invaluable help has come from Vera Liber and Dr David Holohan with their great expertise in the Russian language. Thank you both so much. My thanks also go to Dr Janet Sturgis for giving the work another thorough reading and to Peter Dunne for helping me out with some tricky specialist words connected with hunting. And finally I would like to thank Alessandro Gallenzi for offering me the opportunity to do this translation.

– Dora O'Brien

ALMA CLASSICS

ALMA CLASSICS aims to publish mainstream and lesser-known European classics in an innovative and striking way, while employing the highest editorial and production standards. By way of a unique approach the range offers much more, both visually and textually, than readers have come to expect from contemporary classics publishing.

∾

To order any of our titles and for up-to-date information about our current and forthcoming publications, please visit our website on:

www.almaclassics.com